For my children

CHAPTER ONE

The thin, balding Harbormaster slurped oysters from the halfshell while he perused Raiden's orders, his eyes pinched with concentration. Slimy mollusks disappeared down his gullet one after the other, the empty shells discarded with a staccato clattering onto the massive desk which took up half the stonewalled tower room. Raiden held on to his patience by his fingertips. So far, this tower was all he'd seen of the city of Sicaria, but for a glimpse of bright, pastel-colored buildings marching up the hillsides behind a high, crenelated seawall. A narrow window behind the harbormaster looked out over the bustling docks and caught the occasional waft of salt-air and dead fish. The sun was shining, bright and hot, but the sky held a strange, rose-colored haze.

Not haze. Raiden adjusted the strap of his heavy satchel, peering at the narrow aspect of sky. *It is a Veil.*

From the sea, Sicaria had seemed an ordinary city, but for the strange, translucent dome sheltering her. It had stretched beyond the dense cluster of buildings atop two high hills, obscuring the coast to the north and south like a shimmering bank of fog. But it wasn't fog, it wasn't haze; it was a powerful shield created by magic no one outside this island nation could comprehend, much less replicate. The Veils of Malavita protected its people from the broken, twisted magic which had – eons ago

– laid waste to a once golden, fertile land. And the Brotherhood church which had raised and maintained the Veils for centuries were loath to share their secrets with their newest overlords, the Bhaskar Empire. Which was rather inconvenient as most of Malavita was a deadly wasteland unfit for human habitation.

As he watched a drop of brine land on the Imperial seal, Raiden touched the hilt of his sword and contemplated lopping off the man's hand. It might speed things along. He was an Imperial emissary with diplomatic protection. What's the worst they could do? Charge him a fine?

Finally, the man tossed the last of the oyster shells on a plate and wiped his fingers on a linen napkin. His thin lips pursed beneath an even thinner mustache. "It does not say who you are here to meet, just lists a 'city-prince'. Why hasn't this anonymous prince sent his men to fetch you? It's not every day an emissary from the Empire arrives on our shores. And where are your guards? Where is your retinue?" He frowned at him. "How am I to believe you are who you say you are?"

Raiden bristled at his tone. No one spoke to the Commander of the Imperial Guard in such a rude manner. Not if they wanted to live. Almost immediately, he checked his ire. He was the *former* Commander of the Imperial Guard, and this troublesome little colony was his exile.

Still.

"The order is marked with the Emperor's own seal, and it states very clearly who I am," he snapped. "Captain Raiden Mad, Imperial Emissary to an honorable city-prince of Sicaria. I am here on a diplomatic mission which requires some discretion. Who I am meeting is irrelevant as I have Imperial permission to enter your city, and how I travel is my own concern, sir."

The thin man shrugged. He wore a rich, brocade vest embroidered with tiny gemstones and it sparkled with the movement. "What do I know of seals? Or diplomatic missions? I am a simple agent placed in charge of this port. I can't let just anyone into Sicaria. We have rules here, boy."

"Captain."

The man blinked. "What?"

"I am not a 'boy', I am a captain in the Imperial army, and you will address me by my proper rank."

Another infuriating shrug. "What do I know of rank?"

"Apparently you don't know much of anything." Raiden leaned down and jabbed a finger at the creamy paper in the man's hand. "There is my name in clear letters. In your language, I might add. Can you not read? The gods know we've conquered many illiterate people. I just didn't realize Malavita was counted among such barbarians."

"Conquered?" He chuckled. "No one has 'conquered' Malavita. Empires trade us like a pretty bauble. They come, they go, we stay eternal." He waved a hand. "Yours is the same as all the others."

Nostrils flaring, Raiden gripped the hilt of his sword and decided taking the man's head would be far more satisfying than his hand. But he resisted the urge. This was a corrupt and lawless land, but he was an agent of the Bhaskar Empire. He was here to fulfill his duty. He would not be goaded by a casual insult. Reluctantly, he eased his grip.

"And I can read, captain," the Harbormaster added. He tossed Raiden's paperwork on his desk as casually as he'd discarded his oyster shells and leaned back in his chair, fingers laced over his chest. A smile spread across his face as he eyed the satchel resting against Raiden's hip. "And if you desire discretion... well, I'm sure we can come to some arrangement."

An hour later, his properly authorized documents worn and begrimed from the myriad hands through which they had passed, been inspected, scrutinized, and once refused, Raiden entered the gates of Sicaria. Sweat soaked his crimson uniform jacket. He'd undone the top few buttons of his single-breasted coat, unwilling to open it all the way, though the air was thick, and the sun weighed on his head.

Shoulders back like a proper soldier, he made his way

through streets clogged with people, wagons, carts, and noisy animals of every sort, including a camel or two among the more pedestrian donkeys and goats. Horses were rare. By the amount of manure clogging the gutters, he expected street sweepers were just as rare. The cobblestones were marble, stained and mottled with age and use, and the warren of buildings to either side – shops, homes, warehouses – were built from bright, decoratively carved limestone, or plastered in a myriad of pale pastels. Cascades of roses and geraniums fell from nearly every window and balcony.

In his crimson and gold uniform jacket, snug tan trousers and tall, shiny black boots, Raiden drew looks. There was an air of hostility which followed him like a bad smell. Though they had taken Malavita peacefully, the Bhaskar Empire was still a foreign ruler. Despite a land rich with precious gems, she'd been more trouble than she'd been worth to many of the Empire's predecessors. The Emperor hoped to change all that with the royal charter Raiden carried in his satchel, the first step in a new venture.

A few Imperial Polizia wandered through the packed streets, a small badge of crimson emblazoned with a golden sunburst on their dun-colored jackets. He caught a few rude gestures aimed at their backs. Recruited from the locals, the polizia were rife with corruption. He kept clear of them.

Ahead of him, a disturbance ruffled the throng. The crowd parted for a group of men swaggering down the street shoulder-to-shoulder. These men weren't wearing the simple tunics and trousers of their fellows. They were bare-chested, and wore short, wraparound skirts of pale linen covered by strips of armored leather pteruges, leaving their legs bare but for sandals laced up to their knees. Finely-tooled leather knife belts spanned their narrow waists, long, thin blades resting at their hips. Broad-brimmed hats shaded their hard eyes.

But their dress, strange as it was, wasn't what set them apart. Even the knives at their hips weren't as impressive as the tattoos covering nearly every inch of their bare flesh. Like peacocks among a flock of pigeons, the men shone. The tattoos were full of color and movement – striking snakes, raptors, dragons, tigers, and other predatory animals, or raging flames and lightning bolts. The elaborate ink radiated power.

His hackles rising, Raiden slipped into the shade of a storefront awning. He recognized these men by description. The Empire had entire books devoted to the Bloodwizards of Malavita, those tattooed magicwielders who used gemstone blades to shed their own blood for power, but these men were not common bloodwizards. They were the famous – no, infamous – Corsaro. Marked by their attire, and their swagger, these particular bloodwizards served powerful warlords calling themselves Capomaji. They held this land in thrall, extorting and intimidating people, especially in the more isolated Veils in the interior. They were a dangerous nuisance.

Raiden laid a hand on his sword hilt, watching the Corsaro strut down the street, the people scattering before them like mice before cats. It would be interesting to test them. How would their vile magic hold up against steel? But he eased his grip once the Corsaro had passed. The citizens of Sicaria seemed to release a collective sigh before going on with their business and he left the shelter of the awning. It was growing late, and he was due to meet Safire's representatives soon.

A few inquiries pointed him in the proper direction, and after a dozen turns down the twisting streets he emerged onto a quiet avenue with shuttered storefronts and a taverna with a black rooster on its shingle. A red and white-striped awning shaded a few tables on a stone patio and wide-open doors led into the dim interior. Raiden stepped into the shade, grateful for the respite. He waved to the comely young woman serving a table of four and took a small table for himself. He could hear patrons inside the building laughing and talking, but he and the group at the other table were the only ones seated outside.

His gaze swept them, wondering if they were the

representatives he was supposed to meet. Three of them wore loose, flowing silk shirts tucked into snug trousers, soft leather boots wrapped to their knees, and knife belts with only a single blade each. Blades made of quartz. The Brotherhood church, who created and distributed the gemstone blades, didn't bother working with quartz. Most lesser blades were homemade. Crude and simple and nowhere near as strong as the "blessed" blades. Still, it meant these men could wield bloodmagic.

Their shirts were brightly colored, the oldest in red and the two younger men in blue and green. The shirtsleeves were bloused at the elbows with ribbons, leaving their tattooed forearms bare. Long, wild hair framed their narrow, swarthy faces, and long mustaches drooped around their mouths. Tattoos peaked from beneath their open collars. Not Corsaro, certainly, but bloodwizards nevertheless.

The fourth was a youth. Tall and slim, and dressed like a Sicarian in long trousers, sandals and a long-sleeved jacket, he had neither mustache nor loose, wild hair. His long, dirty-blond hair was contained in a braid, and he wore a broad-brimmed hat pulled low over his eyes.

A person going to the trouble to hide his eyes was usually up to no good. Suspicious, Raiden adjusted the sword tucked into his sash. The youth gave him a slow nod, as if he knew why he had shifted. Raiden looked aside. *Cheeky brat.*

Immediately, he dismissed the four. They couldn't possibly be the representatives of a Malavitan city-prince. Especially one who'd served a year in the Imperial Army and distinguished himself during the Vulcaro Campaign. He had never met Dante Safire personally, but he knew him by reputation as a man of honor and integrity. It was why the Emperor was willing to grant the man a boon – once Raiden determined the feasibility of Dante's request, of course. He wanted an Imperial charter granting him land and rights to raise a new Veil, which, while beneficial to the Empire, was a doubtful proposition. Malavita's ruling class, the so-called "First Families", were as beholden to the Brotherhood as the rest of the people. Strong in magic and the nominal lords of the Veils, nevertheless, they had no choice but to pay the Brotherhood their crippling taxes. Without the Brotherhood and their cryptic magic, the Veils would fail. And without the Veils, life was not possible in Malavita.

It was a frustrating situation for the Empire as vast tracts of Malavita's interior – the blighted Wastes – could be reclaimed by new Veils, yet the Brotherhood was as parsimonious with their Veils as they were with their gemstones. They hadn't raised a new Veil in over a hundred years, and the priests refused to impart their secrets to any bloodwizards outside of their organization. They kept the knowledge as close as their blades.

But when he'd appealed to the Empire for the charter, Dante Safire claimed he had the knowledge and the strength to raise his own Veil, a Veil for the Empire. It sounded too good to be true to Raiden, and he was prepared to refuse the charter. They had been burned before with ill-conceived charters. Not long ago, the Empire had granted charters to some of their own nobility and trading companies in an attempt to establish royal colonies within existing Veils – they'd learned the hard way that the Wastes were uninhabitable, at least by Imperial citizens – but even those attempts inside Veils had ended in disaster. Pit mines had failed to yield any quality gems, crops had fallen to blight, grapes had withered on the vine, and herds of hearty Imperial cattle had wandered into the Wastes to be transformed into twisted beasts. The locals had sniggered and mocked the foreign invaders until they had all fled. Without bloodmagic, the Imperials were at a disadvantage in this land.

Yet, if Dante truly could raise a Veil free of Brotherhood control and dominance, then the Empire would at last have access to their own gem mines. Cutting out the Brotherhood from the lucrative gem trade would be a profitable venture.

When the serving girl approached, Raiden ordered wine. The first glass of the cool, golden liquid soothed his throat and slaked his thirst. The second softened his muscles and eased the tension between his shoulder blades. He stretched his legs beneath the small, wrought iron table and slumped low in his chair, relaxing for the first time in what seemed like weeks.

The journey across the Trincarian sea had been long and dull. Losing himself in the practice of the Thousand Forms had been impossible on the cramped ship, and all he'd been able to do was think. His thoughts had circled around only one thing: the shame of his dishonor. He was – he'd *been* – a shield, born and raised to protect the Imperial family. Born and raised to kill any enemy who threatened them. Even as a boy, barely into his tenth year, he could pick an assassin from the crowd and kill them before they came near a royal family member. He'd always expected to sacrifice his life for his family, but he'd never expected to have to fall on a *figurative* sword. Death was preferrable to this – this exile.

The strain of the day beat against the back of his eyes, and thoughts of his homeland made him weary beyond measure. He closed them. Just for a moment…

A sudden shout of pain jarred his eyes open. He jerked upright, cracking a knee against the table and toppling his empty wine glass. It shattered against the paving stones. The noise made him wince, but no one else took notice. All eyes were on the man groveling on the patio, the innkeeper by his humble garb and snow-white apron. The pretty serving maid crouched beside him, her arms around him, weeping. Blood dripped from the innkeeper's nose, and his hands were raised in supplication. A tattooed man stood over them, bare-chested in a skirt of armored leather strips.

Raiden hissed in a breath. *Corsaro.*

The tattooed man held a long, slim blade against his own forearm. The blade was of a pale green stone and parallel cuts stood out against his painted flesh.

"The tribute was due today, Alonzo," he said. "Not tomorrow, not next week. Today!"

"Please, Vito. Please, I beg you! Business has been so bad this season, and the tribute has increased so much. I have nothing to spare!"

"Nothing? You have nothing for the man who keeps you safe? The man who protects your daughter from rapists and scoundrels?"

With a sob, the girl hid her face against her father's shoulder. The innkeeper paled.

The man, Vito, shook his head. "This is no good. No good." He applied pressure to the green blade. "I already gave you an extra week and still you give me nothing. Do you think my Capo will be gentle with me if I am gentle with you?"

"Please, good sir. Spare me–"

Snarling, the Corsaro man slashed his arm with his jewel blade. Blood ran black against his tattooed flesh. The pale green blade gleamed.

Raiden gasped. It was beautiful.

The Corsaro soldier bared his teeth and his eyes closed to slits.

A wave of force burst from the tattooed man, hot as a summer breeze before a thunderstorm. Raiden felt it, but he remained untouched. The innkeeper, however, ignited. The girl shrieked and recoiled. But she was a quick one and doused him with the contents of her blue ceramic pitcher. The flames vanished, leaving the innkeeper moaning and writhing on the flagstones. His skin was shiny and red through his charred clothing. The tattooed man laughed as if it were the funniest thing he'd seen in days. The four souls seated at the other table beyond the innkeeper watched the tableau in grim indifference.

It was too much.

Raiden stood, knocking his chair over with a loud clatter. The bloodwizard, still chuckling, turned on him. His eyes lit with pleasure. "Ah! Good! A man with a spine. What a novelty. And a foreigner, too. How lucky for me. I hope you have gold in your purse, sir. You'll need to pay for the lesson you're about to receive."

"Is that what you are, you gem-bladed wizards? You so-called Corsaro? Thieves and bullies?" Raiden stepped clear of his table and turned sideways, his hand on the hilt of his sword. "Teach me that lesson, scoundrel."

The man snatched a second blade from his knife belt and stepped around the poor soul writhing at his feet. The world slowed, and Raiden drew his long, slim sword. The man's blade rose, and when it began to fall Raiden's sword flickered. It laid open the man's forearm, severing skin and tendons with surgical precision. Vito shrieked and his pale green blade clattered to the ground.

The bloodwizard whirled away, clutching his injured arm to his chest, cursing. Raiden took two steps toward the innkeeper and his daughter, intending to shield them if the man attempted another attack. It would have been an easy thing to run the tattooed man through, but Raiden chose restraint. He was a diplomat, after all.

His hesitation cost him. The man should have been incapacitated by his wound, but another wave of power burst from him. It wasn't as focused as his first attack. Not fire this time, but wind.

Caught off guard, the table of four were scattered like leaves along with the heavy wrought iron chairs and table. The innkeeper and his daughter crouched beneath the violent gust, pelted by sand and grit. The wind pushed Raiden into the street but didn't knock him down as it had the others. Raiden held his sword at the ready as, wild-eyed and blood-stained, the wizard Vito advanced on him, slashing across his bare chest with his remaining pale green blade. Fresh blood slid down his skin, gleaming with light. The tattoos adorning the Corsaro glowed and rippled, closing the cut almost as fast as Vito made it.

And suddenly, the oppressive heat of the day returned with a vengeance. Raiden's sword hilt seemed to gather the heat within its core, burning his palms like a brand. Raiden cried out, his hands springing open instinctively. His sword fell. Grinning, the wizard cut his own chest again, drawing a new line beneath the first, spilling fresh blood.

The air shimmered in front of Raiden's eyes like the distortion around a raging forge. Invisible flames beat against his face and he staggered back. His gaze flickered to the other men who'd been caught up in Vito's attack. They stood together, watching, the long-haired men gathered behind the youth like an odd set of guards. Raiden blinked sweat from his eyes. He'd get no help from them.

"Why don't you burn?" Vito said, his voice raw and ragged. Vito's knife flashed again, drawing blood from his tattooed thigh just beneath his armored pteruges.

The heat became suffocating. The air burned away in this unseen fire. Raiden gasped, and searing agony greeted his efforts.

With sudden clarity, he knew he was going to die. He couldn't fight this man's magic. His legs collapsed beneath him. He crashed to his knees on the hard cobblestones and lifted his face to the heavens. Bright, the sky was so bright. Even the buildings shone with an inner radiance. The whole world was alight.

Death did not frighten him. He'd delivered death to more men than he could count. Now, it was his turn. All he felt was relief.

The wizard loomed over him, a triumphant look on his face. Then, suddenly, behind the Corsaro arose another figure, this one slim and crowned with radiant hair, an angel come to earth. In the clear sight brought by imminent death, details leapt at Raiden: a wry smile on perfect, pink lips, eyes the color of green agate, the proud tilt of a dimpled chin. A slash of late afternoon sun found and illuminated a figure that was unmistakably female beneath snug trousers and a tight-fitting vest. Raiden knew he had never and would never see anything or anyone so incredibly beautiful.

"Enough!"

Her voice rang like a bell. There was a flash of movement, a blackness in the light, and suddenly Raiden felt a flush of cold wash over him. The terrible burning vanished, the relief so abrupt and wonderful, he nearly passed out. His vision grew white, then dark. Then slowly, the world returned.

The bloodwizard Vito had turned away from him to face the interloper. The brightness had faded, leaving a dust-colored scene: the woman – no angel, he realized now that she was no longer wreathed in light – stood with her legs wide, and two black blades in her fists. Her embroidered vest left her arms, shoulders and midriff bare, revealing elaborate tattoos stenciled on her skin.

Another bloodwizard? A woman *bloodwizard?* As far as he knew, there was only one in all of Malavita, and she came with a warning: *"Beware the witch who wields obsidian, for she is a fiend and a scoundrel. A wanted murderer in league with demons."*

It couldn't be her, but the black blades put the lie to his thought. She carried obsidian...

Her hair was a dirty blonde, and he recognized the long braid. She was the youth who'd been sitting with the three long-haired men. Not a youth, obviously, now that she'd lost the loose jacket and concealing hat. A look of predatory glee stole some of the beauty from her heart-shaped face. Raiden shook his head. He could breathe, but his lungs felt raw.

"Puttana!" spat Vito. He made no move to wield his remaining blade but had hunched in on himself like a dog waiting for a kick.

The woman made a scornful noise. "Now, now. No calling me names. You wouldn't want to upset me."

Her three companions stood behind her, the oldest a step apart from the two younger men. Humor danced in the gray eyes of the young ones, but the elder's gaze held a smoldering rage. His hand grasped the hilt of his single quartz blade. Only the woman had blades drawn, though.

"I am not afraid of you, or the Golondrina scum who lick your boots!" Vito stood straighter, gesturing with his blade. His injured arm was clutched to his belly. "Nor do I fear your black blades, witch. They are glass! Not true gemstone blades."

The woman narrowed her eyes. "Do you wish to test them, Beryl Wizard? Have you so much confidence in your Three Faces against the Four and the Hidden?"

Vito flushed, scowling. His blade hovered above his arm. He spared a glance to where his other blade lay on the cobblestones and seemed to weigh his odds. Suddenly, he relaxed and slowly slipped his blade back into its sheath. With a jerk of his chin toward the burnt innkeeper, he said sullenly, "He still owes my Capo. I can't go back empty-handed, or it will be my skin."

The woman's lips thinned. "How much does he owe?"

"Ten gold. Two weeks' worth of protection."

"Protection," she scoffed. "He only needs protection from the likes of you and your Capo."

"He owes us!"

"Very well, but let this be the end of it. You can tell Capo Valentine this place doesn't need his protection anymore. Cyril. Pay the man."

The eldest of the three men, dark-eyed and swarthy with a handsome mane of black, curly hair touched with silver, reluctantly dug into his belt pouch. With a flick of his fingers he tossed a small leather bag at Vito. The Corsaro man caught it, opened it and turned the contents onto his palm. Three bright blue gems the size of almonds glittered in the sun. Vito frowned as if he'd been struck a bad bargain.

"They are worth more than ten gold, thief," the man called Cyril said in a low, gruff voice.

Wisely, Vito didn't argue, and swiftly tucked the treasure into his own belt pouch – the arm Raiden had slashed at the beginning of the unfortunate encounter had stopped bleeding and looked as well as the other. Raiden gritted his teeth. Strange magic.

Smirking, Vito retrieved his fallen blade and sheathed it,

moving leisurely. "I'll be telling my Capo about this, witch."

"Oh, please do," she said.

Whistling, Vito sauntered down the street. Only when he was gone from sight did the woman take her eyes off him. Her gaze settled on Raiden as she slipped her blades into sheaths along her forearms.

"Petra," she said quietly. "Tend to the innkeeper, will you?"

One of the younger men nodded; his hair was nearly as red as his companion's colorful shirt. He flashed Raiden a grin before turning to help the innkeeper.

"Let's get them inside," the one called Cyril said in his gravelly voice, his eyes on Raiden, evaluating. Raiden felt like he was coming up short in the man's estimation, and he lifted a brow. Cyril turned away and the three carried the injured man into the interior of the taverna, the serving maid following, wringing her hands. She gave the woman a few nervous glances as she left the patio.

The woman was watching him, though, her head tilted. Her green agate eyes took him in with a quick up-and-down glance. And just as quickly dismissed him. Raiden scowled. Few men had dared look at him with such disdain. How had he mistaken this *creature* for an angel?

"You are brave, if a bit foolish," she said finally. "You can't fight a bloodwizard with steel. But I was expecting a diplomat, not a soldier. It's a pleasant surprise. Welcome to Malavita, Captain Mad. Dante Safire sends his regards."

"Dante Safire?" Raiden blinked, thrown off guard. "You work for the prince?"

She smiled as if he'd made a clever joke. "Not quite. I am Shade Nox. I'm–"

"You are the Black Witch!" he burst out. "And in the name of the Bhaskar Empire, you are under arrest!"

CHAPTER TWO

It took a moment for his words to register, and then Shade burst into laughter. It was too ridiculous not to laugh. Dusty and singed as he was, the short, boyish-looking Imperial was deadly serious. It only made her laugh harder. At least he'd had the decency to announce she was under arrest. The Brotherhood would have put a knife in her back then said it. They'd been sending assassins after her since the day she'd crafted her obsidian blades – true blades, not crude approximations – a skill only a Brotherhood Blademaster was supposed to possess. They wanted her *scrubbed* from the world like a nasty stain. The Capomaji and their Corsaro, on the other hand, merely wanted her dead. It wasn't a woman's place to challenge them, after all. And most certainly not a woman's place to be stronger than they were. Being placed under arrest by a foreign emissary whose life she'd just saved was hilarious in comparison.

She was still chortling when she felt the cold kiss of steel beneath her chin. Her mirth died as she followed the length of his sword to his black eyes. Anger lurked in their depths. So, the little soldier didn't like being laughed at? Well, she didn't like having a razor-sharp blade at her throat.

"Put away your weapon," she said. "I am not your enemy."

"No," he agreed. "You are my prisoner."

She couldn't help it, she smiled. His sword grazed her skin in warning, and she clamped her lips together. "What exactly are the charges, soldier?"

"Captain," he corrected her. He held his sword rock steady. This was not a man easily rattled. "It is Captain Mad. And you are charged with murder, heresy, rabble-rousing, and sartorial misconduct."

"Sartorial…? Ah, yes, they don't like it when I dress like a man, but skirts and corsets make it rather difficult to practice my magic. Besides, it's dreadfully hard to get blood out of silk. Well, now that you have me, captain, what are you going to do with me?"

"I'll turn you in to the local authorities, of course. You will be processed and held until an Imperial magistrate can be summoned. Your guilt or innocence will be determined through a fair trial."

"The 'local authorities' call me a witch and an abomination and fabricated most of the charges against me. Of course, I'll get a fair trial."

His lips thinned. "Nevertheless, my duty is clear. There is an Imperial warrant with your name on it and I must follow the law."

"My name? It says 'Shade Nox' on this warrant?"

"The warrant is for the Black Witch, but you are obviously the Black Witch!"

"Am I?" She spread her hands. Carefully, slowly. Trying her best to look innocent and meek. "Why would you assume such a thing, captain?"

"You carry obsidian, you bear tattoos, you obviously practice bloodmagic, and that Corsaro called you a witch!"

"I've been called worse…"

"Don't make this harder than it is. I know you saved my life, but I never asked you to interfere. And I cannot ignore who you are, or the charges leveled against you, because you fought in my defense. It is my duty."

She held his gaze, all-too aware of the blade at her throat. "Your duty is to deliver a royal charter to Prince Safire. I am here as his representative because he is my ally, and my friend. He is also a loyal Imperial subject who served in your army as was his duty. Ask yourself: would such a man ally himself with a criminal?"

"It is not my place to determine your guilt or innocence," he reiterated stubbornly. "I must follow the law."

Faces. An Imperial who actually cares about the law? Damn my luck.

"Let's make a bargain then," she proposed, struck with inspiration. "Let me escort you to Dante Safire as planned. Listen to what we have to say, and when all is said and done between us, I will let you take me to the local authorities."

His forehead wrinkled. "How can I trust you to keep your word?"

"By trusting me to keep it." She gave him her best smile, though sweat slipped along her spine. "Like I'll trust you not to run me through with that very sharp sword of yours."

He regarded her a moment, then with a move as smooth as silk, he returned his sword to the sheath tucked in his crimson sash. "Very well. I will take you at your word. If you are Safire's agent, I must accompany you. But consider yourself in my custody."

Certain he wouldn't stab her in the back, Shade turned away and stooped to grab up her discarded jacket and hat. She grimaced. The plan had been to meet the Imperial emissary as Dante's ward and fosterling, and then escort him from the city without incident. Safe inside Dante's villa, they would have revealed their alliance: a city-prince of Sicaria, the last scion of a First Family, and the Black Witch of Malavita, fiend, rogue and wanted murderer. Cyril had wanted to approach him immediately and deliver him to Dante, but she'd insisted they observe him first to take his measure. This man carried their hopes for a Veil with him. If not for Vito, everything would have gone smoothly. Damn Corsaro–

She spun to face him, her arm in one sleeve of her jacket. "Why didn't you burn?" she demanded.

He blinked. "What?"

"Vito was throwing everything at you. I felt it. He was calling enough of the Southern Face to burn down a building. And yet, you didn't burn."

His eyes grew thoughtful and he rested a hand on his sword hilt. She remembered the speed and ease with which he'd wielded his weapon and regarded it as she would a coiled snake. "Perhaps we Bhaskarans have a resistance to your magic?"

"No," she said slowly. "You aren't the first Imperial to grace our shores. Your people don't do well in my land. Few foreigners do. But you, you're different. What makes you so special, captain?"

He pressed his lips together and lifted his chin. "I am the seventh son of Emperor Suijin, seventh of his name, Divine Ruler of the Bhaskar Empire," he said gravely. "I suppose that makes me somewhat 'special'."

She lifted her eyebrows. An Emperor's son?

"I'm not in line for succession," he added quickly. He ran a hand through his mop of black hair, and added, somewhat bitterly, "I hold no titles beyond my humble rank, and I serve at the Emperor's pleasure. Whatever immunity I might have to your magic comes from the benefit of my father's blood, I suspect. It is merely good fortune."

"I'm guessing the son of an Emperor knows a lot about 'good fortune'."

He stared at her a moment, then for some reason he laughed, though there was little humor in it.

Strange man. Shade turned toward the taverna. Gentle waves of energy pulsed from within. Bloodmagic, but a softer sort than she wielded. A healing magic. Cyril and his nephews, Manoli and Petra, were all natural healers as most Golondrina were, and they would be able to ease the innkeeper's pain and heal some of the damage, but the unfortunate man would be scarred for life. She grimaced, wishing she had stepped in sooner. But she hadn't expected Vito to strike so swiftly, or with such strength. Pain was a good motivator, but a man could hardly work half-burned and in agony. Bastard.

"What are they doing, those men? Your... companions?"

Shade smiled wryly at Raiden's hesitation. "My 'companions' are my family, my clan," she said. "And they are healing that poor man as best they can."

"So, they *are* bloodwizards. But... in all my briefings, no one ever mentioned healers among the Bloodwizards of Malavita."

She threw him a glance. "They are Golondrina."

"Golondrina?" His gaze skipped back toward the inn, his manner alert and curious. "The Swallows of the Wastes? I've read about them, but the stories seemed almost fantastical. More myth and legend than evidence and fact. Is it true they live outside the Veils? How is that even possible?"

"The Golondrina have been Waste-walkers since before the ashes from the last great battle between the Sicani and the Unseen had settled," Shade said, wondering how much of Malavita's history he'd learned before arriving on her shores. More than most, hopefully. "I'm sure the stories you've read are distorted versions of the truth. Veil-dwellers consider us little more than thieves and vagabonds despite their fascination with Golondrina tales and lore, but they take our labor when they can. Our craftsmen are some of the best in the land. Golondrina hands built most of the cities beneath the Veils, though they have no city for themselves. No Veil, either."

In a flash, Shade saw again the vision which had haunted her dreams for years: a broad dome of power rising over a valley between two broken hills, the Razor Ridge mountains looming in the background, and a woman at the center of it, her blades gleaming white with magic. At her feet pulsed four perfect gemstones – an emerald, a diamond, a ruby, and a sapphire. The cornerstones for a Quattro Canto. The foundation of a Veil. *Her* Veil.

But. She had no stones, only a hope for the location she desired (a location *foretold*, by the Faces!), and an Imperial emissary who wanted to apprehend her. So far, so good.

"The stories say the Golondrina are cursed to wander because they are in league with the demons that destroyed Malavita," the Imperial was saying, throwing out one of the most harmful beliefs about her people as if talking about the weather. "That their sins against the Four and the Hidden include cavorting with the twisted beasts of the Wastes and worshipping the dead." He made a disdainful noise. "Most stories like those are born of superstition and ignorance, I've found. Everyone needs an 'other' to hate and fear."

His casual recitation of the Golondrina's so-called sins had made her stiffen with rising anger, but just as quickly she relaxed when he dismissed the tales as the nonsense they were. "We've had plenty of petty rulers to hate and fear," she said, giving him a quick smile and a wink when he turned on her with a slight scowl. "Not your Empire, of course. The Bhaskar Empire has been nothing but benevolent."

"We have," he answered in all seriousness. "We show benevolence to all our territories and colonies, no matter how small or troublesome they may be, hoping they will become productive members of our vast Empire in time. But our patience has limits. Malavita would be wise to learn this lesson sooner rather than later. However, Dante Safire's loyalty and cooperation gives us hope."

Raiden turned his attention back to the taverna, luckily for her. She was having a hard time keeping the disgust off her face. He spoke about her home as if it were a recalcitrant toddler who needed to be disciplined by its parent. Emperor's son or not, he had no right to be so dismissive.

"You called them family," he said after a moment. "Yet you

don't look like them." He eyed her shrewdly. "You aren't one of them, are you?"

Observant little bastard. "No, I am not a Golondrina by birth, but I am one of them. They took me in after I was cast into the Wastes by people who should have helped me. Though I had my blades, I didn't have my wards and I was only a girl, alone and defenseless. Cyril found me when I was a breath from dying. He saved me and gave me a home among his people. They have always treated me as a treasured daughter. I owe them everything."

And I intend to repay them.

A moment later, Cyril and the boys emerged from the inn. Petra was pale, but steady, and Manoli was watching him closely. Although the younger of the two cousins, Manoli had always been the protector. Since he'd lost his mother to a Waste beast last winter, he'd been especially protective of his remaining family.

"He'll live," Cyril said to her raised brow.

"He'll never be the same," Petra added grimly. His gray eyes shone beneath his russet brows. Shade ached for him; he had a kind heart. Sometimes, too kind for his own good.

"Corsaro bastard," Manoli said, and spat. His eyes sparked dangerously, and Shade knew they had to make haste to Dante's villa. If they crossed paths with more Corsaro, she feared Manoli might strike without thinking.

"Let's go," Shade said. "We have to deliver our new friend to Safire. He carries all our hopes with him."

The three Golondrina looked at Raiden as one, and he blinked at them in obvious confusion. "I don't carry anything for you people," he said. "My business is with Prince Dante Safire. I won't speak to it any further until I am in his presence. I only have your word that you are allied with him, after all, and little other proof besides."

Shade exchanged a look with Cyril, who raised an eloquent eyebrow and fingered his knife hilt surreptitiously. She hid a smile. Her old friend and mentor was the closest thing to a father that she had – certainly closer to it than her actual father had been – and she respected him more than anyone else. But his natural suspicion was sometimes a liability. He didn't care for Dante Safire, or any Veil-dweller for that matter. And he cared even less for the Empire. But Shade knew they couldn't succeed alone. They would need someone as powerful as Dante Safire as their ally when they managed to raise their Veil, or the Brotherhood would bring it crashing down around their ears. The Safire name carried weight in Malavita. He was one of the First Families. Other lords would be on his side in this endeavor, too many for the Brotherhood to discount. But even Dante had been doubtful his clout and strength would be enough to keep a fledgling Veil safe. Thus, his appeal to the Empire.

"And I thought we were all friends," she said to Raiden. She shrugged when his expression hardened. "No matter. Trust me, captain, the proof in the pudding is when you taste it, and I've got a fine pudding for you."

Raiden frowned. "What nonsense is that?"

"If your Empire wants its Veil, and the land and gems it will provide, I'm afraid your business is with me as well as Prince Safire."

"I assure you, my lady, the Empire does not do business with criminals."

"Oh, I think it will. If it wants the Veil, as I said."

"Dante Safire promised us the Veil."

"But for all his skill as a wielder of sapphire blades and his ancient blood as a descendent of a First Family, Dante Safire will not raise it." His look of shock made her grin. With a sweep of her hand, and a mocking bow, she announced grandly, "I will raise your Imperial Veil, captain. The Black Witch of Malavita!"

CHAPTER THREE

"You must understand my dilemma, Your Highness," the Imperial emissary was saying as Shade paused outside the doorway to Dante's private study. A fire crackled in the hearth behind the two men, lending an air of intimacy to the cozy, wood-paneled room, but Raiden stood stiffly as he addressed the prince. "As a law-abiding citizen, I cannot turn a blind eye to–"

"Would you care for some port, Captain Mad?"

Mouth half-open in mid-speech, the Imperial stared at the small glass of ruby-colored liquid Dante held as if he didn't quite understand what it was. Perhaps remembering his manners, the black-haired man accepted it with a grumbled "Thank you."

Smiling, Dante raised his own glass in a salute and took a small sip, his bright blue eyes fixed on the emissary. He stood half-a-head taller than Raiden and was far broader in the shoulders. His sable hair was constrained in a long queue down his back and he sported a neatly trimmed beard as was the fashion among the nobility. Dressed in a fine silk shirt the color of cream and form-fitting trousers that flattered his long, muscular legs, high, black boots gleaming even in the dim lighting, he looked every inch the gentleman, even with sapphire blades at his hips. But those fine clothes covered a body painted boldly in the tattoos of his art. Dante Safire was a city-prince, a wealthy merchant, and the last scion of an ancient line, but he was a powerful bloodwizard, as well.

After leaving the Black Rooster, they'd made haste to Dante's villa high on Montesegundo, arriving without further incident, thank the Faces. Leaving her friends to dice with the stable hands, she'd taken Raiden into the main house through the servants' entrance. Dante's staff knew her well in her guise as his fosterling – a broad-brimmed hat, loose, shapeless jacket and long trousers, but more importantly a slouching gait and downcast gaze – and she was greeted with smiles and nods. Everyone liked the shy boy Dante had taken in as a favor to a dying nobleman in some faraway Veil. A nobleman who didn't exist, of course.

On their journey to the villa, she had explained her subterfuge to Raiden: not everyone in Dante's sphere knew he harbored the Black Witch.

"I suppose concealing your identity is the least of your crimes," he'd said, correcting himself with a thin-lipped smile, "*alleged* crimes."

Glad to hand him off to Dante's personal valet after that comment, she'd taken a back hallway and sought her suite on the second floor of the sprawling villa. It wouldn't do to meet Dante as a callow youth. Nor would she appear dressed as a bloodwizard – only a few of Dante's most trusted retainers had seen her dressed in the armored leather skirt and snug vest she wore in the Wastes. Even they thought she was some odd, painted whore, not the notorious Black Witch. Tonight, she would let Lizette, the sole lady's maid among Dante's staff, transform her into a proper lady.

Preparing to make her entrance, Shade smoothed the blue silk of her skirt and checked the lace at her neck and wrists. Lizette had worked her magic with artfully applied cosmetics and perfume, and she'd arranged Shade's hair in a glorious cascade of golden waves. The pale blue silk she'd chosen flattered her curves and skin tone as effectively as it hid her tattoos. It was also Dante's favorite color...

"My lord, there is a warrant for her arrest, and the charges against her are quite serious. Surely, you understand I am required to enforce the law–"

"It's not nice to talk about someone behind her back," Shade said, lifting her skirts to keep from stepping on them as she swept into the room. The two men turned, and Shade suppressed a pleased smile at the looks on their faces. Approval and admiration danced in Dante's eyes, and his teeth flashed white through his dark beard. Raiden's angled eyes went wide beneath his forelock of silky black hair. He clicked his heels and gave a hasty bow, nearly spilling his drink in the process.

Her head lowered demurely, she glided to the fireplace and held her hands above the flames. Although the days were growing hot with the advent of spring, the nights were still cool. She glanced over her shoulder coquettishly. "Have you missed me, captain?"

He blinked. "I'm sorry, but have we met? I don't believe I would have forgotten meeting a lady of such grace and refinement. You must be the Lady Safire."

Shade looked at Dante and caught the mirth in his bright blue eyes. Her lips pursed. Was it so amusing to think she could be the wife of a Malavitan prince? "Prince Safire has no wife," she said. Changing her voice and her expression, she turned away from the fire. "And we have met, Captain Mad. You arrested me, remember?"

Again, his eyes widened in astonishment. But he composed himself rapidly. "Of course. Lady Nox. Again, my apologies, but you look – well, you look quite lovely, my lady."

"Are you saying I didn't before?" she demanded.

"No, I mean, you were dressed like a boy before–"

"And boys can't be lovely?"

He pressed his lips together and raised his glass. "If I say you are lovely in all forms, my lady, will you accept my apology?"

She bowed her head. At least he could take a joke.

"We were just discussing the matter of your arrest," Dante

said, taking a sip of port, his bright blue eyes dancing at her. "The captain isn't quite sure what to do with you."

"I thought we'd come to an agreement," she said. "I am in your custody until all is said and done between us."

Raiden glanced around the comfortable chamber. "Are you? It doesn't exactly feel like it."

"Should I be in chains? Would that make you more comfortable?"

"Of course not–"

"Then I don't see the problem." She turned to Dante. "Can't a girl get a drink in this place?"

"This girl can get whatever she wants," Dante said, and poured her a glass of port from the crystal service on the sideboard. Dante's favorite, not hers, but she accepted it with only a slight quirk to her subtly painted lips. She held his gaze as she took a sip, and he graced her with a small smile before turning his attention back to Raiden.

"Well, now that we have gotten all this 'under arrest' nonsense out of the way, let us move on to the business at hand, shall we?"

"It's not exactly 'out of the way', my lord. Nor is it nonsense. The Empire has issued a warrant–"

"Do you like the port, captain?" Dante asked, waving his own small, crystal glass beneath his nose. "It's an Imperial vintage. One I grew fond of during my school days. Though I'm sure it isn't as fine as what was served in the Imperial palace."

Raiden sipped his port, casting a glance toward Shade. "I wouldn't know," he said. "As I told the lady, I serve at the Emperor's pleasure. I am not a prince. I hope you don't think my Imperial blood has any relevance to your request, my lord. Malavita is, after all, a small, remote colony, and so far, little more than a nuisance."

Shade's eyes widened at his casual disdain and quickly jumped to Dante to gauge his reaction. His jaw was clenched, and his eyes glittered dangerously. Shade tensed. He might have been educated in the Empire as a boy, but he was Malavitan through and through. When his parents had been murdered in a blood vendetta, he'd returned home to protect his only sister, earned his sapphire blades at the tender age of sixteen and set about consolidating his family's holdings. Which involved engaging in a violent war with his parents' killer, the Capomajus Rubeus. The war had cost him everything dear, including his sister and her young daughter, but Capo Rubeus and his vast Corsaro army were no more.

Thankfully, Dante's anger vanished in a flash of bright teeth, and he lifted his glass to the Imperial. "Let this be the first step toward my homeland becoming less of a nuisance then," he said. He gestured toward one of the cushioned chairs beside the hearth. "Please, have a seat so we may discuss my charter."

Raiden looked inclined to argue but took a seat. He shifted on the velvet-covered chair, settling his sword beside him, and moving his satchel to his knees. Shade's gaze locked on the leather bag. She perched on the overstuffed chair across from his and held herself like a proper lady, all stiff-backed and prim. Near them, the fire crackled pleasantly, but did little to alleviate the tension in the room.

"I have the charter with me, of course," Raiden said to Dante. "Drafted by the Emperor's own scribes. It is a boon, as this isn't usually the reward for loyal service to the Empire. Most royal charters are granted to Imperial-born citizens. A land grant to a colonist, even one educated in the Empire, is an odd arrangement. But if you actually have the capability of raising a Veil in the Wastes, cutting out the Brotherhood, and granting the Empire unfettered access to productive pit mines and fertile cropland once the Veil is established, the value of such an enterprise would be immense. The Empire will happily provide legal and political protection to a new Veil. An Imperial Veil. The Emperor hopes it will be the first of many."

"I'm glad you have confidence in my abilities," Shade said with a thin smile.

Dante sighed, giving her an irritated look. "You told him you'd be raising the Veil? Was that before or after he arrested you?"

She shrugged. "After. Didn't seem necessary to obfuscate. We need to know where the Empire stands before we're in too deep to turn back."

"Where we stand is clear," Raiden said, drawing her attention to him. "We want a Veil raised for the Empire, but we have no desire to antagonize the Brotherhood. They are the sole source of the precious gems so highly valued in the Empire, the ones imbued with magic and power. Which is why I've come alone and over the transom, so to speak. If this endeavor fails, I have been instructed to engage in talks with the Brotherhood to renegotiate our arrangement with the church. The flow of gems into the Empire is our primary concern."

"The Brotherhood will never renegotiate their terms," Shade said sharply. Was he really going to run to the Brotherhood if things went wrong? She threw Dante a worried glance. He had remained standing, looming over the emissary's chair, and annoyance clouded his eyes. He returned her look, his expression grim.

"You cannot break their power or their control as long as they maintain their monopoly on the Veils." She leaned toward Raiden like a cat about to pounce. Her voice dropped, forcing him to lean closer, as well. "The Veils are life. Every Veil-dweller believes their safety, their very existence, depends on the Brotherhood, and they pay crippling taxes out of gratitude and fear. The Brotherhood claim the Veils are holy, sacrosanct. But they lie to keep themselves in power. They hide the secret to the Veils' construction to keep us all in thrall."

"Yet somehow, *you* know their secrets," Raiden countered wryly, the shadow of a smile on his lips.

"Why do you think they want me dead?"

"The laws are different in many lands, but in most places, murderers are executed."

It was subtle, the implied threat, but Dante Safire stiffened and clapped a hand to a blade hilt. Raiden barely moved, but suddenly he was showing a foot of steel. It caught the firelight in a golden blaze. The two men locked eyes and the cozy study became charged.

"I am no murderer," Shade said, speaking casually despite her pounding heart. Her own blades were strapped to her calves and she itched to draw them. But she knew how fast Raiden could wield his sword. She'd never reach them. Force was not the answer.

"Why would I kill the man who taught me how to craft my own blades? Why would I kill the man who trained me?" As she spoke, calmly, reasonably, Raiden relaxed bit by bit and Dante eased his grip on the hilt of his sapphire blade. Their eyes remained locked, however. Shade licked her lips and took a sip of port to hide the shaking in her hand. Though not her favorite, the slightly sweet, berry-touched liquid was as fine as promised. But she still wished for brandy. She took a deep breath, and said quietly, "Why would I kill my own father?"

Raiden's sword disappeared into its sheath with a resounding snap. He stared at her, his lips parted. "Your father was a Brotherhood bishop?"

She nodded, catching Dante's grimace out of the corner of her eye. He knew it was painful for her to talk about her father. His torture and murder at the hands of Brotherhood assassins haunted her – the Ruby Pontifex were masters of cruelty – but she'd held little affection for the man who'd taught her all she knew about magic. He'd known every Brotherhood secret and had gleefully bestowed them upon his daughter. But only after she'd spent much of her childhood toiling in a Brotherhood pit mine, her untapped potential allowing her to find the best gemstones for her masters. Bishop Raphael had saved her from that life, true, but he'd raised her as a student and a protégé, not as a daughter.

"A bishop and a Blademaster," she said. "He had his own reasons for betraying his organization, and I was a convenient tool. Nevertheless, I learned what was necessary. I learned how to raise a Veil. I learned things no wizard outside of the Brotherhood knows. And for that, they killed him, and they've been hunting me ever since."

By now, Dante's hand had moved away from his weapon and Raiden had relaxed into his chair, his sheathed sword laid innocently across his knees. The Imperial was regarding her with narrowed eyes. The tension had eased from the room, thankfully.

"So. Even if the charges against you are fabricated—" His tone radiated skepticism and Shade's jaw clenched. He may as well have called her a liar. "Even if you are as innocent as a lamb, the fact remains the Brotherhood has it out for you. And as I said before, we have no wish to antagonize them."

"If we succeed in raising a Veil, believe me, they will be antagonized."

"With our own Veil, and all that comes with it, we won't care if they are antagonized at that point. The concern is if you fail. Imagine their rage if they learn we went to the notorious Black Witch to circumvent their control?"

"Does the mighty Bhaskar Empire fear this tiny island so much?" she asked, waving a hand. "After all, you could raze our nation to the ground if you so chose."

"That is not our way," he replied firmly. "We wish to bring peace and prosperity to our land. Our entire land, even this small part of it. We only engage in war when there is no other option. And, luckily for all involved, Prince Safire brought us that option." He exhaled and scrubbed a hand over his face. "Why not just tell Prince Safire how to raise a Veil? It would certainly be more palatable for him to work the magic for us. He's a lord and a member of a First Family; he's greatly respected by the Empire and a loyal ally."

Shade bit down on a sigh and looked at Dante. He met her gaze and knew what she was asking. She didn't want to say it for him, but it had to be said. Most of the time, she found his arrogance amusing, but sometimes it was annoyingly inconvenient.

"It wouldn't matter even if I wanted her to share the very, very complicated process with me," Dante said. He paused, and for the first time she could recall, Dante Safire looked uncomfortable. "And I hate to admit it, but I don't have the power or the will to raise a Veil myself. It would make me vulnerable in too many ways. Shade is stronger than most bloodwizards, me included. It won't be easy, but only she can raise the Veil."

Shade let loose a breath. When she'd first come to him over a year ago, Dante hadn't believed her a real bloodwizard – not until she'd wielded her blades and proved it to him. Even then, he'd been loath to admit her obsidian might outmatch his sapphire. It was pleasing to hear him admit she was the stronger. Surprising, and oh, so satisfying.

"I had to prove myself to Prince Safire," she said, watching Dante. He met her gaze, his eyes shadowed and unreadable. Her belly tightened at his intense scrutiny. "I can prove myself to the Empire, too." Reluctantly, she took her eyes from Dante and turned to Raiden.

He was silent for a long moment. The firelight limned his black hair and one smooth cheek, casting half his face in shadow. Despite his boyish appearance, a deep stillness emanated from him, a patience unusual in such a seemingly callow soldier. "Very well," he said at last, the words pulled from him grudgingly. "You have backed me into a corner with these revelations, but I am here to speak for the Empire. It is my mission to determine the feasibility of your proposal and either grant you the charter or deny it. The matter of your warrant, my lady, is yet to be determined, but for now we will put it aside."

"How kind of you," Shade murmured, tossing back the last of her port in a most unladylike manner. At his hard look, she smiled and gave him a wink.

"There are several other matters to be determined in the meantime." He raised a fist and lifted his index finger. "One: where will you raise this new Veil? An appropriate site is vital to its success."

"We have some plans in motion..."

And I know where I will raise it, Faces turn to me. Where I must *raise it.*

A second finger. "Two: how will you acquire the stones you need for the so-called 'four corners' necessary to raise the Veil? Or did your bishop father already give you those vital tools?"

Shade bristled. "The Quattro Canto is the sacred foundation of all Veils. They are more than tools. They are the very elements encapsulated and bound by spirit – the Hidden Face of God!"

He blithely ignored her outrage. "Then I take it they are important."

Before she could erupt, Dante stepped in and laid a hand on her shoulder. "I would never have started down this path if I didn't have knowledge of where to acquire the cornerstones we need," he said calmly, giving her a reassuring squeeze. "You need not concern yourself."

Raiden tipped his head, acquiescing, though Shade was less than mollified. Dante still hadn't revealed where he planned to get the stones for the Quattro Canto. Only the Brotherhood had access to the mines containing such rare and powerful gemstones, and they were an unlikely source. But she had to trust him; he'd been a faithful ally so far.

The captain lifted a third finger, continuing as if he'd not been interrupted. "And three: who will populate this Veil once it is raised? Will they be willing to work with the Empire? Or will they choose the criminal Capomaji out of misguided loyalty to the demons they know?"

"My clan will populate the Veil upon its raising, and they have never been beholden to anyone. Once the Veil expands to cover enough reclaimed land," *a shield rising over a valley between two broken hills*, "we will open it to any Veil-dweller who wishes to attempt a life free of their current overlords. The Capos and their Corsaro will not be welcome."

"This is our goal, captain," Dante said. "Not gems or land or power over those dependent on our magic. We want freedom for all Malavitans. We want to expose the Brotherhood and end their oppressive control of our land."

Raiden frowned. "You know that is not our goal. We have no desire to encourage an internecine war in our own colony."

"Nor do we," Dante countered quickly. "Too many wars have devastated Malavita already. Change is always messy, but with the Empire on our side, we believe we can avoid violence. And we've already laid plans to address all your concerns. Shade will be traveling into the Wastes tomorrow to meet with an important representative. Hopefully, it will be the first step toward determining the location of the Veil. We can't just drop it anywhere in the Wastes. We must anchor it at an appropriate place. One with a water source and potentially arable land–"

"And rich deposits of gems, of course," Raiden remarked.

Dante's lips thinned. "Of course..."

"I'll be leaving first thing in the morning with Cyril and the boys." Shade leaned back in the cushioned chair and threw a leg over the armrest, abandoning all pretense of being a lady. There was hardly any point with Raiden. He'd seen her as a boy and a bloodwizard. The subterfuge had lost all meaning. A more direct approach seemed easier. "I'll be gone no more than a day or two. I'm sure Dante can keep you entertained until I return–"

Raiden's laughter interrupted her. It was full of genuine amusement. She dropped her foot to the floor in surprise. What the hells was so funny?

"I'm afraid you won't be going anywhere without me, my lady," he said. "You are in my custody, after all."

"The Wastes are a dangerous and unpredictable place," she

argued. She had no desire to drag him through the Wastes; she wasn't some for-hire bloodwizard protecting a merchant train. "No place for someone without bloodmagic. Your sword won't save you from the twisted magic which infests the unprotected lands. The Unseen's blight will warp your soul."

"I assure you that my soul is already sufficiently warped." Raiden stood, adjusting his satchel and sword with one hand, the other still gripping his glass of port. He quaffed it and settled it on the marble-topped table beside his chair. Clicking his heels together, he bowed to her. "I will see you at dawn, my lady."

Shade stared at him, open-mouthed, but he had already turned toward Dante, effectively ending their exchange. "My lord, might I be shown to my room?"

"Of course, let me ring my valet…"

Seething, Shade waited until Dante's elderly valet had led the Imperial out of the study before jumping to her feet to confront him. "I will not take him into the Wastes with me," she snapped. "It will be difficult enough to negotiate with the Kindred. I can't bring an outsider!"

"He's not an outsider, Shade," he rebuked her gently. "He's our ally. And we need the protection of the Imperial charter he has the sole discretion to grant us. I know you're very hopeful the Kindred will give you access to the land you desire, but I am less sure. Perhaps if they understand we'll have the backing of the Empire, they'll be more inclined to give us what we want."

She wasn't so sure about that. The Kindred were an insular and secretive Golondrina clan almost as ancient as Malavita. They had seen a dozen empires come and go. She pursed her lips, prepared to argue, but he'd moved closer to her. He was quite tall; her eyes were level with his chest. His silk shirt was open at the collar and she could see the swirl of his tattoos in the cozy glow of the fireplace, the vibrant colors muted. Faint scars overlay his wards – he was no soft lord who had never wielded his own weapons. She lifted her face to him, her anger softening. He was far too good-looking, she decided. "Can I boot him into the sun once he signs it?" she asked, smiling sweetly.

He grinned and ran a hand down her arm, giving her wrist a squeeze before he slid away and crossed to the sideboard. She turned to watch him, her heartbeat oddly quick.

"Would you like another drink, my lady?" he asked, plucking a different decanter from his collection. "I believe your favorite is brandy, is it not?"

CHAPTER FOUR

It took the better part of the morning to reach the Veil wall. The Golondrina had opted for a cart drawn by a mule instead of the horses Prince Safire provided. Shade would have ridden in the cart with Cyril and the others, but Dante had insisted she ride with Raiden. The captain had pretended not to notice Dante's sly wink after Shade had clambered onto his horse and settled behind him. She was scandalously clad in a cropped vest and skirt of armored leather strips beneath a thin linen cloak, leaving her long, shapely legs exposed, but he was not an inexperienced boy to be distracted by a half-naked woman. He'd been forced to kill more than one would-be assassin who'd thought her feminine charms would be enough to fool him.

Still, he didn't necessarily mind the feel of her pressed against his back or her long fingers splayed at his hips. The angelic vision of her as he'd knelt on the brink of death flashed through his mind. He grimaced. This woman was not an angel. He felt foolish having to remind himself of it.

She's certainly not an angel, but is she a killer?

Someday, he would have to decide, but not this day.

In the gray light of dawn they passed verdant fields, tidy vineyards, and sprawling orchards, following a winding road between green and gold hills. The Veil was a pale stain across

40

the sky. Where it had been scorched pale near the sea, here it was tinged with rouge. Even the brutal sun held a ruddy hue.

"How expansive is this Veil?" he asked as they followed along behind the painted cart, its three occupants watching him in a decidedly unfriendly manner. Even the russet-haired fellow, who had offered him a tentative smile earlier in the morning, now stared at him with a stony expression. The other two must have squashed his attempt at comradery. Raiden ignored them. It was no different from how his fellow soldiers in the Imperial army treated him. They had shown him the same respect one showed a coiled adder.

"From the sea, it seemed to stretch for miles along the coast," he prompted when he got no response.

She sighed and shifted in her seat, muttering something about "foul horses" before giving a grudging reply. "It does, in a way. The Veils which shelter the coast are many, not one. All together they make up the Golden Crescent."

The Golden Crescent. He nodded. The broad crescent of sheltered coastline contained large settlements and fertile cropland. Maps of Malavita marked each Veil in broad circles drawn over land and cities but did little to express the true nature of the magical shields. Now, within one, he had a slightly better understanding. "How do you know where one begins and another ends? They seemed to overlap in places, especially along the coast."

"For someone like you, I'm sure it's impossible to tell," she said. "But I can sense the edges of each Veil like I can my own skin."

"Is that true of all bloodwizards?"

"No. Just the strongest."

He supposed she had a right to be smug, though he'd only experienced a single instance of her power. That Corsaro, Vito, had certainly seemed reluctant to test her. "I suppose you had better be," he said. "Since you plan to raise a Veil."

"I am the strongest of the strong." She pulled back, her hands suddenly gone from his hips, though her thighs still grazed his.

"Yet you chose obsidian. It is hardly rare or precious. From what I've read, the Brotherhood Blademasters don't yield any stone below emerald. Why choose such a common gemstone?"

She was silent. He could feel the tension in her as she couldn't help but touch him riding pillion as she was. He genuinely was curious why she'd chosen obsidian, and he needed to know her true power. What if she wasn't strong enough to raise a Veil? What if her reputation was based on lies and exaggeration?

"Obsidian comes with risks," she said, after a moment. "It is born from the fires of the earth, suddenly, violently. Compared to the stronger gemstones, it is new and wild and unpredictable. It grants the wielder great power, power over the Four and the Hidden." She hesitated. "And a power most wizards don't dare touch."

He frowned. "What sort of power?"

He felt her move. A shrug? And suddenly she was pressed against him again, her breath warm on the back of his neck. "It's not important. Just hope I never have the need to wield it."

That was hardly a reassuring answer.

The horse stumbled slightly, and Shade grabbed him around the waist, squeezing hard enough to make him wheeze. The fiery chestnut mare Dante had given him to Raiden's delight recovered smoothly, picking daintily over the rutted path, but Shade didn't release her death grip. Her breath was hot and fast on the back of his neck.

Raiden grinned. So, the Black Witch was afraid of horses? He would have chuckled if he didn't think she'd toss him off the horse.

He kicked his mount into a trot, drawing a startled gasp from her. It pleased him more than he could say to feel her arms tighten around him.

At the Veil wall they left the cart and Raiden's mare with the guardsmen Dante had sent to drive the cart. Not Corsaro,

Dante had assured him adamantly, though they were dressed similarly but for baldrics across their chests in Safire blue. Apparently, the noble houses of Malavita all employed their own private armies of bloodwizards. The two men were trusted enough to see Shade in her wizard's garb. The dark-haired one, tall and pale and bearing tourmaline blades, gave Shade a friendly grin as he helped her down from the horse and let his gaze linger on her a bit longer than appropriate as she shed her cloak and tossed it in the back of the cart.

The man's fair-haired partner jabbed him in the ribs. "See to the horse, Matteo," he ordered gruffly, giving Raiden a respectful nod at the same time.

Raiden handed over his reins to Matteo, scowling, and the dark-haired young man ducked his head in chagrin.

"We walk from here," Shade said, oblivious to the interaction between Raiden and the guard. She tugged at the wide brim of her flat-topped hat, drawing it low over her eyes and gave him a sly smile. "The Golondrina are called Waste-walkers for a reason, captain."

Ahead of them, the Veil wall cut across the road in a translucent sheen. What was golden and green and fertile on their side turned russet and crimson and barren beyond it. The rolling hills became jagged and sullen. Blood-red sand replaced rich, brown earth, and twisted vegetation crowned the broken hills or grew thick and tangled between them. The others didn't hesitate to cross the barrier, but Raiden held his breath like he was jumping into a lake. A brush of awareness passed over him like a feather down his spine, then he was on the other side. Heat slammed him. Immediately, sweat slid down his spine and temples. He glanced at Shade; moisture gleamed on her tattooed skin.

The Golondrina had shed their colorful silk shirts to Raiden's surprise, revealing tattoo work as elaborate as a Corsaro's, but otherwise seemed unaffected by the heat. Cyril led the way along a narrow, rocky track while the two cousins, Manoli and Petra, disappeared into the hills to either side of them. Manoli, the black-haired cousin, gave him a fierce look before he vanished, and Raiden saluted him with a fist to his chest. He knew a scout on patrol when he saw one. The man's grey eyes had widened, and Raiden's gesture had drawn the shadow of a smile from him.

So. Not so unfriendly after all.

As they proceeded, the track between the raw, red hills grew steep and treacherous. Navigating the rocky path took some attention, but Raiden found his eyes falling on Shade as she moved effortlessly before him. She was remarkably fit, her body lean and muscular. He couldn't help but compare her to the soft, cultured women of the Imperial court. They were delicate birds kept in gilded cages and Shade was a hawk. Her wards seemed to glow with an inner light even in the harsh sun. He found his gaze lingering on her far too often as they traveled.

Once, when Cyril paused to let them pass ahead of him, Raiden let his eyes feast on her swaying hips a bit longer than he'd intended. Checking himself, he glanced away, and found the elder Golondrina watching him. His gray eyes were narrowed beneath his bushy brows and his hand rested on the blade tucked in his loose trousers, fingers tapping against it rhythmically.

Raiden swallowed and touched his fingers to his brow, feeling no better than the guard who'd ogled her earlier. From that point, he kept his eyes off Shade and concentrated on the land around them.

The Wastes. They were as harsh as he'd imagined. Hot as a forge, arid and broken, with a strange shimmering glare over the blood-red sands that made his eyes ache when he looked too long. But when he looked away to focus on the path beneath his feet, he caught shadows in the shifting light. Those shadows made his hackles rise. At first, he'd thought he was catching sight of the two cousins flanking them, but he grew less and less sure of it as they traveled. This land was demon-blighted, he knew. Perhaps more than blighted? Tales of the dread creatures which inhabited the Wastes had spread to the Empire. Were they more than deformed animals?

As the sun grew higher and the heat rose, he found himself desperate to track the shadows hounding them. His hand hard on his sword hilt, he whipped his head toward any slight movement of dark within the light. Sweat had soaked through his uniform jacket and his breath sounded harsh in his ears. Every instinct was warning him that danger was near, yet he couldn't see it. And to his increasing irritation, his companions seemed oblivious as they led him on a seemingly random route over and through the stark hills, twisting and turning in complete disregard of the terrain. Sometimes, they led him over steep grades and tumbling rocks rather than following the easier routes around such obstacles. He was beginning to think they were doing it deliberately. Were they leading him into a trap? Were those lurking shadows their allies?

He stopped when they reached a narrow, rocky ravine and Shade began to descend rather than take the easier way around. "No," he said flatly. "I won't be toyed with any longer. Why must you always take the hardest path?"

Below him, Shade stopped and glanced back at him, her eyes shadowed by her broad-brimmed hat, and her mouth bent in a frown, but behind him, Cyril barked a laugh. Shade's gaze shifted to her friend and her frown became a scowl.

"You're not the first person to ask me that," she said to him, even as she glared at Cyril. He'd come up to stand beside Raiden on the edge of the ravine. Raiden spared him a look and was surprised to see a smile lighting his face. The grim, dour elder was transformed. Laugh lines framed his eyes and he stood with arms akimbo, gazing fondly at Shade. The smile vanished abruptly when he caught Raiden's eye.

"We follow the qaraz," he said gruffly, once again all business. "Lines and nodes of pooled magic untouched by the taint of the Wastes. They are ancient and incorruptible. Strong wizards can walk the Wastes without following the qaraz, but it costs blood and magic. Traders and travelers, those weak in magic, depend on the strongest of the qaraz for passage through the Wastes. We follow the qaraz for your protection, Imperial."

Raiden glanced at the ground as if he might be able to discern the pathways, but of course saw nothing. He had never heard the term "qaraz", but he was familiar with the concept of ley lines. Imperial sorcerers often advised the Emperor on where to build sacred sites according to ley lines. Were the qaraz the same?

Frowning, Raiden looked at the quartz blade at Cyril's hip. The other Golondrina carried quartz, as well. If only strong wizards could freely walk the Wastes…? "Are your companions safe, flanking us as they are?" He'd only managed to catch the occasional glimpse of the two men: the flash of Petra's russet hair and bright blue shirt wrapped around his waist, or Manoli's tumble of curly black hair and the red kerchief tied jauntily beneath his chin. "I thought quartz was the weakest of the gemstone blades?"

"We are born in the Wastes," Cyril said in his gravelly voice. "The Golondrina can travel where we want. We know every qaraz in the Wastes and every source of clean water. The blight does not touch us, and our warriors slaughter the twisted beasts of the Wastes in droves. My nephews are as safe as you would be in your own garden." His lip curled slightly. "Veil-dwellers can't leave the main roads or travel anywhere in the Wastes without a wizard to guide them and protect them. They've lost their way."

He packed both disdain and pride into his words, and Raiden felt he was included in Cyril's disdain of "Veil-dwellers". Given the dangers of the Wastes, he didn't feel his question had been unreasonable. Yet, somehow, he'd insulted the elder Golondrina. Flushing, he gave Cyril a respectful bow. "I meant no disrespect, Don Cyril," he said, using the Malavitan honorific. "I was merely concerned for your companions."

"Keep your concerns for yourself, boy, and watch your step. This place can eat the unobservant alive."

Shade chuckled softly. "Quite literally," she said as she turned away and continued down into the ravine. "Unwary travelers are often found waist-deep in solid rock. So, step where I step, if you please."

Sweating, Raiden scrambled after her. "Something's following us," he announced.

She didn't stop, but she threw him a disdainful look over her shoulder. "Shadows," she said, turning away. "Shadows of the Unseen. The demons are long gone, destroyed by the Sicani in their terrible war, but their shadows remain. Their blight. It touches this land and is held back only by the power of the Veils."

Just shadows after all. Well, at least I won't be ambushed.

"Yet the qaraz are clean of the blight?" he asked, confused. The broken, pitted ground beneath his boots did not seem very clean. "How is that?"

"Once, they held the spirits of this land," Shade explained. "The spirits are gone like the demon Unseen, but the power left in the qaraz is imperishable. They connect all sacred things left in this land. The Veils, the springs of pure water throughout the Wastes, and pools of ancient power. Not even a Blackstorm can poison a qaraz."

Blackstorm. The word filled him with dread though he'd never experienced one except through others' firsthand accounts. A scourge of terrible, twisted magic leaving destruction in its wake. Even the sanctuary of a Veil became dubious in the face of a Blackstorm. The strongest bloodwizards – priests, mostly – worked in unison to protect the Veil-dwellers from the worst ravages of a Blackstorm. Thankfully, they were predictable.

Curious, Raiden turned slightly to address Cyril. "How do the Waste-walking Golondrina handle a Blackstorm?"

A low chuckle rumbled from the elder. "We run."

* * *

"This is an Emperor's son?"

Atop her pile of cushions and woven rugs, the withered Golondrina crone sounded skeptical, and far from impressed after Shade had introduced him. Raiden kept his features blandly polite, not wishing to rile the obvious matriarch of this clan. The caravan they'd rendezvoused with was camped in a circle around a cluster of rocks which held a small, clear spring. Pavilions of bright canvas shielded them from the harsh afternoon sun and Raiden had no desire to be sent back into the brutal heat and, worse, in view of the hidden watchers – shadows of the Unseen, apparently – which had been making his skin creep for hours. Here, at least, near a sacred spring and atop a strong qaraz – a deep pool of magic rather than a thin line – the shadows had retreated.

The crone squinted at him in the dim lighting, her eyes bright despite her age. "I would expect the son of an emperor to be taller."

"I know he isn't much to look at," Shade replied to Raiden's chagrin; though sweaty and dusty and wild-eyed from the Wastes, he couldn't argue with her assessment. "But he's fast and skilled with his sword, and he has a resistance to our magic which has saved him once already. He is the Emperor Suijin's emissary to Malavita, he speaks for the Emperor himself as his representative. Even you must find that a little impressive, Jolynn."

The old woman grunted, sounding remarkably like Cyril. Though, if he understood correctly, she was his aunt. Or at least he'd called her "aunty" when he'd given her a deep, respectful bow and kissed her hand as if she'd been a lady of court. Manoli and Petra had called her Aunty Jolynn, as well, but had abandoned formality and kissed her withered cheeks and hugged her, lifting her from her feet to her laughing delight. They had vanished soon after to circulate among the pavilions – this trading group was part of their clan – leaving Raiden, Shade and Cyril to converse with "Aunty Jolynn".

"And he brought you the charter Safire's been going on about, has he? The one he *claims* we need if we want our Veil."

Shade hesitated, shifting on her cushion to cross her legs. "He has," she temporized, throwing him a glance. He opened his mouth, but she rushed to speak over him, "But he has yet to sign it." She forced a laugh. "He insists on 'determining the feasibility of our endeavor' first."

Raiden pursed his lips at her mockingly pedantic tone. Did she think he sounded like that?

Jolynn chuckled and gazed at Shade fondly. "I'm sure he'll reach the proper conclusion soon enough," she said, then threw her shrewd gaze on Raiden. "Never underestimate our witch. Trust me, she always gets her way."

"I do," Shade replied, throwing him a glance, her lips quirked, before returning her attention to the crone. "However, I was expecting a representative from the Kindred to be here, Jolynn. That was the whole point of this meeting. Or have they agreed to my request and bargaining won't be necessary?" This last she said with a hopeful lift of her brows.

Jolynn shifted on her mountain and raised a wrinkled hand. A young girl kneeling near her throne leapt to her feet and dashed away. "We should at least have refreshments while we speak," she replied. "I have been rude."

A low noise emanated from Shade, her eyes narrowing. She exchanged a glance with Cyril who sat on the other side of Raiden on his own broad pillow. Both wore matching expressions of concern. As all conversation ceased while they waited for the girl to return, Raiden began to understand. The old woman was stalling: she didn't have good news.

A hot breeze swirled beneath the canvas awning, raising dust and carrying the scent of goat dung. The nomadic Golondrina depended on sturdy herds of black goats for meat and milk and wool, and this group had recently acquired new stock from

Sicaria. Even though their animals withstood the blight as well as the Golondrina, they lost a goodly number to Waste beasts and accidents.

Finally, the child returned, two older boys burdened with laden trays following in her wake. Soon, they were all sharing tiny porcelain cups of tea and feasting on olives and fresh fruit. More goods acquired from the Veils, Shade explained to him in a quiet aside at his whispered question. For all their Waste-walking, the Golondrina depended heavily on the Veils, their goods and bounty. No wonder Shade was so anxious to raise a Veil for her people. He glanced at her. She sat stiffly, gripping her teacup and ignoring the food, her eyes boring holes into the old woman. Jolynn seemed unfazed as she spat olive pits on the ground.

"Quit stalling, Jolynn," Shade said at last, settling her cup on the carpet. She rubbed her hands down her bare thighs as if scrubbing something unpleasant from her hands. "Tell me what the Kindred said."

Cyril rumbled a low warning, but Shade ignored him. Apparently, Jolynn wasn't Shade's "aunty", and she was done being polite.

Jolynn wiped her fingers on a linen napkin, its edges embroidered in bright blues and greens, pointedly ignoring Shade's demand. With another broad gesture, she directed the children to clear away the refreshments. They complied with alacrity while Jolynn settled her gaze on Shade, the silence stretching. Finally, she sighed, her expression heavy. "They said no, my child."

"No? What do you mean, no? We're offering generous compensation for land within their territory. Don't they understand what I intend to do?"

"The Kindred made their feelings known in the message they sent. They think you are attempting a foul magic trying to raise a Veil like a Brotherhood priest."

"And who are they to judge me?" Shade said scornfully. "They hide in their stronghold beyond the mountains, venturing out only to meddle. I should know; my tattoo master was Kindred. Even Satine thought her people had hidden away for too long. This is their chance to help their Golondrina kin. I must raise my Veil beyond the Razor Ridge mountains. We'll be far safer there than anywhere else in the Deep Wastes."

Jolynn seemed to sink into her mountain of pillows. "I tried to make them understand. But they were adamant. The Kindred want nothing to do with a new Veil. Not in their land."

"Don't they understand what's at stake?" Shade's voice was strangled; she clutched one of her blade hilts like a drowning man grasping for a rope. "Can't they see how the Wastes have grown stronger, more violent, more dangerous? Even they will suffer eventually. We all will need this Veil!"

"They say a Veil is not the answer," Jolynn said, sounding pained to be the bearer of such bad news, but also sounding as if she might agree. She cast a look at Raiden. "They believe this empire will go the way of all the others and would make a poor ally, as well. And in that I cannot argue, no offense, Emperor's son. This is not an Imperial problem, but a Malavitan one."

"The Empire holds all the land in Malavita," Raiden said, unable to hold his tongue any longer, though he understood little of this exchange. Why was Shade so adamant on working with these reluctant people? Or raising the Veil on the other side of the imposing Razor Ridge mountains? Still, if she was this determined, perhaps there was more to it than he understood. "These Kindred you speak of are Imperial subjects whether they are willing to admit it or not. If we wish to claim their land for our own use, they cannot stop us."

Shade gave a low groan, but Jolynn met his statement with mocking laughter. "Will you send in soldiers to take it like all the others before you?" she demanded. "Their bleached bones litter the Wastes. They never even made it through the mountains, let alone across the Glass Fields. The Kindred might have been willing to give up a scrap of their land to their own, but they will never allow an outsider near their stronghold."

"I am no outsider!" Shade cried before Raiden could respond. "And any Veil I raise will belong to the Empire as all of them do now – in name alone! It will be for us, for our people first. The Kindred included. Even the oldest and strongest of us will need shelter if the Wastes continue to tip out of balance."

Raiden looked at her sharply, already riled by her dismissal of the Empire. This was the first he'd heard of the Wastes tipping out of balance. Was she serious, or was this a ploy to get what she wanted?

"The Kindred will not give you what you want," Jolynn said firmly. "And you cannot force them to participate in your scheme."

Shade's head jerked back as if the old woman had slapped her. "Scheme? You think this is all some *scheme* I've concocted?" She went still, and when she spoke, her words were hollow. "Do you even believe in my Veil, Matriarch?"

A mask seemed to slip over Jolynn's face, and she was suddenly unwilling to meet Shade's gaze. She lifted her chin proudly. "We have lived in the Wastes for generations beyond counting, my child. If anyone can survive what is to come, it is us. The Golondrina do not need saving." At last, she fixed her sharp eyes on Shade. "Not even by you."

CHAPTER FIVE

When the fiery sun dipped close to the horizon, the Golondrina left the shelter of the pavilions and started to gather great bundles of twigs, grasses, and dung from their herd of sturdy black goats. They placed them at the cardinal points around the camp, and in the raw, red dusk, children carried horns of glowing coals to each of the bundles, setting them aflame. The coals had been kept alive from camp to camp, an unbroken succession from the very first fire set to ward off the night, or so Petra had kindly explained to Raiden before vanishing to help the clan. Of all his new companions, the red-haired man seemed to have warmed to him somewhat.

Even before the fires were set, the pavilions were transformed into tents, and the brightly painted carts and wagons the Golondrina used to cross the Wastes were moved to encircle the camp like sentries.

The clan worked efficiently. A solemn dance of preparation as intricate and rehearsed as the ceremonial drills of the Imperial Guard. It was fascinating to witness, though Raiden felt removed and not a little useless. Shade and the others had left him to his own devices, and he couldn't help feeling as if she had been particularly eager to avoid him after the disastrous meeting with Jolynn. He wasn't about to let her, though.

He caught her as she emerged from between the circle of

carts, her blades in her hands. He quickened his steps, afraid she might bolt back among them rather than face him. But she turned and waited for him. There were cuts on her arms. As he approached her, he couldn't help staring. The cuts were healing in a weaving of light.

"It's not polite to stare, captain."

He cleared his throat and pulled his gaze away. "Forgive me. It's still new to me, seeing your magic at work. Your ability to heal is incredible."

"It's not an inborn ability," Shade said, slipping her blades into their sheaths. "Without our tattoos, we would bleed like anyone else. The wards weave our flesh closed and replenish our blood. They are vital to practicing bloodmagic."

He studied her, noting the swirls and patterns of her tattoos. Some were abstract, but there were vines and flowers twining up her arms, and green-eyed dragons wrapped both her legs, their elaborate scales disturbingly realistic. He thought he caught a face peeking at him from one of her shoulders, but upon closer inspection it was a blooming rose of gold. He took this in quickly, not wanting to gawk, but what he discovered was significant. "You don't have tattoos on your face or neck." He peered at her head. "Beneath your hair?"

She shook her head, her lips pressed thin, as if she knew exactly what he was thinking. He supposed she did, so he said it out loud. "Would you heal as quickly if you were cut where there are no tattoos?"

Her hands settled on the bone hilts of her knives. "Do you plan on cutting me?" she asked softly.

He didn't reply, only held her gaze for a moment. He'd learned long ago that silence often said more than words. Her nostrils flared at his scrutiny, and he had his answer.

"So, you failed to acquire the land you wanted," he said abruptly. No need to mince words. "But the unsheltered Wastes are vast. There must be somewhere suitable for *our* Veil. A location beyond the Razor Ridge mountains seems unlikely, anyway, as they are impassable. I know because many before us have tried. We can't even manage to reach those lands from the sea as the coast along the western side of Malavita is treacherous. Why are you so determined to raise your Veil in such an unlikely place?"

She turned, staring toward the West, squinting against the last rays of the sun as if she could see beyond it to the distant mountains. "The Kindred know the way in and out of the mountains. They venture out to trade with the other clans every season, and they bring stones of exceptional quality. Nearly equal to those produced by Brotherhood mines. Imagine what they could glean from pit mines sheltered by a Veil?" She sighed, and her expression grew clouded. "Why they keep the ways so secret is a mystery. Even my tattoo master couldn't explain it to me. I tried to follow her once–"

Her lips closed on the words and she faced him again. "I know Dante thinks the Empire can protect us, but the Brotherhood's reach is everywhere. I was hoping to raise my Veil as far from their influence as possible. In its nascent state, it will be vulnerable. Dante thinks the legal protection the charter provides will be enough to protect us from our enemies, but I am not as certain. Your Empire is far away, captain, and our troubles and concerns matter little beyond our value as a potential source of gemstones. Do you deny this?"

No. He couldn't deny it. The charter was meant to create a for-profit venture benefiting the Empire. For Shade and Prince Safire, it meant far more. If the Brotherhood destroyed the Veil before it was established, it would cost the Empire nothing more than their initial investment. It might cost Shade and her clan their very lives. The loss would bother his father as much as losing one of his prized stallions. Less.

He did not hesitate to sacrifice me, after all.

Shade's sea-green eyes were searching his face and Raiden hoped she couldn't see the flush in his cheeks. The light from the bonfires flickered across her face and limned her hair with gold. He felt a strange hitch in his belly, then cleared his throat and turned aside, his eyes scanning the Wastes beyond the camp. A soft breeze caressed his face; it cooled his warm skin. It was growing dark swiftly, and he could hear the Golondrina settling in for their evening repast. Men in pairs walked the perimeter, shirtless as his companions had been in the Wastes, keeping watch.

"They seem capable, your people," he mused. "Perhaps your elder was right. Perhaps they don't need a Veil as much as you think they do. You might consider leaving it a venture in profit alone, and not salvation."

"You know nothing of my people," Shade scoffed. "Or what they need. Even Jolynn is a blind, stubborn old–"

A sudden strange wailing interrupted her. It rose on the evening breeze, rising and falling in volume and intensity. Raiden started and Shade grew wide-eyed, her mouth gaping.

"What is that noise?" he demanded. Shouts erupted in the camp and people appeared from between the carts, mostly men but a few women in long skirts and sleeveless jerkins too. They all looked shocked, and not a little frightened. A confused babble of voices carried on the breeze.

Shade's gaze darted past him, searching anxiously. She drew her blades and slashed at her bare arms, and suddenly she was rising into the air. He backed up so he could see her without craning his neck, his hand reaching for his own weapon, though he wasn't sure what he was fighting yet. Above him, Shade twisted on an invisible column of air, stopped when she was facing south and then peppered the air with curses. A moment later, she thumped to a landing beside him. Her face had lost all color. The clarion wail did not stop.

"What is happening?" He took her by the arm, squeezing hard. "That is a warning siren, isn't it? Warning against what?"

She stared at him, stunned. But then she shook her head, and a determined expression hardened her features. "Now you'll see firsthand why my people need a Veil."

"Tell me what you saw!"

"A Blackstorm, captain. Coming fast out of the south. A week too soon and a hundred miles off course." She smiled grimly, her grip tightening on her blades. "And we have no time to run."

Blackstorm. To all Malavitans, there was no more terrifying word. Even the threat of the Wastes paled in comparison to a ravaging Blackstorm. After all, you could cross the Wastes in a merchant train or a caravan, even if you didn't have strong bloodmagic yourself. Trade between the Veils thrived under the watchful eyes of bloodwizards. The Capos and their Corsaro had long ago strong-armed their way into being "guards" over the valuable trade routes, and the Brotherhood allowed it – as long as they got their cut. Only the Blackstorms drove home how terribly vulnerable most Malavitans were in their brutal homeland. Even beneath the powerful, protective Veils, they needed the priests to reinforce the magical shields or risk having them scoured away by a Blackstorm. In the smaller, outlying Veils in the interior, that duty fell to the Capos and their Corsaro soldiers. And thus, all Veil-dwellers bowed to them.

As a young girl, Shade had witnessed her father add his magic to his fellow priests' as they'd worked in unison to protect the Veil from a Blackstorm. It had evolved into an elaborate ceremony over time, to awe the people and remind them how much they owed the Brotherhood. Even knowing all she did about the Brotherhood, remembering those times still filled her with reverence. Since she'd been cast into the Wastes and taken in among the Golondrina, she'd witnessed Blackstorms only from a distance. Her people knew the patterns of the Blackstorms better than even the Brotherhood. Only the unluckiest clan, or unwariest, fell to a Blackstorm.

And now one was descending on them with terrifying speed.

"Leave the carts! Leave the tents! Gather only what you might need to last the night!"

With the Imperial trailing her – and what was she going to do with him during what was to come? He'd be useless baggage at best – Shade strode through the camp to Jolynn's tent, following the sound of her commanding voice. The old woman was leaning on a cane, directing the nervous clan. She was pale in the light from the bonfires, but she moved and spoke with restrained urgency. After decades of Waste-walking, Jolynn was unflappable even in the face of catastrophe.

The clan was listening to her, though their faces were blank with terror. Mothers were swaddling new babes securely to their chests in preparation to run, while toddlers rode their fathers' shoulders. Luckily, this trading caravan had only a few children along.

"What about the kids?" a young goatherd asked Jolynn anxiously, his hands twisting beneath his chin.

"Leave them," Jolynn answered sternly. She touched the youth on the cheek as the only comfort, and he spun away in tears. She raised her voice. "We must make haste, my children! Run north as fast as you can!"

"No!" Shade shouted, a small nick on her wrist allowing her to amplify her voice with wind. Now that the warning siren had stopped, her pronouncement echoed over the group. Startled, Jolynn and the people frantically preparing for departure turned to her as one. Manoli was among them, helping a young mother with her baby, and he grinned at her, excitement dancing in his eyes. Petra appeared behind him, no less excited, though he refrained from smiling. She took a breath now that she had their attention. Jolynn was staring daggers at her.

"There is no time to run," she said, her voice carrying to each of them as if she stood by their sides. "We'll be caught in the Blackstorm and picked off by magic or beasts one by one. Our best chance is to stand together here!"

"We'll be slaughtered if we stay," Jolynn protested. "We might be able to withstand the vile magic of the storm, but it will draw every beast within reach of us. They will come to feast. Hordes upon hordes!"

"As long as you can protect the clan from the twisted magic, I can protect us from the beasts."

"You alone? Your arrogance will kill us all, Shade!"

Murmurs of doubt swept through the clan, and some began to resume their preparations to run, even edging away into the growing shadows. The sound of the approaching Blackstorm filled the air like the buzzing of a thousand wasps.

"I am obsidian! I am the strongest of the strong!" Shade turned slowly to each of her people, willing them to believe. Running was suicide. They had to be convinced. "I have mastered the Four and the Hidden! The Faces of God reside in my blood!" Her voice rose, grew deep with power. "I can touch the Wild Power and bend the world to my will! I am the scourge the beasts of the Wastes fear. I will burn their twisted forms from the earth! Have faith in your witch!"

"How will we protect the children from the storm?" asked a father with a small boy on his shoulders. "They are too young to wield blades. They will be defenseless against stray tendrils of magic, and we cannot stop them all."

"Open the qaraz."

Shade turned to find Cyril emerging from between the carts. Behind him, to the south, lightning forked the black sky beneath a scattering of stars. Night had fallen while they'd dithered and the Blackstorm loomed close. The hairs on her neck and arms began to rise. The twisted magic released by a Blackstorm could warp even the strongest bloodwizard if they were caught unprepared.

"Open the qaraz?" Jolynn echoed, but her gaze turned inward even as she questioned him. For a moment, she seemed to be elsewhere, caught in a trance of sorts. Then light erupted beneath her feet and spread outward in a shimmering pool. A gasp burst from Raiden who stood near Shade, and she smiled grimly. The Imperial was getting quite a lesson today. The light stopped just a few inches from them, and Shade stepped back from it. She couldn't enter the qaraz, not like her adoptive kin. This was a Golondrina skill alone, a holdover from their ancient blood. Once, they had worshipped and protected all the spirits of the land: the Locorum.

At the center of the circle of light, Jolynn opened her eyes. They gleamed golden. "Bring the children to me," she said, her voice resonating. "And anyone who cannot fight. The rest of you, listen to our witch."

Quickly, with hushed tones, the Golondrina sent their children into the light. The few mothers with infants entered, as well. As Shade watched, the youngsters sank into the pool as if it really were water. It swirled about their necks, as they stared pensively back at their parents. Jolynn sank slowly until she was waist deep. She met Shade's eyes, a warning in her ancient gaze. "I'll keep them here as long as it is safe."

Shade nodded. The Golondrina tended the qaraz; they were the reason the magic stayed clean and strong. But it cost them. The qaraz fed on their power. Like shedding blood for one's magic, there was only so much any one Golondrina could give. She would have to do everything in her power to see this storm dissipate quickly.

"Cyril, Manoli, Petra," she called. "To me. The rest of you add your power to the circles of protection. Give all you can. Remember what's at stake."

It was unnecessary to remind them, she saw it clearly in their faces. Even if none of the children in the well of power were directly related to them by blood, they were all one clan. Losing a single soul was unacceptable. The men and women scattered, placing themselves outside the ring of carts. Each would use their lone quartz blade to draw upon their magic. Alone, none of them could master any Face above air, but together, bound by their shared ancestry, they could touch each element, but for spirit, and form a temporary shield around the camp. Only Shade could touch the Hidden Face. And she would need spirit to battle the worst of the creatures the storm would bring.

"Stay close to Jolynn," she ordered Raiden, tossing the command over her shoulder as she dashed away, Cyril and the boys on her heels. They raced to the southern edge of camp, placing themselves in the direct path of the Blackstorm. It was already obscuring the stars as it rose like a mountain against the night sky. Light flickered across its face, lightning stained red and orange and deep pink. Streaks of power blasted outward from the towering clouds, striking the earth and blowing up great gouts of dirt and rocks. Though the storm itself was as black as the lowest hells, a strange light lit up the Wastes. Enough to see a wave of ravening creatures tearing across the ground toward them.

"Catch any that get past me," she said, breathless with fear and excitement. The energies of the Blackstorm crackled in the air around them. It smelled of sulfur and rotten meat. Of death and putrescence.

"We've faced worse than this, boss," Manoli said, grinning as he had been since the moment she'd told them they wouldn't be running. Beside him, Petra flashed a brief smile and gave an encouraging nod. Concern lurked in his eyes, and she knew exactly what had him so worried. He would die before he let a child come to harm.

"We won't let a single beast get past us," Petra said fiercely.

"Get yourselves ready," Cyril growled to his nephews. He'd already stripped away his shirt and had his blade drawn, the others followed suit. His eyes narrowing beneath his bushy brows, he bent close to Shade's ear. "You aren't really going to call the Wild Power, are you?"

She grimaced. "I've avoided it so far, old man. I don't plan on starting today. The world's plenty bent out of shape already." She raised her voice so the cousins could hear her. "Stay close to the circle and hold the line here. I'm taking the fight to them."

Without a backward glance, Shade launched into a run. Straight toward the crawling, surging wave of warped creatures.

The Beasts of the Wastes were the misbegotten spawn of the Unseen's blight. Once simple animals, now demon-touched, they craved blood and pain. Nothing drew them like a wizard's blood, but most were craven and weak. When driven by a Blackstorm, however, they forgot they were cowards and attacked en masse.

Luckily, Shade knew how to kill them. Any bloodwizard who dared walk the Wastes knew how to kill the twisted creatures who inhabited them.

Faces, there are so many of them.

Wielding her blades against her bare arms, she called the Eastern Face – wind – and rose above the horde, riding currents of air. The leading line of creatures howled as the scent of her blood and magic reached them and slowed, the rest of the approaching wave bunching against them, overwhelming them. Like ants, the beasts in the rear climbed over those stopped in front until they had created their own tower of shifting, crawling limbs and fangs and talons. Bunched as they were, there was no distinguishing one beast from the other.

Blood vulpines, lupari, scarab cats or any number of foul beasts, they all die the same.

Held aloft by her power, Shade drew blood again and lifted her arms toward the still-clear sky above her. The Southern Face this time. Fire in its most awesome permutation. Snapping energy filled her and she cast lightning down toward the writhing tower of creatures desperate for her blood. It struck in a blast of blinding white heat, exploding a great rent in the black wave. Shrieks and dying screams nearly drowned the growing cacophony of the Blackstorm. Releasing the wind she'd called, Shade landed among her enemies, her body strengthened by another drawing of blood. Earth, the Northern

Face. The ground erupted away from her, tossing her enemies like discarded toys, clearing a space.

But more came from the dark, driven by the warped energies of the Blackstorm and tempted by the lone wizard defying their bloodlust.

By now, the sky overhead had succumbed to the boiling clouds of the Blackstorm. She could feel the weight and power of the storm roll over her. With it came a new horde of beasts, ravenous and fresh.

Briefly, her heart quailed, and she felt small and helpless even as her power beat through her veins. Her arms and legs were coated with blood – she'd drawn faster than her tattoos could work – and she could feel the cost of her magic in the weariness creeping into her muscles.

Stop. You are obsidian.

She took a deep breath and placed the edge of one blade against her bare midriff. She still had plenty of blood to spend. A sharp laugh burst from her, half-sob, but before she could cut, a wild thunder roared from overhead. Startled, deafened, she looked up to see a new threat descending.

Birds. Hundreds of them. Black-winged with naked blood-red heads and curved silver hooks for beaks, they moved as one in a surging blanket. It dropped toward her with a million razor-sharp talons extended. Desperately, she combined wind and water – the Western Face – fire and earth, adding spirit – the Hidden Face – to form a thin shield around herself. But she knew it wouldn't stop them for long. Feathers and talons and hooked beaks swarmed her dubious shelter. She shielded her head with her arms as they began to break through, dropping to her knees before the onslaught. Pain lanced her as their claws found purchase. She used the drawn blood as best she could, casting fire and stealing water from the nearest raptors, leaving them desiccated.

Too many. Faces turn to me! I can't stop them all.

Shade screamed as one great bird tore a clump of hair from

her head. Their shrill cries were deafening. The wings beat against her from everywhere. They would tear her to bits if she couldn't break away. Using air and fire drawn from her wounds, she pushed the creatures back until she had the space to fully wield her blades. She lifted her head, tears of pain on her cheeks, and screamed at the flock of ravenous birds. She raised a shaking blade to her chest. They screamed back; their glowing red eyes locked on her. There was triumph in their unnatural gazes.

In an instant, that triumph turned to fear as a streak of silver tore through a great swath of them, leaving blood and feathers and entrails in its wake.

Stunned, Shade fell back on her heels. A figure emerged among the now-panicking flock. Clad in a bright crimson jacket and wielding a single-edged sword, Raiden Mad leapt and danced in a display of preternatural grace and speed. His boyish face was set in a grim visage, his dark eyes empty, reflecting the strange light of the Blackstorm as he mowed down the creatures with movements almost too fast to follow. The birds took flight in a desperate heaving. Any left in range of Raiden's sword fell in pieces.

The clatter of talons and hooked beaks striking her pulsating shield brought Shade from her shock. The birds had fled, rising to safety, but a new wave of beasts rushed toward them and the Blackstorm's raging winds and dangerous lightning were making their position precarious. She pulled herself to her feet, dropping her shield and taking back some of the power she'd spent to raise it.

"Fall back to the others!" she shouted to Raiden, who stood in a defensive crouch in front of her. Ready to shield her again.

Damn Imperial. Not so useless, are you?

He glanced over his shoulder at her shout and gave a quick nod, dropping back beside her. Shade sent a blast of super-heated air toward the approaching creatures, calling water as she did so. A wave of boiling steam enveloped the leading edge. Together, she and Raiden turned to run, chased by the sweet music of shrieking death.

They reached the circles of protection just outside the barricade of carts and bonfires well ahead of the swarm. Cyril and the boys were working as one to fight a few stray beasts who'd managed to get past Shade, striking with precision and power. The other Golondrina were holding back the worst of the storm with their combined strength and will, preventing its devastating magic from warping them into hideous malformities. Not a few of the carts had been smashed by vicious bolts of lightning – all the Golondrinas' power was being spent to protect their people, not their property.

"I told you to stay near Jolynn!" Shade snapped at Raiden once they'd reached the relative safety near the carts and blood-drawn circles. He might have saved her life, but he had put himself in terrible danger. And anger was the only thing keeping her going, so she let it fill her, drawing on its strength.

"I do not take orders from you," he said simply, wiping gore from his sword with a small square of silk. He glanced up, towards the Wastes, and tossed the soiled silk aside. "Here they come."

Shade turned, her blades ready, and for the next endless hour, there was nothing but battle and blood. Raiden stayed near her like her own shadow, moving with her, anticipating her strikes before she made them, mowing down any creature that came too close. At times, her power washed over him, and knocked him to his knees. But he rose to fight again and again. Unstoppable. Despite her growing weariness, and with the danger of drawing too much blood looming, Shade felt a strange thrill. A rightness. Her Golondrina companions worked together as precisely and effectively as if they were one person, and suddenly in the midst of a wild fight for survival, she felt the same connection with Raiden. It gave her the strength to go on longer than she would have alone.

Longer than she should have...

Silence.

It fell as quickly as the night. It rang in Shade's ears until slowly, slowly, the world returned: the gentle humming of insects and the soft susurrus of the wind, the crackle of the bonfires and the murmurs of the Golondrina clan. Above them, the sky was clear, but for a few lone, flapping vultures scattering into the night.

A cheer rose from inside the circle of carts, then another. Suddenly, the entire camp erupted into cheering. They had survived the impossible.

But not without a cost. Even among the cheers, Shade could hear the groans of the wounded, and the hideous screaming of goats. She grimaced. Some power would have been spent protecting the herds from stray tendrils of twisted magic, but protecting them all would have been impossible. "Let's see where we can help," she said to Cyril who was looking at her with a furrowed brow while he held onto her arm. As if she needed help standing, which was ridiculous. Petra had already started running for the camp before the words left her mouth but Manoli lingered. His grin had slipped in the aftermath of battle, but his eyes were bright with admiration as he gazed at Raiden.

"I've never seen anything so fantastic," Manoli said breathlessly. His dark hair flew wild in the last lingering wind from the storm. He pushed it back impatiently, his grin returning in full force beneath his long moustache. "You were magnificent, Imperial. Rushing in to save our witch like that." He shook his head, chuckling, and thrust a hand toward Raiden.

Raiden's face was blank with astonishment. He stared at the proffered hand as if he was unsure what it meant. Then, slowly, a smile spread across his face and he grasped Manoli's forearm in a firm grip. "I'm glad I could be of service," he said. "It is part of my training to protect the helpless."

The helpless? And just like that, Shade's good feelings towards the Imperial vanished. It didn't help that Manoli, after staring at her with raised brows, started laughing uproariously at the Imperial's statement.

"Wait one damn minute," she muttered, though she doubted anyone heard her over Manoli. She took a step, intending to shove past Cyril, and instead landed against her old friend's chest, the world spinning around her.

"Easy, little swallow," he said, propping her back on her feet. His thick brows were pinching his hooked nose as he regarded her. "Let us get you some water and something to eat. You'll need to rest after spending that kind of blood."

"Rest can wait," she said, pushing aside her weariness. She watched Manoli take Raiden by the arm and lead him toward camp, gesturing and cavorting about as if he were reenacting the entire battle while the captain followed in bemused silence. She grunted softly. If anyone could charm Raiden to their side, it would be Manoli. *Better him than me.* "I want to talk to Jolynn. I imagine now she'll be more than happy to go along with my little 'scheme'."

CHAPTER SIX

The next morning, after doing what they could to repair carts and wrangle bleating goats, Shade and her companions bade farewell and good luck to Jolynn and her clan.

"I'll send another message to the Kindred, Shade," Jolynn had promised. Something had changed in the old woman's eyes. There was a fear Shade had never seen before, a resignation. Disaster was coming, and she could no longer deny it. "I will try and make them understand."

Shade had embraced her, glad Jolynn had recognized their predicament, but sad to see the older woman so distraught. After all, it had been Jolynn's decision to allow Shade to remain among the clan when Cyril had brought her home with him. She was the clan matriarch, the eldest and the wisest. Her word was law. And now, she was putting all her trust in a foundling.

I will live up to that trust. Our destiny lies beyond the mountains.

With the sun in their eyes, Shade set a rapid pace back to Sicaria. Her head was pounding, and her mouth was cotton, but she pressed onward. Everyone was hurting from the night's battle, but even more from the revelries afterward. The Golondrina knew how to celebrate life, especially after coming so close to death. Even Raiden was struggling to keep up. Apparently, he'd had quite a time among the thankful clan. So far that morning, he had emptied the contents of his stomach twice. His dusky skin had gone sallow, and his mouth was pinched white at the corners. Manoli was shadowing him, cracking jokes and showing remarkable sympathy towards the foreigner, even handing over the kerchief from around his neck so Raiden could wipe his face.

Of course, it was Manoli who'd gotten him so drunk in the first place.

After last night, her friends' attitude toward the Imperial emissary had shifted. His skill and fearlessness fighting off the Waste beasts had impressed all of them, even Cyril. Remembering how he'd fought brought a shiver down her spine. He had thrown himself into a battle of which he had little understanding, facing supernatural creatures to save her. It shouldn't surprise her how quickly they'd come to respect him. Cyril and Manoli were born warriors and Raiden's skill astounded them. Petra, on the other hand, saw Raiden's willingness to throw himself in the face of danger for another's sake as the most admirable of traits.

"Shade, you need to slow down."

Disturbed out of her ruminations, Shade glanced toward Cyril. "Are you serious? Why?"

Grim-faced, Cyril pointed back the way they had come. Several yards below them, Raiden worked his way up the path. Each step seemed a monumental struggle, and he paused often with hands on knees.

"He's just feeling his drink," Shade said. "He'll get better."

"Perhaps. But a rest won't do any harm. We'll still reach Sicaria well before sunset if you're worried."

She fidgeted, her hands kneading her blades. "We're vulnerable out here," she said. "I'm down to my last dregs."

Cyril said nothing, only unhitched his waterskin and took a long drink.

"Fine. We'll take a break. Everyone's got to be bone-dry after last night's excitement."

Raiden seemed grateful for the respite, draining a full skin in a single draft. She watched him as she sipped at her own skin. For a soldier, he couldn't hold his liquor all that well. Her belly roiled unpleasantly, reminding her she'd had a rough night, too. The tension across her shoulders and down her back wasn't helping either. The red sands stretched empty in all directions, shimmering in the heat and haze of the sun, but she knew it was a deceptive emptiness. Enemies could hide in plain sight in the Wastes, especially two-legged enemies armed with magic.

We need to get back to Dante's villa. He has enough men to dissuade even the strongest Capo.

When they resumed their journey, Raiden was a shade less sallow, and they were able to keep to a faster pace. The vast shield over Sicaria was a growing haze on the horizon, a distortion in the hot, clear sky. Unfortunately, it wasn't long after their brief rest that her fears were confirmed. A rider appeared, heading steadily in their direction. The fact that she only saw one rider convinced her there was more than one. A lone wizard had a much better chance of staying hidden. A group less so.

Shade swore softly. The rider disappeared into a gully then reappeared in a strange haze. Other riders materialized beside the first, shimmering like mirages. It was hard to pin down the exact number of their pursuers, and she wasn't about to stop and count them.

"We have company."

Raiden had moved up to match her pace. Somewhere along the way he'd become the soldier she'd first seen in the streets of Sicaria. Cool, calm, entirely professional.

"Riders have been angling to intercept us for an hour or so," he said. "I don't think we can outrun them."

"I know." Shade glanced at him; he was still white-lipped and sweat glistened on his forehead, but he seemed much improved. "I had hoped to outrun them, but it looks like we're in it for sure."

"They'll catch us within the hour. We should stop. It will be better to choose where we will face them."

Her thoughts exactly. She pressed her lips together, her estimation of him growing once again. It wouldn't be long before she started to like him. *Hells...*

"You may be right," she said. She halted and waited for Cyril and the cousins. The older Golondrina looked as grim-faced as usual, though his gray eyes shone with eagerness, and he turned to face the riders with his hand on the blade at his belt.

The terrain had been growing rougher as they neared Sicaria, the red, sandy slopes turning into steep, rocky hills. The hillside upon which they stood was a rugged tumble of rocks, sand, and stunted vegetation with a narrow track the only accessible path. Above them, the track zigzagged sharply over treacherous terrain before it reached the toothed summit. It would be a tough climb on foot, and nearly impossible for horses. Shade pointed. "There," she said. "Up there. We'll have the advantage."

The arduous climb took them off the qaraz, and Shade spent a little blood to keep the worst of the blight at bay. When they reached the steepest portion of the hill, they spread out along the narrow path. There was little in the way of cover, but the terrain would give them an advantage. Hopefully.

Below them, the horsemen no longer sought to conceal themselves as they trotted confidently over the rocky ground. Six riders, some bearing strong blades. At least one or two of them could touch all Four Faces which meant an amethyst wielder, at least, or topaz. The rest carried quartz of varying strengths, possibly jasper or beryl, too. None of them could touch the Hidden, thankfully.

Habitually, her hands went to her blade hilts. The feel of the smooth bone filled her with confidence, yet she knew she hadn't fully recovered her strength. Sweat popped out on her forehead. Shade licked her parched lips and glanced at Cyril. Of all people, he knew better than anyone what her magic cost her. He must have sensed her scrutiny, or perhaps her worry, for her old friend caught her look and gave her a reassuring nod.

When she looked away, she found Raiden was watching her with his brow furrowed. "Are they powerful?" he asked.

"They're strong, but not as strong as we are together. Keep out of our way and let us handle this; don't give them a reason to target you. You have some resistance to bloodmagic, but you aren't immune to it."

He frowned, but nodded, though his hand was on his sword hilt. Would he stay out of it if things turned bad? She doubted it. The man was no coward.

The riders had reached the bottom of the hill and one by one they dismounted. They stood together a moment, conferring among themselves, glancing upward every so often. They had to understand their disadvantage. Would they keep their distance or let arrogance lead them into a mistake?

A stocky man with tattoos the color of earth and fire scowled up at them then began to climb the trail, his steps firm and quick. The others followed, younger men with flashier tattoos and rippling muscles that glistened in the bright sun. Arrogance then.

Shade ignored the youths, keeping her attention on the leader. He was the most powerful among them, older and wiser, presumably. He alone might give them real trouble.

To her left stood the three Golondrina, Cyril between Manoli and Petra, all looking relaxed and indifferent. Lazy, almost. But she knew they'd linked already, joining their magic through the blood bond of a Golondrina clan. Shade could not join in their bond, but she relied on it nearly as much as her own blades. Manoli gave her a wink, his smile broad. After facing a Blackstorm last night and surviving, he was brimming with confidence.

"Lovely day for a stroll," the stocky man called when he and his men were halfway up the hill. He stopped on the narrow track several yards below them, his men scrambling to either side, spreading out across the rough terrain. Smart. A group was easier to target.

"Isn't it?" Shade replied cheerfully. "Though if you come any closer you might find yourself tumbling head-over-ass down this nice hillside."

He showed his teeth, his jowls quivering. "Now, now, that's no way for a lady to talk." His pig-eyed gaze traveled up and down her body. "No way for a lady to dress, either. But you're no lady, are you, witch?"

Shade gave him a languid smile, her hands resting lightly on her knife hilts. "I'm a witch who carries obsidian, amethyst wielder. Who in the lowest hells are you, besides a man who can't touch the Hidden?"

The stocky man bristled, and his smile turned to a scowl. "I am Lorenzo, witch, lieutenant to the Capomajus Errenzo Valentine of Sicaria and the Golden Crescent, your elder and your better in all regards."

"But for the old part, I doubt it." She fanned her face with one hand. "What do you want with us? And hurry up, it's hot out here."

"My business isn't with you. My Capo was clear about that. As much as I'd like to teach you a lesson, witch, I'm here for him." He jerked his chin toward Raiden. "The Imperial."

"Him?" She feigned surprise while inwardly cursing. Of course, Valentine would take an interest in an Imperial emissary – there might be profit in it. "What do you want with him? He's just an emissary, no one of consequence."

Lorenzo's hand crept to one blade, but he didn't draw. "No one of consequence?" he said scornfully. "He's the son of an emperor, and don't pretend otherwise."

Shade winced. How in the lowest hells did he know that?

"You think Safire could bring someone so important into Sicaria, and my Capo wouldn't know? Now, hand him over peacefully, and we'll be on our way. You can have him back once the Empire has paid his ransom." He grinned. "In however many pieces you wish."

"Ransom?" Raiden blurted before Shade could speak. He stepped forward. "How dare you threaten an Imperial emissary! I am an official representative of the Empire, the Emperor's own eyes and ears, not a pawn to be used in your games. The Emperor would answer any request for ransom with fire and storm and utter destruction!"

"I don't fear the fool who sends his only son into a dangerous land without armed escorts. What did he think would happen? I imagine he'll pay once he starts getting you back one piece at a time."

Before Raiden could answer, Shade put a calming hand on his rigid forearm. "His only son? I'm afraid you and your Capo have been sorely misinformed. He's a seventh son, and the child of a concubine. He's not exactly the royal heir. How do you think he got stuck in Malavita?" She gently squeezed Raiden's arm, hoping he didn't take offense. "I suppose you could hold him for ransom, but the Empire will only send a new emissary, not gold."

"Hand him over then if he's so unimportant. After all, you can always get a new emissary. One's as good as another, right?"

Shade gritted her teeth. "You know I can't do that," she said. "I've grown to rather like him." Her hands returned to her knife hilts with clear intent. Beside her, Raiden stepped to the edge of the path, his hands on his sword hilt, ready to draw, looking like he might throw himself down on his enemy.

Instantly, the air crackled with menace. To a man, the Corsaro soldiers grasped their blades and drew. Two of kunzite in deep pink, a rich red garnet, blue topaz and swirling green malachite.

A heartbeat later, Shade yanked her blades free. Cyril and the cousins followed her lead, eliciting a few snickers from the Corsaro soldiers when they saw their single, curved quartz blades. Obviously, they were unfamiliar with Golondrina magic, or they'd have known better than to laugh.

Only Raiden didn't draw; his eyes were pinned on Lorenzo and he was as still as death. Shade both dreaded and hoped she might see him unleash his fury on this arrogant toad.

"Don't get in the middle of this," Lorenzo warned her. He hadn't drawn yet, though he gripped his hilts so hard his knuckles were white. His piggish eyes switched from Raiden to Shade and back as if he couldn't decide who was the bigger threat. He settled on Shade. Maybe he wasn't so stupid. "My Capo wants him, witch. I'll cut right through you if necessary and give my Capo a surprise gift. So, give him up!"

"I am not hers to give," Raiden said, drawing his sword and stepping sideways. The long, single-edged blade caught the sunlight, shining like a flame. "If you want me, then come and get me!"

A few derisive laughs erupted from the soldiers, and Lorenzo drew his amethyst blades with a sneer. "My Capo said to take you alive, Imperial, but he didn't say you had to be in one piece!"

"Don't be a fool," Shade interjected, still hoping to avoid violence no matter how futile. She pressed a blade against her forearm, suppressing a tremble. "You're outmatched. Take your men and go."

Lorenzo glared at her. "Put away those toy blades before you hurt yourself, whore!"

Toy blades? Shade narrowed her eyes. Rage gave her strength. With practiced ease, she sliced her forearm and called fire from the thick, hot air. A ball of flames roared toward Lorenzo's face, wiping away his haughty expression as he scrambled to defend himself, purple blades flashing. The fireball veered to the side mere inches from his face and slammed into the hillside between two of his men. The soldiers sprang for cover, their blades flying to counter the flames.

Shade didn't let Lorenzo recover – earth was his strongest

element and she was on treacherous footing – but drew
additional blood from her thigh. A wall of fire descended from
her perch, sweeping toward her enemies; she felt Cyril and the
cousins lend their strength to the flames. Perhaps she could
end this quickly.

The Corsaro defended themselves as best they could. The
strongest managed to shield themselves, but one man was
singed, and another – one of the wielders of kunzite – burst into
flame. His hideous scream made her wince, and it continued
even as the earth lifted beneath her feet, threatening to send
her tumbling down the hillside. Lorenzo was the only wizard
strong enough to call water, but he'd chosen to attack her
rather than save his man. Cruel bastard.

Beside her, Raiden fell to his knees on the shaking earth.
Shade leapt off the path and called the Eastern Face, riding
a current of air to more stable footing. Unfortunately, she
was closer to Lorenzo and his Corsaro thugs. Luckily, her
Golondrina friends were outside the range of his attack and
managed to keep their feet.

The unfortunate kunzite wizard was still ablaze when Shade
regained her footing, and she called upon the Hidden Face, a
difficult and costly magic, to put him out of his misery. Water
wouldn't have done anything for him now, so she gave him
mercy instead. A hard kill. It made her vision dim briefly.

Her compassion cost her. Rocks and chunks of earth flew
at her from all directions as Lorenzo took advantage of her
momentary weakness. Blades flashing, she countered the
onslaught as best she could, leaping out of the way of some of
the missiles when magic failed.

A sharp stone caught her on the shoulder, drawing blood
and numbing her arm to the wrist. She barely kept hold of her
blade and scrambled backward to avoid a storm of rocks.

Fucking amethyst wizard!

Attacks flew at her from the Corsaro soldiers, as well:
pathetic balls of heated air or stiff winds or loose rocks under

her feet. Cyril and the boys defended her from the more minor attacks, leaving Shade free to deal with Lorenzo.

Deal with him she would, too. She slashed her midsection, drawing blood from her gut. Power roared through her. Power over earth.

A crack appeared between Lorenzo's wide-spread legs, quickly widened into a crevasse, and swallowed him whole. His startled shriek was music. Shade whooped as he disappeared, but her cry of triumph turned to a shout of dismay as the fissure raced toward her.

Too fast!

The earth split beneath her. She threw herself to the side, catching the edge, trying to bury her blades in the hard earth, but her feet couldn't find purchase on the smooth, steep slope and she was sliding, sliding–

A hand caught her forearm. It was enough to stop her slide, slow it at least, so she could dig her toes into the earth. She looked up to find Raiden over her, his face screwed up with effort. Desperately, she scrambled out of the crevasse, the earth rumbling beneath her. Lorenzo was countering her attack from within the fissure – it was already closing on her end. Face set with determination, Raiden backpedaled, dragging her. Her feet had barely cleared the edge when the crack sealed shut with a boom.

There was no time for thanks. Lorenzo rose from the still-open hole she'd dropped him into, working his blades over his muscular forearms.

"Is that the best you can do, witch?" he cried mockingly. "I was calling the Northern Face before your father even thought about spilling his seed in your whore of a mother."

Coughing out a lungful of dust, she gathered herself and readied her blades.

But suddenly Raiden was in front of her, his blade drawn. Cold determination hardened his profile as he dropped into his now-familiar, sideways stance. This time, however, he didn't hold himself in deathly stillness. Instead, he charged Lorenzo with lethal grace.

The Corsaro lieutenant reacted instantly, calling his magic in short, sharp slices across his chest and torso, attacking Raiden with fire and ice and shaking earth. The onslaught slowed him when it should have killed him, but Lorenzo seemed to expect that. He was already dashing away as the last of his attacks poured over Raiden. His final blow with wind and fire managed to knock Raiden to his knees.

Cursing, Shade clambered over the broken landscape to get a clear shot at Lorenzo, praying to the Four Faces Raiden would stay out of the way. Two Corsaro soldiers appeared in her path, knives flashing green and red. With a snarl, she knocked them aside with a burst of wind. One managed to catch her with a tongue of searing hot air. She hissed and stumbled.

Then Cyril was there, and Manoli, and Petra. They shielded her from the three remaining able-bodied Corsaro soldiers, leaving her free to tackle Lorenzo. With a quick glance to Cyril, she leapt down the treacherous slope toward Lorenzo and Raiden with the elder Golondrina following.

Raiden's uniform was singed, and blood trickled from one ear, but he climbed to his feet using his sword as leverage and flung himself at Lorenzo. His sword snaked out, a flickering of light in the bright sun and a deep slash appeared across Lorenzo's torso. The Corsaro man screamed and his amethyst blades clattered to the earth as he clasped his hands to the wound. Bright blood pulsed between his fingers, and Shade caught a glimpse of pale intestine as she raced toward him. His tattoos worked in a scintillating weaving, but the cut was too deep. It was a fatal blow, a massive bloodletting.

Power crackled around the dying Corsaro. His eyes snapped up, his lips drawing back from his teeth in a rictus. Blood pumped from him in great gouts.

No, no, no, no, no...

Raiden had stepped back, already turning to engage their

remaining foes. Shade cursed silently even as she and Cyril raced toward him. The elder Golondrina easily outpaced her, barreling toward Raiden with single-minded focus. The Imperial didn't understand the danger. She opened her mouth to shout a warning–

–and a violent burst of power exploded from the dying bloodwizard, all Four Faces combined into one wave of force.

"No!" The scream tore from her throat but was drowned out by Cyril's bellow as he slammed into Raiden, knocking him out of the path of Lorenzo's death strike. The wave of power struck Cyril, lifting him and flinging him across the hillside. Raiden was caught in the wake of it; it spun him violently, leaving him in a sprawl.

Her heart pounding and her mouth dry with fear, Shade scrambled over the broken landscape to where Cyril had skidded to a stop. His bright red shirt was singed black and smoldering, his face was white and streaked with ash and blood. A roaring started in her ears as she reached for the pulse point beneath his chin. Her bloody fingers felt nothing. Feeling a choking panic rise in her throat, she managed to roll him onto his back. She dropped across him, her ear to his chest. Nothing. He wasn't breathing, he was still as death.

Come with me, little swallow. I'll take you home...

Her vision dimmed. *Dead, he's dead.* Cyril had plucked her broken and terrified from the Wastes; he'd given her a home, a future, a life. A sob threatened to rip its way out of her. Rage and grief built into a black wave too big to hold, too violent to contain. Sense shattered before it, and Shade rose, her black blades flying, slicing deep again and again.

Power welled through her, building and building as she continued to draw blood. Her blades gleamed, no longer black but blazing like the sun. Slowly, she turned to find the still corpse that was all that remained of Lorenzo. Tears blinding her, she unleashed a wave of destruction, burning him to ash. His body disintegrated in a black cloud lit by flames. Blood dripped freely down Shade's arms and legs, glittering with light. The power poured through her, unstoppable, fed by her rage. In quick succession, she targeted the other Corsaro soldiers, taking out two while the remaining man made a mad dash to the horses.

Strength filled her, the energy of a voicano, the deep, Wild Power only obsidian could reach. Turning, she tracked the Corsaro as he mounted clumsily and kicked his horse into frantic gallops. The air filled with menace as her rage rose. There would be no survivors to report back to Valentine. She would end this here and now.

"Shade, stop!"

It was Manoli, screaming at her from somewhere far, far away. Suddenly he appeared in front of her, raising his hands, his features slack with panic. "He's alive, Shade! Release the magic before it consumes you."

Deep in the grasp of her blades, touching a power which filled her with boundless energy, Shade had no desire to release it. This was the Wild Power, the power she'd always feared to handle. It charged the atmosphere, making her hair rise and gooseflesh ripple across her skin. It was beyond the elements, something more than spirit. It was glorious. With it, she could bend the world, turn time upside down and inside out.

With it, she could bring the dead to life...

"He lives! Please, boss, listen to me. Cyril is alive!"

Alive. Cyril was alive.

She heard the words, absorbed them. Relief shuddered through her, but it was distant, drowned by the power flowing in her veins.

And suddenly she was clinging to the Wild Power by her fingertips, trapped in the center of a vast maelstrom straining to be unleashed. Fear replaced her rage, icy cold. Her muscles trembled and her blades felt strange in her grip. She was already weakened; she should never have reached for the Wild Power. By the Faces, how had she fooled herself into believing she could control this? The power had to be unleashed – it demanded it!

But she had no idea how to release it without destroying everything and everyone around her.

There was only one thing she could think to do, one desperate act to keep the magic contained. She had to take the magic back–

Before she could hesitate at the sheer insanity of it, Shade plunged her blades into her thighs. A flood of agony broke her hold on the magic, and it was released back into her blood. A circle snapped closed, the wild energies spinning into a loop. The air grew still, the magic returning to her core, leaving her blades empty.

Shade waited, hunched over the searing brands plunged into her legs. Slowly, her tattoos began to work, healing all her minor wounds, absorbing all her spilled blood. The pain was unbearable, and she screamed, aware of every small cut and slice stitching closed. Only when the wounds in her thighs began to heal around her blades did she yank them from her flesh. She tossed them away, fearing the call of magic. Blood spilled down her thighs, but the wards worked quickly to seal the deep puncture wounds.

She swayed; Manoli caught her and lowered her to the ground, shouting for Petra.

"Easy, easy, we've got you."

She felt pressure on one leg, and then the other. There was the sound of tearing cloth. Pain made her head swim. Her wards worked doggedly to stitch up her many cuts and lacerations, but she'd already lost a dangerous amount of blood.

"How is he?" she asked weakly, her throat dry and her lips cracked. Faces, she needed water.

"Petra is attending him, my lady." Raiden knelt beside her, his pale face streaked with blood. He took one of her hands in his, grimacing. "This is my fault…"

The world was growing dark around her. Damn it. She couldn't pass out. Not here. "How bad is he?"

"He's alive," Petra replied, his voice thick with grief. "That's the best I can tell you, boss."

Alive. It was her only thought as she fell into darkness.

CHAPTER SEVEN

Drawn from his study by shouts and the thunder of hooves, Dante Safire arrived in his stables to a scene of chaos. His guardsman, Angelo, was trying to calm a wild-eyed, lathered horse so an equally wild-eyed Manoli could unstrap the rider on its back – a white-faced Shade with bloody bandages around her legs. She was clinging to the saddle like a burr which wasn't helping Manoli or Angelo.

Nearby, Raiden held on to a second horse with Cyril on its back and was having a much easier time. Petra, shirtless and covered in dust and blood, threw himself from a third horse as it trotted into the barn. Unconcerned for the beast, he went to help his uncle dismount. Looking half-dead, blood-covered and scorched, Cyril collapsed in a heap.

Angelo, usually a more-than-competent horseman, seemed unable to bring the unruly horse to heel, and Manoli's angry cursing wasn't helping. Stepping in, Dante grabbed the horse's bridle, clamping down on his own anger and fear so he could calm the animal. He caught Shade's eyes – blank with fear and exhaustion – and shoved Manoli aside. "You are not helping," he growled sharply.

The Golondrina glared at him, but obeyed, albeit reluctantly, leaving Dante and the fair-haired Angelo to deal with the horse and rider.

Finally, they got the animal settled. Angelo stroked its muzzle and murmured comfort while Dante focused on removing the straps binding Shade into the saddle. Where had they even gotten the beasts? The horse shuddered and huffed but held still long enough for him to haul Shade off its back and into his arms. She clung to him, trembling, and he feared to put her on her feet lest she collapse.

"Shade," was all he could manage to say.

"It wasn't my fault." Her voice was faint, but defiant, and he felt a rush of relief. He had never seen her so weak, but he recognized the effects of blood loss and overuse of one's power.

"We can talk later. You need to rest."

Weakly, she nodded, and her eyes drifted shut. She went limp in his arms, and he called to Matteo who had followed his brother Angelo into the chaos. The man's usually pale face was paper-white and it was hard to hand her over to him, but he trusted Matteo more than most.

By now, the stable hands had arrived to tend to the horses, and he directed Angelo to help him with Cyril. Raiden and Petra were lifting the older man to his feet. The Imperial's dusky face had gone sallow and was twisted with concern. Dante could hardly blame him. The residue of the power used against Cyril radiated from his limp frame, and he could hardly believe the man was alive. He would need a healer of great skill, one who surpassed even the Golondrinas' abilities.

"Send for Korin," he ordered his valet who'd followed him from his study. He handed Cyril over to an anxious Petra. "Take him to the east suite; Angelo can show you the way. Have Korin meet me there, Marco."

"Yes, m'lord." His white-haired valet sketched a hasty bow and departed, his steps quick though Dante knew his knees had to be aching after they'd spent the day overseeing the fields and vineyards. They'd had to race home when he'd felt an unexplained surge of power from the Wastes. Now he knew it had been Shade.

Once she and Cyril had been carried out, calm settled over the stables, and Dante rounded on his emissary.

"What in the lowest hells happened out there?"

"We were ambushed, my lord," Raiden explained stiffly, standing at attention in his torn and bloodied uniform. "A Capomajus sent men after me. They thought they could get a hefty ransom for the Emperor's son, the insufferable fools. We were forced to fight. I struck down their leader. I slit him open stem to stern."

Dante grimaced. "You should have gone for his heart, captain. Or his head."

Raiden fixed him with a dark glare. "I will next time, my prince. I assure you." He took a breath, and his features crumpled with sudden guilt. "Cyril took the blow for me. I wish he hadn't. He's..."

"Did they say which Capo gave them their orders?" Dante asked.

Ever the soldier, Raiden straightened and smoothed his expression. "Yes. A Capomajus named Valentine."

"That opportunistic bastard," Dante growled. Valentine had been a thorn under his saddle for years, but he'd never thought him a fool. To go after an Imperial emissary was madness. The Empire was not Malavita where kidnapping was a way of life. He rounded on Manoli. Tears streaked his dust-covered face, but suppressed fury lurked in his eyes. "How did a bunch of Corsaro lackeys get the better of Shade? She should have been able to handle them in her sleep."

"We faced a Blackstorm last night," he said, his hands rising in fists. "Shade called power like I've never seen, and she was rightfully exhausted. Those Corsaro bastards didn't get the better of her! She burned them all to ash."

"How? If she was as weak as you say?"

Looking stunned, Manoli dragged a hand through his tangled hair. "When Cyril was struck down, Shade lost control. She... She unleashed such incredible magic. I thought we would all be destroyed before she managed to control it." His voice dropped as if he were afraid to speak too loudly. "She touched the Wild Power."

By the Faces. So, that's what he'd felt. The Wild Power. "Faces turn from her," he said, his voice faint. "How are you still alive? How are any of us still alive?"

"She took the power back into herself," Manoli said, a hint of awe in his voice. "It was the only way."

It took a moment for him to understand, and when he did he let loose a string of curses. Manoli and Raiden stood in stoic silence, letting him vent, until at last Dante couldn't think of another bitter word to express his rage and terror and he sputtered to a stop, feeling utterly exhausted.

"My lord, we must discuss–" Raiden began, but Dante stopped him with a gesture.

"Clean yourself up, captain. We will speak later."

Raiden's mouth clicked shut, and he bowed his head.

"What about Cyril?" blurted Manoli. "Can your man heal him?"

"If Korin Illario cannot heal him, then no one can."

By the time Dante reached the suite where he'd sent Cyril, Korin had arrived and was tending to him. Cyril lay stretched out on the bed, his ruined shirt stripped away. His barrel chest rose and fell shallowly, and his face was as pale as the cotton sheet beneath his splayed salt-and-pepper hair. The old healer stood over him, a small lump of amber in one hand, his face scrunched in concentration.

A tall man with skin as frail as parchment and hair as fine and white as silk, Korin Illario had been the Safire family's healer for generations. For a man his age – he had to be ancient, having delivered Dante's own father – he stood straight as a sapling and possessed remarkable strength. His skill as a healer was unparalleled. Dante flexed his hands as he approached

the bed, hands shattered long ago by a brutal enemy. Only
a pale network of scars, and a dull ache during Blackstorms,
remained to remind him of the injury. As to the enemy who'd
broken them, he and his Corsaro were dead or scattered to the
far corners of Malavita.

"You should be helping Shade," Cyril rasped as Korin moved
the stone over his limp body. The man's gray eyes were bright
with pain, yet he stared daggers at the old healer. His gaze
shifted to Dante. "Send your pet Sicani to her, Safire. I'll be
fine."

"Don't be a fool, Cyril." Dante moved to stand across the bed
from Korin, mostly to distract the elder Golondrina from his
work. "Let Korin help you."

Cyril writhed on the bed, futilely trying to right himself. "He
should help Shade!" His demand was a strangled gasp, and he
subsided, panting.

Korin's lips pressed into a grim smile. "Your witch is as tough
as diamonds," he said. "Hold still. Your need is greater."

Cyril groaned in agony. His eyes fluttered closed and he
seemed to shrink into the vast bed.

"Will he be alright?" Dante asked, feeling surprisingly
anxious for the man's well-being. Cyril had only ever shown
him scorn, but he was important to Shade. Dante didn't want
to be the one to tell her he couldn't save her old friend. She
wouldn't weep as other women might; she'd most likely stick
a blade in him.

"His pure, dogged stubbornness will keep him alive. I have
no doubt."

There was a touch of grudging respect in Korin's voice.

The amber cupped in Korin's long, elegant hand began to
gleam and his eyes glowed with a matching radiance. Awe filled
Dante, as it had since he was a child and he'd first witnessed
Korin's gift: golden, healing light. A power deeper and purer
than bloodmagic, born from Sicani blood, the first people of
Malavita. Possessed with deep wells of power, they had dwelt

peacefully in a land brimming with magic and fecundity for centuries, until invaders arrived on their shores. Having no wish to engage in violence, the Sicani had gradually retreated to the more remote interior of their island.

But the people who'd come to make a life for themselves brought a terrible magic with them. They shed the blood of innocents for power. Such dark magic corrupted the spirits of the land, giving rise to the Unseen. Unwilling to fight human foes, the Sicani had no such reservations against these demon adversaries. Unfortunately, their cataclysmic battle had destroyed the golden heart of their land, leaving the survivors doomed to a slow, agonizing death.

The Sicani had given Dante's ancestors the secret to the Veils, had shown them how to practice a better bloodmagic using gemstone blades against their own flesh and not that of innocents. They had shown these misguided people mercy and compassion in the hopes they would cleanse Malavita of the Unseen's blight. But the Brotherhood's sacred pact to build and preserve the Veils had become something far different, far more self-serving and corrupt.

Cyril mocked Korin by calling him Dante's pet Sicani. But Korin had never claimed to be an actual Sicani, only strong in Sicani blood. Most of the true Sicani had sacrificed themselves in their battle with the Unseen, and the rest had vanished long ago. Korin had served the Safire family for decades as a healer, a mentor, a friend. Dante owed him his life ten times over and trusted him above all others.

"There are many places within him that are broken. So much damage." Korin clicked his tongue. "Falling off a cliff would have produced similar results."

The healer fell silent, all his concentration centering on his patient. It was a trance of sorts, and Dante expected it might last well into the night. He made himself comfortable in one of the cushioned chairs by the hearth. There was a low fire to stave off the coming chill, and Marco had brought him wine and a tray of food, expecting a long night. The wine he gulped down eagerly, but he ignored the food. His stomach had been in knots ever since he'd felt the surge of power from the Wastes, knowing without a doubt Shade had been in the center of it.

He saw her pale face again, felt her limp frame in his grasp, and clutched the arms of his chair, willing himself not to race to her side. Petra was tending to her. She was fine, after all, just exhausted. She'd known not to cut anything vital in her desperate act of madness. She would heal quickly. It brought him little solace, though. Since their unlikely alliance had begun months ago, he'd grown to enjoy her company very much. Even with all the dangers they faced, it had never occurred to him that anything could harm her. Her strength had seemed boundless.

And when was strength alone enough to keep anyone safe in Malavita? His sister had been strong. Fiercely intelligent and utterly fearless, but for the conventions of their society she would have been his equal as a bloodwizard. Korin had been training Mercedes to be a talented healer and had placed great hope in her young daughter to follow suit.

And it had all ended in fire and blood...

Brooding, Dante stared into the hearth, mesmerized by the glowing coals. When Shade had first come to him with a proposition anyone else would have considered madness, Dante had jumped at the chance. A new Veil. The first in over a century. Raised, not by a Brotherhood priest, but by a witch and a prince of Malavita. It *was* madness. But she had sought him out because of his reputation as an honorable man, a man determined to break the Capos and expose the Brotherhood's lies. He knew her, of course. She was the Black Witch, a fiend, a rogue and a murderer. And also the wielder of obsidian blades, obsidian blades she'd crafted herself. She'd been inked with tattoos more elaborate and beautiful than anything the Brotherhood had ever produced, as well. How could he not believe in her power?

His eyelids grew heavy and his thoughts scattered. Visions of Shade danced with memories of his sister amid bright flames, shadowed enemies surrounding them...

Pale light seeped through the room's thick curtains and his fire was nearly ash when a thumping on the chamber's door pulled him from a half-doze.

Dante rose as the door swung open, pushed by a tall, slender woman in a pale blue robe with a tangle of dark golden hair around her shoulders. Shade staggered into the room toward the four-poster bed, her eyes wide in her white face. She stopped before she reached it and lifted a hand to her lips, looking like a lost child.

"Is he...?" she started to ask, speaking in a near-whisper. She swayed and Dante went to her, offering an arm for support. Barely acknowledging the help, Shade clutched his forearm and leaned against him, her eyes never leaving Cyril.

"He lives," Korin said. A golden aura enveloped him and when he turned to Shade his amber eyes glowed like coals. Slowly, the light faded. The room turned dim and ordinary. A great sigh rolled from Cyril, one free of pain. Color returned to his face. In the expectant silence that followed, his strong, steady breathing filled the room.

Trembling, Shade pulled away from Dante and straightened, feigning strength. Dante was surprised she'd let herself show any weakness at all, especially in front of Korin. She despised him more than Cyril did. Obviously, her fear for her old friend had affected her greatly.

"You have my gratitude," she said through her teeth, refusing to meet Korin's gaze. "But don't think this changes my opinion of you or your so-called Coterie."

Korin sighed and gave Dante a wry look. Dante made no reply. On this subject, he had to side with Shade. He didn't understand Korin's association with the secretive underground cabal of bloodwizards who worshipped the ancient Sicani and swore the Unseen still touched the land. Not through the blight.

They meant actual demons still threatened the land. Shade hated them with a fury. Those fools had turned her away from their door in her darkest need, casting her into the Wastes with the hope she'd politely die. When she'd discovered Korin was a member of the Coterie, she'd nearly broken their alliance. Luckily, he'd managed to convince her to continue.

Unfortunately, he had yet to tell her it was the Coterie who would be providing her with the cornerstones she needed for the Quattro Canto. Even more unfortunately, it was time to tell her.

"I could sooner change the path of the sun than your opinion of anyone, young lady," Korin said.

Dante cringed at his tone, waiting for Shade to explode. It didn't take much from Korin to set her off. She stiffened instantly, but before she could respond, Korin spoke again, "The Kindred wouldn't let you into their stronghold, would they?"

Bright spots appeared on her cheeks. The glance she gave him told Dante all he needed to know. His jaw tightened; he'd feared her mission had been a failure but had still maintained a small hope despite everything. But Shade wasn't well-practiced at hiding her emotions, not like a true Malavitan highborn lady. Her failure was written plainly on her face. Worse, it had been Korin who'd warned her she would fail to get what she wanted from the Kindred.

"It's merely a setback," she said after a pause. Looking aside, she tightened the sash of her robe and ran a hand through her tangle of hair. "If the Kindred won't come to me, I'll have to go to them."

"Go to them?" Dante took her by the arm and turned her toward him. "You mean to cross the Glass Fields like the Brazen Monk and his Doomed companions?" he asked. "Or do you know the secret ways through the mountains, and just failed to tell me?"

A stubborn look settled over her features and her arm went

rigid in his grasp. "I will do whatever it takes. I promised you I would secure a safe location for our Veil, one with rich sources of gemstones, and I will. Please, Dante, you have to trust me." And suddenly, she was leaning toward him, her eyes soft and pleading. "Please, I will find a way. Don't let him manipulate you."

Korin chuckled humorlessly. "Who's doing the manipulating, my child?"

Shade spun toward Korin, somehow managing to press herself against Dante at the same time. He could smell the lavender soap she preferred wafting from her tousled hair. It sent an unexpected shiver through his belly, but he kept his expression blank. The knowing look in Korin's eyes, however, told him he wasn't fooling his old friend. Korin had warned him more than once not to grow attached to Shade.

Too late for that.

"I am not a child," she said sharply. "And most certainly not *your* child. I made a mistake coming to the Coterie all those years ago; I won't make that mistake again." She gave him a bitter smile. "You were right to turn me away. It made me strong. Stronger than you could possibly know."

"Oh, I know." His gaze turned stern, cold. "I know your strength, your power. We all know. Every bloodwizard within a hundred miles felt you touch the Wild Power. And we felt you almost lose control of it, too."

Again, those bright spots of color appeared in her cheeks and her eyes grew troubled, her brow furrowed. Was she recalling that maelstrom of power she'd nearly unleashed upon the entire land? Dante shuddered at the memory, though he had only felt a bare brush of it.

On the bed, Cyril stirred and muttered in his sleep. Korin frowned and stepped away from him, moving closer to Shade and Dante. He lowered his voice and took on a more persuasive tone. "The Coterie has been working against the Brotherhood for far longer than you know," he said. "No matter your unfortunate past with them, your goals align. They want to see the Wastes brought back into balance and a new Veil raised. They have been waiting and hoping for someone like you to appear, ever since we lost–"

He stopped, his eyes flickering to Dante. "Shade knows about Mercedes," Dante said, and Shade's grip tightened on his arm. "And my poor little niece, Elena."

He looked down at her, a familiar loss welling in his heart. Sympathy darkened her agate eyes. She knew how his sister and niece, along with Mercedes' husband and entire household, had died in a conflagration set by assassins at their villa. She also knew how the Coterie had manipulated his sister's child in the womb, hoping to create a bloodwizard who was also strong in Sicani blood. It had not improved her opinion of the Coterie, or of Korin. She blamed them almost as much as he'd blamed the Capomajus Rubeus for their deaths. They had made his poor niece a target, she'd insisted more than once, by making her some sort of potential weapon.

"Yet when I did appear at your door, you tossed me to the wolves," she said bitterly.

"If I had been among that sect of the Coterie, I would not have treated you so poorly. The Wild Power does not frighten me as much as it does them. And it was fear which led them to act so dishonorably. But, your continuing animosity toward us serves no useful purpose. Not when we have what you need to raise your Veil."

Dante braced himself. Shade had grown still against him, her gaze locked on Korin. "What could the Coterie possibly have that I would need?" she asked dismissively.

Korin straightened his fine blue tunic, his expression grave. "When you first approached Dante with your wild idea, I thought it a fool's quest. Even with the knowledge to raise a Veil, how would you manage to do it without the sacred stones for a Quattro Canto? Perhaps your father had provided you with the stones along with the knowledge? But, alas, he had not."

"He would have," she said defensively. "He was murdered before he could manage it." She cast her eyes up at Dante. "It wasn't a fool's quest. I had hoped I could find the stones I needed beyond the mountains. Among the Kindred mines. Or I would have stolen them from the Brotherhood if I had to, as my father had intended."

"And I told you I would provide the cornerstones," Dante said softly. His brow furrowed as he gazed into her eyes, feeling as if he was about to betray her. Would she hate him after this? His heart contracted at the thought. "But I don't have them, Shade."

Her eyes searched his face in confusion. "I don't understand…"

"The Coterie have the stones you need," Korin said gravely. "And they will give them to you. With conditions."

Shock and anger crumpled her features and Shade pulled away from him, stumbling on her injured legs. Dante reached for her and she shoved a stiff arm at him, keeping him at bay. Her hand flew to her eyes as she hunched over as if in agony. "I would sooner crawl across the Glass Fields than take anything from your Coterie," she growled. "They can shove their stones straight up their backsides!"

She kept her voice low for Cyril's sake, though Dante imagined she wanted to scream. "Shade," he said, attempting to approach her again, his hands open in supplication. "Please, I never meant to mislead you. I didn't tell you at first because I knew your feelings about the Coterie. They've had the stones for some time, you see, but they had no idea what to do with them. And then you appeared. Like a miracle."

"As if the Four and the Hidden sent you to us," Korin added. Dante threw him a dark look, wishing he would stay quiet. He feared anything his old mentor said would only enrage Shade further. "They came to me soon after you met Dante. I had no idea they possessed such powerful relics, either."

She didn't seem to even hear him. She remained hunched, her hands over her face and her shoulders shuddering.

"Shade…" Dante said.

"You know you have no choice, obsidian wielder." Korin's voice had deepened, grown resonant. Power seemed to fill the air, and not the gentle gold of healing. Dante's hand snaked to one of his blade hilts, even as he shrank away from the healer. "If you wish to raise your Veil and save your people, you will accept what we offer. You have no choice!"

Slowly, Shade straightened. Her shoulders squared beneath her thin robe, and she shook her hair back from her face before spinning to face him. "You've well and truly backed me into a corner, haven't you?" she said, her expression cold. She glared at Korin. "What conditions will they demand of me?"

"None you won't be willing to agree to," he assured her, sounding normal once again. The air was still, calm. Beyond the drawn curtains, Dante could hear the soft trill of birdsong. A shuddering relief filled him, and his hand dropped from his blade hilt. He tried to catch Shade's eye, but she wouldn't look at him. His relief turned sour.

A grim smile bent her rose-pink lips. Her hands settled near her hips, grasping imaginary blades. "We shall see," she said, and her eyes narrowed. "And be aware, Korin Illario, there is always a choice."

CHAPTER EIGHT

The poorer sections of Sicaria lay outside her high stone walls, warrens of stone and timber buildings crisscrossed by streets both paved and muddy. It was an area Shade and her Golondrina companions knew well, so when Korin described the rendezvous point with the Coterie, she knew exactly where he meant. A broad canal inched along the southern wall of the city, providing access to the vast estuary leading into the ports of Sicaria. A few arched bridges crossed the waterway, allowing free passage from one side to the other, and one such bridge led to the outfall pipe of Sicaria's Great Sewer. She'd smirked when she'd realized it; what better place to meet the Coterie than at the entrance to a sewer?

"I don't like it," Cyril had complained when Shade told him her plan. Propped up on a narrow cot in the head groomsman's apartment over Dante's stables, the elder Golondrina had looked much better since his ordeal. He'd lasted a day in the manor before insisting he be moved to more fitting accommodations. He would have had Manoli and Petra pitch the tent they used for Waste-walking in Dante's manicured gardens if Shade hadn't talked him out of it. As tough as he was, he needed real rest in a real bed.

"I'll have the boys with me," she countered, gesturing to the cousins dicing at the groomsman's table. Manoli made a face and rolled his eyes at his uncle's concern, and she moved her stool so Cyril couldn't see his cheek. "And we aren't walking down the streets like doves. We'll be keeping to the sewers."

"Where we belong," Manoli added with a soft snicker.

Shade shot him a warning glance and moved her stool another inch. Luckily, Cyril hadn't heard Manoli, or he was choosing to ignore him. "You should wait until I'm on my feet," he insisted. "I'll be up and about by tomorrow at the latest."

In reply, Shade poked him in the side, eliciting a gasp and turning him a lighter hue of bronze. "I'd rather not wait, Cyril. The sooner we get our hands on the cornerstones, then the sooner we can return to the Wastes. If the Kindred won't let us into their stronghold, then we'll have to find a new location for our Veil. It won't be easy, and I fear waiting any longer. The Wastes are tipping into chaos as we speak."

Cyril's grim expression showed his agreement, but he wasn't done arguing. "I don't trust those people, and I don't trust Korin Illario."

Shade sighed. As if she did? She didn't like any of this. She tapped her toe on the well-sanded floorboards, frowning. She felt backed into a corner, and she hated the feeling. The Coterie would manipulate her for their own ends, she had no doubt. And where exactly had they gotten their cornerstones? She intended to find out whether they planned on telling her or not. If they had managed to obtain the rare and precious stones, then maybe she could, as well.

"If I can't be with you," Cyril growled finally, "then take the Imperial."

"Raiden?" she said, surprised. "He's the one who put you in that bed!"

Stubbornly, Cyril shook his head. "I was the fool who threw myself in the path of danger. There were a hundred other ways to counter, and I chose the worst one."

"Nonsense. I—"

"Shade." Cyril laid a hand on her knee and captured her gaze with his sharp, gray eyes. He lowered his voice. "The lads are brave and would die for you, but the Imperial can protect you like they cannot. Take him with you."

In the end, it hadn't been up to Cyril. Dante had already told the captain their plans, and Raiden had insisted on accompanying her.

"Because I'm in your custody?" Shade had asked him with a sarcastic roll of her eyes as they'd left Dante's villa with Manoli and Petra flanking them.

Walking beside her, his uniform and sword concealed by a cloak, the hood drawn over his sleek black hair, he'd peered at her askance. She was wearing a cloak, as well, to hide her bloodwizard garb. She'd refused to enter the Coterie's lair dressed as a callow youth. She would face the Coterie as herself.

"I owe a debt. To you, to Don Cyril." Raiden had sighed, his gaze returning to the crushed quartz road beneath his boots. Their crunching steps were in unison. "I have served my whole life as a shield to others. My own father made it clear I was always expected to be a sacrifice. Always. I never expected another to make a sacrifice for me."

His words had made her grimace in empathy. "Sounds like your father took lessons from mine. I was never a daughter to him, only a means to an end."

"And what was that end?" he'd asked, curious.

"Revenge."

They crossed a stone footbridge as evening fell, the city's curtain wall casting deep shadows over them, leaving behind the bustling warren of homes and businesses. Shade had kept her cloak closed when they'd passed through the streets, but once they were on the bridge she tossed it back from her shoulders. She wanted easy access to her blades. It wouldn't surprise her if Korin had led her into a trap with the promise of cornerstones. Dante might trust him, but she never would.

Dante. She clenched her teeth. Her feelings toward him had grown topsy-turvy. Just when she was beginning to really care about him, he'd sprung this nonsense on her. But he'd been right to keep it secret; if he'd told her about his connection to the Coterie earlier, she never would have agreed to their alliance. Now, though, she was in too deep.

Raiden followed her example, throwing back his cloak from one shoulder and loosening his sword in its scabbard. Guilt clouded his brow for a moment, and he glanced back at Manoli and Petra who trailed them across the bridge. "I am sorry about your uncle," he said quietly. "I should have apologized sooner…"

Manoli laughed at Raiden's heart-felt apology. "If we were afraid of getting hurt, Imperial, we wouldn't be following the Black Witch."

"Right?" Petra seconded to Shade's annoyance, shaking a thumb in her direction. "We figure the boss'll get us all killed one day, anyway. Then we'll walk the Green Meadows together."

A look came into Raiden's eyes at his comment, one of understanding. He touched his fingers to his brow and bowed deeply. "May we all meet again in the heavens of my father's gods," he said reverently.

Shade's exasperated sigh broke the moment. "Let's not rush it," she muttered.

The outfall pipe of Sicaria's Great Sewer was a stone archway half again as tall as a man. They approached the shadowy recess along a narrow towpath beside the curtain wall. Shade dropped her hood. Someone moved in the shadowy depths of the giant pipe, creeping along the brick edges above the flow of fetid water. He stepped into the fading light, cloaked as she was but with a rough canvas hood covering his head. Ragged holes had been cut for his eyes and mouth. It gave him an ominous look.

"Greetings, Shade Nox. We've been expecting you." His voice was deep and sonorous, as if he spoke from the bottom of a well. From where she stood, Shade could just feel the draw of blood he'd made to produce the effect. "Please, come with me." He gestured imperatively with a gloved hand.

"Come where?" she asked, crossing her arms over her chest and leaning indolently against the arch of the tunnel pipe. He stood on the other side of the tunnel, and she would have to leap across a few broken stones peeking from the foul water to reach him. Behind her, her companions spread out in a loose arc, Raiden keeping closest to her.

"To our lair." The masked stranger reached beneath his cloak and drew out a bundle of cloth. "From here, no one can see the way to our sanctuary."

He tossed it to her, and she caught it, letting it slither open in her hand. A hood. Shade smirked to hide the sudden pounding in her heart. "There's only one," she said, and heard Manoli growl something low and hostile. "You expect me to go with you alone?"

"You are the Black Witch, are you not? Are you afraid?"

"Only a fool fears nothing, and I won't walk alone into a trap."

"Only you will proceed from here, witch." His tone turned haughty behind his tattered mask. "We cannot allow a representative of the Empire near our organization." His horrid mask turned toward the cousins. "And we do not allow oath breakers into our sanctuary."

Shade snorted derisively at the man's accusation, but Manoli and Petra each let loose a curse, Manoli going so far as to step forward with a hand to his blade. Shade sighed. She'd forgotten about this nonsense. The Coterie had it in their heads that the Golondrina had somehow betrayed the Sicani long, long ago and were cursed to wander the Wastes because of it. In that, they were as bad as the Brotherhood.

"Faces spit on you!" Manoli's long mustaches quivered with anger, his teeth bared. "We have broken no oaths. We keep the old ways! We watch over the qaraz!"

"You watch over ghosts, boy. Your people failed to protect the ancient spirits, and the blight has grown." It was hard to say if the man was angry or frightened behind his mask, but Shade noticed his hands had disappeared into his cloak.

"Ignore him, Manny," she said, laying a restraining hand on her friend. "We already know these people are idiots."

Her words sparked a laugh from Petra. The masked man stiffened. Manoli smiled at him. Grimaced, really, but he relaxed.

"Nevertheless, your companions must wait for you here. We are risking everything to bring you into our sanctuary."

"We won't just let you take our boss down a fucking sewer without us," Manoli said, his nostrils flaring and his hand on his knife again.

The man shrugged. "Then your 'boss' will never get the cornerstones she needs for her Veil. The choice is yours."

Hells. Shade exchanged a look with her companions. She held Raiden's worried gaze for a moment. "Shade," he said, a weight of caution in his words.

"Stay with the boys, Raiden. I'll be back soon." Before she could change her mind, she jumped from the towpath onto the broken stones in the outflow. Another leap had her beside the masked stranger. She turned to her friends and gave them a crooked smile. They wore matching looks of horror and concern. Swiftly, Shade pulled the hood over her head. It took all her self-control not to wince away when the man took her by the arm.

"If you don't see me by morning, boys," she couldn't resist saying as he led her along the bricks, the rush of water somewhere beneath her feet. "Then you have my permission to kill Korin Illario."

"As you wish, boss," Petra said, though it was Manoli's guffaw which brought a smile to her lips.

* * *

After a nightmare journey through the foul stench of the sewers, her feet cold and her sandals wet from the ankle-deep filth they'd passed through, and her nerves shot from the impenetrable darkness suffocating her, Shade was allowed to remove her hood. Her guide left her in a small, windowless chamber with a pitcher of water and a basin in which to wash her feet, and footwear next to a small table with two ladder-backed chairs. It was an ascetic space with white plastered walls devoid of decoration but for a quartered mask adorned with colored stones.

"Not a very impressive sanctuary," she muttered as she took a seat. She threw her cloak back to make it easier to reach her blades, and began to wash her feet, and, as best she could, her sandals. She'd expected something grand, at least. The Coterie had spent decades building their cabal of magic-users rich in Sicani blood, and then seeded the Veils with cells of operatives. In her father's home, the staff had whispered among themselves about this secret society determined to destroy the church, though Shade had never seen much evidence of their work. Still, after Bishop Raphael had been murdered, she'd gone to them, desperate for protection. Who better to save her from the Brotherhood than their sworn enemies?

Shade dried her feet with the edge of her cloak, her lips tightening. When she'd appeared on their doorstep after days of searching, her "saviors" had stared at her like she was a cockroach floating in their soup. A stern, hawk-nosed man had laid a hand on her head, declared her "unworthy" after a moment, and then sent her on her way. But she remembered the shadows in his eyes as he'd shut the door in her face. Not just disdain, but fear.

As she was strapping on her damp sandals, the door to the room opened with an ominous squeal of iron hinges. Shade stiffened and jumped to her feet, her hands hovering near her blade hilts. A hum of power preceded the group which entered the chamber. It set her teeth on edge and made the hair on her neck rise. It reminded her of the Golondrinas' combined power, but this wasn't born from a natural bond, this had been forced.

It was an odd group: three women and two men, young and old alike, both rich and poor. One tall, broad-shouldered man wore the silks and linens of a merchant while the man beside him was dressed as a laborer. Bearded and rough-looking, the laborer gave her a smirk and she knew instantly he'd been the man who'd led her through the sewers. The rich man evaluated her as if she were a particularly fine broodmare. She ignored them both and focused on the women. The eldest of the three smiled at her. "Welcome, Lady Nox," she said, her voice smooth and cultured. Her clothing marked her as a noblewoman, full skirts of satin and lace in lovely shades of purple. Matching amethysts hung from her ears and circled her throat and even adorned her long, slender fingers. Her skin was smooth and fair, her neck long and unlined though she appeared to be of middle years. The ash-blonde hair piled on her head had a touch of gray and there were small wrinkles at the corners of her blue eyes. "I am Celeste."

"Are you in charge?" Shade asked.

Celeste's smile tightened. "You are blunt, aren't you, my dear? Korin warned me you might be difficult."

"Did he also warn you the sun might rise in the morning?"

One of the younger women flanking Celeste snickered, and quickly put a hand to her mouth. Shade glanced at her, her lips quirking. At least someone appreciated her humor. The woman – girl, really – was dressed as finely as Celeste, though in a snug, nearly sheer gown which revealed far too much. Not exactly a noblewoman. The other woman was dressed simply in a drab wool gown common among the poorer folk in Malavita. Her plain face was unsmiling. All of them, the men included, had beadwork sewn on their clothing. On the shoulders and collars of their shirts, at their waists in broad belts. Beads fashioned from tiny gemstones. She tensed. Small though they were, the gems were numerous and fine. A vast well of power.

There was little reason any of these people would ever gather in a room together, and yet a common cause and common blood had brought them all to the Coterie. People willing to overlook societal barriers to support a dogma were a dangerous sort. Fanatics.

"I understand why you are reluctant to deal with us," Celeste said. "What happened between you and certain members of our organization was unfortunate, but it shouldn't color our future endeavors. We want the same things, child. And if we overlook past slights, perhaps we can come to a mutually agreeable arrangement."

Every word out of Celeste's mouth filled Shade with a simmering rage. She spoke as if Shade had wanted to join their club and been denied membership. "Do we?" she asked sharply. "Want the same things, I mean. Because I have no idea what you want, lady, except to bring me to heel in your so-called cause. Korin told me as much. If you didn't want me before, why in the lowest hells do you want me now?"

Celeste glided closer, her hands clasped before her skirts. The hum of power reached a level that made Shade's teeth ache, and she glanced at the others. Not one had their hands in sight, but buried in pockets or hidden slits in their skirts. They were drawing blood. She gritted her teeth and kept her hands away from her blades.

"Let's not play games," Celeste said. "Korin came to us with your plan to raise a Veil in the Wastes. Somehow, you've discovered how to do it. Or so you claim."

"You think I'm lying?"

Celeste lifted her shoulders in a delicate shrug, every movement as elegant and refined as her clothing. "If Korin believes it, I will take his word, but others will only believe it when it is done."

Fair enough. Shade crossed her arms over her chest, mostly

to keep from gripping her blades. She didn't want them to think she was rattled. "He told me you're offering me the stones I need, so enough of you must believe I can do what I say."

"True. We are prepared to give you our cornerstones. Cornerstones we acquired through great risk of our own."

Shade's heart raced. "And what will it cost me?"

Celeste pulled out a chair and took a seat at the table. She gestured for Shade to join her. Reluctantly, Shade returned to her seat but angled it so she could keep an eye on the room. The other members of the Coterie spread out around them, silent and watchful. The hum of power lessened fractionally.

"It was a mistake to send you away all those years ago," Celeste said softly. Her pale eyes regarded Shade with something like regret in their cool depths. "We lost a valuable ally in our arrogance, our shortsightedness. I admit, you frightened us when you appeared on our doorstep. Your power is... unusual."

"I've always thought I was special."

"We were right to be afraid." Celeste's tone grew less sympathetic. "We felt you out there in the Wastes. We felt what you almost loosed on the world." A small shudder racked her slim frame. "It was always your attraction toward the Wild Power we couldn't abide."

Shade flushed. "I controlled it," she said, her voice suddenly hoarse. She cleared her throat. "I have it under control."

"Barely."

"If that were so we'd all be ash, wouldn't we?"

"Will you touch the Wild Power when you raise your Veil?" Celeste spoke coldly, and the power in the room pressed against Shade until she twisted in her seat.

"Stop it!" Shade slapped her hand against her thigh, itching to draw a blade. "If you want to see whether I have control over my power, keep pushing me."

Celeste stared down her nose without a trace of fear. "Are you a savior, obsidian wielder, or are you a destroyer? We thought the latter all those years ago and hoped the Wastes would correct whatever mistake the universe made in your creation. Yet you survived. You survived and thrived. You crafted blades – obsidian! Faces turn from me! – you found a tattoo master more skilled than the best among the Brotherhood. And now you dare to create a Quattro Canto and raise a Veil. No one outside the Brotherhood has achieved such a thing."

Her voice had risen, grown excited. The pressure in the air made Shade's ears throb and her head pound, but she withstood it. This was a test, nothing more. There was no true menace aimed at her. Nevertheless, she was about to punch Celeste in the face if she didn't get to her point soon.

"You know nothing of the plans we've had in place for decades now, the pain and blood and magic we've spent attempting to right what has gone wrong in this land. Not fifteen years ago, we thought all our plans ruined, all our hope lost, and for all those years, we mourned. And then you appeared. The unexpected witch." Celeste laughed and there were low murmurs from the rest of the Coterie. They might have been prayers. "You've given us new hope."

Through gritted teeth, Shade asked, "Hope for what?"

"Hope for victory." Her eyes were alight with religious fervor. "Finally, we will finish the battle against the Unseen our Sicani forebears started centuries ago. We will cleanse their blight from the land and wipe them from the world forever."

CHAPTER NINE

Despite her discomfort, which was bordering on pain, Shade laughed. "The Unseen? Are you mad? The Unseen are no more, destroyed by the Sicani long ago. Only their blight remains to trouble us. I thought you wanted me to help you destroy the Brotherhood – which I would gladly do – but you want me to fight imaginary demons?"

Celeste pursed her lips. "They are as real as the ground beneath your feet. As real as your blades and wards. Only a fool would believe otherwise. Only a fool would believe the Brotherhood's lies that all that remains of the Unseen are shadows stalking the Wastes. The Brotherhood itself has long been infiltrated by demons. They use susceptible humans as avatars, and have found a wealth of corrupted souls among those priests."

"I know firsthand the corruption among the Brotherhood. My father taught me, a bishop and a Blademaster. He taught me how to fashion gemstone blades and how to raise a Veil, something the Brotherhood has feared to do for a century. I will restore balance to the Wastes. That is the hope I bring! Isn't it enough for you? Why must you make it a part of some grand ancient battle?"

"Because you must understand what is at stake!"

"I understand what's at stake. Better than you, in fact. My

people, the Golondrina you so disparage, are bearing the brunt of the Brotherhood's failings. They walk the Wastes, tending the sacred qaraz, the qaraz which are the last true magic of this land, but the Wastes are growing more unstable and dangerous. Blackstorms rise where they shouldn't, and the beasts grow ever more ravenous. I am raising a Veil to save my people!"

"It does not matter for whom you raise the Veil, only that you raise it," Celeste snapped, clearly irritated by her mention of the Golondrina. "It will be a blow to our common enemy, the first blow against them in ages. You may not wish to become involved in our war against the Unseen, but if you raise a Veil you will have no choice. Are you ready to face such a consequence?"

"I am ready to face whatever may come. I am not afraid of my enemies," and she smirked, "not the real ones, or the shadows."

"Will you agree to our terms in exchange for the cornerstones you need?"

"What terms?" Shade asked cautiously, though excitement built in her belly. Did they really have the stones she needed? Or was this some elaborate trick?

Celeste stood, lifted a hand, and made a swirling motion in the air before her. Light followed her fingertips, forming a sparkling circle, a blending of Fire and Air. The light became a pattern, intersecting lines which formed a bright node. The image expanded until Shade could see that it was a map of the Wastes. There were the Razor Ridge mountains to the west, and that harsh, pulsating blur near the node was the Glass Fields.

"You must raise your Veil as soon as possible," Celeste said, her voice deep and amplified by magic. "We are well aware of the state of our land. The Veils grow weaker with every passing day and the blight grows stronger. To save our land, you must raise the Veil at the Nexus, nowhere else. If not there, then all could be lost."

"The Nexus?" Shade whispered, her eyes glued to the bright node of power. It was a place where several qaraz crossed, a place deep in the Wastes and dangerously close to the unstable Glass Fields. The amount of power coalesced in this one spot would make it difficult to work the Veil magic. She would be calling on all Four Faces and the Hidden and working with – hopefully – immensely powerful gemstones. If anything went wrong, it could be disastrous for her. Her lips pressed into a line. Were there even potential mines at this location? As far as she knew, no one had dared prospect so close to the Glass Fields – the sight of the final battle between the Unseen and the Sicani.

"It is the perfect place," Celeste said, breathless with triumph. "When you raise your Veil, all of Malavita will be touched by its power."

Her eyes gleamed golden through the map of light, an expression close to ecstasy on her face. It made Shade's skin crawl. Her gaze slipped back to the Nexus, noting Celeste was correct about one thing, at least: the knot of qaraz at the Nexus. Its tendrils radiated outward across all of Malavita, touching each and every Veil in the whole of the island, including all those along the Golden Crescent and those few that sheltered Brotherhood strongholds along the southern coast. The strongest and oldest of all the Veils.

But this couldn't be the place of her vision, she was sure of it. She was meant to go beyond the mountains.

"It's impossible," she said. "It's too dangerous to attempt a Veil so near the Glass Fields. Besides, I've already chosen a location. Beyond the mountains, in Kindred territory."

Celeste's ecstatic expression slipped. "No," she said. "You must go to the Nexus, or we are all lost!"

Shade frowned. There would be no convincing a fanatic. But she had to go to the Kindred lands. The certainty of it had driven her since before she'd ever thought about raising a Veil. It wasn't as if the places beyond the mountains were any safer as far as the Wastes went, but she'd dreamt of her Veil rising like a vast shield over a valley framed by two broken hills, the Razor Ridge mountains looming in the background. In her dream, she'd known what it meant – where it meant.

"Show me the cornerstones you claim to possess," she temporized. "And then I'll decide."

Celeste raised a hand. The power filling the room receded, and the map made of light vanished. Shade let loose a breath, trembling in relief. Faces. They were strong.

The man who'd led Shade through the sewers left the room abruptly, throwing her a smug smile as he did. A moment later, he returned bearing a narrow box made of tin. He settled the box on the table. Leaves and vines were etched on its hinged lid, but she felt a strange blankness from it.

Reverently, the man lifted the lid, and power flooded the room. Her heart began to pound and her mouth went dry. Nestled within on black velvet sat gemstones. Each was the size of a robin's egg, uncut, rough and jagged. The depth of color in them astounded her, and even uncut, the diamond held the promise of perfect clarity. The ruby, emerald, and sapphire shone with inner light, the elements encapsulated. They sang to her, and she knew them.

A memory surfaced: she knelt by her father before a glass-encased shrine, within the case four jewels were held suspended by layers upon layers of power. Power she could see even as a child. Like a dream, she heard her father whisper in her ear, *"Patience, little one. The day will come when they will be yours."*

"Where did you get these?" she asked dully, feeling an emptiness open within her, something deep and hot at its center.

"Your father, the Bishop Raphael, was not the only Brotherhood priest to despise his order for their secrets and lies." Celeste spoke triumphantly, unaware that each word she uttered fed the tiny ball of heat forming in Shade's core. "Our agent put himself in grave danger to remove these ancient stones from the Brotherhood's citadel. But he managed to bring them to us without betraying our organization. It was a remarkable feat of–"

"You *stole* them," Shade said, recognizing the heat in her belly at last: rage.

"The Brotherhood weren't likely to part with their treasure willingly."

Shade let her rage fill her. "These were meant for me!" she roared, rising to her feet, her hands itching for her blades. She slammed both hands on the table. It shuddered with the force of her blows. "These stones were mine! My father promised them to me, and you stole them!"

Celeste jerked, white-faced with shock. The Coterie's power filled the small room again, less unified than before, and Shade could taste their sudden panic. Good, let them be afraid!

"You fools, you unbelievable fools! Your rash stupidity cost my father his life. They sent a Ruby Pontifex for him, accusing him of theft." Tears of rage blurred her vision, yet she managed to reach out and grip one of the stones. The blood-red ruby. Its power throbbed against her palm. It made her ill. "They tortured him for hours, but he wouldn't confess." The screams of her father echoed in her memory. She'd witnessed all of it, the pain, the blood, hidden in a secret panel in the wall of his library. She pressed her fist to her lips, the ruby like a hot coal against her palm. "I thought he was protecting me, but he never had the stones, did he?" She glared at Celeste with murderous rage. "Did he!" she screamed.

"We... We did not know they would accuse him." White-lipped, Celeste backed away. She lifted her chin and tried to regain her composure. Her trembling hands smoothed her skirt, and her companions closed in around her, their power coalescing. It slammed against Shade, causing her sight to dim. She shook her head, swaying.

"They are yours now, witch," spoke the wealthy man, his

disdain of her turned to desperation. "The stones are yours! You have what you need to raise your Veil–"

Shade spun on her heel and raised her fist, the ruby pulsing in her grasp. Power crackled around her even though she had not drawn blood. It reached out to envelop the other stones. They rose in the air, spinning, orbiting her like stars. "Yes, they are mine. They have always been mine, you foul thieves!" With her free hand, she drew one obsidian blade. It gleamed white in the dim room, casting their shadows against the walls. The cornerstones spun around her faster and faster. The earth began to tremble beneath her feet.

"Stop, witch!" screamed the young whore as she yanked a platinum knife from her skirts. Blood dripped from it. "You'll draw every priest in the city to our door!"

"Let them come," she said, "I will burn them into ash along with all of you!"

The man who'd led her through the sewers raised a hand toward her. His eyes were wide, but he spoke calmly, if quickly. "Will you burn your friends to ash along with all of us?" he asked. "They are in a taverna just over the river."

Shade hissed, his warning reaching her through her rage. As much as she wanted to, she couldn't unleash her power in Sicaria. The Brotherhood would come for her and destroy everyone within the vicinity to get to her. Nevertheless, she held onto her power, letting it fill the room. "I'm walking out of here," she said, fixing Celeste with a glare. "With the stones. And I will raise my Veil where I see fit!"

All her composure had vanished, and Celeste bared her teeth at Shade like a wild beast. "So be it! Let Korin deal with your obstinance. Sheath your weapon and begone from our sanctuary!"

"You won't stop me?"

Celeste shook her head, her neat hairstyle whipping loose with the movement.

"Swear it! Swear upon the ancient Sicani, our most blessed saviors."

"I swear upon the Sicani, demon witch!"

Shade smirked and sheathed her blade. Only then did she release the magic of the stones. They ceased their spinning and settled into her open hands like birds alighting in their nest. Keeping her eyes on the others as best she could, she stuffed them into her belt pouch. "Now, if someone could show me the way back to my companions...?"

A vicious look settled on Celeste's face. "Take her back the way she came, Armand."

The rough-dressed man approached her, his eyes lit with gleeful spite and the canvas hood in his hands. "With pleasure, my lady."

The interior of the seedy taverna was smoky and dim, and overly warm from a crackling hearth. The smell of woodsmoke and the savory notes of fried sardines couldn't quite conceal the sour tang of spilled ale or the distinctive odor of urine. His nose wrinkling, Raiden kept a hand on his sword hilt as he followed his companions. Both Manoli and Petra threw jolly greetings to the man behind the bar – if a plank on two barrels could be considered a bar – but they each kept a hand on their blade hilts, too. The barkeep, a sullen-looking man in a dirty apron, waved and turned to fill tankards of ale from the cask behind him.

Manoli led them toward an empty table in the back of the cramped common room and they wedged themselves around it, keeping their backs to the wall. There were a few other patrons in the place, solitary men mostly, hunched over plates of fish and pints of ale. None were dressed as Corsaro, fortunately, but all of them displayed tattoos and carried simple quartz knives.

A moment after they sat down, the barkeep dropped three tankards on the scarred tabletop. Petra grinned and tossed him a coin, but the man's sullen mien remained the same. He tucked the coin in his belt and shuffled away. Petra shrugged at Raiden's raised eyebrows. "He has good ale," he said.

"And he knows how to keep his mouth shut," added Manoli ominously as he reached for his tankard. His brow was furrowed and his lips were turned down beneath his long mustache. "We should have followed them."

Petra sighed, but didn't disagree. While his cousin quaffed his ale, he sipped his, and kept his attention on the men around them. Raiden followed Petra's example, finding him to be a thoughtful, cautious man slow to anger and quick to help. It had been his fast thinking which had kept Shade from bleeding to death in the Wastes. A slight stirring of guilt made him shift on the hard bench, but he squashed it. He'd been forgiven. It wouldn't do to continue to wallow in self-loathing, no matter if he felt he deserved it.

"I don't think Lord Safire would knowingly send her into danger," Raiden said, though even he found his words unconvincing. They should have followed her. *He* should have. Uninterested in his ale despite Petra's endorsement, he toyed with his tankard and watched the other patrons. He'd tossed back the hood of his cloak and not a few of them were eyeing him. His delicate features, smooth cheeks and short shock of silky black hair marked him. The looks thrown his way weren't exactly hostile, but they weren't exactly friendly either.

"Safire only cares about raising a Veil for the Empire," Manoli scoffed. "He'd throw us all to the wolves, Shade included, to get it. All the First Families value profit above their people. This endeavor will surely line his pockets as much as the Empire's. At the least, he'll avoid paying Capos their tribute and the Brotherhood their tithes." He shook his head. "But Shade is the one putting herself at risk for the rest of us. It is her power and knowledge which will raise the Veil. I don't know why we need him, or the blasted–" He stopped abruptly and threw Raiden an embarrassed glance.

"The blasted Empire?" Raiden finished for him. He smiled at

Manoli to show he hadn't taken offense. "I admit the Empire's interest in the Veil is purely selfish. But," and he paused, searching for the right words, "I may represent the Empire, but my motives are my own. I have seen with my own eyes why Shade is so desperate to raise a Veil for her people. Not for gems or land or some new enterprise for profit, but as a shield against the horrors of the Wastes." He shook his head, still in awe over all he'd witnessed. The Golondrina had fought as one, protecting the weakest among them. Not as an army but as a family. His very breath escaped him when he recalled how Shade had risen on invisible tendrils of power to face a horde of beasts alone. At the time, chasing after her, his heart had been lodged in his throat and he'd felt something he hadn't felt in years: fear.

Warmth rose into his cheeks and his heart began to thud. He'd faced more enemies than he could count, killed more men than he cared to remember, and suddenly he was afraid. For a woman he barely knew. Raiden gripped his tankard. He was a weapon, a shield, an assassin. He was a tool to be used. And discarded when necessary. But, here, perhaps he could be more.

"Shade has been our only shield for a few years now," Petra said. "Her power has kept us safe as the Wastes have tipped further and further into chaos. But even her power has limits, and she can't be everywhere at once." He grimaced. "We are Waste-walkers. It is our sacred duty to tend the qaraz, our purpose. We have lived in the Wastes since the Final Battle destroyed our land and never quailed from our task. We don't want a Veil, my friend, but we need one."

"I know. And Shade has proven her power to me. I believe she can deliver what Safire promised. A new Veil raised in the Wastes. A Veil for the Empire." He fixed his companions with a serious gaze. "Are your people willing to work with the Empire in this endeavor? You will be the ones living in the Veil. Will you mine gems like the Brotherhood? Grow crops and tend vines like Veil-dwellers? Can you give up the freedom of the Wastes?"

Petra looked aside, his brow wrinkled but Manoli returned his look, his grey eyes dark. "When it is between life and freedom, my people will choose life. We have faith in our witch." He grinned, showing his teeth like a wolf. "She's never killed without cause, you know. She has more honor than every Capo and Corsaro soldier combined."

Raiden lifted a brow. Of course, they would know about the warrant. And he had "arrested" their witch the first day they'd met which was why they'd been so hostile to him. At first. Things had changed. However, it really wasn't his place to decide her guilt or innocence.

Still. Would he really turn her over to the polizia after all was said and done between them? The thought made him cringe inside. He had seen her kill, yes, but only when attacked. She'd shown mercy to Vito when he himself would have chosen to kill. Was it so hard to believe she'd been framed for a murder she didn't commit?

Raiden grunted softly, lifting his tankard. Isn't that what had happened to him? Though it hadn't been necessary to frame him. He'd willingly taken the blame for a crime someone else had committed.

The door to the taverna opened with a jangle of bells, letting in a wash of cold air. At first, no one stood in the entrance. Perhaps the wind had opened the door? But, as one, every man in the place tensed. Alerted, Raiden straightened and adjusted his sword. On either side of him, both Petra and Manoli reacted identically. Tension settled heavily throughout the tavern. The regular noises of quiet conversation, and the soft sounds of eating and drinking ceased abruptly.

Two men entered dressed in the long robes of Brotherhood priests, black robes instead of the usual crimson Raiden had seen from a distance. They carried blades, these priests. A single knife at their belts, though longer than those carried by other bloodwizards. Their sharp, black eyes shifted around the room then arrowed to Raiden like hounds catching sight of a fox. Raiden gritted his teeth as the men strode toward their table with grim purpose; they moved smoothly, effortlessly. Like living shadows.

He tensed, his hand slipping to the hilt of his sword hidden beneath his cloak. Petra laid a hand on his arm. His eyes were wide, and his face had paled. "Your sword won't help you," he said in a strangled voice. "Be still, and don't antagonize them."

"Who are they?" Raiden murmured.

"Ruby Pontifex."

Raiden frowned. They were high-ranking priests as far as he knew. But whatever they chose to call themselves, he knew what they were: *assassins*.

"If they'd come to kill you," Manoli added rapidly. "You'd be dead already."

The two priests reached their table and stood shoulder-to-shoulder, their hands tucked demurely in the sleeves of their black robes. Tall and lithe, the man on the right bowed his head to Raiden, his thin mouth downturned. He was clean-shaven and his dark hair was cut short. Thin, pale scars marked his high, narrow cheeks. His companion was similarly shorn and scarred, though shorter and broader with a round face which appeared almost babyish. Both men had eyes as black and emotionless as a snake.

"Captain Raiden Mad, seventh son of Emperor Suijin, honored Emissary of the Bhaskar Empire, welcome to Malavita," the tall, narrow priest intoned flatly. "His Excellency, the Bishop Arturious of Sicaria, requests your attendance at his palace. His Excellency is most eager to discuss our future relationship with the Bhaskar Empire."

Raiden blinked. He'd expected threats, perhaps subtle, perhaps direct; he hadn't expected an invitation. And he had no real reason to refuse them. In fact, he was authorized to deal with the Brotherhood Church if Dante failed to deliver a Veil to them, but he highly doubted it would come to that. Having witnessed firsthand Shade's power and will and determination, he had no doubt she would succeed in raising a Veil. At this point, he was actively rooting for her. When she returned with her cornerstones, he was more than ready to sign the charter.

Refusing to meet with the Bishop of Sicaria would reflect poorly on him, and thus the Empire. He wasn't royalty, but he wasn't exactly a simple emissary, either. Being the seventh son of the Emperor, even a disgraced, illegitimate son, was no small matter. Malavita was an Imperial colony and deserved respect... even if it was a lawless, chaotic mess.

"I thank you for your invitation," Raiden said, pulling himself up straight and trying to sound somewhat professional. "I would be happy to meet with His Excellency as soon as I am able. I am here only as a simple messenger, however, so I don't believe he'll find me very impressive. But I will give the bishop my Emperor's greetings to show respect and honor." He smiled pleasantly, hoping once the bishop discovered how little use he was he'd give up on the idea of a meeting. "Perhaps in a week's time I could attend your bishop at his residence?"

The two priests exchanged a glance, and their faces hardened. The tall one, apparently the spokesman of the two, returned his snake's gaze to Raiden. "You misunderstand, captain. Bishop Arturious requires your attendance. Now."

On either side of him, his companions tensed. Raiden swallowed, afraid for them. Up close, he could see the priests carried ruby blades. The Golondrina were outmatched. Even with Cyril, he didn't know if they could face such strong bloodwizards. He took a deep breath. How was he going to get out of this without violence? For he knew if he went with these priests and met this bishop, he'd never leave until they let him. What man sent assassins to carry out a mission of good faith?

The dim, smoky tavern had grown quiet and tense, the other patrons suddenly finding their tabletops or mugs of ale intensely fascinating. Maybe if he could get these priests outside, he could slip away–

The jangle of the door chimes sounded as loud as thunder in the silent common room. No mere breeze had blown it open this time. Every soul in the place turned as an apparition staggered inside. Foul-smelling water as dark as ale dripped from a stooped figure in a sopping wet cloak. A white mask of fury rose above the filthy cloak, dark blonde hair plastered to it. More putrid liquid oozed down its horrifying visage. The apparition bared its teeth at the ruby-bladed priests. A hand emerged from the cloak, stabbing a finger at them. "Your kind isn't welcome here!"

Raiden gasped, and beside him, Manoli swore softly. There was no mistaking that voice.

The Ruby Pontifex turned as one, and menace filled the room as they grasped their blades. "Witch," the taller one hissed. "Brother Jacobis warned us you might be with the Imperial emissary and you have proven his suspicions correct. Your alliance with Dante Safire is obvious now, foul creature. Show us your hands and we may show you mercy."

"I'll show you something better," Shade growled. Her hands disappeared into her cloak and she stood straight. Her eyes narrowed and her pale face grew flushed. Water dripped from her chin when she grinned at them. She looked like she'd just crawled from the sewer–

Gods of my father, that's exactly what she's done!

What had happened with the Coterie? The thought was a fleeting one, then Raiden's mind went blank. Emotion vanished in a cold, red haze as the assassins drew their blades and Shade tossed back her water-logged cloak, her hands clutching her own, black blades.

Power crackled through the cramped taverna; the smoky fire in the hearth roared suddenly. Gasps broke out among the patrons. The bitter stink of terror filled the place. A battle between such powerful wizards in such a small space would be disastrous.

Raiden moved instinctively. A lifetime of training compelled him. He leapt over the table, one hand flat on its sticky surface, launching himself across it, the other drawing his sword. Silently, he dropped behind the two priests, his sword flashing in a shining, unstoppable arc even as they touched their blades to their forearms–

Blood sprayed, and the two priests crumpled to the floor, their heads following a second later to land amidst their black robes. Sightless eyes stared at the ceiling. Death had come too swiftly for surprise to register in their dimming gazes.

Shocked silence descended. Then there was a scraping of chair legs against the floor and a jangle of bells as every patron scattered. Only Shade, the cousins, Raiden and the barkeep – passed out in a sprawl beneath his makeshift bar – remained.

Shade stared at him, her lips parted and her eyes wide, her blades poised to draw blood. Behind him, he heard Manoli say softly, reverently, "Fucking hells..."

Standing over his kill, Raiden gulped in great draughts of air. The danger had passed, but his body was tense, his muscles on fire. Not a drop of blood stained his gleaming sword so swiftly had it sliced through flesh and bone. He met Shade's eyes, saw the shock, and his stomach lurched. Now, she would see him for what he was...

But the shock in her bright eyes faded as he watched. Her full lips quirked and she regarded him with something close to admiration. "Well done, Captain Mad," she said, and sheathed her blades with a snap. "I would have been forced to blast this place apart. Looks like you saved me the trouble. Unfortunately, the death of a Ruby Pontifex never goes unnoticed. And two of them?" She shook her head, her grin belying her serious tone. "We'd best be on our way, I think."

Manoli and Petra appeared beside him, no grimmer than Shade. Their demeanor was almost festive. Manoli clapped him on the shoulder. "I like your style, my friend. Uncle Cyril will be sorry he missed this!"

"Right, well, we'd better get back to him in one piece so we can tell him about it." Shade was peering out the door of the tavern onto suspiciously empty streets beyond. "Let's scatter to the winds before more priests arrive," she suggested. "Out the back, all of you."

Petra shook his head. "We'll make a ruckus in the Warrens, boss," he said. "And draw away pursuit while you get Raiden home. He's the one they came for, you were a happy accident."

Shade frowned. Raiden imagined these two rarely contradicted their "boss". But she nodded an instant later. "Good thinking, Petra. I'll take Raiden with me. You two get back safely, alright? Or I'll send Dante Safire and all his guardsmen after you."

The two cousins exchanged a pleased glance then dashed out the front door, Manoli pausing to give her a flippant salute. "See you soon, boss." His nose wrinkled and he waved a hand beneath it. "Have that prissy lady's maid get you a bath. You smell like you just crawled through the entire sewer system of Sicaria!"

"It was well worth it, Manny!"

She was still laughing as Raiden followed her out the back of the taverna, and despite the danger, he felt a thrill of excitement. She had the cornerstones. And when they were safe in Safire's villa, he would sign the royal charter. The Empire would have its Veil.

CHAPTER TEN

Dawn broke on a scene of chaos at Dante's villa. Polizia swarmed the halls and grounds, searching for evidence that he was harboring the Black Witch. Keeping the reins on his temper was difficult as Dante watched the smug bastards ransack his home and disrespect his guardsmen. The fiery Matteo nearly started a fight when a group of them got in his face demanding access to Dante's study, but luckily his brother kept him restrained. Always the more stolid of the two, Angelo managed to diffuse the situation and keep the polizia from entering Dante's private office, as well.

Already rattled by Shade's failure to return the night before, he had greeted the polizia at his door with seething anger. Drawing upon the deep arrogance of a prince of a First Family, he'd forced them to wait over an hour in the pre-dawn chill, feigning disbelief and outrage, and swearing he'd bring them all up on charges when the council of the First Families met in the winter. It was no idle threat. The polizia had little true power in Malavita. The sergeant in charge seemed ready to back down – until a Brotherhood priest appeared bearing a new warrant for the Black Witch which now included the charge of murder of two Ruby Pontifex. Clad in long crimson robes with a pair of crossed blades embroidered on his left breast, the Blademaster Jacobis was not so easily turned away.

He'd directed the search in near silence, his dark eyes ever watchful, his red hair tied back in a tight queue, making his features sharply vulpine. Dante had crossed his path only once and had done all he could to avoid him since. There was something about the priest which set his hair on end. Those watchful eyes of his seemed to see right into his soul. Giving him free rein of his home, hoping and praying Shade wouldn't show up in the midst of the search, he'd retreated to his study to wait out the invaders.

Finally, the search having produced only a pile of fine women's clothing and a vast collection of cosmetics, the polizia had left. But there had been a promise of more to come in Brother Jacobis' cold eyes. With the morning sun flooding his private study, setting fire to dust motes, and limning the dark wood of his desk, Dante sat tipped back in his chair, his feet up and grinding the warrant beneath his boot heels. *Two Ruby Pontifex.* He scoffed. *What rubbish. Half the city would be in ruins if Shade fought two Ruby Pontifex.*

Shockingly, the polizia had done little damage to the villa, though poor Lizette had been beside herself when the thugs had confiscated everything from the most elaborate gown to the last drop of perfume. Shade's alter ego, the Lady Nox, would have nothing to wear to the next ball. Dante had sent the lady's maid to her chamber with an order for a sleeping draught. He was tempted to take one himself to blunt his nerves, but he'd chosen brandy instead. Fear and rage rolled through him in unending waves, and the liquor was doing little to calm him.

When Shade returned, he would wring her neck for putting him through this ordeal. If he lost her now, he would never get his Veil. If he lost her now...

His heart contracted and he squeezed his eyes shut. Where was she?

"My lord!"

His eyes snapped open. Angelo had thrust his head into the

study. He and Matteo were standing watch outside his door, unwilling to leave him unguarded even though the polizia had withdrawn. Grim excitement lit the fair-haired man's face. His heart leapt into a gallop and Dante's feet dropped to the floor. "What is it?" he snapped, though he already knew the answer.

"She's here, my prince. The witch has returned."

"Where is Korin?!" Shade's shout echoed in the foyer. She'd burst through the main doors, sending the footmen backpedaling and a maid into squeaking flight as Dante descended the grand staircase to greet her. "I'm going to kill that bastard!"

Taken aback by her appearance – she was covered in filth, her hair a wild tangle around a face twisted with fury – Dante paused. He'd spent a sleepless night waiting for her return, worried for her safety more than he dared admit. The polizia had raided his very home in search of her mere hours before. *Because* of whatever had happened in the city. Whatever had gone wrong. Because of her.

His relief at seeing her safe, his worry and fear, all of it evaporated like dew before the hot sun. Anger to match hers filled him.

"What in the lowest hells happened?" he demanded. "Do you have any idea what I've just endured? The polizia invaded my villa. The Brotherhood sent a Blademaster to my very door! All searching for you. And now you return at last only to scream death threats against my most loyal retainer? What madness has possessed you?"

Shade threw her soiled cloak back from her shoulders, holding herself like a queen, unaffected by his anger. Behind her stood his Imperial emissary, looking slightly chagrinned. Dante's lips thinned. What part had he played in all of this? Dante knew Raiden didn't hesitate to throw himself into a fight. He was beginning to think the Emperor had played a joke on him, sending such a volatile diplomat.

Crossing to the staircase, Shade grasped a carved finial as if she intended to tear it loose and stabbed a finger at him. "I am going to kill your pet Sicani. He sent me to bargain with a den of thieves. They tossed me into the sewer because I wouldn't accept their conditions!"

Dante blinked, aghast. That explained her appearance. "What conditions? Tell me what happened." He started down to her one slow step at a time, horror overriding his anger. "Please, tell me you acquired the stones we need? All is lost if you didn't!"

"Of course I have the stones. They were mine to begin with." Her face grew flushed. "They stole those stones. Their thievery killed my father. Korin knew before he sent me; he knew what their actions cost me, yet he sent me anyway. For that, I will make him pay."

"You will do no such thing," he said sharply. Two more steps took him to a riser just above her. She looked up at him defiantly, her jaw set in a stubborn line. Now that he knew she had the stones, he struggled to let go of his anger. She'd done what was asked, even if she'd kicked a hornet's nest in the process. He gripped the banister as hard as he could, attempting calm. "What conditions did they demand in exchange for the cornerstones? What did they ask that was so difficult?"

"They wanted me to raise my Veil in a place of their choosing and I refused." She jerked her chin disparagingly. "Tell your loyal retainer I won't be raising my Veil at the Nexus. I'll raise it where I planned to from the start. Beyond the Razor Ridge mountains, in Kindred lands."

Dante blinked. The Nexus? He knew the place. To his family, to all descendants of a First Family, it was a sacred place. It had once been the golden heart of Malavita before the war and the blight and was still a confluence of power and ancient magic. But it lay close to the Glass Fields, subject to the warp and weft of that unstable stretch of broken horror. Not even the

Brotherhood had dared raise a Veil at the Nexus and nothing was sacred to them any longer.

Yet, he could understand why Korin and the Coterie would have chosen it. A strong Veil at the Nexus would have far-reaching consequences. It would touch all the qaraz in the land, and its strength might feed the ancient pathways, and thus strengthen every Veil. It might restore the beating heart of Malavita and stabilize the Wastes themselves.

Dante stepped off the final stair, looming over her. "Where we raise our Veil is not your choice alone," he said. "The Nexus has advantages you should consider, advantages I'm sure drew Korin and the Coterie to their choice. Korin is wise, and I trust him more than anyone. Don't let your anger cloud your mind to what's best for all of us."

"My mind is clear," she countered in a hiss. "It will be my power which raises the Veil. My knowledge! Without me, you have nothing. So." She jabbed a thumb to her filthy chest. "I decide where to raise it. I decide where it is safest to anchor my Quattro Canto!"

"And you think that place is in lands you've never even seen?" he scoffed.

She grew still. "I have seen them," she said softly, almost reverently. Her expression grew distant, picturing something in her mind's eye. "I have seen the valley which my Veil will shelter. It calls to me in my dreams." The vague expression left her face and she fixed him with a sharp look. Anger and determination burned bright in eyes as green as grass. "I won't let Korin or the Coterie force me from my path. This is my vision. My destiny!"

He stared at her in disbelief. Her vision? Her destiny? He'd never heard her sound so much like a zealot. He shook his head. Was her hatred for the Coterie driving her to this extreme? Or was it something else?

Aware he was treading on dangerous ground he threw her past in her face like a bucket of cold water. "Is this about

Satine?" He said it quietly, calmly. It wouldn't do to accuse her like a raving madman. He didn't want her to think he was speaking out of jealousy. "Do you so desperately want to chase after the lover who spurned you, you would ruin all our plans?"

She blanched at his words. She'd pretended her dalliance with her tattoo master had been nothing, but he'd caught the sorrow in her eyes when she'd related the tale. He ignored her hurt, though he felt a twist in his belly at the look on her face.

"This has nothing to do with Satine," she said, brushing aside his accusation with a wave of her hand. But he could see the color high on her cheeks. It contrasted sharply with the sudden paleness of her skin. "But I'm glad you have expressed your true feelings. Imagine, all this time, I thought you had faith in me."

She backed away from him, her head twisting toward the hallway which led further into the villa. "It has been a long night, my lord," she said stiffly, far more formal than she'd ever been with him. With a deep regret, he felt a wall rise between them. "Do I have your permission to take my leave?"

"You don't need my permission–"

"Very well, my lord. I'll be in my rooms if you have need of me." She paused, half-turned toward the hallway and escape, and glanced back toward the main entrance. "Oh, and Captain Mad has some news for you."

Dante faced the Imperial who stood like a sentry beside the wide-open doors. He'd been so still and silent, Dante had forgotten he was even there. But those sharp black eyes had missed nothing of his exchange with Shade. They scrutinized him yet revealed nothing of Raiden's thoughts. "What news?" he asked.

Shade answered for him. "He has agreed to sign your royal charter."

* * *

"Her foolish stubbornness will be the ruin of us all."

Korin reached for the bottle of brandy on Dante's desk, his eyes bright with anger and deep frown lines around his mouth. The bottle was half empty. Dante had been steadily working through it when his mentor had barged into his study. The news that Shade had refused the Coterie's conditions yet taken the stones had driven Korin into a rage. He'd paced the room, wearing a path in the fine woven rug and excoriating Shade relentlessly until Dante had begged him to stop. The brandy had removed the last remnants of his own anger and he was tired. Beyond tired. His alliance with the Black Witch had been exposed far sooner than he'd hoped, and his own emissary had managed to kill two Ruby Pontifex. It was only a matter of time before the Brotherhood struck. The polizia raid had been a gambit. He'd already instructed his people to be ready and doubled the guards patrolling the grounds.

Yet, I sit here getting drunk like a fool.

He'd wanted to warn Shade, as well, but feared she might slam the door in his face if he tried. He winced and ran a hand over his beard. He never should have brought up her old lover – she'd told him about Satine only after they'd shared one too many bottles of wine. She'd confided in him, fighting tears, trying to laugh it off as a youthful transgression, but the incident had obviously wounded her deeply. And he'd thrown it in her face. The look of betrayal in her eyes haunted him.

She brought home our cornerstones and managed to get the charter signed all in the same day.

The Imperial royal charter lay spread out on his desk, the ink barely dry and the wax seal still warm. He perused it again, the terms and conditions. The Empire had been generous, granting them autonomy in their governance. As long as they delivered on the promised gemstones. A hefty lavishment, true, but one he felt confident in fulfilling. Everything was falling into place.

Except my witch hates me.

"She is as stubborn a woman as I've ever met," Korin

continued angrily, pouring himself a drink without so much as a by your leave. "What does it matter where we acquired the cornerstones? It's not as if Celeste and the others knew what would happen when their agent took the stones. Of course, there were risks. We are all prepared to die for our cause, why should her father be any different?"

"I doubt Shade sees it that way…"

He made a rude noise. "She sees what she wants to see. Fool girl." He took a swig from his glass, and his lips pinched as he swallowed. "Did she really say she had a vision about where to raise the Veil?"

Dante nodded. It had been a strange revelation. Shade wasn't the most spiritual of women. Visions and destiny seemed out of character for such a pragmatic soul. But, if she said she was being led by a vision, he had to believe her. He looked at Korin, frowning. "Why does it matter where she wants to raise the Veil? If she can find a way through the mountains, such a secure location might be to our benefit. Besides, the Nexus is sacrosanct. Did you ever consider you and the Coterie are wrong in your insistence she raise it there?"

Korin's brow furrowed and his eyes took on a brooding look. Rhythmically, he tapped his fingers against his cut-crystal glass. "I don't like this talk of visions," he murmured, as if he hadn't heard a word of what Dante said. "Why is she so driven to oppose us? One must ask who, or what, sent her this vision."

His ominous statement sent a shiver up Dante's spine. "And who do you suspect might have sent it?"

Korin snapped out of his introspection, pinning Dante with his bright eyes. "I have warned you how the Unseen can influence pliable souls. They could be using your witch against us."

"You think *Shade* is pliable?" Dante laughed humorlessly. "I doubt even immortal demons could force Shade to do anything she didn't want to do. And you called *her* a fool!"

His face flushed. The suspicion didn't entirely leave his gaze, but he waved a hand, dismissing his concern. "You're most likely right, my son. Nevertheless, she must raise her Veil at the Nexus if we hope to stabilize the Wastes and strengthen all the Veils. You must persuade her to do as we wish. Use your influence and push her toward the proper path."

"Shade walks her own path," Dante said. "And why do you believe I could persuade her to do anything? Right now, after what I said to her, I'd be surprised if she ever speaks to me again, let alone listens to my suggestions."

Korin tilted his head, a knowing look on his face. "Come, my boy, don't be dense. I've seen the way she looks at you, the way she flirts and teases. If anyone can persuade her, it's you."

Shock sobered him instantly. Dante blinked, staring at Korin as if he'd never seen him before. "It's an act," he insisted. "She plays the coquette to allay suspicions. There's nothing more to it." He rolled up the royal charter, checking first to make sure the ink had dried, and kept his face carefully blank. "Besides, I told you no one can persuade her to do anything she doesn't want to do. Not demons, not you, and certainly not me. And right now, Shade wants to go to Kindred lands. I have no choice but to help her. Without her, there is no Veil."

"Hmm." Korin settled his glass on the darkened wood of Dante's desk, but made no move to refill it. "I may have misread the situation." His expression grew stern as he eyed Dante. "It is Shade who is the persuasive one, apparently, if she's convinced you to let her go on this fool's errand."

"She did not *persuade* me of anything–"

"I had no idea your judgment had become clouded by your feelings. It is a mistake to care for her too deeply, Dante. I fear you will regret it."

"My regrets are my own, old man." Dante looked away from his sharp gaze. Korin was wrong; his feelings toward Shade were nothing more than a natural regard for an ally. It didn't quite explain the heat rising into his cheeks, however. He shoved his chair back from his desk with a squeal of wood and stood abruptly. "And regarding Shade, my judgment is no more clouded than yours. Your animosity toward her has been clear from the beginning. You and the Coterie can't stand the fact that she won't be your willing pawn."

"You know nothing of our cause, Dante, of the importance of our work–"

"And I don't care to," he snapped. "I know my best chance for a new Veil lies with Shade, and I will do whatever she asks of me. I'll go to the deep Wastes and help her find the Kindred myself if I have to!"

"No," Korin said quickly, lifting a hand toward him. His face had gone pale, his eyes suddenly sunken. "No," he repeated, slowly lowering his hand, his fingers tightening into a fist. He thumped it on Dante's desk, his shoulders hunching as if in defeat. "It's far too dangerous for you to traipse off into the Wastes. You are the last Safire. I won't lose you as I lost your sister and–" his voice grew rough, "–And the child."

"I appreciate your concern, Korin, but I carry sapphire and I'm no unblooded boy." He softened his tone, aware his old mentor was merely concerned for his safety. Korin's fear for him had only intensified after Mercedes' murder. His sister had been Korin's favorite, and the one strongest in Sicani blood. Though years had passed, the pain her death had caused hadn't. "I won't put myself at risk unnecessarily, but to raise our Veil, I am forced to take risks. Can't you see that?"

"Of course I can, but this is an unnecessary risk. You do not have to go to the Wastes with her. She can go alone."

"Then you do support her quest to reach the Kindred?"

"No," he said. "But it's our only choice, thanks to Shade. You don't need to help her find the Kindred; I already know the way." A haunted look entered his bright eyes, a swirl of shadows. "I would know my own way home, wouldn't I?"

CHAPTER ELEVEN

There was a low fire burning on her hearth, and a covered tray and a bottle of wine waiting on the table before it. With a sigh, Shade made her way to the cushioned chairs beside the fireplace, seeking warmth. Her hair was damp from her bath and she wore only a shift beneath her silky robe. She silently thanked Lizette for her tyrannical insistence on cleanliness. The lady's maid had taken one look at her in her disheveled state and marched her to her chambers for a hot bath. Shade had protested, too angry and upset to be reasonable, but there was no resisting Lizette when she was on a mission.

Scrubbed raw, her hair lathered and rinsed a half dozen times, and her cloak and clothing whisked away to be burned – or so Lizette had claimed – Shade had soaked in a copper tub of hot, clean water until it had cooled around her. Reluctantly, she'd risen from the bath grateful for the pile of soft towels Lizette had left her, and equally grateful to be dripping with clean water and not sewage.

Shade had settled herself on a chair and was reaching for her wine when there came a soft knock on her chamber door. She sighed. What now? Had Dante returned to argue with her again? Or throw her past in her face? Bastard. She never should have told him about Satine. She still wasn't sure why she had, and too much wine was hardly an excuse. Only Cyril knew the whole story, and only then because he'd had to deal with her afterwards.

It couldn't have been easy for him. Keeping my blades from my wrists.

She grimaced, the memory making her belly tense. A hard way to go for a bloodwizard. You really had to *want* to die to if you managed it by slitting your own wrists.

And I did. For a time...

There was another knock, louder this time. Groaning, Shade stood up and crossed to the door. She leaned against the dark, heavy wood, her fingers touching the thick whorls on the carved panels. "Who is it?"

"Captain Mad."

Shade sighed. *Faces.* What must he have thought about her fight with Dante? They were supposed to be allies, united by a single purpose, a single goal, and they'd bickered like children in front of him. She pushed off the door and rearranged her robe to best effect before reaching to pull it open. Beyond, in the dim light of the hallway, stood Raiden. He'd shed his uniform and wore a wrapped shirt of soft ivory cotton with wide-legged trousers. His feet were bare on the honeyed floorboards. She gave him her best smile.

"Who is Satine?" he asked.

Her smile slipped. "Please, come in, captain. You have to be as weary as I am." She left the door open and returned to her couch, her nerves afire. Would he doubt her motives too if he knew about Satine? But she had to tell him. He had to understand this had nothing to do with her old tattoo master. For all she knew, Satine was with a caravan somewhere in the Deep Wastes and not in Kindred lands.

And if she never saw her again, she would die a happy woman.

"I only have one glass," she said, filling the goblet with a generous pour. She lifted the bottle in a salute as he took a seat on the opposite couch. "I'll keep the bottle, if you don't mind."

Raiden reached for the offered glass, saying nothing, watching her. Patiently, but also implacably. There would be no avoiding this. She took a deep breath, steeling herself. It had been so long ago. Why did the memories haunt her still?

She ran her hand along one arm, feeling the whorls and patterns of her tattoos, remembering those long-ago days when Satine had inked her. It had transformed her into who she was today. What she was: an obsidian wizard, the only one in all of Malavita. Even though she'd had her blades, without the proper wards she would have died trying to wield her magic.

"I told you before that obsidian comes with risks," she began, slowly, feeling each word. Trying to explain. "When Cyril saved me in the Wastes, I had my blades. I had tried to use my magic to survive. But without tattoos." She shrugged, fingering a scar along her forearm, a pale seam that had healed naturally. Lasting evidence of her desperation. "My clan had tattoo masters, and one of them managed to ink my first ward." She grasped the v-shaped opening of her robe and pulled it aside to reveal a golden rose in full bloom just below her left shoulder. "It was a strong tattoo, but it cost her dearly. Wielding obsidian had opened unexpected power in me. It made it difficult for the tattoo master. She feared to ink any more wards and urged me to seek a tattoo master among the Kindred."

A line appeared between Raiden's finely arched brows. "You've sought out the Kindred before? Yet you don't know the way to their lands?"

She shook her head, staring into the fire. "I never found the Kindred. Not even one of their caravans on this side of the Razor Ridge. They found me. Or, rather, *she* found me."

"Satine."

Her throat tight, she could only nod. "Somehow, she had sensed my power from miles away. She was waiting for me as I made my way to the mountains, at one of the springs along the qaraz. At first, I didn't believe her, didn't understand how she'd anticipated my route. I was suspicious. I'd already been through so much. But," and she couldn't help smiling at the memory, though pain lurked close beneath it, "Satine had a way about her. A quiet strength, a certainty. She seemed so wise, though she was only a few years older than me, so sure of... everything. She had laid out all the tools of her art in preparation for my arrival. I was so desperate at that point, and so helpless without proper wards, I set aside my suspicion and submitted to her needles and ink. It was the best decision I ever made."

"Her work is extraordinary," Raiden said softly. He cleared his throat at her raised eyebrow and took a drink of wine, but she could see the color on his dusky cheeks. It made her smile.

"Satine was extraordinary," she said. "Beautiful and kind. And playful when she wasn't buried in her work. Though the work itself was an intense, intimate experience." She exhaled, her hand tightening on the neck of her wine bottle, remembering the silken fall of Satine's dark hair through her fingers. She'd never felt anything so soft. Until she'd touched Satine's skin. "By the second day, I was in love. It wasn't hard to love her. Not for me. I was young, lonely. My own father had treated me as little more than a student. A project. My time among the Golondrina was still new and having someone so focused on me and me alone..." she shook her head, "... How could I not fall in love with her?"

She fell silent, finding it a struggle to breathe. A stick had lodged in her throat and her vision was blurry. She blinked rapidly. She wouldn't cry, not for Satine. Not ever again.

"What happened when she finished inking your tattoos?" Raiden asked. His tone was matter of fact, lacking the sympathy she had expected, and she was thankful for it. She took a swig from her bottle to give herself a moment. The wine nearly choked her, but she forced it down. Next came the hard part. The humiliating part.

"When Satine was done, we were done," she said, unable to keep the bitterness out of her voice. "She left me in the middle of the night. I thought she'd been dragged off by a beast or something, but her tools were gone, too. No trace of her remained, so I figured it had been deliberate. Like a fool, though, I didn't take the hint. I tracked her down. I had my wards and my blades, and I used my magic to find her. She was with a caravan of other Kindred, heading back toward the mountains and their stronghold." She grunted ruefully. "If only I'd been a little slower, I never would have found her. I never would have declared my undying love for her in front of her husband and her son."

Raiden spoke a word she didn't know. But she guessed it was an oath of some sort. His face screwed up with sympathy. "I am sorry, Shade." He leaned back on the couch, his wine goblet balanced on his knee. "It must have felt like a terrible betrayal. Such a thing is not easy."

"No. It is not. But I don't know if it was a betrayal. She never promised me anything. She never even told me she loved me."

"Still." His hand squeezed the stem of his goblet and his eyes were hard. "No matter what was said or unsaid, she led you to believe there was something between you. She made you feel important then she cast you aside. It is cruel and unfair. She should have made it clear from the start that it was all temporary. That you were expendable to her."

The level of anger in his voice surprised her. "I suppose I was expendable," she said, wincing at the unpleasant thought. She narrowed her eyes at him. "So. You know what it's like to be betrayed by a lover, too, I suspect."

He looked aside, his gaze boring into the hearth and his brow furrowed. "Not a lover," he said, his words drawn out in a growl. "I was not allowed to love anyone besides my family. My loyalty had to be singular. *My* loyalty, not theirs."

Now Shade understood his anger. Betrayal by your own blood was far worse than by a lover. She recalled the words they'd exchanged the day before on their way to Sicaria. "You were raised to be a sacrifice."

He nodded, his lips pressed in a hard line. "But my sacrifice was not my life as I had always expected. Instead, I was forced to sacrifice my honor to save my eldest brother, the treasured heir. Who would believe the Imperial Prince, so strong, so honorable, so perfect, could murder a child in such a horrific manner? But the seventh son? The son of an enslaved foreign sorceress? The son born and trained to be a cold-blooded killer? That son could do such a thing."

She sat in stunned silence, staring at him. His lean frame was rigid, his shoulders stiff. He radiated pain, despair, and her heart ached for him. "You took the blame," she said. At his father's command, she deduced. Which would explain his anger, and his hurt. "And how are you here instead of hanging at the end of a rope?"

His smile was bitter. "My blood is royal. I was spared execution, but my father had to send me somewhere. And I could no longer be trusted to lead men into battle. So. I was given a mission far, far from home."

He didn't say it out loud, but she knew. "This is your exile."

A heartbeat passed, another, and then he relaxed with a deep exhalation. The anger had faded from his eyes when he turned to her. "I no longer think of it as an exile," he said. "I've found more than I expected in this troublesome little colony."

She grinned. "If it helps, the boys adore you. Even Cyril, the old crank, and he hates everyone. They admire your courage, and your skills. To them, you are honorable and strong and perfect."

Eyes downcast, he lifted his wine glass to drink, but she caught the smile tugging at his lips. "You are no murderer, my lady," he murmured into his cup. "I know that now. Even though all is said and done between us, I won't be taking you to the authorities."

"Who says things are done between us?" she scoffed. She stretched her legs along the couch, feeling surprisingly light. The fire and the wine were working magic on her sore muscles.

She leaned back and drank from her bottle. "Nothing's done until the Veil rises over the place of my choosing. And you'll be there when I do it." She pointed a finger at him. "Swear it, Captain Mad."

He chuckled. "I swear on the gods of my fath... on the gods of my mother," he said, his chin lifted proudly. "I will be there when you raise your Veil."

Her fire had burned down to coals by the time Raiden left her room. They'd finished the wine and discussed their plans to leave the villa as soon as possible. Raiden was more than willing to accompany her to the mountains and beyond. Where before she'd thought him a burden in the Wastes, now she knew what an incredible asset he was and was glad for his choice. He was Dante's emissary, of course, but the Veil was the priority. It made sense he would be there when she raised it.

And will Dante Safire be there? She scowled. *Only if he learns to trust me again.*

She was exhausted, but her mind was racing. The room had grown uncomfortably warm even though the fire was dead. Probably the wine. She passed a hand over her face. Eschewing her bed, she went to open the doors to her private balcony. There was no moon and the stars shone through the haze of the Veil. A soft breeze caressed her as she stepped onto the stone balcony, drying the sweat on her skin. Below her stretched darkened orchards and an expanse of manicured lawn. She leaned on the stone balustrade and breathed in cool, sweet air.

A shadow moved on the hillside below her. Man-shaped. She straightened, suddenly alert. She shook off the fog of wine. Who in the hells would be wandering through the orchards at this time of night? A guardsman?

Without a lantern, skulking from tree to tree...

And then the shadow reached the manor wall far below her. She leaned over the balustrade as far as she dared, her heart thumping, and watched the shadow scurry up the brick wall effortlessly. What the hells? She followed the path of its trajectory. The shadow man was heading up to Raiden's room unerringly.

Assassin. Furious, Shade pushed off the railing. She needed her blades. Heart pounding, she started to turn when a shadow rose above the balustrade. A man-shaped shadow. Dressed all in black, it dropped onto the balcony, a long, ruby blade clutched in its fist.

Ruby Pontifex!

Before she could utter a sound, he leapt at her, blade descending in an unstoppable arc. The ruby blade sliced empty air as Shade flung herself backwards through the open balcony doors. The hardwood floor slammed the air from her. Compelled by fear, she rolled to the side. Without her blades, she was next to helpless. Her knife belt – the leather pouch containing her cornerstones threaded securely onto it – hung on a peg near her bedside. She had to reach it.

Gasping, stars in her vision, she scrambled to her hands and knees, intending to run. Able to suck in a breath, she opened her mouth to shout for help when air wrapped around her and lifted her off the floor. Her limbs hung frozen in position to run, but she couldn't move. It was useless, but she fought the magic around her. If she could kick him…

Panic slammed inside her chest like a broken-winged bird. The assassin appeared in front of her, his face concealed, only his eyes showing. They were black and cold, and insufferably pleased. He lifted his ruby blade and placed it against her throat. Not magic, then, just a blade in the dark.

"And so dies the Black Witch. Trapped like the insect she–"

A sliver of silver emerged from the center of his chest, thrusting forward like a blade of grass rising from a field.

Shade's eyes widened – the only thing she could move – then crossed as the blade sprang dangerously close to her nose.

It vanished with a slick, metallic ring, and the Ruby Pontifex crumpled. Her bonds disappeared abruptly. She dropped to the floor like a sack of potatoes, the breath knocked from her again.

"Shade, are you alright?"

Raiden.

"A guardsman said there might be trouble. I was coming back to check–"

Shade grabbed his leg, trying to warn him. "Another!" she managed to gasp.

"What?"

"Assassin!" she screamed, catching sight of the shadow slipping into her suite from the hallway. Raiden spun, his sword raised.

The assassin froze at her shriek, but only for a split second. Then he flung his blade at Raiden. Amazingly, the Imperial caught it, flipped it end over end and threw it back.

The ruby blade caught its master square in the chest. His eyes widened above the concealing mask and he staggered back, clutching at it. Shade scrambled from the floor and grabbed her knife belt from its peg, yanking one blade free. A slash along her thigh filled her with power. She called wind and fire and water, wrapping the would-be assassin in a violent tempest. She wanted to be sure he couldn't escape.

The Pontifex's clothes went up in flame, instantly doused by the water, and the wind slammed him to the wall, his mask and most of his clothing gone. The tattoos emblazoned across his body was some of the Brotherhood's finest work, and the four colors in a quartered shield over his heart marked his allegiance. His own ruby blade was buried in that shield. Shade met his dark gaze just in time to see the light fade from his eyes. He was smiling…

"Shit," Shade muttered, grabbing for Raiden's arm, screaming "Run!" as the room filled with ominous power.

The death strike of a bloodwizard killed by his own blade, one who had mastered all Four Faces and the Hidden, was a force of destruction not even her magic could counter. It would make Lorenzo's demise seem a soft breeze in comparison.

They raced down the hallway. Behind them, the power built. A hum filled the air. Terrible in its potential. It rattled her bones and made her teeth ache. Shade shoved Raiden down a side corridor; they had to reach the stairs. They passed no servants, thankfully. She hoped they were all downstairs in the servants' quarters at the opposite end of the villa.

They reached the stairwell and she pulled Raiden over the banister to the main floor. She drew blood and cushioned their landing and then they were off, racing down the grand hallway. If they could reach the back portico, get outside–

The explosion was silent. Light and heat enveloped them. Raiden pulled her to him and wrapped his arms around her. Power lifted them, flinging them down the hall. Shade landed hard, Raiden atop her, her head slamming into the floor, leaving her stunned. Wood and stone shattered around them. Debris rained from above. Ears ringing, Shade squeezed her eyes shut while the world exploded.

More wreckage dropped around them, on them. The noise of cracking wood and breaking glass deafened her. The whole villa was collapsing!

She tried to rise from beneath Raiden, but something hard and heavy struck her forehead and the world went black.

The world was smoke and ash and darkness. Flames crackled nearby – he could feel the heat, hear the increasing roar. Raiden pushed against the floor, shaking off the broken timbers and plaster pinning him. On his knees, he wiped dust from his eyes and gasped in a breath, only to gag and choke. Retching, he spat out a lungful of plaster dust.

A pale, limp hand poked out from the debris beside him – a hand resting atop a black blade. Raiden tore at the wreckage to reach Shade. She groaned as he freed her from the worst of it. He smoothed her hair back from her filthy face, his hands shaking. Her eyelids fluttered, but didn't open, and when he pulled his hand back it was covered in blood. The growing flames allowed him to see the deep gash on her forehead near her hairline.

"Shade," he said. He felt her arms and legs for broken bones then gently probed her torso. Another groan slid from her, and her eyes opened at last. They stared at him, glassy and unfocused.

"Shade," he said again. "It's alright, you're fine. I just have to get you out of here…"

There were shouts and the sounds of people moving through the destroyed villa. Rescue? How many people had been caught in the blast? He took stock of himself; he was bruised, and bleeding from several lacerations, but he had no serious injuries. He stood on shaky knees, using his sword as a cane – he'd kept his grip on it through the whole event. And Shade's knife belt lay near her on the floor. He returned her blade to its sheath and strapped the belt around her slim waist, manhandling her a bit. She would want her blades on her, even if she couldn't use them.

A man approached through the flames and smoke, and Raiden lifted his hand to wave him closer. But the man paused and raised something at his waist–

The twang of a crossbow string was his only warning. Instinct made Raiden twist, and the bolt sliced along his side. He hissed, but battle-fury allowed him to ignore the pain. In two long strides, he was close enough to slice the man open. A bloodwizard wouldn't be using a crossbow. His enemy made a strange gurgle and fell face-first onto the wreckage. He wore a dark jacket of a familiar cut, like Raiden's own coat.

Imperial polizia!

More shouts and shadows moved through the devastated house, and flashes of fire and blasts of wind rattled the air. Even in the darkness, he could see Safire blue on some of the men fighting. The invaders mostly wore polizia garb – though he caught glimpses of bare-chested Corsaro, too – and carried crossbows rather than jewel blades. Those compact, handheld weapons were surprisingly effective against Dante's men, though. Especially in the darkness and chaos. The screams of the injured and dying added to the mayhem.

Raiden dropped to his knees beside Shade. He needed to get her out of this mess. Taking her by the arm, he lifted her. She wasn't completely unconscious, thankfully, but she was dazed and disoriented. He slung her arm over his shoulders and took her around the waist. Hoisting her to her feet, he searched for a way out. The walls had been blasted apart, and there were no recognizable doorways anymore. He started toward the nearest hole, catching sight of stars and the silhouette of trees beyond it.

A shadow rose in the opening, blocking the way. Gripping Shade tight, Raiden raised his sword. A burst of light blinded him momentarily, then it faded to a globe of fire. Blinking tears from his eyes, Raiden watched the globe rise. Its light filled what was left of this wing of the villa. The blast had broken through all three floors as if a fist had punched through the house. The fighting men froze in the sudden illumination, but only for a moment.

Dante Safire stepped into his house, guardsmen rushing around him to engage the enemy.

The prince strode to Raiden, his face a mask of fury and his blades in his fists. The sapphire blades flew across his flesh, drawing blood and power from his bare arms and chest. His long, sable hair hung loose around his shoulders, and though he was shirtless, he wore snug trousers and riding boots. He struck down those polizia closest to him like he was flicking away flies. Behind him his loyal guardsmen, Matteo and Angelo, followed closely. The two brothers looked just as angry as Dante, shadowing their prince like stalking lions.

Nostrils flaring, Dante sheathed his blades when he reached Raiden, his eyes on Shade. "Apparently the Brotherhood blames me for the deaths of their priests. They have sent the polizia to arrest me."

"Arrest you?" Raiden cried. "They sent assassins! They were after Shade!"

Dante's blue eyes turned to ice and he lifted a hand toward Shade.

"My prince, we must leave," Angelo said urgently. "It's not safe here!"

The creak and groan of straining timbers echoed around him. Something crashed to the ground and flames crawled across the ceiling. The fighting had moved away from them, but they could hear more shouts and blasts in the distance.

Dante shook his head. "This is my home. My people are inside, fighting. I must help them. But the rest of you need to leave." His icy eyes fixed on Raiden. "Take her out of here, captain. Get her on a horse and go." He turned to Matteo and Angelo. "Make sure he reaches the stables, understand? Both of you. Then make for the Veil wall as fast as you can."

"Where do we go from there?" Raiden asked, holding Shade as if she were an injured bird. "How will we find you again?"

"You'll go to the Wastes. Tell every man you pass to do the same; they'll know what you mean. I'll follow when I can, if I can. But if anyone is to survive tonight, it has to be her."

"But, my lord, we can't abandon you," Angelo protested.

"You can and you will." He put a hand on Angelo's shoulder, holding his gaze. "Ride hard and fast, son, and keep her safe."

The man pressed his lips together and nodded. Matteo, following his brother's lead, grasped his tourmaline blades and pulled them free. Raiden met Dante's eyes and understanding passed between them. With a short nod, Raiden lifted Shade into his arms. "I'll see her safe, Prince Safire."

Dante nodded sharply. "I'm counting on you, Captain Mad."

"By the gods of my mother, I will not fail you."

They emerged from the villa into more mayhem. Across the grounds, men fought. Crossbow bolts and magical attacks flew, punching through flesh or tearing up the earth in great gouts of power. More Corsaro had appeared alongside the polizia, and it was obvious Dante's men were outnumbered.

Angelo called to his fellows, shouting, "To the Wastes! For your Prince! To the Wastes!" as they navigated the chaos. Dark-haired Matteo wielded his blades with deadly precision, keeping most enemies at bay. Hampered by Shade, Raiden let the brothers clear a path, focusing all his energy on keeping his feet over the hummocky ground.

The sky had taken on a gray cast in the east. The shadowy bulk of the stables loomed against the brightening horizon, and flames licked from the tall, narrow windows lining its gambrel roof. The screams and shrill whinnies of horses rose on the wind. Groomsmen pulled panicked animals from the burning building while Dante's guards protected them from attack. As soon as they got them clear of the stables, the grooms began to saddle the horses. So. They'd taken heed of Angelo's shouts.

The fighting was intense near the stables. Men grappled hand-to-hand within the burning building, and it was unclear who was who. Raiden thought he caught a glimpse of Petra's russet hair among the fighters, but he couldn't be sure. He sent his friends a quick prayer.

A blast of incredible power rocked the earth just as they reached the horses, knocking them off their feet. Shade tumbled from Raiden's arms. The animals screaming and rearing around her, she staggered to her feet, a hand to her bloody forehead. Raiden scrambled up beside her. She stared at him, swaying. Blood streaked her face, and her eyes were pinched with pain.

He grit his teeth. She was in no condition to fight. And now a new enemy had arrived to attack them. A red-robed priest was leading a group of Corsaro up from the vineyards – he had been the source of the powerful blast. The priest had a ruby blade in his fist and was directing his magic at the stables and the men trying to escape. Even in the predawn dimness, his red hair shone like flame.

The priest spotted Shade, and his blade flew across his wrist, drawing black blood. Matteo leapt in front of Raiden and Shade, defending them against the initial attack. The priest scowled as he attacked again, a ruby amulet gleaming on his chest. It was so deep red it looked almost black. "Kill the witch!" he screamed.

"Get her on the horse!" Angelo shouted, dragging two wild-eyed horses with the help of a white-faced young groom. "Captain! Get her to safety!"

"No," Raiden said, he pushed her toward Angelo. Startled, Shade stumbled but the guardsman caught her. "You take her. You and Matteo." He stood back and drew his sword. Behind him, he heard Matteo grunt and curse. The boy was fading fast. "Do what Dante ordered; keep her safe."

"Raiden...? What are you doing?" Shade took a step toward him, but Angelo held her back. She struggled weakly against his grip. "Let me go! Raiden, what in the hells do you think you're doing?"

"What I was born to do," he said, and he turned toward their enemies. He grasped a staggering Matteo by the arm and pulled him back. "Go with your brother," he ordered. "I'll keep them back."

"Captain?" Matteo said, his face scrunching in concern.

"Go!" Raiden shouted, and he broke into a run.

"Raiden!"

Shade's shout rang in his ears, but a calm had settled over Raiden. Ignoring the blasts of power rushing over his skin like the heat of an open forge, he closed with the Corsaro flanking the red-headed priest. There was no dance of steel with these so-called soldiers, no thrust and parry. He struck to kill. He took the head off one unfortunate amethyst wielder before the others recognized the danger. His sword flashed and two more men fell. Their magic slowed him but didn't stop him. He struck through the heart of another Corsaro, and by then the others recognized him for what he was: death.

Abandoning the priest, the surviving Corsaro soldiers turned and bolted.

Grinning savagely, the priest faced him alone; the gem was a horror on his chest, throbbing with black light. Remarkably, he dodged Raiden's sword, moving with lightning quickness. Too fast. Impossibly fast. No man moved so fast…

The shell of calm encasing him began to crack, and Raiden grew aware of his labored breathing. Suddenly, he felt his injuries from the assassin's final strike. Digging deep for every last bit of energy, Raiden unleashed a flurry of blows. Incredibly, the priest laughed and dodged every elegant thrust and slash.

Sweat stung Raiden's eyes, blinding him, and his sword dipped toward the ground. He stepped back, gasping for breath. Weariness slammed him, and the priest smiled. The red-black ruby on his chest began to pulse. Unable to take his eyes from it, Raiden dropped to his knees.

Had he given her enough time to escape? He looked away from his enemy to make certain. The grounds around the stables were clear, and all the horses were gone. Only the injured remained. The villa was a smoldering wreck, and the stables still burned, but relief shook through him. He slumped to the ground, his sword resting in the grass beside him. The priest approached, staring down at him in grim satisfaction. "Do you surrender, heathen?" he asked.

Panting, Raiden drew himself straight though he was on his knees in the dirt. "I am Captain Raiden Mad, Imperial Emissary of Emperor Suijin IV, may He live forever. You have attacked an Imperial citizen without cause. Sent assassins against a prince of this city! I will not surrender to you! Kill me if you must, but you will face the consequences of your actions!"

The man scowled, but he sheathed his ruby blade. "You consort with heretics and witches," he said. He raised a hand

and gestured. Suddenly, they were surrounded by polizia. A dozen crossbows trained on Raiden. "Imperial Emissary or not, you are under arrest!"

Despite his predicament, Raiden tipped back his head and laughed.

CHAPTER TWELVE

By the time they reached the outskirts of Sicaria's Veil, the sun had risen. It had been a necessary risk to drive the horses at a gallop before full light, and only luck had kept either from breaking an ankle or a leg. All Shade could do was cling to the pommel of the saddle and pray to the Four and the Hidden she wouldn't fall. Every leap and stumble of the beast set her teeth to chattering. She was battered and her head ached, and she'd left her friends behind to die…

She would have forced Angelo to turn the wretched beast around and return to Dante's villa if the thunder of hooves and the wind in her face had allowed for conversation. Instead, she let them carry her farther into the Wastes, farther away from Cyril and the boys, from Raiden, from Dante, too weary and hurt to prevent it. As the sun rose, and neither man showed signs of stopping, she felt herself slipping…

Beneath her, the horse huffed laboriously, and began to slow. Dropping from a gallop into a quick trot was jarring. A small whimper emerged from her, and she felt Angelo's arm tighten. The horse, thankfully, slowed to a walk.

"I've got you, my lady," Angelo said. His voice was hoarse with fatigue, but full of kindness. Shade fought the urge to weep.

"We can't stop yet," added another in a vaguely familiar voice. She turned her head to find Matteo riding beside them.

For once, the dark-haired man didn't flash her a grin when she looked at him. His sharp-jawed face was grim and pale.

"I know. But soon. She's about to collapse."

Matteo frowned at her. "We'll make for the Redstone Spring." He looked ahead, his broad-brimmed hat shading his features. "And pray to the Faces no one's following us."

"No, we have to go back," Shade insisted. Or tried to. She could barely speak above a whisper, and her companions ignored her. They kept going, and the swaying gait of the wretched horse lulled Shade into a doze.

The pounding in her head had receded to a dull ache, and her mouth was dry as dust when Angelo finally pulled the beast to a halt. When her feet touched the ground, she collapsed in a heap.

"We have to go back," she said to Angelo as he knelt to check on her. She grabbed his arm, half-rising. "That priest will kill him!"

Grim-faced, Angelo shook his head. Behind him, Matteo was busy leading the horses to the tiny pool of water hidden in the cluster of red rocks. He spoke in low, soothing tones to the nervous, weary creatures. Shade wanted to scream at him to mount up and ride, but the thought of climbing atop a horse again made her knees give out. She slumped in defeat.

"He's strong, and important. They won't kill him. We need to look to ourselves now. Or at least until we meet up with Prince Safire."

Shade scrubbed a hand over her face. Dried blood flaked off and stained her fingers. She stared at it, her vision blurring. So much blood. She'd never had a head wound before now. Her wards couldn't close this cut.

Frowning, Angelo pushed her hair aside to look at her wound. Too tired to protest, she sat meekly and let him probe the gash.

"If Dante managed to escape," she said dully. "He stayed behind to fight. Like Raiden. Like I should have done…"

"The prince did what he thought was best."

Angelo took a kerchief from his belt and dampened it with his waterskin. At least one of them had been smart enough to bring a few supplies. Shade had nothing but a thin shift and a tattered robe to her name. No, she had her blades. Seeking comfort, she grasped their bone handles while Angelo cleaned her wound. Beside her right blade hung a leather belt pouch. She had the cornerstones, too. All was not lost. But her vision of a new Veil rising above a wide valley seemed as distant as the moon.

She winced as he pressed the cloth into the gash. "Do you think it was for the best?" she asked him quietly. "Saving me?"

"He cares for you a great deal," Angelo said, which was no answer at all. Avoiding her gaze, he busied himself with his task and Shade fell silent, wondering herself if Dante had made the right choice.

One of the horses whinnied suddenly, and there was a scuffle by the spring as both beasts jostled each other. Angelo handed Shade the damp cloth and rose to help his brother, reaching for a topaz blade in case there was danger. Matteo had pulled the animals away from the spring and was stroking one lathered horse on the nose. Both beasts' eyes were showing white.

"What is it?" Angelo asked. "What's spooked them?"

The younger brother turned a stricken gaze toward them. "The water... it's no good."

Angelo stopped, his back and shoulders stiff with shock. "What?"

"That's impossible," Shade said, rising to her feet. Her legs felt better, still stiff but stronger.

"Come see for yourself," Matteo said. "The spring is stagnant. I–I've never seen anything like it. Not here, not along a qaraz."

He was right. A layer of scum covered the pool, and the water itself was black as tar. Shade dropped to her knees beside the spring. She knew this spring; she'd stopped here more times than she could count. Fresh water was rare and precious in the Wastes, but it was always drinkable. It was always clean. She stared at the fouled pond, confused and disturbed.

"This is not possible." She stretched out a hand and brushed her fingers across the surface. The layer of scum moved and swirled like oil beneath her fingertips. The foulness clung to her. It burned slightly. She rubbed her fingers on her robe in disgust.

"We have to find water," Matteo said. "The horses won't last much longer without it."

She nodded, standing on her sore legs. Faces, she hated traveling by horseback.

"Shade, we'll have to leave here and go a little farther," Angelo said. He was already checking the cinch on his saddle. "It will be rough, traveling this time of day. But we have no choice."

Shade drew a blade and stepped away from the befouled spring. The tumble of rocks enclosed a smooth stretch of sandy earth, a few small shrubs and tufts of grass existing in its shelter. She kept to the shade, near a looming rock wall. "If we leave this place, the horses will die."

"They'll die here without water," Matteo snapped. "I'd rather take the chance and move on!"

Shade gave him a sidelong glance. His face was scrunched with anger, and not a little fear. It had rattled her, too, finding a ruined spring, but she knew what to do. She raised her blade and sliced the back of her arm, letting her blood drip to the cracked earth. Where it landed, light erupted.

Matteo's eyes widened and his mouth fell open. "You can touch the Hidden Face," he said, sounding strangled.

"Of course I can. And with it, I can touch the qaraz." She felt the magic swell within her; her senses expanded, deepened. Focusing on the stream of magic beneath her feet, she sent Spirit *down*.

There was a dissonance in the qaraz. It made her bones hurt. It took her a moment to recognize it – the blight. She shuddered. Somehow, the blight which infected the Wastes had entered this qaraz. *Impossible.* Calling more Spirit, she delved deeper. She no longer saw the earth and rocks around her, rather she saw a gleaming stream of ancient magic. A thin film of blackness overlay the bright light of the qaraz. With spectral hands, she swept it up like dust from a smooth wood floor, gathering it into a pile. She couldn't pick up all of it – small flecks remained. But for now, it was the best she could do. For now, the qaraz ran nearly clean again.

Releasing a deep breath, Shade rose from the magic. She was shaking as she surfaced. It hadn't cost her much blood, but Spirit always drained a wizard. Her two companions were staring at her, agape. The horses had grown calm – one of the beasts let out a soft whicker as if it sensed what she'd done. "Let them drink," she said. "The water is safe now."

"How?" Angelo asked, letting his brother tend the horses. "How did you do it?"

Sheathing her blade, Shade hid the trembling in her limbs. "I learned a few tricks among the Golondrina. They watch over the qaraz, you see, and keep it free of the blight. They have a knack for it. I can't do all the things they can, but if you can touch the Hidden, you can affect the qaraz."

He shook his head. "If you can touch the Hidden," he repeated in chagrin. He put a hand over his heart. "Forgive me, my lady, I never believed you were a true bloodwizard. I–I am ashamed of my doubts."

"Don't worry about it. You were right: I'm not a true wizard." Confusion wrinkled his brow and she grinned. "I'm a witch."

By the time they'd rested and recovered somewhat, a cloud of red dust had appeared on the horizon. Cursing, Matteo rushed to ready the horses for flight, but Angelo watched the growing cloud with resignation on his face. Heart sinking, Shade stood beside him. The horses had rested, but they were worn and listless after the wild gallop from Dante's villa. They couldn't outrun a herd of goats much less determined pursuers. The rocks might protect them for a time, but the three of them were as weary as the horses and in no shape for a prolonged fight.

"If you take one of the horses," Angelo said softly. "You could run while we hold them at bay. When Lord Safire says go to the Wastes, he means for us to go to Enrice Veil. It's to the southwest, at the edge of the Deep Wastes and near the Razor Ridge mountains. He will be waiting for us in Enrice Veil, hiding in a little village just inside the southern edge of the Veil. You can make it on your own, I'm sure of it."

"I won't let you two be martyrs for me," she muttered angrily, gripping her knife hilts. She turned on him with a scowl. "I'm stronger than both of you together, Topaz wielder. Maybe you should run?"

Angelo scrubbed a hand through his hair. "Please, lady witch. Lord Safire would never forgive us if we let anything happen to you."

"Then fight with me." She yanked her blades free, forcing herself to stand straight, to appear strong. "I am the Black Witch." She let her mouth quirk. "I'll protect you."

Humor danced in his light eyes, and he drew his own blades. "It would be an honor," he said. Then he turned and called to his brother. "Matteo, leave the horses hobbled. We won't be running anymore. Not today."

His order was unnecessary. Matteo had already abandoned the animals, and was walking toward them, blades drawn. He gave Shade a wink and flashed a smile. There wasn't a trace of fear in his blue-green eyes. "Never did like to run."

By now, the cloud had coalesced into riders. Several riders. The three stood together, shoulder-to-shoulder, facing their enemies as one. A peace settled over Shade. Unexpected, but welcome. It reminded her of the time she'd fought beside Raiden against the beasts of the Wastes. There was a rightness to it.

The riders thundered near, and against the red wash of the Wastes shone flashes of blue. Angelo cried out in triumph, thrusting a fist toward the sky. Beside her, Matteo began to laugh, but Shade could only stare. The men racing toward them on horseback wore Safire blue, and leading them was a bearded man with a gash on the side of his face, his fine clothes ash-stained and tattered. The gash down his face was raw and ugly, and he looked like he'd walked through the lowest hells. Blood streaked his torn silk shirt in a broad fan.

Dante Safire rode his horse to within a few feet of them, reining in the beast so hard it went on its heels. He leapt off its back in a cloud of dust and sand and strode to Shade, his eyes locked on her. Trembling, she sheathed her blades, her shock and relief exposing her deep exhaustion, and braced herself for a tirade. She'd brought destruction on his house. Would he ever forgive her?

But when she met his bright, cobalt eyes, joy shone from their depths, joy and relief. Not anger, not blame. She opened her mouth to speak, and he grabbed her around the waist, pulled her to him, and kissed her hard on the mouth. Her exhaustion burned away in a sudden rush of fire. It roared up from her belly and filled her heart to bursting. Heedless of the eyes on them, she wrapped her arms around his neck, and returned his kiss with all the strength left in her.

Great heaving shudders racked him, his arms tightening to the point of pain. She tasted salt on his lips, and realized he was weeping. She broke their kiss and buried her face in the crook of his neck. "Why, my dear, sweet prince," she said, her lips pressed to his skin. "I never knew how much you cared."

He squeezed her until she could barely breathe. "Neither did I, my dear, sweet witch. Neither did I."

CHAPTER THIRTEEN

"No, I absolutely forbid it."

Shade stared at Dante as he shuffled papers on his makeshift desk – some farm wife's kitchen table, old and worn, but polished to a sheen – and murmured to the village men coming and going from the hovel he'd commandeered. Her announcement that she was returning for Raiden had barely ruffled him, and his casual refusal left her mute. It was bad enough he'd been ignoring her ever since they'd arrived at this far-flung Veil, but for him to *forbid* her from saving Raiden? It was too much.

"You forbid it?" she finally managed to say. She put a hand on a blade hilt and gave him a look she reserved only for idiots. "Since when did the Faces grant you the power to forbid me anything?"

Dante sighed impatiently, gathering sheets of parchment to hand to one of his attendants. Orders for supplies and equipment, everything he needed to outfit what was left of his men. Preparing for war, or so it seemed. Not that he'd included her on any of the planning.

She watched him, seething silently. His dark hair was pulled back into its usual neat braid, and there was no trace of the devastating wound he'd taken to the skull, one even worse than hers had been. After digging him from the wreckage of the villa, Korin had healed the deep crack in Dante's head, most assuredly saving his life. Poor Marco, his valet, hadn't been so lucky – he'd shielded his lord with his own body. It had broken her heart to learn the sweet, old man was dead, but she'd been comforted knowing Lizette had escaped. The elderly lady's maid had led the villa's staff to safety amid the chaos. For all her frippery and feminine airs, she was iron.

Shade touched the scar at her own hairline, her fingers tracing the pale mark. Like Dante's wound, it was faint and nearly healed, thanks to Korin. Normally, she would have let it heal on its own, but she itched to return to Sicaria. The fact that Cyril and the boys had also survived, and opted to stay behind in Sicaria, was her only consolation. They would watch out for Raiden, she was as sure of it as her own blades.

Meeting her gaze at last, Dante leaned back in his chair, gesturing for the village men to leave them alone. They scurried from the room, bobbing respectfully as they exited. One threw Shade a satisfied smirk. Maybe he thought Dante was about to chide her for her impudence? She bared her teeth at him, and he flounced out with his nose in the air.

Dante sighed. "You shouldn't antagonize the locals. They don't know what to make of you, and I can hardly blame them."

"They can all go to the lowest hells."

Since they'd arrived, the "locals" had shown her only disdain, giving her hostile stares when they weren't snickering behind her back. Children dogged her heels only to run shrieking when she turned on them with a snarl. It had been amusing... the first day. Even most of Dante's men didn't know what to make of her, having known her as the Lady Nox. But she wasn't about to hide behind a dress again, or even in tunic and trousers as Dante's callow fosterling. No, she would be herself. And she would wear her blades like a bloodwizard.

She adjusted her knife belt, settling it comfortably on her hips. The village tailor had scowled through her specifications for more suitable garb, muttering under his breath about the "scandal" it would cause for her to parade around in a snug-fitting vest and skirt of leather pteruges. But he'd produced the clothing. Having Angelo and Matteo scowling at her shoulders had encouraged him.

At some point, the brothers had decided to become a sort of honor guard for her and were never far away. They had stood side-by-side with her after their wild ride from Dante's villa, facing what they thought had been an enemy at the time. She would forever be grateful to them, and if she couldn't have Cyril and the boys at her back, at least she had them.

"Nevertheless," Dante continued. "We don't want to bring suspicion on us. We need time to regroup."

She scowled. She wasn't worried about these Veil-dwellers. Tales of the Black Witch hadn't reached this insular village within Enrice Veil, luckily, so most of the villagers thought she was some painted whore. He had made no comment about her choice of clothing, just given her a raised eyebrow before returning to his work. Also infuriating. Of course, he was dressed as a Corsaro soldier, too: bare-chested, skirt of armored leather strips, knife belt, and sandals. The people of this interior Veil knew him as "Capo Donatello", never suspecting he was a city-prince of Sicaria, and the last scion of a First Family.

Forcing her scowl into a smile, Shade sauntered around the makeshift desk. It pleased her to see his eyes linger on her legs. The short kilt left a scandalous amount of tattooed skin exposed. He'd seen her dressed this way before, of course, but since their kiss he hadn't bothered hiding appreciative glances anymore. When he'd bothered to give her glances…

"It won't matter much longer," she said, perching on the edge of the desk, her leg nearly touching his. "I'll be leaving soon."

He regarded her, lacing his hands behind his head, his long legs sprawled beneath the table. "I agree, you will be leaving soon." He clucked his tongue at her sudden grin. "But you won't be returning to Sicaria."

"I won't abandon Raiden. You can't ask me to do such a cowardly thing."

"Do you think Raiden Mad would appreciate you racing into a den of lions to save him? Do you think it would please him to see you die at the hands of the Brotherhood for his sake?"

"You know Cyril and the boys stayed behind to keep an eye on him. Even if he's being held in the deepest dungeon in the Brotherhood citadel, they'll find a way to reach him. And if they can get to him, I can get to him. I'll have him out of there, and into the Wastes before the Brotherhood has a clue."

"There isn't time for you to go running back to Sicaria, and you know it." He shifted forward in his chair, lowering his hands to take her by the waist. Surprised, she bit her lower lip and held still as if she might frighten him with sudden movement. She could feel the warmth of his hands through her vest. "You wanted to raise the Veil in Kindred land, and Korin has shown you the way. We have the charter. We have the cornerstones. You have a path to follow, and it doesn't lead back to Sicaria. Don't forget your vision, now, Shade. Not now, when we're so close."

Shade looked away, her heart sinking. He was right, but she couldn't admit it. Time *was* short. The qaraz were being touched by the blight. She had to raise her Veil soon. Without the qaraz, life in the Wastes would be impossible even for the Golondrina.

And yet...

"I can't let Raiden die for my sake," she said. "Not if I can save him."

"The Brotherhood will not kill him, not the son of an emperor. Not even they are so foolish, or mad."

"Can we take such a chance? He stayed behind and fought so we could run. I can't abandon him now. I can't. If I don't go back for him, who will?"

"Do you think so little of me?" he asked. Hurt laced his soft words.

"What?" She blinked, taken aback.

"The Imperial is my emissary; I owe him my protection." His hands still at her waist, he moved closer to her, his arms resting on her thighs and his chest against her knee. A flush rose to her cheeks at his nearness. "I will be going after Raiden. Not you. It's my turn to ride to the rescue." He fixed her with a stern look. "You are going into the mountains, to find the way to the Kindred. Korin gave you the maps he promised even though he disagrees with your choice. There's nothing stopping you now."

Uncertainty and guilt twisted in her gut. She wanted to save Raiden, but she *needed* to raise her Veil. Before the attack, she'd already decided to go into the mountains, and now she had maps showing her the way. The fact that Korin had provided them was the source of her hesitation. At every turn, he seemed to be there to push her in a certain direction. Had she decided to go to the Kindred, or had he decided for her?

But he had seemed so reluctant to hand over his maps…

Shade clenched her teeth. It was her decision. She'd made it days ago, before she even knew Korin had maps.

"I know," she said, resting her hands on his bare arms. They were solid and warm, his skin like velvet beneath her fingers. "I'll leave for the mountains as long as you promise you'll go after Raiden."

He smiled wryly. "You need a promise from me? Haven't you learned to trust me yet?"

Her heart leaped into a gallop. "I trust you." She shifted toward him, sliding her legs around him. A spark entered his blue eyes, and he pulled her hips to the edge of the desk. Her heart thudding, Shade lowered her forehead to the top of his head, breathing in the scent of him. Lavender soap and sunlight.

Dante had the simple farmhouse to himself, though it was

hardly luxurious. But it was cozy and clean, all stone and warm wood, shutters open to the breeze. A door behind his impromptu office led to a second room where a wide bed sat beneath a window, this one looking out over a flower-strewn hillside. Shade found her eyes slanting toward the other room as she stroked his muscular arms, her breath coming faster.

For the last few days, she'd been sleeping in the loft of a barn, not wanting to give these people any more fodder for their rumors. Suddenly, it seemed a ridiculous reason to avoid a comfortable bed. She nuzzled his hair, drawing a low moan from him. The soft noise made her grin. Her hands moved up his arms to his shoulders, and she clasped him with her thighs. She exclaimed in surprise when he stood suddenly, lifting her easily from the desk.

"Are you done ignoring me?" she whispered in his ear, her arms clasped around his shoulders.

"It's called restraint, my dear," he growled back, nuzzling her neck as he carried her to his bedroom. "I was protecting your reputation."

She laughed, low and throaty, and he nipped the delicate skin beneath her ear, turning her laugh into a gasp. Her nails dug into his broad back as his teeth teased her flesh, sending ripples of heat through her. Wrapped together, they fell onto the soft featherbed. Somewhere between laughing and gasping, Shade sought his mouth while her hands roamed his body. His fingers worked deftly at the laces of her vest, and she started to tug his knife belt loose.

With her hands at his narrow waist, she pulled back to meet his gaze. "They'll think I'm your whore for sure, now."

His fingers paused. "We can stop... if you want..." His words came out strangled, and the fire in his eyes belied them.

She smiled sweetly. "Stop, and I'll break your fingers, my prince."

* * *

Dante woke in a cold sweat, gasping for breath. Visions of blue fire faded, and the feel of crushing timbers across his chest eased. He wheezed, dragging in air as the dream released him. He blinked, and found a ceiling of pale, water-stained plaster above him. Soft light seeped through the tatted curtains beside his bed. He turned toward the open window, and took a long, deep breath, remembering where he was. In Enrice Veil, safe and whole, not trapped in burning wreckage, the body of his valet across him like a shield. His memories of that night were vague, but his nightmares brought it back to him in vivid clarity. He knew Korin had dragged him from his home, saving him, but he couldn't recall exactly how the old man had managed it. It left him feeling ashamed. He should have been the one to save all of them.

Breathing easily again, though the memory of suffocating lingered, Dante rolled to his side. The bed was empty beside him, the covers tossed back. He ran a hand over the crumpled sheets, wondering if she'd just risen to visit the privy. But the linen was cold, and he knew she'd been gone for some time. Gone. And not just from his bed.

Pain lanced his heart, and Dante squeezed his eyes shut. His hand closed to a fist on the empty sheets. *I sent her away. What was I thinking?* For a moment, he doubted everything he'd said to her: he shouldn't have sent her off alone. He shouldn't have volunteered to chase after Raiden Mad. He should have gone with her, protected her. What Shade had gone to do was more important than anything. She would need him beside her when she fashioned the Quattro Canto.

Dante tossed aside his blankets. There was still time. She'd be traveling on foot. On horseback, he could catch her in no time…

He had his horse saddled and loaded with supplies before the sun had cleared the treetops, his confused men following his snapped orders without question. He'd called for Angelo initially, but the man had been nowhere to be found. Him, or his brother. Too bent on his own mad goal, and driven by haste, Dante barely gave their unusual absence a thought. He had plenty of other men to follow his orders.

His people would wonder at his departure, Dante knew, but his lieutenants could keep everyone in line while he was gone, however long it might be. They had nowhere to go for now, anyway. Sicaria was too dangerous for anyone swearing allegiance to Dante Safire. It would be best if they laid low in Enrice. They might be glad to see him gone, after how badly he'd bungled things. He'd failed them as badly as he'd failed Shade. And Raiden. And poor Marco...

His fingers trembled as he tied another waterskin to his saddle, and his vision blurred. He'd failed everyone...

"What are you doing, Dante?"

Dante stiffened, but finished tying the leather thongs before turning to face Korin. His old mentor was staring at him, his face wrinkled with concern. They stood beneath a tall, glossy-leaved pear tree behind the hovel he'd been using as his base, and a pleasant breeze rustled through the leaves above them. Birds chirped and sang nearby, and the sounds of the waking village drifted to them. It was peaceful, bucolic, but Dante felt only a yearning to run. A burning need shivered through his limbs, possessed him. He ached to be away, to be racing through the Wastes. He ached to be useful.

"I'm going after Shade," he said, his voice remarkably calm considering the roiling stew of emotions in his belly. He adjusted his knife belt and tugged down his broad-brimmed hat. "She left before dawn, I suspect. She'll need my help to find the Kindred. And once she reaches the place in her vision, she'll need me when she raises the Veil."

"Matteo and Angelo went with her," Korin said, shade dappling his face. His golden eyes shone in the dim light, holding Dante captive. "She is going where she needs to be, Dante. She doesn't need your help, not in this."

Dante scowled, filled with sudden fury. "Those two went with her? I gave no such orders!"

Korin drew himself up, his face stern. "I sent them with her," he said. "I told Angelo you gave the order."

Shock made him gape. "You? You sent them – who are you to send my men anywhere without my say?"

"Would you rather she fulfills her destiny alone, my boy?" Korin's expression softened, and he raised a hand toward him. His brows dipped toward his long, straight nose. There was sympathy in his golden eyes. "I know how you feel about her, but this is for the best. I sent her to where she belongs, but I didn't send her alone. Trust me, you must let her go. Your place is not with her, Dante."

"What are you talking about? Where did you send her? She's going to the Kindred, isn't she?" Sudden suspicion gripped him, and he took two steps and grabbed Korin by his shirt. The white silk crumpled in his hands. "Shade never trusted you," he hissed, fury rising in his gut. "Was she right? Where did you send her? What have you done?"

Despite Dante's grip on him, Korin remained unflappable. "I told you. I sent her where she needs to be. There is no pass through the mountains, not where I sent her. When she finds her way blocked, she'll have to go to the Nexus." He settled a hand on Dante's fist, his eyes boring into him, compelling and bright as the sun. "I told you she must be forced. When she realizes there is only one path left to her, she will take it."

CHAPTER FOURTEEN

Raiden flowed across the smooth varnished floor of the training salle, sweat sliding down his dusky skin, his hands and bare feet moving in elaborate patterns almost too fast to follow. Sunlight from the high clerestory windows made the wood glow like darkened honey and it gleamed off the silver glaives of the spectators – armed men dressed in skirts of black leather pteruges wearing baldrics chased with silver across their tattooed chests. Finely tooled knife belts sat at their hips, holding a rainbow of blades – their true weapons, not the sparkling glaives. The bishop's Noble Guard never left Raiden's side. Though the Bishop Arturious had declared him an "honored guest" since retrieving him from the Imperial Corso after his arrest, Raiden knew he was a prisoner in this opulent palace as surely as if he'd been in a cell at the polizia's fortress.

The red-haired priest who'd arrested him, Brother Jacobis, a Blademaster and a fanatic, had not been pleased when the bishop himself greeted them at the Corso with a phalanx of Noble Guard. The polizia who'd accompanied the good brother on his raid had mysteriously vanished when they'd arrived, leaving Raiden alone with the Brotherhood priests. Still recovering from the blast and the subsequent fight, Raiden had swayed with exhaustion while they'd argued with one another in the courtyard of the fortress. The Brother Jacobis had been loath to release him to the bishop.

"He is a heathen from a foreign land who consorted with apostates, your Excellency! Because of him, I lost the Black Witch!"

"You forget yourself, good brother," the bishop warned, his hands buried in the dagged sleeves of his brocade and linen robes. He was shorter than the red-haired priest, his cropped hair was almost entirely gray, and his elaborate vestments hid an ample belly, but his simple words brought the brother's tirade to a sputtering halt. "Captain Raiden Mad is an Imperial Emissary and protected from arrest or religious persecution. You cannot throw him into a cell like a common criminal. He will be an honored guest in my own home." He fixed the other man with a grim look, his nostrils flaring. "Or do you wish to continue with your insolence?"

Though red-faced with rage, Jacobis had nonetheless subsided. Tossing Raiden a last, murderous glance, he'd bowed to his bishop. "No, your excellency. I apologize…"

The bishop's outrage had seemed genuine to Raiden in his dazed state, and he'd been relieved to be escorted to Arturious's palace, hoping he would be able to convince the man to let him go. But he'd spent days wandering the palace, feasting at the bishop's table, enduring inane small talk about trade and weather and taxes, and he was no closer to freedom.

Even though he was trapped, he was consoled knowing Shade had escaped, as well as Dante Safire. He worried about the Golondrina, having last glimpsed them in the burning stables, but felt a strange certainty they had managed to escape unscathed. They were resourceful fellows, after all. So far, he'd been given relatively free rein in the bishop's palace, including use of the expansive gardens and the impressive library, and his chambers were far grander than his rooms at Safire's villa. But he found himself in the Noble Guard's training hall the majority of the time. Only when he lost himself in the arduous practice of the Thousand Forms did he manage to find relative peace.

Raiden moved through the Forms with ever-increasing speed, his feet leaving the ground in impressive kicks, his hands striking unseen enemies with lightning speed. Murmurs and soft exclamations rose from the men watching. At first, hostile and suspicious, the guardsmen who used the training hall had given him a wide berth. They'd laughed behind their hands at his practice and sneered at what they deemed "dancing". Only after he'd fought them ten-to-one and soundly beaten them all had they looked on him with grudging respect. Little did they know how much he'd held back.

Now when he practiced the Thousand Forms, several of the guardsmen found themselves with free time and a desire for extra combat training. They'd even gone so far as to invite him to watch their magical training in return; he'd learned a bit more about bloodmagic and discovered how to better utilize his natural resistance. And how to kill them more efficiently, though he kept that to himself.

Coming to a finish after a flurry of kicks and blows, only slightly winded though his skin glowed with sweat, Raiden strode from the center of the salle to where his jacket was flung across a bench along the walls. One of the spectators, a burly fellow with thorny vines twining up his arms, handed him a towel. Raiden murmured thanks and wiped the sweat from his bare chest. The man stared at him for a moment, his eyes roving. Raiden was used to the scrutiny; his smooth, naked skin seemed to fascinate them. Even men without bloodmagic wore tattoos in Malavita.

"You should find someone to ink you," he said, his brow wrinkling. "You're small, but you're tough. You deserve a strong tattoo."

Since the man topped him by a head, Raiden didn't take offense. He shrugged. "Maybe I will."

A murmur took up among the men milling about the salle.

The man he was talking to suddenly looked beyond him, his eyes widening. He ducked his head and made a swift retreat. Calmly, Raiden continued to wipe his skin dry.

"Brother Jacobis…"

"Good brother…"

"Blademaster, may the Faces turn to you…"

It didn't surprise him that the red-haired priest had hunted him down. He'd shadowed Raiden for days now. Bishop Arturious had assured Raiden the brother meant him no ill will and had merely let his zealotry get the better of him. But he remembered how the man had moved with preternatural speed, and his palm itched for his sword. Hearing the retreat of the men around him, Raiden reached for his jacket in an unhurried manner before turning around.

"Good afternoon, captain," the priest greeted him stiffly, his hands tucked into the sleeves of his crimson robe. Up close, without rage to contort his face, Jacobis looked younger than Raiden recalled. Freckles stood out on his smooth cheeks. "The bishop has informed me I must make things right between us. Therefore, I apologize for my previous actions. I was blinded by my desire to apprehend a heretic, and a murderer. You were merely in the way."

"I see," Raiden said slowly. "When I send my official report to my father, the Emperor Suijin, may He live forever, I'll be certain to include your heartfelt apology."

The priest's gaze darkened. "Do you think your Emperor frightens me? I have seen true evil. No man born of this world frightens me. Only the Unseen make my heart quail."

Raiden lifted an eyebrow. "I have seen the monsters in the Wastes, the twisted beasts made wrong by the blight. But are they demons, good brother, or just misshapen animals?" So, he truly was a fanatic. Like the Coterie, he believed the Unseen still stalked the land. Even the holy scriptures taught that the Unseen were gone from Malavita. Only their shadows remained – he'd seen those himself.

The priest scowled and drew closer, his greater height forcing Raiden to look up at him. "In Malavita, demons are as real as the earth beneath our feet, my son. It is part of a great lie that they only exist as shadows. Their war with the Sicani destroyed our land and for centuries the Brotherhood has fought their blight. Yet the Wastes grow stronger and the Veils grow weaker. The Unseen are rising. We must be ready!"

This last he said with great fervor, his hands clasping into fists at his sides. Raiden nearly stepped back, but he held still. Despite himself, he felt a shiver rush up his spine. Hadn't Shade and the Golondrina been telling him the same thing? The Wastes were growing stronger, and the Veils weaker. The Coterie had warned Shade about the Unseen, too. She had scoffed. But. Was it possible…?

"Why hasn't the Brotherhood raised a new Veil in a century?" he asked quietly. He'd asked Arturious the same thing but never received an honest answer, just obfuscation and deflection. "Why have they stopped pushing back against the blight? Why have they abandoned their vocation?"

Shadows haunted Jacobis' dark eyes and he looked aside, his lips pressed into a line. "It's not so simple."

"If you won't raise new Veils and reclaim more of the Wastes, why not let someone else if they are willing?"

"You speak of the witch."

"And why not her? She already possesses the knowledge, and she's more than strong enough. What is there to fear if she succeeds? Or is it merely your pride which compels you to block her efforts?"

Expecting anger and outrage, Raiden was surprised when the priest's face lost all color and his eyes widened in abject fear.

"It is not pride. It would be a disaster," he said in a strangled voice. "You don't understand the danger, and neither does your Emperor. If the witch raises a new Veil, all the Veils in the land will fall!"

Raiden stiffened. "Because you think she's evil, but you're wrong. I know her."

"You misunderstand. Perhaps your witch isn't evil, but what she plans to do would doom us all. This I know." He raised his hands when Raiden opened his mouth to object. "Listen to me, please, captain." His voice dropped to a near-whisper, forcing Raiden to lean in close. "We have not raised a new Veil in over a century because the magic is failing us. The more recent Veils in the interior are far weaker than the coastal Veils. We do not understand why or how the magic has gone wrong. The knowledge was passed down from one priest to another at the highest levels of the church. But it is an oral tradition. Perhaps something was lost over the years, but the fact remains we are too afraid to attempt a new Veil."

"Why?" Raiden asked, surprised at his sudden honesty. "Even a weak Veil would reclaim wasteland and push back the blight. Perhaps, with enough of them–"

Jacobis shook his head vehemently. He stepped closer and Raiden had to stop himself from stepping back. An odd spicy scent wafted from the priest's crimson robes. Not unpleasant, but it made Raiden's hackles rise. "The last time the Brotherhood tried to raise a Veil, it collapsed before completion in a great implosion of power. The shockwave reverberated along the qaraz, damaging the Veils near it until they eventually fell. It killed the priests who raised it, and many hundreds of innocent souls. The truth was hidden, buried, and the Brotherhood stopped raising new Veils, claiming our foreign rulers prohibited it. Which is why Dante Safire went to the Empire, I suspect."

"The Brotherhood refused to work with us on the matter," Raiden said. "We had no choice but to work with Prince Safire." Understanding why they had obfuscated did nothing to raise his opinion of the church. Rather, it filled him with outrage. "You could have told us the truth. You *should* have told us the moment we claimed dominion over your wretched land."

Brother Jacobis pulled back, his nostrils flaring. "The Veils are our dominion. Malavita survives because of our diligence, our power. You have no right to anything here, no matter what you claim on a map."

"You have hidden the truth from your own people to keep them dependent on you. You lie to save face! I see nothing but cowardice and avarice in your actions. You should let Shade raise her Veil. She possesses awesome power. Perhaps where your magic failed, hers will succeed!"

His freckles stood out clearly on his pale face, and Jacobis' eyes were dark pools. "We cannot allow your witch to raise a Veil, not when it could collapse. If she is as powerful as you say, such a backlash could damage even the oldest, strongest Veils. Are you willing to risk the lives of hundreds? Thousands?"

"Shade is trying to save her people. She won't fail. I have faith in her."

Jacobis' gaze grew shrewd. "Then let me ask you this: are you willing to risk the life of your witch? We are determined to stop her, captain. One way or another. You can stop her from raising the Veil. Or we can. Which do you think would leave her alive in the end?"

Within the cool interior of the Duomo di Sicaria sat countless rows of wooden pews stained dark with age. Dressed as a pilgrim in a simple tunic, trousers, and soft boots, a travel-stained cloak about his shoulders, Dante Safire knelt in worship in a dark alcove far from the altar of the sprawling Duomo, his head bent to his clasped hands as he whispered in rhapsodical prayer. Beside him, another pilgrim sat stiffly on the pew, his hood drawn over his silver hair, leaving his face in shadows but for his frown. Tall and straight-backed, his arms crossed over his chest, this pilgrim seemed more annoyed than worshipful.

Dante threw Korin a glance, pausing his prayers to mutter,

"You can at least pretend to be awed. Even you have to be able to feel the power of the Quattro Canto beneath us."

Korin sniffed. "The Four and the Hidden are sacred, here most of all, but they are not a god. And this place has been twisted to oppress, rather than enlighten. I cannot pretend to be awed by hypocrisy."

"For the Faces' sake, the Duomo is not the place for religious debate. Just bow your head like a good pilgrim."

Reluctantly, Korin uncoiled from the bench and got to his knees beside Dante. He rested his arms on the pew in front of them and bowed his head. "You know I hate these places," he said crossly. "I don't understand why I couldn't wait outside. I'd rather pretend to be a beggar in the streets than a false pilgrim."

"Because I wanted to keep an eye on you," Dante said, shifting on his sore knees. He shot his old mentor a dark look. "I know you want to race after her. I practically had to drag you here by your hair."

"Any of your men would have happily helped you retrieve the Imperial. Instead, like a fool, you brought only me. I'm not a soldier, I'm not even a bloodwizard." He hunched over hands clenched so tightly his knuckles had whitened. "If you'd let me go after her, maybe I could have convinced her to stay on the right path."

"She chooses her own path. And if I were you, I'd stay out of her sight until she's raised our Veil."

"*If* she manages to raise it," he said bitterly.

Dante bit his tongue, refusing to have this argument again. Back in Enrice Veil, as Korin had confessed he'd sent Shade on a fool's errand, hoping to force her into using the Coterie's gemstones at the Nexus, Dante had listened in stunned silence.

"Shade will never do as you wish!" Dante had finally exploded, shouting at his mentor and startling his horse. The beast snorted and shied away from them, and it took Dante a few minutes to calm him. He was still shaking with fury, though, when he was able to confront Korin again.

"You know her," he said, forcing his voice to normal levels. He stroked his mount's soft nose, and glared at the tall, regal man. "How do you think she will react when she discovers your duplicity? Do you truly believe she will just shrug her shoulders and do what you want?"

A flash of uncertainty darkened his gleaming eyes before Korin shook off his doubt. "It is the only way," he said firmly, reiterating what he'd been saying all along. "Shade wants to raise her Veil above all else. She *must* raise it – you heard her report about the tainted qaraz. The Wastes grow stronger every day. The Unseen grow stronger! There is no time for her stubbornness. She must act now, or all will be lost."

Emotion crept into his voice, at last. Desperation, and not a little fear. It shocked Dante. He'd seen the healer angry and frustrated, concerned, even, but never, ever afraid. He felt no sympathy. Because of his fear, Korin may have pushed Shade too far this time, and it would cost them all. There was no way she would meekly do what she was forced into doing. She'd cross the Glass Fields on her hands and knees first–

"By the Faces." A sudden realization turned his blood to ice. "That is exactly what she'll do."

"What? What will she do?"

Dante stared at his mentor grimly, surprised Korin hadn't considered the possibility himself. "You backed her into a corner," he said. "So, she's going to do what she's always done – tear the walls down." At the look of confusion on Korin's face, Dante bared his teeth in a vicious smile. "She'll get to the Kindred's stronghold, you old fool. She'll cross the Glass Fields!"

Watching Korin's expression crumble with horror had given Dante little satisfaction. In his bones, he knew that was exactly what Shade was going to do, and it made him sick. But instead of racing after her to try to convince her to take some other route, he'd ordered a second horse saddled and supplied. In one thing, Korin had been right – it was not his place to go after Shade. He had promised her he would save Raiden Mad, and he would keep that promise.

It had been difficult convincing his men as to the soundness of the plan. His lieutenants had argued vehemently, insisting they return to Sicaria in strength. But, even if they'd just ridden to the edges of the Golden Crescent, a force of bladed men would be noticed. Dante had to calmly explain that it would be much easier for two men to infiltrate the city, that he wasn't returning to Sicaria to start a war, not yet. He was only going to retrieve his emissary.

To mollify them, he'd told them to keep preparing for war while he was gone, vowing they would reclaim all they'd lost to rousing cheers. And they would, one day.

The great bells of the Duomo rang for midday. The deep, sonorous tones throbbed through the building, making the pews vibrate. He tensed expectantly, hopefully, as he had every day since arriving in Sicaria. The Duomo was a prearranged meeting place, one the Brotherhood would never suspect.

As the bells sounded overhead, Korin nudged him in the ribs and jerked his chin toward the aisle between the pews. A brown-skinned man in black and silver livery strode down it, twirling a driver's cap on his finger. His salt-and-pepper hair was contained in a neat braid and his drooping mustache was waxed into jaunty points. Dante watched him halt before the altar and make a perfunctory bow to the quartered sign of the Four and the Hidden, then cross to the colonnade along the southern wall.

His heart thumping, Dante rose from the kneeler as the bells echoed into silence. "Stay here," he ordered Korin.

Behind the towering, fluted columns, in the deep shadows of the cathedral stretched a line of confessional cabinets. Curtains provided privacy for the penitent, but the priest sat behind a locked door. Dante could hear the fervent whispers and mournful weeping of the confessors, and the stilted, rote responses of the priests as he walked down the line until he came to a door with a jaunty cap hanging from the handle. The alcove for the penitent was empty, and Dante slipped inside, dropping to the kneeler and pulling the curtain closed behind him.

"It's about time, Safire. I was beginning to give up hope."

Though he'd recognized Cyril even in his driver's disguise, Dante still felt a surge of relief upon hearing his familiar, gravelly voice. "I came as quickly as I could," he said, grinning. He could just make out Cyril through the screen between them, and another figure wedged into the corner of the booth. A priest. His head was slumped to his chest. "Faces, you didn't kill the poor fellow, did you?"

Cyril's teeth flashed white in the shadows. "He's just taking a nap."

"Good. Not every Brotherhood priest is an enemy."

He was answered with an eloquent grunt which made Cyril's opinion clear. "Where's Shade?" he asked.

"Shade is on her way to the mountains. And she's tasked me with rescuing our mutual friend."

"I guessed as much. I just wanted to be sure she was safe."

Safe. Dante prayed he was right. "So, I'm assuming by your livery, Bishop Arturious has my emissary. How quickly can we retrieve him?"

"We've been laying our plans, me and the boys, but we've had no way of warning Raiden. He's kept under watch by the Noble Guard and a bevy of hand-picked servants." Cyril huffed. "Even Manoli couldn't charm his way close to him."

"That is surprising." The young Golondrina was popular among his staff, men and women alike. "What are your plans, then?"

"The bishop is throwing a great ball in Raiden's honor," Cyril said, his broad smile gleaming through the screen. "He has announced some 'surprise' in store for his guests. I figured if he wants a surprise, we'll give him one…"

CHAPTER FIFTEEN

Miles west of Enrice Veil, the Razor Ridge Mountains grew steep and jagged, rearing against the white-hot sky in an unbroken wall. Abruptly, the imposing peaks vanished as if a colossal fist had obliterated a great swath of the mountain range. Left behind was a field of shattered glass, extending for miles in menacing ripples. The fragments littered the red sands, razor-edged shards like thousands of broken bottles heaped atop each other, ankle-deep at the edges, but rising into a forest farther within.

It was hard to discern the true nature of the Fields, at least from the outside. Strange magic distorted the land around them, and no qaraz led into them. No qaraz anyone could find, anyway. Staring into the Fields was like staring into the sun, and it made Shade's eyes ache. But she found herself unable to look away. From her vantage point on a sheer ridge overlooking the menacing Fields, she stared down at the destruction until her eyes burned with tears.

"Shade."

The sun glared off the riot of crystal shards, both beautiful and captivating and infinitely dangerous. She narrowed her eyes against the brilliance, forcing a tear down her cheek.

"*Shade.*"

The voice was firmer this time, too firm to ignore. "Yes?"

she asked quietly, though she didn't move. She couldn't move.

"We have to return to the qaraz below. There's nothing here but rocks."

It had taken them days to reach this place, she and her honor guard. Days of hard travel on foot, following a faint qaraz through increasingly rough territory, spending blood to draw circles of protection each night and fighting off the occasional surge of Waste beasts had left them all drained. The qaraz led to the Nexus, eventually, a fact which had filled her with a vague suspicion when she'd studied Korin's map. But she'd convinced herself she was being foolish and letting her distrust of the Coterie affect her. What good would it do Korin to lead her astray now? He still wanted the Veil, as did his Coterie.

So, she'd continued to lead them on this path. It had been a difficult journey, but her companions were strong, good with their blades, and good company. The two brothers worked together well, their efforts coordinated and efficient. They laughed and talked and teased each other much like Manoli and Petra, and she found it comforting and easy to travel with them, despite the hazards of their journey. But even they had reached their limit. This dead-end climb through the broken foothills had whittled them to the bone.

A tumble of boulders blocked the pass through the mountains. The only pass, according to her maps. And it wasn't a fresh rockfall. Weeds and scrub had grown up among the cracks where dust had settled over the years. No one had passed this way in quite some time, least of all the Kindred in their caravans. The map Korin had given her had been a lie.

With the sun dipping behind the mountains, leaving them in shadows, they'd stared at the riot of boulders in stunned disbelief. The useless map had fallen from Shade's limp fingers, fluttering to the ground to join the dust, and she had retreated to the edge of the plateau to stare at the Glass Fields far below them.

"Maybe we can find another way," Angelo continued hopefully. "If we return to the qaraz, perhaps it will lead us to a better path." He'd remained calm upon discovering their way obstructed, though his brother had cursed and ranted and proposed smashing through the mountains with magic. They could have drained every drop of their blood, however, and made no more than a dent, and they all knew it.

"There is no other path!" Matteo insisted, his voice cracking with exhaustion. He was especially quick with his blades and had fought admirably the whole journey. All for nothing. "The Glass Fields are to the south of us, an impassable mountain range to the north of us. Where do you suggest we go? How long should we wander the Wastes looking for another way?"

Shade heard steps behind her. "Shade, please," Angelo said. "What do we do? Where do we go, now? Perhaps there's a different map, a better map."

She didn't reply, and Angelo made a sound of frustration.

"There has to be a way," he muttered to himself, and she heard him rustling through her pack which lay abandoned on the ground nearby. Slowly, she turned to look at him. He was crouched over her pack, pulling out her spare clothes and leather map tubes. She wanted to tell him to stop. Korin had given her several maps leading her to this place. But only one map showed the pass through the mountains. And it was a lie.

She felt like a fool. The Coterie had cast her into the Wastes when she'd been a girl, hoping she would die. And they had done the same again. How had she been fool enough to fall for their lies?

He sent me here, hoping to box me in. To force me onto his *path.*

She could feel the Nexus. It lay close to the Glass Fields, somewhere in the Wastes to the south of their position, its power like a pulsing heart buried in the earth. If not for her vision, and the calling which pulled her in the opposite direction, she might have been willing to raise her Veil there. Despite the danger, it was tempting. Perhaps…

A shudder racked her, and she held herself tightly, her arms crossed beneath her breasts. She had to resist this urge. Something wasn't right and she had to trust her instincts. Whatever their past, it wasn't why she couldn't trust the Coterie. There was more to it, she just wasn't sure what. Not yet.

Beside her, Angelo was opening the map cases, and pulling out scrolls to lay on the ground. He would find nothing useful among those ancient, crumbling maps. Some were older than the Wastes, showing a Malavita which no longer existed. Muttering to himself, Angelo took one of those maps and shuffled it aside for more recent surveys. But the one he'd dismissed caught her eye.

It was stained dark with age, its edges ragged, one corner torn away, but it was a map of the Razor Ridge mountains. The range in its entirety, before the Final Battle had blasted, melted and shattered a great portion of it into glass shards. Golden threads winked at her, seemingly random tracings across the renderings of mountain and plains. A knot of shimmering gold sat exactly where she would expect the Nexus to be in this time.

Finally, she recognized those golden lines. Qaraz. The threads traced the path of the ancient qaraz, unchanged even after the war had lain waste to Malavita. And one such thread wended its way through the mountains, mountains which no longer existed. Her arms loosened and fell to her sides as she took a step toward the edge of the cliff, her eyes watering as she stared again into the abyss of the Glass Fields. Could it be?

Heart pounding, she grabbed up the discarded map and held it before her, comparing it to the land around them. There, the high jagged peak above them was clearly marked, and she could feel where the Nexus lay in her very blood. Slowly, she turned the map in her hands, lining up the landmarks, though she had to guess at the scale. A golden thread snaked through the mountains on her map. She lowered the parchment, still seeing it in her mind, and imagined it winding through the Glass Fields below her. Her breath caught. Was it still there?

"What are you doing, Shade?" Angelo asked, rising to stand beside her. An edge of impatience touched his voice. "That one is too old, and it shows nothing, anyway."

"You're wrong," she countered, hope alighting in her thundering heart. A flash and pulse erupted from the Glass Fields far below, shaking the very ground beneath them. Always in flux, the Fields undulated and twisted like a tortured beast. It was madness to enter them. Even the strongest wizard would drain themselves of blood keeping the gnarled magics at bay. But, on a qaraz, it might be possible to cross them.

The white burning of the Fields beat at the back of her eyes, but she couldn't look away. It was there, even after all this time; she was sure of it. She checked the map once more, a burning imprint of the Fields marring her vision. The gold lines on the map pulsed and she lifted her gaze back to the Fields. There. A glimpse. A sliver of gold among the blasting white. A thread. There, and then gone.

A path...

"The way," she said hoarsely, wondering if she'd only imagined that thread of gold. Hope rose in her. She threw her arms wide, the map fluttering in a sudden, hot breeze. "There is a way!"

Shade drew the circles of protection around their camp as the dying sun washed the Glass Fields an angry crimson. It was not an ideal spot, high on the mountain with only rocks and scrub for shelter, but none of them had the strength to hike back down to the qaraz they'd followed to the mountains. The small burst of energy she'd gained from her excitement over spotting a qaraz in the Glass Fields allowed Shade to draw the circles, leaving the brothers to find fuel for a fire.

By the time she finished, a small pile of tinder burned bright and hot at the center of her overlapping circles, a kettle hanging on a tripod over it. Matteo was sprinkling tea leaves into it. He'd already spread their bedrolls for the night, and Angelo was unwrapping a moldy cheese and cured meat for their meal. Lines of weariness framed the elder brother's mouth, and Matteo was pale and wan, but neither spoke a word of complaint.

Shade sheathed her blades, her hands lingering on the hilts. The two men had agreed to follow her through the promised pass. Neither had agreed to follow her into the Glass Fields. It would be asking the impossible of them. According to legend, only one person had ever crossed the Glass Fields: the Brazen Monk. It was a popular legend. A brave holy man and his two loyal companions had dared to cross the Fields – a true hellscape even worse than the Wastes. All for the hopes of finding some hidden paradise. The story ended in triumph for the Brazen Monk; he'd found a green land littered with gemstones. As for the others…

Shade dropped to her bedroll, sitting cross-legged. Gratefully, she accepted a cup of tea from Matteo. Despite his drawn face, he flashed her a smile. She caught his wrist before he could move away. "I'm sorry," she said. "For dragging you to this dead-end. I know it must seem like madness to consider crossing the Glass Fields."

Matteo dropped to one knee beside her, a line between his brow. "Korin told us to keep you safe, lady witch. To accompany you to your destiny, or so he put it." The line deepened, and his bright eyes darkened. "But he said Prince Safire told us to guard you. And I know he didn't. Illario lied, and I don't like liars. Never have. I understand why you don't trust him. Can't trust him. Even so, I'm glad he sent us with you." A flash of teeth and his expression brightened. "We probably would have followed you even without being ordered. My brother and I will follow you anywhere."

She jerked her chin towards the cliff's edge. "Even into the abyss?"

"Yes, m'lady."

"I am no lady," Shade said, giving his wrist a squeeze before letting him go. She sipped her cooling tea. "I am the Black Witch, a fiend and a scoundrel, a coldhearted murderer, and a madwoman. I might lead you to your deaths, or worse." She fixed him with a hard stare, and raised her voice so Angelo could hear, as well. "Do you still wish to follow me?"

Across the fire, Angelo stood, his hands resting on his blade hilts. Not in a threatening manner. She recognized a man seeking comfort. "My brother already told you our choice. Do you doubt our word?"

"Never. But... legend says the Brazen Monk entered the Glass Fields with two companions. But when he emerged on the other side, he was alone."

"We know the tale," Angelo said grimly. "The qaraz way was difficult, costly. The Fields demanded blood from the trespassers. Sometimes, it required more. Sometimes, it required sacrifice."

Sudden anger filled her. Was he so eager to die? "The Brazen Monk murdered his companions to find the way. You'd follow me knowing that?"

The brothers exchanged a glance, and Shade watched their resolve solidify. Angelo's grim expression relaxed into a smile. "We aren't following the Brazen Monk," he said. "We're following the Black Witch. And she would never cross the Glass Fields on the corpses of her companions."

Her throat tightened at his words, at the certainty in his voice. She gave them a sharp nod and buried her face in her teacup. Without a word, the brothers returned to their tasks. Shade swallowed her bitter tea and prayed she could be as certain as Angelo that she wouldn't need their corpses to reach her destiny.

CHAPTER SIXTEEN

With dawn still a few hours away, Shade led her companions down the mountain and to the edge of the Glass Fields. With her honor guard trailing her in silence, she stalked the black emptiness, every sense open to find the qaraz she'd only glimpsed. She clung to her hope as doubts assailed her. What if she had imagined it? The idea of reaching the Kindred lands beyond the mountains had possessed her for so long, she couldn't imagine failing now. Had that fear driven her to imagine a way? Had her longing for Satine disguised itself as her vision? It wasn't too late to go to the Nexus–

There. She knew the moment she stepped upon it. The familiar clean pulse of a qaraz. It was faint, but as she focused, a narrow, golden path of light snaked away from her and through the Fields. Good thing it was still dark. She didn't want the others to see her trembling in relief.

"Stick close to me. I don't want to lose anyone."

"We'll stick like burrs, lady witch," promised Matteo. She could practically hear his grin. It heartened her. With a deep breath, she stepped forward.

They advanced into a strange, unsettling darkness, the path beneath their sandals a faint luminescence, and when the sun broke the edge of the Glass Fields in a blinding array of red and gold, all three breathed a small sigh of relief. Pitch black and empty, the Glass Fields had nevertheless been full of disturbing echoes and soft, unidentifiable cries and whispers.

The frigid black night gave way to a scintillating brightness stretching in all directions. The broken, malformed glass radiated a strange heat, promising a brutal day ahead, and even with the qaraz to guide them it was a halting, stumbling progress through piles and hummocks of razor-sharp fragments. Shade could feel the warped magics of the place pressing against the power of the qaraz with every step.

The qaraz took them on a twisting, meandering track. At times, it seemed they were making little progress. But they persisted. Disturbingly, the qaraz tended to vanish behind them. It was soon apparent that there would be no turning back. It was forward, or nowhere.

After an hour of daylight, Shade's eyes ached from the glare. Eyes watering, she kept her gaze on the qaraz. She felt exposed in the vast emptiness, especially forced as she was to keep her head down. Her companions followed in her wake, Matteo keeping his hand on her pack and Angelo gripping his brother's belt. Unfortunately, neither brother could see the qaraz. She was glad she'd warned them to stick close.

As the sun lifted above the horizon, the heat rose. Shade felt as if she'd fallen into an inferno. Would they bake alive in this place once the sun reached its apex? She drew a blade. A small cut on her wrist gave her enough magic to bend the air around them, manipulating water and wind to shield them from the worst of the heat. She heard Matteo's relieved exhalation behind her, and Angelo muttered thanks to the Four Faces.

"They had nothing to do with it." Shade sheathed her blade and concentrated on the path before her, a thin, twisting way barely wide enough to keep them from touching the shards on either side.

The deeper they moved into the Fields, the higher the "glass" rose. The land sloped steadily downward, and the shards began to tower over them. It became a dance of sorts to avoid the razor-sharp edges, bending and twisting and slipping sideways along the qaraz. At times, they were forced to crawl beneath great arcs like frozen waves of glittering ice.

Sweating, Shade emerged from one such tight squeeze, and she stumbled, nearly falling into a lovely tower of knife-edged crystal. Matteo's quick hand on her arm steadied her. She blew out a breath, every limb shaking. The jagged glass would have sliced her to ribbons. And who knew what magic it would have called.

"Maybe we should rest," Angelo suggested.

Shade nodded. She led them farther until the path widened, giving them just enough space for all of them to sit. Great waves of glittering glass arced overhead.

Angelo dropped to his knees, shrugging off his pack. On the ground, they were at least spared the worst of the sun, sheltered in the dubious shade of the ever-growing trees of broken shards. Shade eyed the "trees". Had they formed this way? In the cataclysmic final blast? Or were they living somehow and still growing? Angelo dug in his pack a moment before pulling out a canvas-wrapped parcel of dried meat. He handed Shade and Matteo their portions, keeping a smaller piece for himself.

"I saw that," Shade grumbled around a mouthful of tough meat. "You get a double-ration tonight, Angelo. There'll be no martyrs on this trip. We all need to stay strong."

He shrugged. "I'm not that hungry, that's all."

Matteo snorted, and grinned at her. "I once saw him eat an entire suckling pig on Feast day. He's always hungry."

Shade chuckled, trying to imagine the trim Angelo devouring a roast pig on his own. "When we get through this, I'll roast you a whole boar, Angelo."

He cleared his throat. "Forgive me, lady witch, but I can't see you cooking a boar."

"Why? I know how to cook."

Angelo glanced at his brother, who stifled a snicker. "Uh,

there's a reason we've been doing all the cooking since you made breakfast that first day."

Shade gnawed on her ration in disgruntled silence. You burn one pot of porridge and suddenly you can't cook. She smirked and pointed at Matteo. "In that case, Matteo can roast it for you. I'll just carve it." And she patted one obsidian blade.

Their laughter echoed through the glass like the tinkling of a wind chime. It returned to the clearing strangely distorted. Two voices transformed into many, and none of them friendly. They fell silent, eyes wide in the gloom.

"Let's get moving," Shade said. "The faster we're out of this place, the better."

They continued, somewhat refreshed, in a growing forest of twisted crystal. Each step forward took them down. To where, Shade could only guess. Into the lowest hells? It made her grip the bone handles of her blades more tightly than ever. She had a strong desire to open her skin and blast a way through the glass forest, but she resisted the urge. Drawing enough blood to ease their way was one thing but calling real power in the midst of such distorted magical energy would end in disaster.

Power she couldn't comprehend had created this place, and its residue kept it dangerous. Unpredictable. Though the Sicani had been victorious over the Unseen, the cost had been tremendous. For the first time in her life she had to wonder: Had it been worth it? Most of Malavita was a terrible wasteland continually ravaged by Blackstorms. The Veils held back the worst of the blight, sheltering enough land for many to thrive, but those with strong bloodmagic held dominion over those without. The Veils were prisons to some. It was a vicarious existence, growing ever-more unstable.

We need to finish what we started. Strong Veils raised over all the land until the blight is pushed into the sea.

Her Veil would be the first, but it wasn't just the Veil she wanted. The Empire craved the gems it would provide, but so did Shade. She kneaded her knife hilts, seeing a future she'd only dared imagine: an army of bloodwizards bearing a lethal rainbow of blades – blades she would fashion for them – working together to cleanse the land of its blight. A blight of both supernatural and human sources. She'd told no one of this ambition, not even Dante Safire, but it drove her as much as her vision.

A shattering crash broke the stillness of the glass forest. They froze as one. Shade's heart thudded at her breastbone like a caged bird. She'd drawn without even realizing it, but so had Matteo and Angelo. The green and pink of Matteo's tourmaline blades, and the deep blue of Angelo's topaz reflected a thousand times over in the diamonds. Shade's blades were streaks of black within the shining forest.

The shattering grew closer, louder.

"Should we run?" Matteo asked breathlessly.

"And expose our backs to only the Faces know what?" Angelo shook his head. "Stand ready."

"Do nothing until you see an enemy," Shade warned as they faced the approaching sounds. "Strike at it, not the trees. The glass will disrupt our magic or twist it in unexpected ways."

A shadow appeared among the shimmering glass, gigantic and lumbering. Shade swallowed, unsure as to what it could be. What could live out here? It was huge, she could see that much. A lupara? An ursus? Both were large, carnivorous predators of the Wastes. But this wasn't the Wastes, not exactly.

A deafening roar battered their eardrums, louder than the shattering of the trees.

"Wait!" Shade shouted above the noise, though every instinct told her to unleash her magic. "Wait!"

The glass forest before them splintered, sending razor-sharp pieces flying. Shade felt the fractured stones slice her. Blood slid down her arms and legs, and magic raged beneath her skin. Ready to be released. But she didn't dare until she had a target.

A creature, vaguely horse-shaped, barreled onto the qaraz

a few feet ahead of them, missing Angelo by a hair's breadth. Four-legged with a horn as long as Raiden's sword, the beast bellowed, swinging a massive head in all directions, a head more skull than living flesh. Bones peeked through scraps of skin clinging to its frame. It looked like a half-rotted corpse. Its bulging eyes were milk white and it lifted its bony snout as if tasting the air.

"It's blind," Shade said.

She'd kept her voice low, but its head swung toward them, and with a bellow, it charged. They scattered. Angelo and Matteo dove off the qaraz and into the surrounding forest, Angelo giving a shout as he shoved Shade aside, drawing the creature after him. They vanished into the trees. The creature hit the gleaming structures, crashing after the two men.

"No!" Shade screamed, and the creature turned toward her, roaring. "Come and get me, you bastard!"

With an enemy clear in her sights, Shade called her magic. She slashed at her belly with one blade and her thigh with the other, unleashing fire and wind and earth. The obsidian took her offering, followed her will, and gleamed white-hot.

The creature took the brunt of her attack. But it shook off the fire like sand, scrambled across the pit she'd opened at its feet, and ignored the spray of earth she'd blasted at its face.

"Shit." She said it like a prayer and flung herself out of its path. Its rotted coat brushed against her as it passed; the force of its passage sent her spinning.

Her feet left the qaraz. She knew the moment it happened. The earth beneath her no longer hummed with welcome but set up a violent discord. It throbbed through her soles, up her legs, a deep vibration that made her teeth rattle and her bones ache. She hadn't fallen into the glass forest, yet, but it loomed too close for comfort.

The beast had barreled into the trees on the other side of the qaraz but seemed none the worse for it. The shattered crystals cascaded off it, leaving only a few scratches. Shade stumbled back onto the qaraz and felt immediate relief shudder through her body. She shrugged off her pack and tossed it to the side, the map cases and cooking utensils within landing in a clatter. The beast snorted at the ruckus, its long ears swiveling and its massive head swinging toward the noise. Shade readied her blades, holding herself rock-still.

With a trumpeting bray, the beast charged again. Toward her pack. Thank the Faces! She held her blades over the skin of her forearms, poised to strike, though she doubted it would do any good. The creature had shrugged off her magic like a ratty cloak.

It reached her pack and skidded to a stop, its head lowered to the earth, snorting and sniffling at the canvas bag, tearing it asunder, spilling travel rations – ground meal and meat and dried fruit – across the earth. It squealed furiously, raising its head, searching for a victim.

Shade inched away from the creature, her blood rushing in her ears and her heart thudding painfully, expecting it to turn on her at any moment. Her feet crunched over shattered glass and she winced at the noise. How sensitive was its hear–

Its massive head swung toward her. She froze. A deafening bellow blasted from it, a noise that reverberated through her bones. Behind her, she could hear glass crashing to the ground. She risked a glance over her shoulder – there was a path opening in the trees, a shadowy space in the glistening forest. Could she lose it among the trees? Matteo and Angelo had disappeared so thoroughly.

I'll find them.

Shade stepped to the left, choosing to stay on the qaraz rather than risk the forest, but the beast tracked her unerringly. It pawed at the ground, readying for a charge. She had one choice left to her. Heart hammering, she turned and dashed into the forest. The creature's enraged blaring followed her then abruptly ceased as the shadows closed around her.

Right. Shade stopped on the path which had so conveniently

appeared for her. The dissonance of the place had lessened somewhat, but it was still there. Lurking.

"Matteo," she called, and her voice echoed back. She tried again. "Angelo!"

Her words were swallowed by the impenetrable jungle of twisted crystals. She blinked sweat from her eyes. How would she ever find her friends in this alien place? There was no horizon, no way to see the sun. She didn't even know in what direction she was traveling. And even if she found her companions, how would they ever find the qaraz again? Would they be lost in this place, doomed to wander until they died of hunger or thirst? Frustrated, and not a little frightened, she held herself still and listened.

Silence. She heard nothing but her own stampeding heart. And then – a faint cry. Shade spun toward the sound.

"Angelo?" she whispered. She folded her lips closed and listened.

A scream, so feeble it was a puff of air against her eardrums. She turned toward the sound and broke into a slow jog. The forest opened before her – drawing her in – and ahead of her a shadow appeared among the bright and shining crystals. She slowed. What if it was another misbegotten illusion of a creature? No. This shadow was shaped like a man.

The forest widened around a massive crystal column. Its surface was smooth, and the man-shadow lay within it. Tall, broad-shouldered with a narrow waist. Matteo. Shade stopped, eyes widening. He was *inside* the crystal, his eyes closed, and his arms crossed over his chest, tourmaline blades in his hands, shining brightly.

"Matteo," she breathed, reaching to touch the crystal encasing him. It was hard and slick, completely solid. The bright gleam of his blades grew more intense. She squinted against the brightness, trying to see his face. Her eyes watered, and she looked aside, blinking away spots.

A glow appeared on the ground beneath Matteo's crystal

tomb; it grew into a pathway, cutting straight through the forest. It was broad and smooth, practically a road. Bright sunlight shone at the end of it, in a sky of deep blue over distant mountain peaks. It was the other side of the Razor Ridge mountains.

The way out...

Stunned, Shade took a step toward the path. It was a qaraz. Strong and pure. It would be so simple to leave. To be free of this place. Torn, she wrenched her gaze back to Matteo. The glow from his blades seemed to be fading; she could see his angular face clearly. The color had drained from him. As she watched in horror, his lips turned blue, and dark circles appeared beneath his eyes. He was dying...

And as he died, the path grew firmer, brighter.

"No," Shade said. She slammed the butt end of her blade against the crystal tomb. "I won't leave him! Faces turn from you, let him go!"

Shade beat against the crystal until her fists grew swollen. Not a mark marred the smooth surface. She was wheezing, sobbing through clenched teeth. Her tears mingled with the sweat dripping down her cheeks and stained her lips with salt. Matteo had grown cadaverous during her useless tirade, his blades dimming. The path pulsed enticingly.

"Damn you," she muttered and fell back from her friend's prison. She raised her blades, no longer caring if her magic might kill her in this deathtrap. This twisted place was letting her through, granting her safe passage, and the price was Matteo's life, most likely Angelo's, too. The magic in their blood was what sustained this field of glass that wasn't glass. Like some giant sea anemone feeding on the fish that wandered into its grasp, this place fed on random travelers. The Brazen Monk had fed his companions to it in order to cross unmolested. So simple, so cruel.

"Fucking trees!" she screamed, her blades flashing as she drew blood from arms and legs and torso. The obsidian gleamed like twin suns, eclipsing the qaraz, turning the crystal trees into black, shifting shadows. She called all Four Faces, combining wind and water, fire and earth; she called the Hidden, the Fifth Face, spirit in its purest form.

A maelstrom rose around her, but she knew it wouldn't be enough. The glass would take her magic and twist it. She would most likely only succeed in killing herself. But she couldn't let Matteo die.

In desperation, she reached for the Wild Power.

Thunder rumbled through the clear sky; the earth shook beneath her feet. A geyser of violence rose in her blood like the hot, liquid magma of a volcano, seeking a crack, a way to break free. The world would bend before such power. Time itself paused in anticipation. To go forward, to go backwards, to go nowhere

"Stop."

The simple command doused the power flaring within her. Like a bucket of cold water dropped over her head. Suddenly, Shade stood in a sphere of calm, Matteo before her, free from his crystal prison. He was pale, but he was always pale. Silence and stillness surrounded them, sheltered them. From the trees, four strangers in hooded robes appeared. They approached slowly, and Shade tensed, her heart thundering.

"I told you she wouldn't sacrifice my brother," Angelo said, appearing from behind a tall person in a green robe and looking both anxious and relieved.

They stood within a clearing; the trees had retreated. Soft, dense grass covered the ground. Life teemed in the soil beneath her feet. What was this place? Were they still in the Glass Fields? Her hands tightened on her blade hilts. Had she even called her magic? Or had everything been an illusion?

Angelo reached his brother and grasped his arms. "Are you alright?" he asked, scanning him for injuries.

"I'm fine. Stop, Angie. What the hells is happening?" He shrugged away his brother's hands and moved nearer Shade.

"Who are these people?" he asked her, keeping his eyes on the hooded strangers and his hands on his hilts. "Are they the Kindred?"

"I don't know," she said hesitantly, feeling strangely hollow. She'd called enough magic to level half of Sicaria and it had vanished as if it had never been. The Kindred were an ancient tribe of Golondrina, strong in their healing and qaraz-tending, but not in bloodmagic. They would not have been able to stop her so easily. And what was the purpose of this subterfuge? Confusion gave way to anger.

"Do you control this cursed place?" she demanded. "Who are you? *What* are you?"

"We are the guardians of this 'cursed place'," one of them said, a tall, slim man wearing a blue cloak. He lifted hands spotted with age, and dropped his hood, revealing a narrow face lined with wrinkles. A long, drooping mustache as white as chalk nearly hid his pursed lips. "One of our tasks is to watch the Glass Fields and repel the unworthy. It is a sacred task we do not take lightly. Those who attempt to enter our sanctuary are often misguided in their motives. They must be dealt with harshly to discourage others."

"Harshly?" Matteo sputtered. "Did you send that beast to force us from the qaraz? Would we have proved unworthy if it had torn our guts out or trampled us into paste?"

"The creatures which inhabit this place are more shadow than substance. You were never in any *real* danger," added another of them quickly. This one wore a rich scarlet cloak. His voice was deep, melodic. Kind. He seemed mildly embarrassed by his companion's comments. "But we had to make sure. We had to test your resolve. Finding the qaraz proved you were strong, but not whether you were worthy."

Matteo took a step toward the robed man, his muscles bunching. "I couldn't *breathe*, you bastard!"

"I am sorry for that," the man in red said. He drew back his hood, revealing a portly face only slightly younger than his companion's. A full, white beard hid his wrinkles, but for the ones crinkling the corners of his bright green eyes. "It seems not that long ago when we were on the same path as you. The tests we faced were... difficult. But in the end, we proved ourselves worthy and found our purpose."

"And now you judge the worth of others?" Shade scoffed. She could sense power from these strangers, but she was stronger. All of them carried blades but for the one in white who held back from the others. She kneaded her blade hilts. Somehow, they had tricked her. Clouded her mind. They were not Kindred. But they were in her way. "We came to find the way to Kindred lands, not prove ourselves to the likes of you. My worth is not yours to judge. Only the Four and the Hidden can weigh my soul."

"You are as arrogant as I expected, obsidian wielder." The tall man wearing green pulled back his hood. Towering above the others, his shoulders broad and his body perfectly balanced, he was clearly a warrior. His face was stern and relatively unlined beneath a thatch of short-cropped black hair shot with silver. He scowled at her. "We should never have let you enter the Fields."

"As if we could have stopped her," the last of them said in a low murmur, the one in white. Shade narrowed her eyes, trying to see inside the woman's concealing hood. Hair as black as a raven's wing spilled from beneath it to lie on the snow-white robe. There was something familiar about the odd lilt in her silky-smooth voice.

"She saw the way," the woman continued. "She found the qaraz. What right did we have to stop her? No one stopped you, Brother Elias."

The man in the scarlet robe chuckled softly. "True, Lady Diamond. But my boldness came with a price, did it not?"

"Yes. A badly-woven tale," the green warrior said, grimacing. "At least you survived it to reach a so-called 'treasure', brother. The rest of us met rather ignominious ends."

"At least you died in dignified resignation," the blue-robed man added petulantly. "I went kicking and screaming."

"It was my idea to cross the Fields in the first place," Brother Elias said. "Of course, I was the hero. And you two had to die. It was a cautionary tale, after all. A warning to those who might follow in our footsteps."

"Wait. Are you claiming to be the Brazen Monk?" Matteo exclaimed, agog, his eyes leaping from one of them to the other. "And his doomed companions? Alive? After all this time?"

"Ah, good." Brother Elias clapped his hands, pleased. "You know the tale!"

"Know it?" He exchanged a look with his equally astonished brother. "I think we just lived it," he added faintly.

Shade stared at the old man, shocked. It was impossible. The tale was over a hundred years old. This had to be another trick. But she recalled the characters from the tale: a fallen monk, a disgraced nobleman and a forsworn knight. The Glass Fields was a place of strange and unpredictable magics. And yet…

"I don't believe you," Shade said, frowning. "And I've had enough of your trickery. If you're trying to confuse me, well done, but it doesn't dissuade me from my goal. I am meant to be here. Meant to find my way beyond the mountains. Try and stop me at your own peril!"

Brother Elias snorted, his thick white eyebrows drooping over his eyes like fuzzy caterpillars. He shook his head. "You cannot force your way into the Last Bastion, young woman."

She bared her teeth in a smile. "Why don't we find out, good brother?"

"I see you haven't changed, Shade Nox," the woman said, her voice still teasingly familiar.

Shade glared at her. "Do I know you?" she demanded, frowning, a strange sensation crawling across her skin. Her breath quickened and sweat dampened her brow, cold and clammy. That voice…

"Of course, you do, my dear." Lady Diamond threw back

her hood, at last, revealing a face both young and beautiful. She was smiling wryly, a twist of pink, perfect lips that were oh, so familiar. "I see you finally crawled over the Glass Fields to find me."

Shade's knees buckled, and she landed on the soft, moist earth, the blood draining from her face, leaving her skin chilled. The world swam in her gaze. She feared she might faint. Light-headed, stunned, she managed one, strangled word, *"Satine."*

CHAPTER SEVENTEEN

Night fell across the Glass Fields while Shade grappled with her shock, plunging them into the deepest darkness. Light flared suddenly, and she blinked, her eyes watering against the brilliant glow emanating from Satine's palm. Beside her, Matteo let out a low curse. Angelo took her by the arm to help her rise, but he kept his eyes on the others. Tension ran through both of them, and they flanked her protectively. She barely noticed. Her thoughts raced in the same circle: *Satine, Satine, Satine.*

Behind the blue glow flickering atop her palm, Satine smiled at her, a small, secretive smile. It made Shade's belly tighten unexpectedly. Satine's amber eyes gleamed, reflecting the strange fire. Shade rubbed her eyes, unsure she could trust them. Was this really Satine? For all her skill as a tattoo master, Satine had never exhibited any bloodmagic, had never carried any blades. Her smooth, pale skin had been free of wards, as well. Yet now, blue fire was dancing on her hand.

Faces turn from me, what is happening?

The glow from the tiny flame expanded, pushing back the darkness surrounding them. The glass trees sparkled at the edges of the clearing, strangely beautiful in the eerie light.

"We lingered too long," the blue-robed man said, frowning. Fear had crept into his voice. He peered at the looming forest, his hands sneaking inside his robe. "We won't reach the Bastion tonight."

"We are perfectly safe," the green warrior said. "You are always jumping at shadows, Lord Azure."

Lord Azure frowned. "Shadows have a way of killing you in this place, Sir Julian. We've all seen it happen."

"I have set the circle of protection," Satine said. She tossed the ball of fire into the air. It stopped above their heads and hovered there benignly. "Nothing will harm us."

Shade eyed the blue flames – anything to take her gaze off Satine; it *was* Satine, after all this time – and wondered what kind of wizard crafted fire without gemstone blades, or drawn blood, or protective wards. She gripped her blades. Matteo moved closer to her, his hard eyes on Satine, while Angelo turned slightly, his hand going back to his hip to rest on a hilt. She felt their rising edginess, their blooming suspicion.

"What is she?" Matteo whispered. "You know her. Is she… is she one of the Kindred?"

"I thought she was," Shade muttered. "But now, I'm not so sure. I've never seen such magic. I–" and she made a small sound of frustration. "It's invisible to me."

It was true. She couldn't sense the fire above them, only see it. Their bloodmagic was elemental, but this fire was invisible to them. Her gaze settled on Satine again, Matteo's question echoing in her head: what *is* she?

"You are not one of the Kindred." Shade jammed her blades into their sheaths – they wouldn't do her any good anyway. "You only pretended to be one of them. What in the lowest hells are you, Satine?"

"I am one of the last of my kind," she said softly, a look of sadness on her fair face. "The Kindred keep our secrets for us as they have since the Final Battle. They are the only Golondrina tribe allowed into our sanctuary. Sometimes we travel among them to the outside world, seeking signs of our enemies. Those we could not contain. They are few and they have learned how to hide. They use humans to do their bidding, possessing them from afar. We hunt down these avatars when we can, quietly eliminating them, but we never engage their masters. We have no desire to renew any sort of war between us. We must fight them in other ways." She fixed Shade with a firm gaze, smiling her secret smile again. "Sometimes, we find treasures hidden in the land, and we feel compelled to take greater risks. But, it's best the people of this land believe we are gone from the world."

"What are you?" Shade repeated, practically growling the words through her clenched teeth. She remembered this about Satine. The woman had always spoken in riddles. At the time, she had thought it mysterious, enigmatic. Now, she just found it annoying. She had risked too much and come too far for mysteries. "I dared the Glass Fields seeking the Kindred," she said, her anger growing. She took a step toward Satine. "I sought their help in the first place because I thought one of their own had aided me once. They refused to deal with me, and now I understand why. You aren't one of their tattoo masters. You're… I don't know what you are."

"Are you dense as well as arrogant?" asked Sir Julian disdainfully.

Shade glared at him. He was big, and he carried strong blades from what she sensed, but she felt confident she could squash him if she chose.

"Lady Diamond is a Sicani, my child," Brother Elias said gently.

"A Sicani?" Shade frowned, rounding on Satine again. Her eyes narrowed. "Are you completely mad? Or just a liar? All the Sicani are dead!"

Satine said nothing, only gazed at her with one delicate eyebrow lifted. The blue flame overhead pulsed hypnotically, casting strange shadows across the grass. Brother Elias cleared his throat pointedly as he raised his eyes to the shell of protection covering them.

"If you are trying to convince me you are one of the legendary Sicani, you have to do more than toss a shiny blue ball into the air."

Brother Elias threw his head back, laughing.

"She's a hard one to impress!" Azure said, scowling.

"Yes," growled Sir Julian. "Why not blast her to bits, Lady Diamond? That might convince her."

Angelo and Matteo both dropped into fighting stances at Julian's threat, drawing their blades. "Try it, try anything," Matteo said, smiling a wolf's smile.

"She won't hurt me," Shade said. Matteo glanced at her, and reluctantly sheathed his blades. Angelo followed a second later, though doubt and suspicion clouded his eyes. He threw her a side-long glance. "Are you so sure, lady witch?" he asked.

Satine's laughter was like a tinkle of bells in the clearing. "Lady witch? Oh, I like that, I like that very much."

Shade bristled. "What game are you playing? It's no accident you were here, waiting for me. Are you working with the Coterie? Trying to force me to do their bidding?"

Satine's expression darkened. "The Coterie has their own agenda. They think they carry on the interests of the Sicani, but they do not. They are agents of chaos. They would see the whole world burn to destroy our ancient enemy. We do not agree with their tactics."

"And what are the Sicani," Shade countered, feeling a need to be cruel, "but a dead people?"

"Watch your tongue, child," snapped Lord Azure. "The Sicani sacrificed themselves to save this land. We are to blame for what befell them."

"Blame? What blame do I bear? I was born long after their war destroyed this land. And now you're telling me the Sicani aren't gone, that they're hiding in some secret sanctuary while the land falls to blight?" Her hands curled into fists. "I came here seeking the Kindred, seeking a place for the creation of a new Veil. My dreams led me here. A vision I could not ignore, a vision sent by the Four and the Hidden as far as I know. Not even all the Sicani left in the world will stand in my way. Do you understand me?"

Satine was no longer smiling. "It was not the Four and the Hidden who sent you your vision, Shade. It was not the Faces of God haunting your dreams. It was me. I called you here."

Shade recoiled as if she'd been slapped. "You? You sent me my vision? You called me here?" The memory of Satine turning her away from the Kindred caravan flashed through her mind. An ache settled in her throat, humiliation as fresh as the day it happened coursing through her. Her face felt aflame. Grief and anger hoarsened her voice. "I would have followed you into the lowest hells if you'd asked. I came to you, and you *scorned* me! And then you torture me with visions and dreams? You cruel, scheming *bitch*."

Sir Julian growled low in his throat. Shade ignored him. Beside her, Matteo laid a hand on a blade hilt and ran a finger casually across his windpipe. The old warrior's expression didn't change, though a gleam entered his dark eyes. It almost seemed like approval.

"Why?" Shade said, tears stinging her eyes. She refused to let them fall. Not for Satine. Never again. "Why now and not then?"

Sympathy softened Satine's features. "You had your own path to follow. And it was not my place to bring you here, you had to be ready first." She lowered her voice. "This was never about us, Shade."

"Then what is it about? Tell me you sent me more than a lie, that my vision was real. Tell me this isn't just a vicious game!"

"It is not a game. I needed you to come to me so I could show you what to do. I needed your will to be strong for the trials to come." Satine held her gaze and her voice grew firm. "You bear powerful stones – I can feel them. Born from the bones of the earth and imbued with the ancient magic of our land, they contain vast wells of energy."

Shade laid a hand over her belt pouch as if to shield its precious cargo. Satine's tone had grown ominous.

"For centuries, the Brotherhood depended on such stones to raise their Veils, unaware that the true knowledge had been lost. I fear the Unseen worked among them to obscure and deceive and pervert the magic. If you were to raise your Veil on their stones, it would be weak. Or it would fail entirely, releasing devastation."

Shade bristled. "That can't be true. My father would never have misled me. He said my Veil would be strong because I am strong. He said the Brotherhood had grown weak and venal and wanted only power, not salvation. Why should I believe you over him?"

The blue fire flared above Satine's head, a sudden, raging globe. Beneath it, the black-haired woman seemed to grow larger, taller. Her white robes gleamed, and her amber eyes flashed. "My people created the Veils to save this land and we entrusted the Brotherhood with this sacred mission. They have failed in their duty. They have allowed themselves to be corrupted. The true way to create a Quattro Canto must be restored to someone who is uncorrupted, or the Wastes will continue to tip out of balance until everything is lost."

"And you think I am uncorrupted?" Shade scoffed. She clasped her blade hilts, mostly to hide the trembling in her hands. Satine's transformation had startled her. This was power she didn't understand. A strange dread began to fill her.

Satine shook her head. "Not like that. Uncorrupted by the demon Unseen. Trust me, I know you are not." Her bright eyes held Shade's and it felt as if she could see into her soul. Shade quailed at the scrutiny. She felt laid bare, and she did not like it.

"Show her, Lady Diamond," Brother Elias prompted. "Show her why you brought her here."

"Yes, show her," added Sir Julian gruffly. "I want to see if there is more to her than arrogance and bluster."

Matteo stiffened, and Angelo spat a curse. Shade was no less annoyed by the man's insult, but was gratified by her companions' reaction to it. Manoli and Petra would have reacted the same way. *Faces, Cyril, I wish you were here.* Her heart ached for her Golondrina friends, a sharp, sudden pain, and she touched the two men on the arms.

"Be easy," she said softly. "I'd rather have him eat his words than your fists."

A laugh burst from Angelo, and Matteo grinned. The tension flowed from them, but they remained alert.

Across the clearing, Satine had returned to her normal self, though Shade couldn't help but look at her askance. She beckoned her closer. "Come," she said. "Take my hands, Shade. See the truth."

Shade's heart leapt into thunder as she locked eyes with her old lover. Once, she had stared into those amber depths for hours, glad to be lost in their beauty. Her eyes were still beautiful, but she stared into them now with an edge of fear. Satine was a Sicani. A legend come to life.

Reluctantly, Shade approached Satine and grasped her hands, brutally suppressing the memories her touch rekindled. Her skin had always felt like silk.

Dante's skin had felt like silk beneath her hands, too, she recalled with sudden clarity. A rush of blood filled her cheeks, and she hoped Satine didn't think it was because of her. She lifted her chin to stare down her nose at her old lover. Satine's amber eyes trapped her, and she was swept into a golden light.

The gold faded to green. She stood alone on a gently sloping hill. In every direction lay green grass, towering trees, and clear streams. Turning slowly, she stared in wonder, amazed by the green and fertile land.

To the west, a line of black marred the horizon.

She went cold, her skin rising in gooseflesh. *A Blackstorm!* Hissing in a breath, she reached for her knife hilts. Only strange, soft fabric met her grasping hands. Her heart filled her throat, thumping madly, as she ran her hands over the simple red kirtle covering her torso. Soft, dark boots peaked from beneath the skirt, footwear unsuitable for Waste-walking.

This isn't the Wastes. Not yet. She looked up. The Blackstorm had grown closer, and now effaced the western horizon. It seemed big enough to swallow all of Malavita. It reached into the sky, looming as high as a mountain. Flashes of lightning burst across its boiling surface. The day darkened as it blotted out the sun.

This was no ordinary Blackstorm. Deep in her soul, she knew it was the First.

The First Blackstorm had laid waste to nearly half the island of Malavita, or so the scriptures claimed. Blackstorms were a continuing scourge. Their power threatened even the Veils, but now – *whenever* she was – there were no Veils.

Screaming broke the stillness. Shade turned and found a small collection of brightly painted wagons in the valley below her hilltop. Their dress was different and the wagons larger and more elaborate, but Shade knew them. The Golondrina. They huddled together, pathetically few. They had no idea what terrible power was descending on them. Her heart contracted with fear.

Stop. This happened long ago.

She turned away. The Blackstorm was almost upon her. Lightning speared the ground, tossing up great hunks of earth and sod. The wind howled like a thousand Waste beasts, whipping the trees into a frenzy. She felt nothing, untouched by lightning or wind. Her thumping heart slowed; she was only a witness to this horror.

The Storm hit the cowering clan, tearing apart their fragile wagons. She wondered why no one had blades, then cursed her own stupidity. They hadn't needed them, not yet.

The people on the edges were the first to be swept away. Dark shadows snaked from the storm cloud, snatching a woman from her husband's grasp, taking the screaming man a moment later. Some weren't taken at all but fell in writhing heaps only to rise as misshapen creatures with long fangs and sharp claws. They leapt on their neighbors, rending them with talons and gnashing teeth.

But a small group had managed to retreat into a stream feeding the valley. It kept the beasts off them and the worst of the storm. She started. Of course. A qaraz flowed beneath the stream. Even before the disastrous war, the Golondrina had worshipped the spirits of the qaraz. This day, it had saved at least a few of them.

Satine's voice spoke in her head:

"That was the beginning of the end. The First Blackstorm was caused by the Sicani's war with the Unseen. And while my people fought those demons, the people of this land fought to survive."

Shade felt the land shift. The green grass and verdant trees vanished, replaced by a land scorched and smoking. A different group of people struggled in what had once been a valley but was now a smoking patch of broken earth. She was dressed as they were – in tattered scraps more rags than clothing. Her feet were bare, the earth beneath them blackened.

The survivors of the land's breaking huddled around a man with a rose quartz knife. He gestured with the blade. Some of the people wept as a different man dragged a struggling child forward. A woman shrieked, and she tried to reach the small boy, but others held her back. Shade's heart constricted. It was this sort of foul bloodmagic which had caused the rise of the Unseen in the first place.

The man had raised his blade over the boy's chest. Shade opened her mouth to shout—

"NO!"

Startled, she snapped her lips closed. She hadn't screamed. Someone else had. Another man forced his way through the huddled mass. He wrenched the knife from the wielder and glared at his people in disdain. She couldn't hear what he said to them, but whatever it was made all of them hang their heads in shame. The man holding the child wept at his words. He let go of the boy, who scrambled back to his grateful mother. The second man laid a hand on the first's shoulder, holding his knife in limp fingers.

Suddenly, the first man lunged at him. They both grappled for the quartz knife. The first man prevailed, the one who would have murdered the child. Shade held her breath, waiting for him to go after the child again. Instead, shockingly, he plunged the knife into his own chest. Blood welled from the wound, staining the rags covering him, unleashing power.

With his last breath, the man directed the power he'd called. Even as he fell, dying, he pushed the magic away from him, manipulating it. He made a circle of protection with his mortal blood. A permanent circle.

A Veil, she realized with awe. A very primitive type of Veil, at least.

Born of death, of self-sacrifice.

Dread filled her. Satine had mentioned sacrifice. Was this the true way? Did she have to die to raise a Veil? No wonder the Brotherhood had abandoned the true magic. Who among those self-serving, powermongers would sacrifice himself for the good of all?

Could she?

Faces spit on me. She stared at the dead man, and the people sheltered by his sacrifice. All of this had been for nothing; she couldn't do this, she wouldn't–

"Wait. There is a sacrifice to be made, a price for such magic, but not necessarily death."

"What then?" Shade said, speaking to the broken land. "I have always been willing to die fighting. But I won't sacrifice myself like a lamb to the slaughter. There has to be another way."

"There is, impatient one." Satine's chuckle was a feather brush down her spine.

The charred, smoldering ruins vanished, replaced by flat,

open marshes. The grasses here were sickly yellow and gray green. The water pooling in depressions among the weeds looked black as sludge. She could hear surf in the distance and spun in a slow circle until she found the ocean to the east.

The vast, endless water glistened bright blue until it washed onto the shore. There it rolled in red, frothy waves, swelling and receding. Shade knew where she was, at least. Someday, this would be the Golden Crescent, home to the oldest and strongest Veils in Malavita.

There. Humans. Not far from her. These people were not struggling villagers. There were no women or children, just men. Five men in all. One wore a simple white tunic and leather trousers. His long, dark hair hung loose to his shoulders, framing a remarkably handsome face. She could see that his eyes were a deep amber, just like Satine's. He had no blades, no knife belt, no weapons of any kind. The other men, tattooed and dressed in simple woolen kilts and crude knife belts, stood in a ring around him listening intently as he spoke and gestured.

She could hear him, but she didn't understand his language. Those golden eyes and uncommon beauty marked him as a Sicani. The others had to be the descendants of the previous groups. Those who had survived had mingled their blood with the ancient Sicani, she knew, producing a new kind of wizard.

The four bloodwizards carried blades. One each, slightly curved, and long like those the Brotherhood wore. She noticed amulets at their throats, too, each quartered with white, red, green and blue stones. The blades in their hands were crudely fashioned, like the relics in some Brotherhood citadels. One man held garnet, the other tanzanite, the third peridot, and the fourth quartz. All of them together could yield all Four Faces, but each alone was relatively weak.

The Sicani finished speaking and raised his hands to the sky. He began to glow a soft blue. The light spread outward to encompass the men. First, the garnet-wielder drew blood, slashing open his chest, slashing across a tattoo of an open rose. Shade felt the air grow hot.

So, she was meant to feel this. Why now?

The tanzanite-wielder called his magic next. Water. The air grew heavy. Sweat dripped down her skin. Luckily, Shade was dressed in her own clothes, though she had no blades. She clenched her teeth and ignored the flip in her belly. Focus. She knew she needed to not only see this but feel it. This was what she'd come to learn.

Next, the quartz-wielder drew from his thigh, striking deep. Blood dripped down his leg. The few tattoos adorning it came alight. Shade's hands closed uselessly on the air – air now dense as water. It was a struggle to breathe. The men working magic heaved and sweated as she did, but they did not stop. The Sicani at their center had his eyes closed, his face lifted skyward, his hands still reaching toward the sun.

At last, the peridot-wielder added his blood to the mix. Through her sandals, she felt the earth tremble. A booming sounded in the center of this rising maelstrom. Like the thud of a giant heartbeat, the magic pulsated with it.

She felt it when the Sicani added his magic: Spirit, the Hidden Face.

A dome of light enveloped the group, and the Sicani threw his arms out to the sides, palms facing away from him. The dome expanded, engulfing Shade, pushing across the marshes in all directions. The far side moved over the ocean.

And there it stopped. Most of the newborn Veil lay over the land, perhaps a mile in circumference if she had to guess. The edges were blurry where they touched the earth.

Amazed, Shade turned back to the wizards, her heart thudding rapidly. It wasn't over yet. She could feel the power building between the four men. A stabbing pain lanced her gut. She doubled over, gasping, and heard the same gasps from four throats. Fighting the debilitating agony, she looked up, blinking back tears. The pain lessened, thankfully, grew distant as if she were only feeling an echo of it.

The four wizards had no such relief. They shrieked and dropped to the ground, writhing in pain, losing all control of their limbs and blades. She watched in horror, breathing shallowly against her own pain, as one by one they sank their blades into their own guts, moving the hilts as if digging for something. Their screams made her ill. What in the name of the Four were they doing to themselves?

The Sicani shouted something. Encouragement? His voice was strong, steady. The men's frantic motions grew more controlled, the burrowing blades more directed.

Tanzanite wrenched his blade free first, and then plunged his fingers into the hole left behind. His teeth were clenched, his lips pulled back in a grimace, but he curled his head forward so he could see what he sought.

After an eternity, he withdrew his fingers. Pinched between them was a bright blue gem. Shade knew it was a sapphire by its color and quality. It was huge – the size of a robin's egg. Once it was free, the wound in his side began to close, and she saw that he'd plunged his knife through a tattoo. The ward would save him, thankfully. But, by the Faces, what agony he'd endured for–

She gasped. A cornerstone!

This is the sacrifice a bloodwizard must make for a true Quattro Canto.

The others had also retrieved gems from their living flesh. A diamond, an emerald, a ruby. Priceless, enormous, cut and polished. They floated in the air before them, spinning gently. The men swayed with shock and exhaustion. Each looked diminished somehow, thinner, weaker. The Sicani gazed upon them, his eyes gleaming. He gestured with one hand and the stones that each man had produced flew to him. Again, the nascent bloodwizards called their respective magics, spilling blood with dangerous rapidity. The stones merged into one great ball of light, pulsing like a living heart, drawing power from their creators.

Shade watched, feeling the pain and exhaustion the others felt. The men stayed standing, fighting against the blood loss, calling power like nothing she'd ever seen. She could hardly believe what she was witnessing. The cost of this terrible magic was immense. Light streamed from the stones, a blinding radiance. She had to close her eyes against it.

And when she could open her eyes again, she beheld a glorious sight. The men were gone, but the cornerstones remained. Bound together, four as one, in a setting of light. Each massive stone took up a quarter of the whole, pulsing with color and depth: diamond, emerald, ruby, and sapphire. It settled on the ground like the first stone of a new building. Shade recognized it, feeling dazed. A Quattro Canto. The heart of a Veil. Its anchor and foundation.

It pulsed with light, and the dome overhead pulsed in response, a sheen of red spreading across its surface. Her heart began to beat in rhythm to the Veil's pulse. She felt connected to it in ways she never had to any Veil. In awe, and a growing horror, she realized the price those men had paid, the price she must pay if she wanted to succeed: the Veil contained a part of their souls, they were tied to it. Leashed.

Panic made her breath short, and she fought against the rising tide, cold sweat standing on her forehead and upper lip. A wizard was bound to the Veil he raised. Even unto death. Every Quattro Canto resided in the crypt of the Brotherhood priests who'd created it. Holy places, sacred and revered men. Buried in their own prisons.

"Faces spare me this," Shade whispered. The world spun around her. Shifted.

Golden eyes stared at her. Shade yanked her hands from Satine's grasp, stumbling backwards, her legs weak and trembling. Hands grabbed her, held her up.

"Lady! Be calm. Shade!"

She stared at Angelo, clutching his arms, at first not recognizing him. Where was she? *When* was she?

His brow was creased in concern. "You're safe," he said softly.

Shade let out a guttural sob. "The price is too high," she said, tears blurring her vision. "Too high…"

"Do you still think she is the one to fight for us?" Lord Azure said bitterly.

"Quiet, Azure," snapped Sir Julian. He was standing on the other side of her, helping Angelo hold her upright. Her own legs didn't seem to be working. "It is a high price to pay for even the bravest souls."

"She needs time," Brother Elias said. "And rest. Perhaps, come morning…?"

Only Satine remained silent, watching her. Shade could feel her regard. Like hot coals on her skin. She shuddered, trying to shake off the memory of pain, and worse, the memory of being tethered.

"Should we still take her to the Last Bastion, Lady Diamond?" Sir Julian asked. His hands were warm on her, and surprisingly gentle. "What if the Elders–"

"There is no going back through the Glass Fields from here. We have to bring them to the Last Bastion," Satine said. "I will deal with the Elders. There will be no hiding them once we leave the Glass Fields." She paused, her voice dropping. "I had so hoped…"

Shade pulled away from the men helping her. Dashing the tears from her eyes, she faced Satine. In a voice roughened by sobs and exhaustion, she spoke. "I said the price was too high. I never said I wouldn't pay it."

CHAPTER EIGHTEEN

The grand ballroom of Bishop Arturious's palace swirled with Malavita's elite. Finely dressed men wore blades in ornate sheaths with cutouts in the leather to expose the type of gemstone. All members of their families wore corresponding gems sewn into their clothing, stacked on their fingers, or dropped like stars in their hair. The lower the gemstone, the more ostentatious the exhibition, it seemed.

Tattoos, on the other hand, were kept hidden by the nobility. Not all the guests were noble, however, and those men of lesser blood wore garments which displayed their impressive ink. Some even chose to go bare-chested, strutting like proud peacocks across the ballroom floor. They seemed almost primitive next to their well-dressed fellows, but the highborn kept any disdain well hidden. The Capomaji, for all that they were criminals, held power in Malavita.

Dressed in his Imperial uniform, crimson jacket heavy with braids and medals, Raiden stood out among the guests even more than the Capos and their skulking Corsaro. Slender, his straight black hair cut short in military-fashion, his skin a few shades darker than even a Golondrina's on a beardless face with high, fine cheekbones, Raiden was an obvious foreigner in this insular nation, a nation which had an unfortunate history with invaders. He was also the son of an emperor. All eyes found their way to him, and the guests either displayed bald curiosity, venal speculation, or open contempt.

Positioned at the foot of the bishop's dais, flanked by the Noble Guard, Raiden could almost pretend he was attending his father at an Imperial banquet. But the strangeness of the people, and the many stares he was collecting, put the lie to his fantasy. He was here on display, not to serve his duty. An Emperor's son, a man of influence and power – supposedly. A man at the bishop's beck and call. He'd been allowed to carry his sword, at least. It added another exotic element to him since no one in Malavita bothered with swords.

Since his conversation with the Brother Jacobis, he had been even more eager to quit this place, and this farcical grand feast in his honor only added to his frustration and impatience. He felt like an exotic animal, similar to those on display in the Imperial menagerie. Arturious sat above him on the dais, and the steady line of guests ascending the steps to kiss his rings gawked at him as they passed.

The bishop wore his finest robes, and an elaborately decorated miter towered on his head, resplendent with gold and jewels. The wealth of the Brotherhood church was on full display, and Raiden assumed it was for his benefit. It was more pathetic than impressive. The Emperor exuded power dressed in even the simplest garments, and his banquets were the height of sophisticated simplicity. By comparison, this feast was a circus.

Raiden didn't hide his contempt. He peered down his nose at everyone seeking the bishop's favor. The guests noticed, and their glances and whispers were filled with consternation. It was a small win, but it was all he had.

Soon, he grew bored being on display. None of the guests dared approach him. Even the Capos merely eyed him challengingly rather than engaging him in conversation. Raiden scowled. To all those in attendance, he was the bishop's guest, not his prisoner. A guest was free to move about wherever he chose. He plucked a glass of wine from the tray of a passing servant and stalked away from the crowded dais, creating a ripple as guests moved out of his path. He gripped the stem of his wine glass like he might use it as a club and ducked through an archway into the gallery along the west side of the ballroom. Tapestries graced the walls of the long promenade, along with plinths holding busts of previous bishops. Alcoves with padded benches and tall, lead-paned windows provided a welcome retreat from the crowded ballroom. A few guests strolled along the gallery, admiring the art or taking advantage of the semi-private seats.

Relatively alone, he sat on an empty bench. The lead-paned window was open and the scent of jasmine and gardenia tickled his nostrils. Beyond the walled gardens, he could see the city below, ablaze with a thousand torches. His glass trembled in his hand as he leaned toward freedom, but he knew the Noble Guard still watched, and the Ruby Pontifex patrolled the gardens. He would have to kill a hundred men to–

"Good evening, captain."

The pleasant greeting pulled him back from the window, and he raised his glass to his lips, pretending he hadn't been startled. He schooled his features before turning to greet the man behind him.

A man without a coat.

His tattooed torso shone softly in the dim light, swirling with flames and rampant dragons. Golden armbands encircled impressive biceps and a heavy torq lay around his neck, its ends capped with sapphires. He wore fine black trousers and tall boots rather than the armored skirt and sandals of a Corsaro soldier, but an elaborately tooled leather belt bearing twin blades spanned his narrow waist. He was smiling, but his hands rested on the hilts of his blades.

"Good evening, lord…?" Raiden said, raising an eyebrow.

"Valentine," he said. "Errenzo Valentine. And I'm no lord."

Valentine. Raiden stiffened as the man took the bench across from him. He moved fluidly, dangerously. Two other figures lurked in the shadows nearby. Dressed in battle gear, not formal wear. Corsaro.

"I've been trying to make your acquaintance for some time, Imperial," Valentine said, making himself comfortable.

His relaxed pose didn't put Raiden at ease; this man had tried to kidnap him. Gray shot through his dark hair and fine lines framed his eyes and lips, but he was well-muscled and lithe. A man in his prime. Raiden gave the Corsaro soldiers a sidelong glance and shifted to make his sword easier to draw.

"Now, now, we're all friends, aren't we?"

"In my country, friends don't try to kidnap each other." Anger simmered beneath his words, and his fingers tightened on the stem of his wine glass.

"Ah, yes, I take full responsibility for our earlier... missteps."

"Missteps? Is that what you call blatantly attacking me and my companions? Did you really think such an ill-conceived plot would win you any favors with the Empire? As I told your men, my father would have seen this entire land razed to the ground if you'd managed to kidnap me. You could have captured the heir to his throne and gotten the same treatment. We do not bargain with criminals."

Valentine eyed him shrewdly. "Only witches," he said, never losing his smirk. "And now bishops, as well, I understand."

"With whom I do business is none of your concern."

Valentine raised a hand, gesturing with two fingers. One of his men appeared from the shadows with a small glass of spirits. The Capo accepted it without taking his eyes off Raiden. "You pretend your Empire is incorruptible, yet you auction off royal charters on a whim," he said. "How much did Safire pay your Emperor for his?"

"We do not auction royal charters," Raiden said, insulted at the implication. "Dante Safire earned his charter through loyal service to the Empire. If you or any of your fellows choose to give us a year of service, you might earn a reward yourself."

Valentine's eyes glittered in the shadows, and his free hand slipped to a knife hilt, tightening subtly. "I would sooner spend a year in the lowest hells than serve your Empire." He waved his glass beneath his nostrils, inhaling sharply but never taking his gaze from Raiden. "And as for royal charters up for auction, what do you think the purpose of this feast is?"

Raiden blinked, taken aback. "What do you mean?"

A look of glee brightened his face. "Ah, you actually didn't know, did you?" He chuckled and sipped from his glass of golden liquor. "This feast is in your honor nominally, but the real purpose is for Arturious to announce an end to the moratorium on Veils. He made sure all the First Families, the merchant class, and the Capomaji learned there was a prize to be had: an Imperial charter granting rights to a new Veil. For such a prize, the strongest of the strong will go to war. The streets will run with blood. Innocents will die for their greed, and I will stand aside and watch. In the end, you see, it will belong to me. That is the way of Malavita."

For a moment, Raiden couldn't speak. The bishop was going to offer a royal charter? One that didn't even exist, and for a Veil they wouldn't dare raise? To what end?

"There is no royal charter for sale," he said at last. "It's a lie."

Valentine shrugged dismissively and rose. "A lie is more powerful than the truth, Imperial. And a war built on a lie just as deadly. Enjoy the feast."

For a time, Raiden didn't move, his pulse racing and his breath hard and fast in his chest. Arturious would start a war over the promise of a new Veil? A Veil that would never be raised. The true depth of Arturious's cunning and duplicity struck him like a brick. The contenders would fight for the hope of land and gems in a country where such things were rigidly controlled. A new Veil in the Deep Wastes would give access to potential riches. And the Brotherhood would sit back and bask in bribes and tributes while their flock murdered one another for the chance to profit most.

He couldn't let Arturious continue this deception. The Empire wouldn't stand idly by and let one of their colonies devolve into an internecine war. They would intervene with their full might to squash it. All involved would face a terrible reckoning. And one criminal witch might be rounded up in that reckoning. He doubted the next Imperial soldier to cross her path would be so reluctant to put her in a hangman's noose.

Drawing a deep breath, Raiden took one last look out the open window, and returned to the bishop's ballroom like a soldier marching to war.

Dante watched Raiden Mad emerge from the gallery while he refilled the wine glass of a city-prince he'd hunted with more times than he could count – who nevertheless looked right through him in his servant's livery with his clean-shaven face – and wondered how he'd be able to warn him help was near. Manoli and Petra moved through the crowd as well, having masqueraded as servants nearly the whole time Raiden had been held at the bishop's palace. Neither one of them had managed to infiltrate the army of servants tending the Imperial emissary, however, to their frustration.

Unfortunately, none of them were allowed near the high table either. Arturious had his own personal attendants, all scrutinized by priests concealed in hooded black robes. They moved with far deadlier grace than the ostentatious Noble Guard. Ruby Pontifex. It added a new wrinkle to their plans, but there wasn't much to be done for it. He wondered if Raiden realized he was surrounded by those elite assassins, and then shook his head at his own stupidity. Of course Raiden knew.

His only hope was Raiden would realize rescue had come when Korin and Cyril started their commotion outside among the guests' carriages and horses. In the ensuing chaos, they should be able to reach him and lead him into the gardens where Manoli had found an abandoned postern gate in the high wall days ago.

Trumpets announced the start of the feast, and Dante made his way to the edges of the ballroom while the guests took their seats. There was a seat for Raiden to the left of Arturious, and he marched to it stoically. In his crimson uniform with its sparkling medals and gold braid, he cut an impressive figure.

Dante took a place against the wall among the other servants, waiting for the service to begin. He tried not to fidget with impatience. His blades were tucked into his boots, well-hidden, but they called to him. It would be oh-so-satisfying to interrupt this tedious event with violence.

Soon, Petra sidled up beside him, a tray tucked beneath his arm. An exuberant smile played about his lips and his cheeks were flushed. He and his cousin were enjoying this immensely. Dante envied him; he felt nothing but a queasy suspense.

The feast began: course followed course, each more elaborate than the last, in a well-coordinated dance of dozens of servants and kitchen staff. A simple, soft-boiled quail egg started the feast, a dollop of shiny black fish roe adorning it, a dish of fried lark wings followed slathered in a shimmering, red sauce. A course of sweet ice led into a course of bitter greens tossed in tart vinegar and honey. Meat courses followed the greens and a flight of vegetable dishes which ranged from tender pea shoots to earthy mushrooms each with complementary sauces. Savory sweetbreads led to roasted veal, and after that Dante was hard-pressed to identify the type of animal he was serving. The sauces and presentations grew more elaborate and varied, and different libations were offered with each course. He gave each guest healthy pours when it was his duty to serve the drinks. Let them all get drunk.

The crowd grew raucous with each subsequent course, losing themselves in the abundance of food and drink. Only after the fifth sweet course did the dishes finally cease to flow from the kitchens. Grateful for the reprieve, Dante took his place at the wall and sagged against it. It had never occurred to him how hard it was to serve. He'd forgotten to be worried about his peers recognizing him after an hour into the feast. Not one had made eye contact and he'd been too busy to care. Beside him, Petra grinned. "Not as easy as it looks, eh?"

Dante grimaced. "My people always made it appear effortless."

"That's the hardest part..."

People began to rise from the tables, and the army of servants rallied again to clear the tables and benches away, leaving a grand space for dancing and entertainment. Dante took the opportunity to slip into the gallery and make his way closer to the bishop's table while the musicians, who'd played softly throughout the entire meal, struck up a lively tune. Many of the younger partygoers squealed and shouted with delight as they took to the floor. The bishop and his entourage, including Raiden, remained seated. The bishop was smiling and clapping his hands along to the music. Every so often he would lean over and make a comment to Raiden who sat beside him, stiff-backed and expressionless.

Suddenly, during an energetic round, the bishop stood and tapped the stem of his wine glass with a silver fork. He may as well have blasted a trumpet; the music died in a discordant jangle, the dancers whirled to a halt, and all eyes turned to Bishop Arturious.

"Greetings, my blessed children," he said, speaking at a conversational level, though his voice reached every remote corner and dark alcove of the vast ballroom. Dante felt the familiar tingle of bloodmagic, and knew he'd used air currents to magnify his voice. "Welcome to my home. I have gathered you all here to celebrate a grand occasion. The Bhaskar Empire has sent to us a royal son, a treasured son, in the hopes that our land will become strong again, and free of blight."

A rising excitement rippled through the crowd.

"For this son brings a gift." He smiled, his arms wide in benediction. "At long last, after so many of our overlords have denied us our sacred right to raise new Veils, the Emperor Suijin has given me a charter granting land and mining rights to anyone brave enough to take a chance on a new life. Our long-suffering is at an end."

He paused portentously and the entire room held its breath. "Malavita will have a new Veil!"

CHAPTER NINETEEN

Exclamations of disbelief, wonder, and excitement erupted in the ballroom. The bishop continued to smile benevolently – triumphantly. A Veil meant arable land, safe access to valuable mineral and gemstone mines. It meant new opportunity in the blighted Wastes.

"And who gets this Veil charter?" demanded a highborn lord from the crowd, Prince Lucian. Though he carried only garnet, he was a man of wealth and influence. His family claimed three Veils, though the Capomajus Victorious took a sizable chunk in tribute and the Brotherhood collected its substantial tithe, as well. Nevertheless, the income from those three Veils had kept his family powerful for centuries. "Or are you keeping it for yourselves?"

Arturious shook his head. "The Brotherhood claims ownership only of the Southern Veils, the Veils which produce our most sacred stones." He gave them all an oily smile. "The stones used in the creation of your holy blades, my most blessed children. For this new Veil, we will provide the land, of course, and we will raise it, but it will belong to whoever wins the charter. It is our sacred duty to raise Veils, not to gain wealth."

Dante glanced around the grand hall with an ironic lift to one eyebrow. Apparently, wealth was just a happy by-product of their "sacred duty". Not a few of the other highborn had the same look on their faces. The Brotherhood church was exempt from Imperial taxes, as long as they only collected income through tithing. And they dominated the trade of their "sacred" gemstones. His gaze returned to Raiden. Had he really given Arturious a royal charter? What good would another Brotherhood Veil do the Empire? The church would keep iron control over any gems it produced.

"Then it should go to the families that have governed Malavita's Veils since they were first raised," added Prince Diamante. Of course, *he* would say that; his family owned the Veil which held Sicaria and some of the most fertile land in Malavita. He claimed, often and loudly, he could trace his family back to the First Veil. "One of the First should have the charter!"

"You already own all the Veils in the land," cried a well-dressed merchant outfitted in a rainbow of gemstones and platinum jewelry. "Give the rest of us a chance to claim our piece of Malavita! My family has been here as long as yours. They just didn't murder their way into power!"

Prince Diamante, and several others, shouted in angry denial, inciting the merchant folk to scream insults in return until the whole grand hall erupted into cacophony. Dante watched Arturious's eyes narrow and a slight smile touch his lips before he put on an expression of dismay and called for silence. His voice boomed over the chaos, cracking like thunder. A collective gasp took all the air from the room, and quiet followed.

"You all have a right to this charter," Arturious said. "Whoever proves most worthy will be granted the cornerstones needed for the Quattro Canto. The Brotherhood will work the magic as we have since the First Veil was raised. Tomorrow, we will hear claims for the charter from appropriate candidates." Smiling, Arturious took his seat and gestured to the musicians to resume playing. "Now, please, enjoy the ball!"

This last was lost in the renewed arguments and hurled insults. The highborn and the merchant class were too busy eyeing one another to pay attention to the music. Dante watched the scheming begin among the crowd, watched the guests take sides, and understood at last why Arturious had done this. The Church would dangle the charter like a prize and feed the competition for it. Lords and merchants would beggar themselves for the chance at a new Veil, and the Brotherhood would reap only reward.

And by the dark look set on Raiden's face, he'd figured it out, as well. Arturious was using him. Dante moved closer to the dais, slipping from archway to archway. He had to get near Raiden; he was running out of time. Cyril and Korin would launch their plan soon and light the incendiaries Cyril had been collecting and concealing in the bishop's own stables. The method of attack had given Dante grim satisfaction, but he'd made sure the two would clear the place of horses first. A fire would distract the Noble Guard and the palace staff, but the Ruby Pontifex lurking in the shadows wouldn't be so easily distracted.

Suddenly, Raiden rose to his feet. Arturious, looking startled, grasped Raiden by the arm and hissed something at him. With a shake of his wrist, Raiden broke his grip and hoisted himself onto the table, knocking over goblets and sending them crashing to the floor, his face a mask of fury.

It took a moment for the guests to notice him standing there, but when they did all eyes fixed on him. Conversations and arguments faded to curious whispers. Dante paused behind a column. His heart thudded against his breastbone. What was he doing?

"I am Captain Raiden Mad of the Bhaskar Empire, seventh son of Emperor Suijin, may He live forever, former Commander of the Imperial Guard, and Imperial Emissary to Prince Dante Safire! My word is my life, and I cannot condone these lies your bishop spews!" He paused, his fierce gaze sweeping the room. "There is no royal charter to be sold to the highest bidder. There will be no new Veil!"

His ringing statement was greeted with an angry chorus of demands and curses. Behind Raiden, Arturious had risen to his feet and was gesturing to the Noble Guard as he retreated from the table. Dante hissed a curse. If they took Raiden into custody, how would they ever get him out?

"We never forbade the Brotherhood from raising new Veils!" Raiden shouted above the angry mob, his hand outstretched to quell their anger. "That was a lie! Everything the Brotherhood has told you for a century has been a lie. Their magic has failed them. The Brotherhood can no more raise a Veil than I can! You will fight over an imaginary piece of paper, and the Church will bleed you dry in reward!"

The cries from the crowd became dismayed, confused. Doubt rippled among them, and eyes began to turn toward Arturious. Their voices rose and their mood changed. A threat of violence rippled through the ballroom.

"The church's sacred mission is to cleanse the land of the Unseen's blight!" Arturious cried from where he hid behind his guards, his magic-enhanced voice thundering over the cries of the crowd. "We alone have kept you safe from the Blackstorms and the Wastes. But we have been chained by foreign dogs for a century. The Bhaskar Empire is benevolent. They have chosen to reward us, but I fear their emissary has fallen under dark influences."

Raiden spun toward him, the table shaking under his feet, one hand on his sword hilt. "I will not let you deceive these people! They will hear the truth."

Raiden's words were faint; Dante could barely hear him from the gallery. He doubted many of the grumbling crowd heard him either. And at the mention of "dark influences" they began to eye Raiden with suspicion. He wouldn't be the first Imperial who'd come to Malavita only to be warped by the blight.

Ignoring Raiden – though he kept himself behind his wall of Noble Guard – the bishop rose above the ground on magic, his arms spread beseechingly to his audience. "I should have suspected it from the beginning. He has spent time in the company of the Black Witch! She has twisted his heart with her foul influence."

At the mention of the Black Witch a collective gasp of horror took the air from the ballroom. Dante gritted his teeth and stepped from the gallery. There was no sneaking away quietly now. They'd have to fight their way out.

On the dais, Bishop Arturious glared down at his guards. "Take him into custody! Now!" He fixed Raiden with a snarl, his voice no longer enhanced. "Perhaps you'll like an oubliette more than your suite, Imperial dog!"

Despite Arturious's orders, the guards held back, well out of reach of Raiden's sword. They were armed with jewel blades but had to be aware of Raiden's resistance to bloodmagic and his skill with a sword by now. None had drawn. Instead, they shuffled forward in half-steps, their ceremonial glaives before them like the bristles of a hedgehog. Snarling, Arturious made small gestures with both hands.

Dante felt magic unleashed from more than one spot in the vast ballroom. Power arrowed toward Raiden, a fierce wind. Knives rode its currents. Snatching his blades from his boots, Dante shouted a warning. "Behind you, captain!"

The wind struck Raiden first, but barely ruffled his hair. He was already turning, though, alerted by Dante's shout, his sword flashing. With preternatural speed, he swept several blades aside using steel and the flat of his hand. Only one managed to touch him, slicing a streak of blood along his cheek. Seeing him occupied, the Noble Guard found their courage and surged forward, their long weapons thrust low to tangle in his legs.

Dante shredded the sleeves of his uniform, his blue blades flashing as he ran toward the high table. He drew on the fire of the gilded lamps behind the Noble Guard, attacking their rear with roaring flames. They shrieked and scattered away from the heat, and it broke their charge on Raiden. The Imperial dashed down the table, knocking over goblets and dishes and sending the bishop's guests fleeing in panic. Those Noble Guard not scorched pursued him.

Drawing more blood, Dante called earth and lifted the stones beneath the floorboards. Wood splintered and shattered beneath their feet, sending the Noble Guard toppling. The thunder of pounding feet tore his attention from the dais. Backpedaling as more guardsmen charged down the gallery toward him, Dante slashed at his chest. Air slammed into the first ranks of the men, the rest bunching behind them as if they'd hit a wall. He would have laughed if he'd been able to spare a breath. Magical attacks burst from their ranks and Dante spent the next few draws countering them.

By now, the ballroom had erupted into chaos. Raiden had reached the end of the table and vaulted off it, twisting in midair like an acrobat before taking down two guardsmen with precision kicks. Another felt the kiss of his sword before his feet touched the ground. Their shrieks of pain were swallowed by the screams of several highborn ladies who subsequently fainted in dramatic fashion. The male highborn were slower to react; a few had drawn blades but seemed reluctant to get involved.

With Dante and Petra's interference, Raiden had a clear shot to the windows along the gallery. He disappeared into the promenade. Blades flashing, Dante covered his escape, yelling at Petra to follow him out. A screen of smoke and heat roared in a crescent between them and the rest of the room, forcing more guests to shrink back, screaming and shouting. Coughing and shielding his face, Dante fell back from the billowing hot cloud. The screen held back the Noble Guard, but a few figures in flowing black moved through it effortlessly.

Ruby Pontifex.

Wishing his friends luck, Dante ran.

* * *

The gardens were a tranquil pool compared to the chaos in the grand ballroom. Raiden blinked smoke from his eyes, wondering which way to run.

"Raiden! Here! To me."

It was Manoli. He was at the verge of a carefully tended hedge maze, gesturing frantically. His black uniform made him hard to see among the dark foliage, making Raiden all too aware of his own bright clothing. The crimson and gold made for poor camouflage in the moon-washed garden. He ducked into the maze after his friend.

After unerring twists and turns, Manoli led him out into a less-manicured part of the garden. There, Petra waited beneath the dark, waxy leaves of a fig tree, grinning.

"How did you beat us?" Manoli demanded, but Petra only shrugged. His eyes bright, he looked at Raiden. "That was bold!" he exclaimed. "The bishop will never forgive you for humiliating him."

"I hope he doesn't," Raiden said, breathless with excitement. "He won't get his war now, I suspect."

"Come on," Manoli said. "We have to leave the grounds before the Ruby Pontifex find us."

"What about Lord Safire? Should we wait for him?"

Petra shook his head. "Dante's drawing off pursuit, but don't worry about him. He has his own escape plan. You need to follow us."

Behind them, explosions rocked the palace and the sounds of screaming drifted to them on the breeze. Raiden grimaced as he chased after the cousins, feeling guilty for causing such chaos.

I stopped a greater war, at least—

From the shadows to his left, Raiden caught a glimpse of red. A flash, then gone. He hissed a warning to his friends. Alerted, Petra and Manoli slowed, their quartz blades drawn.

Another stirring. To his right this time. Not just movement. Blood had been drawn. Raiden moved, sidling sideways away from the buildup of heat. His natural immunity would protect him to an extent, but evasion was the best defense. Flames burst across his path, close enough to singe the hair on his knuckles. Raiden scrambled backwards, falling against the gnarled trunk of an olive tree. It knocked the wind from him, and he rolled to the side, gasping.

Light blazed all around them, torches and balls of fire illuminating the orchard. Manoli ran to Raiden and helped him up while Petra shielded them in a crouch. Men in hooded robes surrounded them, bearing torches or holding fire in their hands. Ruby Pontifex. They closed in on them, moving with purpose. Raiden readied his sword as Manoli stood back-to-back with Petra. They would have to fight their way out.

"Hold!"

The disembodied voice thundered from the darkness. The robed men startled, and their hidden faces swiveled, searching.

A man emerged into the light, a man with flame-red hair. Brother Jacobis.

"The bishop has no further use for the captain, and no desire to draw the ire of the Bhaskar Emperor. Stand down."

Slowly, they backed off, none speaking. Raiden licked his lips, not daring to hope Brother Jacobis was helping him. The red-headed priest had his own motives. Manoli and Petra pressed closer together, and Manoli hissed a low warning. An unnecessary warning.

"Do you control the Ruby Pontifex?" Raiden asked once the hooded priests had left. They took the light with them, but for a torch Jacobis held. "Why do they answer to you, brother?" He layered the address with disdain.

Jacobis approached him. "They answer to the man who trained them," he said.

So, another hidden layer – priest, fanatic, assassin. What did he want if not to drag him back to his master? But, Raiden knew.

"Now is your chance," Jacobis said softly, as if he'd read his mind, his eyes slipping to the Golondrina then back to Raiden. "And I'm willing to let you go to see it done. I trust you, Captain Mad, to do what is right."

"You'll just let us go, then? No one follows. No one stabs us in the back, from the dark?"

"No one follows. No one attacks you. You have my word."

In front of him, Manoli snorted softly. Jacobis glared at him, his lip curling in disdain. "Send the heathens away so we may speak as civilized men."

"Careful, brother. These heathens are my friends." Raiden stepped toward Jacobis slowly and lowered his weapon at the same time. "Now. We are going to walk out of here, and no one is going to stop us. Correct?"

Brother Jacobis nodded. "As I promised. But…before you leave, I want a private word with you." His narrowed gaze found the cousins. "Without them."

His hackles rose at the request, but Raiden feared it might be the only way to avoid a fight. He exchanged a look with Manoli and gave him a nod. The Golondrina didn't look pleased, but he took Petra by the arm and edged past Jacobis.

"There," Raiden said. "We're alone. What do you need to say to me?"

"You remember what I warned you about the wi– the woman?"

Raiden nodded. How could he have forgotten? The Veil she planned to raise might lead to disaster.

"I wanted to make sure you understood the danger she represents. Through her ignorance, not any true malice!" He lifted his hands when Raiden scowled. "Please! Don't take this the wrong way. I fear for my land, that is all. I'm only asking you to talk to her, to convince her to desist in her efforts to raise a Veil. Nothing more."

His suspicion faded in the face of the priest's seemingly sincere concern. He appeared truly frightened. But Jacobis didn't know Shade at all if he thought she could be convinced not to raise her Veil. He temporized. "If I can, I will warn her about your concerns. I can promise nothing else."

Jacobis nodded, giving him a tentative smile. "I am so glad to hear you say it," he said. "I wish to give you something, my son, to protect you from the dark forces in my land. Malavita is a dangerous place, as you've learned the hard way."

Raiden narrowed his eyes, his suspicion rising again. Slowly, Jacobis reached into his robe with one hand, keeping eye contact the whole time. Raiden tensed, his sword ready. But the red-headed priest pulled out an amulet, not a blade. A simple garnet set in a gold sunburst. A garnet the size of a baby's fist...

Reverently, Jacobis held out the amulet to Raiden: a gold chain dangled from it. "It is a talisman meant to shield its wearer from the Unseen's blight. A small token, I admit, but it might be enough to keep you safe in the Wastes without a wizard's help."

Reluctantly, Raiden reached for the amulet dangling from Jacobis' hand. The gems of this land had power; it might prove useful. He loathed trusting a priest, especially this priest, but Jacobis had called off the Ruby Pontifex. Perhaps–

A shock raced up his arm at first contact, and his fingers closed over the amulet convulsively. A burst of light blinded him, and when he could see again he was alone in the dark orchard, a simple amulet in his fist. Without thought, he tossed the chain over his head and settled the amulet against his chest, tucking it inside his jacket. It felt right; it was warm against his skin, almost...comforting. His suspicion and doubt faded. For the first time in days, he felt clear-headed. Peace settled over him. It was a feeling he hadn't had for years; there were no questions, no confusion. The world became crystal.

With the amulet warm against his skin, he turned to find his friends and leave the bishop's palace behind. It was time to find Shade.

CHAPTER TWENTY

They left the Glass Fields with the sun high overhead in a sky that was a deep, clear blue. The land beyond the shattered place opened into tranquil pastures and rolling hills, verdant and rich, a distant smudge of ocean at the horizon.

Amazed, Shade stopped and stared at a landscape she'd only seen beneath a Veil. There was no trace of the blight here, but no Veil sheltered this place. How was this possible?

"What is this place?" she asked breathlessly as Satine crested the hill to stand beside her. Satine had thrown back her concealing cloak to reveal a trim body dressed in fitted leather trousers and a wrapped silk shirt both as black as her hair. Hardly the flowing skirts and colorful blouses Shade remembered. The clothes hugged her curves in a disconcerting fashion.

"My home," Satine said, giving her a small, secret smile. Shade felt a familiar tingle ride up her spine and squashed it ruthlessly. She couldn't allow herself to be distracted. She did not know this woman. This... Sicani. "The Last Bastion is the only remaining land in Malavita which is untouched by the blight. We retreated here when the war ended to–"

"To hide from the world?" Shade interrupted sharply.

Satine's expression became dismayed. "You don't understand..."

Shade stared at her in disbelief. In a single night, the entire world had shifted around her. She shook her head. "I don't understand any of this," she snapped, and continued down the track they were following. Matteo and Angelo dogged her heels, and she was grateful for their presence. She didn't trust any of these... strangers. Or this impossible place. They walked through orchards of healthy trees laden with young fruit, descending into a broad valley of green and gold. The hills surrounding it were terraced, and she could see people working among the bounty. To the east rose the Razor Ridge mountains. They had done it, they had made it beyond the mountains, but Shade felt anything but triumphant. Nightmares had plagued her sleep, the memory of agony keeping her from peaceful slumber. She'd never once been afraid of raising a Veil. She'd always been prepared to work the difficult magic required. Her father had taught her the way. The wrong way, unfortunately. Now she knew the true way, and it frightened her more than she cared to admit. Not the pain, not the plunging of her blade into her own flesh – she'd already done that – it was the idea of giving so much of herself to the creation which worried her. It demanded pieces of her soul. And then she would be tethered like a dog tied to a fence. She shuddered.

And now, to find this place. A place clean of the blight. The settlement which crowned one of the hills was not a huge one, but as large as any village in an interior Veil. Clusters of small, stone houses marched up and around one of the hilltops at the edge of the valley. Bright, terracotta-tiled roofs capped the houses, and flowers spilled from boxes beneath nearly every window. The village had a commanding view of the valley and was only accessible by a narrow switchback road lined with tall cypress.

This was not the valley from her vision. She was sure of it. And disappointment was bitter on her tongue. Why would this place even need a Veil? It was free of the blight. Her jaw clenched. Was this why the Kindred had refused to show her the way to their lands? Did they enjoy this bounty alongside the last of the Sicani? The betrayal made her stomach hurt.

Villagers going about their daily lives paused when they appeared on the road, curious, but not alarmed. A few waved, and Satine and her companions waved back, calling greetings. Shade glowered at them, anger filling her as they made their way up the road. The Sicani lived in a paradise while the rest of Malavita languished beneath the Veils.

Satine led them through the village to a large, stone cottage near the top of the hill, surrounded by a garden full of wild red geraniums and yellow witch's broom. A pale orange cat greeted her upon their arrival, yowling. It twisted between her legs, its back arching. She murmured a low greeting and bent to pet the animal's head. More cats lay on the front stoop of her house, basking in the afternoon sun. A few thumped their tails and gave their mistress a slit-eyed glance, but only the tabby begged for attention.

Shade eyed the animals askance; cats were particularly susceptible to the blight. She'd never seen one that wasn't a raving, distrustful beast. These seemed harmless, except for the one doing its best to trip Satine as she entered her cottage. Still, Shade gave the creatures a wide berth as she followed.

The house, thankfully, was empty – Shade had feared to find Satine's husband and child waiting for her. Satine led them into a cozy parlor while she went to fetch tea. Surprisingly, Lord Azure volunteered to help. Shade raised an eyebrow to Angelo, who shrugged. How many times had Dante offered to help with tea?

"Lord Azure has been a servant longer than he was a nobleman," Sir Julian said, catching her bemused expression. "As we all are, now. Who we were has no bearing on who we are."

"You're a servant?" Matteo said, surprised. He narrowed his eyes at the imposing warrior. "You don't seem like one."

With a shrug, Sir Julian removed his green cloak and hung it on a peg. As Shade had expected, there was a knife belt slung low on his hips. Emerald peeked at her through patterns in the tooled leather. Other than his blades, though, he didn't dress as a bloodwizard. He wore a deep purple tunic atop a pale linen shirt, breeches, and low, soft boots. The garb of a merchant, or craftsman. Still, how he wore his blades and held himself like a coiled snake told her all she needed to know.

"Service comes in many forms," Brother Elias said. He tucked his hands into the sleeves of his fine, red robe and made his way to a velvet-covered chaise beneath a window. "All those years ago, we came seeking adventure, and wealth. There had always been tales of untold treasures hidden in the Glass Fields. At the time, we had little to lose. We were a band of outcasts – a lord of one of the First Families who'd gambled away his fortune, a knight of a sacred order who'd broken his vow of chastity, and an exiled priest who'd been more devoted to wine than the Four Faces and the Hidden. We were more desperate than brazen, I'm afraid."

Shade perched beside him on the couch and gave Sir Julian a speculative glance. Broken his vow of chastity, had he? It was hard to imagine him as some sort of sybarite. Or, even more unlikely, in love.

"It was a long time ago, lady witch," Sir Julian said. He had remained standing, his hands resting lightly on his blade hilts, forever on guard. "We stumbled upon the qaraz through sheer luck, but we were not worthy of it. Our journey was difficult. The Fields tested us in unexpected ways. Yet, somehow, we made our way through."

A broad smile lit Elias' face. "Not by deceit and trickery," he said, "but by friendship, and trust. We were not worthy when we entered, but we earned our worth at the end. And our treasure."

"What sort of treasure is it to be servants for a hundred years?" Matteo asked, scoffing. He stood near the cold hearth, halfway between his brother, who'd taken a seat in a wing-backed chair, and Shade. Ever the more high-strung of the two, he was balanced on his toes and fidgeting with his blades.

"There are more kinds of treasure than gems and gold, my son," Elias said. "We found our purpose among the Sicani. We have dedicated ourselves to the most important work in all of Malavita."

"And what work is that?" Shade asked, wanting to fidget like Matteo, and holding herself still out of sheer will. This place was free of the blight, but something dark simmered beneath the surface. Her unease was more than just bitterness.

"We stand guard against the darkness, my sweet girl."

The breath snagged in Shade's chest. Satine stood in the doorway bearing a porcelain tea service on a wooden tray. She gazed at Shade, her golden eyes serene in her pale, perfect face. Shade had thought nothing could shock her as much as seeing Satine again after all these years, but a simple endearment threatened to break her all over again. She struggled to draw a breath, to speak normally. Her cheeks grew warm, and she couldn't tear her eyes away from Satine.

"What darkness?" Matteo demanded, stepping between them. Whether it had been intentional, or not, his action freed her from that amber gaze. She could breathe again. She looked aside, and found Angelo watching her, his brow creased. Lips pursed, he stood abruptly, another shield between her and Satine. "Don't be rude, Matteo," he said. "Help the lady with the tea."

As they busied themselves clearing a small table of books to make way for the service, Lord Azure appeared from the kitchen with a basket of bread and a pot of butter. Brother Elias rose to help him, leaving Shade alone on the couch. She scraped her fingernails across the soft fabric and stared out the window. Yellow flowers waved gently in the breeze. Fat bees danced between the blossoms. Her thudding heart began to quiet. The thickness in her throat eased.

"You stand guard over paradise," she said, turning away

from the window and the bucolic scene. She looked at Satine and saw again a stranger. Not her lover, not a tattoo master of the Kindred. A Sicani. These people were legendary, their magic was stronger than any bloodwizard's, and they were *hiding*. She sat straighter and waved away the cup of tea Matteo offered her. If she was going to have a drink, it would be something stronger than tea. "Tell me why you hide here while my people sacrifice to tend the qaraz. Tell me why I must risk my blood and soul to raise a Veil when there is land free of the blight right here!"

At her words, Satine paled. "No matter what you might think, the Last Bastion is no paradise."

Relieved Satine hadn't called her "sweet girl" again, Shade sneered, determined not to be moved by her distress. "Should I deny the evidence before my own eyes? You've twisted the truth before, Satine."

"Keep a civil tongue, witch," Lord Azure snapped, taking Satine by the elbow solicitously. "Be at ease, Lady Diamond," he said to her gently, casting a dark gaze in Shade's direction. "She speaks to wound. And she speaks from ignorance."

Ignorance? Shade tensed.

Satine lifted her chin, staring down her straight nose at Shade, as regal as a queen. "The Last Bastion is a prison, not a paradise. We used the power of the last clean place to contain the Unseen, to cut them off from the blight. After our final cataclysmic battle, they were weakened but not destroyed. They are forever seeking escape, forever testing our power, our resolve. They want to spread their blight to the entire world, and we are all that hold them in check. With each passing year, there are fewer of us to stand watch. Children are rare. Even rarer are those souls daring enough to cross the Glass Fields." She smiled at Lord Azure and the others, gratitude shining in her eyes. "They call themselves servants, but they are Guardians. As am I, as are the strongest among us. The Elders choose who is worthy of the task." Her bright eyes fell on Shade. "They will want you to stay, to join your power to ours. You would be a strong Guardian. It was a risk, bringing you here, but I believe I can convince the Elders to let you leave–"

"Let us leave?" Matteo exclaimed while Shade struggled to understand what Satine was saying. "What do you mean, *let* us leave?"

Satine gave Sir Julian a pleading look. Stone-faced, he addressed them. "We were given a choice all those years ago. We could stay and add our blood and magic to the power containing the Unseen, or we could return to the Glass Fields."

Matteo spat a curse and Angelo gestured sharply. "What choice is that?" he demanded. He pointed at Satine. "She already said we couldn't go back through the Fields."

Sir Julian did not reply, but his grim expression said it all.

"So, your choice was servitude or death," Matteo said bitterly. He took a menacing step toward the ancient knight, his chest puffed and his gaze dangerous. Sir Julian topped him by half a head, was built like a bull, and carried blades far stronger than his, but it made no difference to the younger man. Behind him, Angelo made a subtle shift, preparing to defend his brother. "Force such a choice on us at your own peril!"

"Back down, pup." Julian tapped a finger against his blade hilt, but otherwise made no threatening move. He seemed more amused than alarmed.

Matteo's nostrils flared, and he bared his teeth. "I've taken down Capos stronger than you, old man. Remember, I gave you fair warning."

"Please, there's no need for this," Satine said, stepping between the men. "I assure you I can intercede on your behalf. The Elders must see you will serve our cause far better beyond the Bastion than within it."

"We didn't come here to serve your cause," Shade said. She rose from the couch. "If you or your Elders try to keep us here, you will regret it." She stared at Satine's stricken face and hardened her heart. "Don't think for a moment that what we once shared will stop me from fighting you."

A mask dropped over Satine's face. The regal queen had returned, cold and distant. "Believe me, Shade, I have no desire to keep you here," she said flatly. "The Elders will be swayed, have no doubt. Then I will gladly see you gone."

She nodded stiffly. "Good. When?"

"Come morning I'll take you to the Elders and speak on your behalf." Her voice remained cold, but her golden eyes were pure fire. "You will stand in the shadow of what we guard, and you will see what lies at stake."

Bristling, Shade snapped, "I know better than anyone what lies at stake. The blight grows stronger every day, even the qaraz are touched by it. If I can't raise my Veil, my people will die."

"Oh, my sweet girl," Satine said. "If you can't raise your Veil, I'm afraid all of us might die."

CHAPTER TWENTY-ONE

A soft breeze carried the whir and buzz of insects through the window but brought Shade little peace. She tossed on the wide bed, Satine's bed, a bed large enough for two, and far too big for one, imagining Satine entwined with her husband beneath the cool, linen sheets. Where was the man, anyway? Satine hadn't spoken of him once, or her child. Either Satine was hiding them, or they didn't exist.

"... I have no desire to keep you here."

She kicked off the thin blanket wrapped around her legs. Why had she agreed to take Satine's bed? She should have slept outside with Matteo and Angelo. After a mostly silent, uncomfortable meal in Satine's kitchen, the brothers had gathered their bed rolls and left the cottage. Matteo was on the back portico, and Angelo was taking his chances with the cats on the front stoop. Elias had chuckled at their precautions, bidding them a pleasant goodnight before venturing to his own cottage. Lord Azure had rolled his eyes, but Sir Julian had simply nodded approvingly. Something like respect had crossed Matteo's face, and he'd returned the nod to Shade's surprise. She doubted Dante Safire would have reacted so graciously after someone called him "pup".

Imagining his haughty sneer made her smile, and a sudden longing filled her, her heart aching. She *missed* him. Most of the time, she could push thoughts of Dante to the back of her mind. Her feelings for him were complicated at best, and she couldn't afford to be distracted. Finding Satine again was bad enough – she didn't dare throw Dante into the mix.

Satine was the least of her shocks this day. Now she understood the unease in her belly. The sense of darkness beneath this shiny place. Once she'd grown aware of it, she couldn't shake off the feeling of dread, of fear. The blight didn't affect the land, true, but the balance here was far more precarious than in the Wastes. Even lying in a cozy bed with the sounds and scents of a lovely night to sooth her, she felt perched on the edge of a cliff. One wrong move…

At last, Shade gave up on sleep and slid out of bed. Perhaps Satine had a bottle of brandy hidden in the cupboards. She slipped on a thin robe over the shift Satine had given her and padded into the darkened parlor, threading between the tables and chairs to the kitchen. Satine had taken the couch for the night, and she didn't want to wake her. She glanced toward it and stopped. The couch was empty but for crumpled blankets. Across the room, a thin line of light leaked from beneath a doorway. Taking a deep breath, Shade went to it and knocked softly.

"Come in, Shade."

Her heart thudding, Shade opened the door to a small study. Shelves heavy with leather-bound books lined most of the walls, various collections stuffed among them – carved, painted nesting dolls popular among the Golondrina, a four-quartered plaque heavy with gems, sea glass from the shores along the Golden Crescent, red rocks from the Deep Wastes, carvings and paintings from the interior Veils. The collections of a traveler. A writing desk sat against one wall, covered in papers, pens and ink jars. One large, wing-backed chair sat beneath a window, blankets and pillows adorning it as if someone used it for a bed at times.

"You couldn't sleep either?" Satine smiled at her from where she leaned over a large table, braced on her arms. She wore her soft, white robe, and her hair was loose around her shoulders, falling in ebony waves. Shade swallowed and crossed to the table.

"What is this?" she asked, her discomfort replaced with curiosity. The tabletop had a landscape built atop it, complete with hills and ridges, lakes and rivers. She'd seen table maps before in the Brotherhood churches, but never one so detailed. The whole of Malavita was laid out across it in topographical relief. Magic had gone into its construction, she guessed, though it was magic unlike her own. The map seemed to pulse with an inner light, and lines of gold crisscrossed the land, shining just below the surface. Small translucent domes rose over the eastern and southern coasts and other sites in the interior. All the Veils in the land.

"Our land," Satine said softly. "The whole of Malavita."

Fascinated by the map, Shade stepped closer, studying the faint lines. "Those are qaraz, aren't they?"

Satine nodded. "All the ones which remain untouched by the blight. They have lasted far longer than we ever dared hope. The Golondrina have done their duty well, but they were given an impossible task. They could never replace the Locorum."

The Locorum? Shade rubbed her chin, her eyes tracing the lines on the map. "The church speaks of the Locorum only as minor spirits who reward the righteous and punish the wicked."

Satine made a small noise of disgust. "The Locorum *are* spirits, but not in the way the Brotherhood think. The greatest loss we suffered in our long and horrible war was their corruption by the Unseen. They were the spirits of the land, the source of her light and magic. The Unseen ripped them from the qaraz and twisted them into creatures of darkness, using them to spread the blight. Of all the forms our enemy takes, the twisted Locorum are the worst. Yet even with their loss, we managed to keep the qaraz pure. With the help of the

Golondrina, of course." Her delicate brow furrowed, and her eyes grew distant. She spoke in a low voice and Shade had to strain to hear her. "But for some time now, the balance in the Wastes has been shifting. As precarious as it was to begin with, it has reached a tipping point..."

Shade nodded, feeling chilled. "The qaraz are being touched by the blight," she said grimly. The lines on the map seemed to pulse, as if agreeing with her assessment. A sudden understanding struck her, and horror followed. "They're failing, aren't they?"

Satine leaned on her hands as if the strength had left her. "You always saw things most struggle to see. I have tried to warn the others, but they don't want to hear it. Mostly because they feel helpless to do anything about it. It costs all we have to maintain the prison, and sometimes even that is not enough. My parents, and my beloved brother–" Her words caught in her throat for a moment, then she raised her eyes from the table. Tears silvered her lower lashes. "Sometimes there is a crack, you see, a... a... fissure in the shield. Before we can seal it, the dark power arrows free. Anyone in its path is destroyed. Horribly. My parents were burned beyond saving, and my brother... my brother disappeared entirely."

"I'm so sorry, I didn't know." Sympathy swelled Shade's heart, and she slipped around the side of the map to stand near Satine. With every step, she felt like she was walking backwards in time. "You never told me about your family. I only–" and now it was her words catching in her throat. She swallowed past the ache. "I only met your husband, and your son."

Satine's cheeks colored, and her eyes grew shadowed with guilt. "I–I don't have any children, Shade," she said softly. Her lips pressed together briefly, before she added in a rush, "Or a husband."

Though she had suspected it, hearing it was different. Shade gripped the edge of the table to steady herself. Betrayal ripped through her gut like a sharp blade. "Why?" she said, the word scraping her throat. Tears pricked her eyes, and this time she didn't fight them. "Why did you lie? Did you hate me so much?"

The words sounded so pathetic, but Shade couldn't help herself. She needed to know.

"I didn't expect to find you," Satine said, her voice small. "But when I did, I had to help you. Your wards, Shade, no one else could have inked you as I did. Not even a Brotherhood master. You... You needed my magic, my expertise. With the Wild Power in your reach, you would have died without proper tattoos."

"Is that all I was? A task?" Shade couldn't look at Satine. She stared at the table map, her gaze blurred by tears. She swallowed her hurt. "I guess I was rather pathetic. Broken, lost, a girl desperate for friendship, for love. I suppose I should be thankful for your attention." She lifted her head, blinking rapidly, and pinned Satine with a hard glare. "You didn't have to make up some imaginary family. You could have told me the truth and sent me on my way."

"My... husband and son were part of my disguise," she said. "I couldn't tell you the truth without revealing my secret to the rest of the caravan. Only a select few of the Kindred know we travel among them. They stand guard to protect the Bastion, but they never enter it, and it is safer for them not to know we leave it. And I didn't expect you to come after me. It was such a shock. I... I thought it would be easier for you–"

Shade erupted in bitter laughter. "Oh, yes, Satine. It was so much easier for me, thinking I'd never meant anything to you."

"Oh, my sweet girl, you know that isn't true..."

Sweet girl...

Suddenly, Shade couldn't breathe. It was even worse than in the parlor. How many times had Satine called her that? It hurt to the bone to hear her say it, but it melted her anger in a rush, leaving only the hurt.

"Shade." Satine spoke gently. "I am bound to this place. I am not free to love you like you deserve. If I'd brought you here before you were strong, you would have been trapped. And that would have been a tragedy. You are meant for a far greater destiny than to be a Guardian. But. Don't ever think there isn't love in my heart for you. Don't regret our time together, don't recall me with bitterness. Please…"

Something loosened in her chest, and Shade found she could breathe again. The burn of tears threatened to overwhelm her. She put a hand over her eyes, and then Satine was beside her, pulling her into an embrace. Shade stopped fighting. Tears washed down her face as Satine held her, washing away her pain, her bitterness.

"I loved you," she said, wrapping her arms around Satine's slim torso and burying her face in her silky hair. "You saved me. You… You brought me back to life."

"Oh, my sweet girl, I loved you, too. Never doubt that. You were my treasure, my jewel. I would have kept you if I could have. But you were never mine to keep."

Satine stroked her hair, cradling her head to her shoulder. The house was silent, the night beyond still. Shade took a shuddering breath, the ache in her throat easing. Satine's slender, graceful body was pressed against hers, and every curve of her was achingly familiar. Her breath quickened. She buried her face in the crook of her neck, drawing in her scent. Jasmine and spice, clean soap and fresh herbs. It sparked her memories, and she was a girl again in her first lover's arms.

"Satine," she whispered, moving her lips to her soft earlobe. She nipped it lightly. "I have missed you…"

Satine's warm lips brushed her neck. "I've missed you, too." Her arms tightened, squeezing hard, but then she broke free. Her face was flushed, but there was a sad smile on her full, rosy lips. "But you are not here for me."

Shade clasped her wrist, not wanting to let go. "We could

have tonight," she said breathlessly. "Just one last night together..."

"We already had our last night together."

There was deep regret in Satine's golden eyes, but her words held a finality that cooled Shade's ardor. She waited for the pain to hit, for the rejection to crush her. Instead, she felt strangely relieved. She rubbed her thumb along the bottom of Satine's wrist, feeling her pulse. Rapid and strong. So, it wasn't easy for Satine to turn her down. But it wasn't wrong...

Shade released her and adjusted her thin robe. "I don't recall you being the more inhibited one," she said, smiling to take the sting from her words. "I think you might regret your choice in the clear light of morning."

Satine sighed, long and deep. "I imagine you're right, though *regret* is too small a word..."

Laughing softly, Shade pulled her into a quick, fierce hug. "Thank you for saying that," she said and released her. She ran a hand over her eyes, and felt a lightness enter her as she let go of a burden she'd carried for years. Satine had *loved* her.

A glint of light made her turn toward the map table. The lines of the qaraz brightened as she gazed on them, and a sudden certainty filled her: she had loved Satine, too, but staying with her *would* have been a mistake. She was meant for *more*.

"They are all connected," she said, her finger hovering over the line of one qaraz, tracing it from the coast to the Deep Wastes. She walked around the table, her fingers passing over nodes of light burning at the intersections of multiple qaraz. Many were covered with the dome of a Veil. And all the lines eventually passed through one spot on the map – a bright, shining brilliance not far from the Glass Fields, but one without the representation of a Veil above it. Like a spider at the center of its web, it touched every bright line. She leaned over the table and held her hand over it. "What is this?" she asked, though she already knew.

"The Nexus," Satine said. She stood on the other side of the table, watching her. A delicate line appeared between her brows. "A very powerful place."

Suspicion tugged at her. "Why has no one raised a Veil there?"

"The Brotherhood did, long ago. Their new Veils were growing weak, flawed. They thought raising one in a place of power would help. It did not. The Veil collapsed almost instantly, killing the priests who'd raised it and damaging several other Veils nearby. Another Veil at the Nexus – as they understand how to raise one – would lead to catastrophe."

Catastrophe...

Satine's answer didn't shock her as much as she'd thought it would. "What sort of catastrophe?" she asked. "What would happen?"

"If you raised your Veil there with cornerstones torn from the earth and not born from your flesh, you would have tipped the balance entirely. It would have caused a chain reaction leading to the fall of every Veil in Malavita."

Her head spun and the table map blurred. "That's where the Coterie insisted I raise my Veil. Those fools. I'm glad I refused them."

Satine turned pale as a ghost. "The Coterie wanted you to raise your Veil at the Nexus?" At Shade's nod, she sagged against the table. "Our agents warned them years ago to cease their quest for a Veil. Threatened, actually. Thankfully, they didn't have the knowledge to raise one using Brotherhood stones. It isn't part of Sicani lore. It was the only thing stopping them."

"And then I came along," Shade said. "Bastard," she growled. "He knew what would happen. They all did. Why? Why by all the Faces would they lead me down a path to destruction?"

"I always knew they were twisted in their ambitions. But this is madness. If the Veils fall, it will disrupt all the magic in the land. The qaraz will be tainted, and the blight will consume even the Last Bastion. If that happens, the Unseen will break free." She raised a trembling hand to her lips. "War would consume Malavita once more."

"And that is want they want," Shade said flatly. "They want to finish the war with the Unseen. No matter what it costs." She crossed her arms, staring hard at the Nexus. "I'm glad I thwarted their plot."

"But, Shade, my sweet girl," Satine said reluctantly. "You must raise your Veil at the Nexus."

"What? You just said it was madness!"

"A true Veil at the Nexus will touch every qaraz. Its power will cleanse the lines of power and restore the flawed Veils of the Brotherhood. Balance will return to the Wastes."

"And if I fail?"

"If you fail… If your magic fails, or your will, then it will be as if you'd raised a false Veil."

"Every Veil destroyed," Shade finished for her. She held herself tightly. She hated being backed into a corner. "You called me beyond the mountains, and now you're telling me my destiny lies at the Nexus?"

"I had to bring you here first," Satine said apologetically. "Not just to impart knowledge about the Veils, but about the Unseen. You need to understand the danger you face."

"From demons?" she scoffed. "I have enemies enough as it is, Satine." Sudden anger made her grind her teeth. So, she'd end up raising her Veil where Korin wanted, anyway. But her Veil would stand despite his duplicity! Faces spit on that old bastard.

"Korin Illario is a dead man," she said.

"Korin Illario?" Satine exclaimed, startling her.

"You know him?"

Horror widened Satine's eyes. "Korin Illario was exiled from the Last Bastion decades ago for trying to break the Unseen's prison. He is one of us, Shade. He is a Sicani!"

CHAPTER TWENTY-TWO

The following morning, Satine led Shade and her companions deep into the valley of the Last Bastion. They were joined by Brother Elias, Lord Azure, and Sir Julian. The old men wore their robes as they had in the Glass Fields, as did Satine.

"You're certain you can convince your Elders to let us go?" Shade asked Satine.

"We will all speak for you, witch," Julian interjected. He was ahead of her and threw her a glance over his shoulder. Stone-faced as always. She couldn't tell if he was confident of their chances, or dismally pessimistic.

"We will do our best," Elias added from behind her, which was hardly a resounding vote of confidence. And he was the most optimistic of them all.

"I can't imagine the Elders would want you to stay anyway," Azure grumbled. He was walking beside Julian and didn't bother to look at her. She grinned at his back, strangely reassured by his derisive comment.

They followed a narrow track beyond the village to a vast lake. Trees lined its far edge, taller and thicker than any forest she'd ever seen. The lake itself reflected the sun in shimmering ripples, and the water was clear. Satine took them around the verdant shore to a clearing in the reeds. A sandy beach abutted the water. Here she stopped and faced them. An expression of concentration settled over her face, and she held her hands over the sand beneath her feet. Suddenly, Shade could feel the qaraz which lay under this entire region. It flowed beneath her feet, moving parallel to the lake shore. A gasp from Angelo told her he felt it too.

"What's happening?" Matteo demanded. He had his hands on his blade hilts. Shade resisted the urge to grip her weapons. It was an odd sensation, but she felt no threat. The power flowed faster and faster, and she realized it was moving in a spiral. Like a whirlpool of sorts and they were at its edge.

"Be at peace, my child," Satine said to him. Her eyes had begun to glow with an eerie golden light. The lake behind her rippled as if in a stiff wind. "I am opening the qaraz."

Light appeared beneath their feet. The sand turned to liquid gold. Angelo gave a startled yelp as they sank into the earth. Amazed at the beauty of the light, Shade let the qaraz absorb her in silence, unafraid. She had always envied the Golondrina ability to travel the qaraz. Her heart pounded with excitement at the sudden unexpected chance. The light enveloped them and there was a sensation of movement.

"Though the Locorum have been corrupted and expelled from the qaraz, these lines of pure magic withstand the blight due to the Golondrina's vigilance." It was Satine. Her voice seemed to emanate from the light itself. "Here, they are strongest because we tend them and we use them to shield the Unseen's prison. If the qaraz outside the Last Bastion become corrupted, eventually, that corruption will reach here, too. I fear what will happen if we do not stabilize the qaraz soon." Satine's golden eyes turned toward Shade. "I believe your Veil may be our best chance, Shade. And now we must convince the Elders."

Ahead of them, a black spot appeared in the radiance. It grew larger, closer. A wall of black suddenly loomed. Satine held Shade's gaze until she came abreast of the wall, then she turned toward it and was swallowed. Fear choked Shade, and she reached out. Someone clasped her hand and then it was her turn to be swallowed.

They were dropped into darkness. Blinded, fighting panic, Shade clung to the hand in hers. There was solid ground beneath her sandals, but around her was a nothingness as vast as the Wastes. For a moment, she felt overwhelming vertigo. Her breath came hard and fast. The hand she gripped squeezed back just as hard.

"Is it still you?" Matteo asked. Fear laced his words, and somehow it quelled her terror.

"It's me," she said, sounding remarkably calm in the pitch blackness. "Angelo?"

"Here," came Angelo's strangled answer. "Wherever here is."

"Did she lead us into a trap?" Matteo whispered.

"Don't be ridiculous." A soft light filled the darkness, revealing Satine. The light encompassed her and her companions – the Guardians. Even their robes seemed to gleam.

"You have nothing to fear from us," Lord Azure said indignantly.

No longer blind, she released her death grip on Matteo's hand, though not without reluctance. "Where are we? Is this the Unseen's prison?"

As one, the Guardians turned away from her; they didn't move, but the space shifted around them. Shade experienced the odd vertigo again and swayed. Matteo reached out with a steadying hand, and Angelo braced his legs wide for balance. They were moving swiftly, though the darkness didn't change, then the world grew stable again.

"This is the space which holds the Unseen's prison," Satine said, lifting an arm in a sweeping gesture. She pointed into the darkness. "That is their true prison."

Another light emerged from the darkness, a sphere of glowing red.

At first, it was the size of a lamp, as if hanging from a ship across a vast ocean. Again, the vertigo gripped Shade, and the sphere grew from lantern-sized to bonfire-sized. She gasped as the feeling of movement increased. She was speeding toward a glowing red light. It grew larger and larger until she feared it would swallow all of them whole. Flames moved across its surface, ripples of black and orange streaking the crimson globe. There was no heat, but power beat against her face. A twisted power, as unlike the Sicani power as rot was unlike growth. Disturbingly, it was a familiar power.

The blight. The blight that infected the Wastes also inhabited this globe. It pulsed and throbbed, seeking a way out. But something held it back, as the Veils held back the Wastes.

When she was able to turn her attention away from the giant, pulsating ball of flame and darkness, she noticed the Guardians had spread themselves in a circle around it. She could see each of them, though she sensed a vastness in this place beyond comprehension. Others had joined Satine and her fellows, people in robes like theirs. Two men and two women with ageless faces, though their hair had gone silver. Power exuded from them, making Satine and her companions seem like their shadows.

She licked her lips and touched a bone handle of one blade. On impulse, she slid it free of its sheath. The obsidian gleamed as if she'd called magic. More so. It glowed with an inner flame as bright as the earth's fire that had birthed it. The magic in her blood answered its call, aching to be freed.

Slowly, Shade turned her blade toward her raised forearm, though she couldn't remember lifting it. Her heart hammered against her breastbone, clattering like the hooves of a runaway horse.

"Stop!" Satine cried. But she wasn't talking to Shade. Instead, she was facing the man beside her. His robe gleamed as white as hers. Her counterpart? Or he was the master, and she the apprentice? The man was exceedingly handsome, his white hair long and shining, held back by a leather cord around his forehead. His high cheeks and fine brows, his stature and proud bearing, reminded her of Korin Illario, though his face was smooth. He was watching her, his golden eyes shining.

"Do not speak so to an Elder," admonished a woman in blue robes. She stood beside Azure, short and apple-cheeked but no less beautiful than her companion. Her white hair was captured in a thick braid which hung to her hip. "We can sense her strength. Longinus must do what is best for all of us."

The best for all of them. Yes, it made so much sense. Shade found herself nodding. Her blade trembled above her arm. It would be so easy to draw...

"Release her!" cried Satine desperately. "This isn't why I brought her here! Elder Longinus, please listen to me."

"Lady Diamond, remember your place," the woman beside Sir Julian said. Her skin was a few shades darker than Julian's, and her hair was a mass of white curls. "You better than anyone know what is at stake."

"Yes, Elder Beryl, I do." Satine clutched the folds of her robe, her eyes darting from the Elders to Shade, full of panic. "I've already lost everyone dear to me, and the sacrifice still isn't enough. But she will not be another sacrifice to our cause. She will be more than this. Shade Nox must be sent to the Nexus. She must raise her Veil!"

"A Veil at the Nexus?" cried the woman in blue. "If she tries and fails, she could doom us all! Do you have so much faith in this... this witch that you would propose such a perilous endeavor? Surely you realize we stand on a precipice. Now is not the time to take a leap!"

"Elder Sapphira, it is you who does not understand." Brother Elias spoke this time. His deep voice resonated. "Shade Nox will pull us back from the precipice. Her Veil has the potential to stabilize all the others, to strengthen the qaraz! She will give us what we so desperately need: time."

The short, plump monk stood beside a red-robed man half a head taller than him with fierce eyes and a hawk's nose, yet he spoke with such conviction, he overshadowed the scowling Elder.

"In that you are correct, Elias," Elder Longinus replied. His bright eyes remained on Shade. She felt sweat pop out on her upper lip. His was the power pushing her to draw blood. "Adding her strength to ours could help us hold the gates for a hundred more years."

"Her power would be wasted here," Sir Julian countered, a touch of disdain in his voice. He towered over the slim, dark woman beside him, but he stood a step behind her in obvious deference. She turned to look at him, her smooth, attractive features slack with surprise. His lips thinned as he met her gaze, and he ducked his head. "Forgive my rudeness, Lady Beryl, but I cannot remain silent. With all due respect, Revered Elders, you are wrong."

"Do all of you feel this way?" the fourth Elder exclaimed, the man in red. He strode closer to the vast, red sun dominating the emptiness, and lifted his hand toward it. "Do you truly believe ours is not the more important work? Lord Azure? What say you?"

Lord Azure bent his head, grimacing. "Elder Rosso, the witch is reckless, arrogant, rude and uncivilized." He lifted his head, and his eyes blazed. "And I truly believe she will save the land from tipping into chaos. She must be allowed to try!"

His statement sent ripples of shock through the Elders. They began to squabble among themselves. Shade, too, was surprised by Azure's support, but she took the chance to push back against Longinus while he was distracted. He glared at her, his handsome face growing pale and almost gaunt, but she felt the pressure on her ease.

With sudden clarity, she realized the power flowing from him wasn't only directed at her. Her eyes fixed on the pulsing horror of the Unseen's prison. Even as the Elders and Guardians argued, power bled from them. All of them fed the prison, giving their strength and magic to the task. She hadn't even noticed Elias and the others yielding their blades, but she could feel their bloodmagic feeding the great, coruscating globe. They were tied to it as firmly as a wizard to their Veil, but the cost, the sacrifice was far greater.

Beside her, Angelo's gaze was locked on the guardians in their circle. The Elders were still arguing with Satine and her companions, but their energy and strength faded visibly as they fed the prison. "Look what they give to that thing," he said softly. "They are trapped by it as much as it traps the Unseen."

Unseen. Shade felt her gaze drawn to the angry red sphere; it fought against the power containing it. Somewhere beneath its swirling surface a vast horde of creatures teemed riotously. A hive of hornets struggling to find an opening, to overwhelm the enemies attempting to restrain them and sting, sting, sting!

"It is a noble sacrifice," Matteo said. He had gripped his blades fiercely, and his bright eyes were pinned on the prison hovering above them. An expression close to rapture shone on his face. Angelo eyed him with concern.

"Yes," Shade agreed. A battle raged in this strange, empty place, an unending fight. The evil imprisoned here had destroyed her home, her land. The foul blight of the Unseen continued to infect Malavita, rendering most of it a wasteland. If the Sicani failed to keep them trapped, they would poison everything. The land would descend into darkness and ruin. The world…

Here was the true fight, the true sacrifice. How could she walk away?

Her blade hung a hair's breadth over her forearm.

"This is not your fight, witch. Don't give into the call as we did."

It was Sir Julian, speaking to her from across the vast, empty expanse, though it sounded as though he stood in front of her. She could even see his dark eyes, gleaming red with power.

"What if I fail?" she asked, surprised to so willingly admit her deepest fear. And when she spoke it aloud, she understood it wasn't just Longinus' power pushing her to make a choice. It would be so easy to stay here...

A gentle smile graced his lips, softening the hard angles of his face. "You won't fail. If Lady Diamond has such faith in you, how can you?"

"You are far too stubborn to fail," Azure added cantankerously. "And I for one would like to see the back of you, thank you very much."

"Your fate is not with us, my child," Elias said, smiling his broad, kindly smile. "You belong to the world outside our Bastion. Your Veil will bring new life."

Reluctantly, Shade turned to Satine. Here was the true temptation, she knew in her heart. Her pain and grief at losing Satine had eased, but she still loved her. Desire uncurled in her heart, a wanting that would never entirely vanish.

"Your place is not with me, Shade." Satine drew herself up in her silver robes, her black tresses flowing like living things in the wake of her power. "Only you have the chance to restore balance. Adding your power to this prison would be worse than failing to raise a Veil. Our power is fading, this prison cannot hold. There is nothing here but a slow death."

The last of Shade's uncertainty faded. She returned her blade to its sheath, her limbs trembling as if she'd just climbed a mountain. She might very well fail at raising her Veil, but Satine was right: she was the only one who had a chance. She faced Elder Longinus. "I've made my choice. I must go to the Nexus."

Elder Longinus' face crumpled. "We need new strength." The Sicani Elder no longer looked ageless or serene. The other Elders appeared just as distraught, just as diminished.

These people are fading. She felt a touch of pity for the loss. The legendary Sicani were no more. The reality was a shock, and a cruel disappointment. They were not the answer to Malavita's problems. It would take all they had left to keep their Bastion strong. And, eventually, it, too, would fade. And fail.

But it was not her fight…

"Will you let me go?" she demanded.

Wearily, Longinus nodded. Satine laid a gentle hand on his arm. "Thank you, Elder Longinus." She turned shining eyes on Shade.

A sudden wave of power shuddered past Shade, and she started, thinking Longinus had gone back on his word. But the Elder had his hands raised and golden light had appeared beneath his feet. He was opening the qaraz as Satine had done. Someone else had released that power, and it hadn't been directed at her.

And it had not been Sicani power…

She searched for the source and met Sir Julian's dark eyes. He had an emerald blade drawn and blood stained the sleeve of his robe. He smiled sadly. "We need new blood, I'm afraid. The young pup is strong."

"Shade…"

Full of dread, Shade spun toward Matteo. His blue eyes shone strangely, and he was smiling. "Someone has to make the sacrifice…" and he raised a tourmaline blade.

A stab of unexpected fear struck her heart. She inhaled sharply. "No."

"Someone does," Angelo said softly, and he stepped in front of Shade to take his brother by the wrist. "But it won't be you, little brother."

Confusion wrinkled Matteo's features. His mouth gaped as he stared at his older brother. Angelo kept a firm hold on his wrist, keeping the sharp blade from Matteo's flesh. "You have to protect the lady," he told him, then he pulled him into a fierce embrace. He forced Matteo's tourmaline blade back into its sheath. His brother didn't fight him. Twisting, Angelo shoved Matteo at Shade. She caught him as he stumbled.

"You watch over him, too, lady witch!" he said gruffly, and he drew his topaz blades. Grief crumpled his features. "I'm all he has in the world." Tears spilled down his cheeks. He raised his blades. "All he had."

"Angelo, don't let them force you." But his eyes were clear, and she felt no new wave of power. He smiled at her through his tears, and she knew he'd made his choice. "Angelo…"

"Huh," Julian grunted, respect clear in his voice. "A worthy older pup will do even better."

By now, Matteo was coming back to himself. His eyes screwed up with confusion to see his brother standing with drawn blades. "Angie?"

The golden gleam beneath Longinus stretched to include Shade and Matteo. Angelo stood outside it, watching them with resignation. And not a little fear. He met Shade's eyes and took a deep breath. His tears had dried. His bright blade sliced across the back of his arm. Blood and magic slid free; it arrowed toward the ball of red fire, connecting Angelo to it, and in turn connecting him to the Elders and their Guardians. A glowing aura surrounded the robed figures, extending to encompass Angelo, as well.

Joy replaced the fear in his eyes, the grief. A smile split his face and he laughed.

"No," Matteo said, and he stepped toward the edge of the qaraz. But it was already too late; they were sinking into golden light. He shouted and lunged toward his brother, but Shade held him back, grappling with him. "It's too late!" she cried, but he was wild with anger and grief.

"Why!" he screamed, reaching out to his brother even as Angelo's aura grew brighter, stronger. "Angie! Please! Don't do this!"

"Go with our witch, Matteo. Keep her safe."

"Angie!"

Shade clung to Matteo, holding him with all the strength in her. Suddenly, he wasn't fighting her, but reaching for his own blades, trying to draw. "No!" she shouted, terrified she would lose them both.

"You are free, Shade," Satine said, her voice inside her head. "Both of you. Stay safe, my sweet girl…"

The qaraz swallowed them. Vertigo gripped her. She clung to Matteo as they seemed to fall through the earth. This was different than before; they plunged into a maelstrom of swirling light and energy. Something great and powerful took hold of them. The world *shifted*…

CHAPTER TWENTY-THREE

The west gate of Sicaria had been untended, most of the polizia drawn off by the fire at the bishop's palace. The stampede of highborn fleeing the chaos had given Dante and the others perfect cover to make their escape – even the Ruby Pontifex hesitated at slaughtering innocents to stop them.

Against Cyril's objection, Korin had managed to abscond with three fine horses from the bishop's private stock, and they'd ridden doubled up through the open gate and into the countryside. The roads beyond had been clear, thankfully, but for the occasional lone traveler or loaded wagon tied down for the night. They'd managed to reach the Veil wall without any signs of pursuit, but they'd kept to a reckless pace even in the Wastes. Dante knew Arturious wouldn't give up on them so easily, not after such a humiliating catastrophe.

Forcing their mounts over the dangerous, darkened terrain had been a gamble, and had cost Dante more blood and magic than was wise, but when the sun rose, they were far enough from Sicaria to risk a more sedate pace. There was no sign of pursuit, but Dante wasn't naive enough to think they were free. He led them on relentlessly even as the sun became a white-hot orb overhead, beating down on them like a hammer.

Finally, though, Cyril forced them to stop, overruling Dante's objections.

"The beasts will die," he said gruffly. "I don't care for horses, true, but I don't like seeing any creature suffer needlessly. Only a fool walks the Wastes during the height of day."

Swallowing his angry retort, Dante forced himself to assess the horses. The beasts' coats were darkened with great swaths of sweat. They stood on trembling legs, their heads hanging, their flanks heaving. Their eyes rolled with terror to be in the open Wastes. Cyril was right.

One thought mollified him as Cyril led the way to shelter: any pursuit would be forced to do the same. Still, he chafed at the delay. Now that he had Raiden, there was nothing stopping him from riding to Shade's side but the inconvenience of the murderous Wastes. He was ready and willing to chase her into the Glass Fields if need be.

Shade, Shade, please be safe…

At last, a thorn grove came into view, tucked at the base of a tumble of rock slabs. Dante could feel the qaraz flowing beneath them the moment they stepped upon it. They'd been taking a more dangerous direct route before, avoiding the qaraz to throw off pursuit and cover more distance. Almost immediately, they all felt the difference. Even Korin sighed in something like relief, though he wasn't a bloodwizard. Being strong in Sicani blood had to give him some sensitivity.

Drawing blood with his rose quartz blade, Cyril opened a way through the dense, twisted grove. The leaves clinging to the wiry branches were a sickly purple, and a viscous goo dripped from palm-length thorns. Teeth gritted, Cyril made sure to push the limbs back enough to let the horses enter well-clear of the lethal barbs.

"We can rest through the worst of the day. The water within is pure."

While Cyril had opened the thorn grove, Dante and the others had dismounted and loosened the girths of their horses' saddles. The beasts were trembling with fatigue. Raiden took their reins and followed the cousins into the shade of the grove.

Cyril remained outside the shelter, a suspicious frown beneath his long mustache. He was staring at Korin. The tall, elderly man stood stiff-backed in the blazing sun, staring westward.

"What is it, Korin?" Dante asked, alarmed. Sometimes he forgot how old Korin was, he always seemed so ageless, so strong. Had their rough passage been too much for him? Worried, he approached Korin and put a hand on his shoulder. "Are you ill?"

Korin dragged his attention to Dante, a distant look in his golden eyes turning to a gleam of triumph. "She is no longer in the Glass Fields," he said eagerly, clasping Dante's forearm with long, elegant fingers. His eyes blazed. "They sent her away, I suspect, cowards that they are. I believe she is on her way to the Nexus. I can feel her through the qaraz. She will have no choice but to raise her Veil where we intended. At last!"

"She would never let herself be forced," growled Cyril. He stepped toward them, a hand going to the hilt of his blade. He grunted, sounding pleased. "If she's out of the Glass Fields, then she must be beyond the mountains. In Kindred lands!"

"Did she reach the Kindred?" Dante demanded, excitement rising within him along with a deep, abiding relief. Thank the Faces, she'd made it across the Glass Fields.

Korin let go of his arm. "She is on this side of the mountains, not beyond. She could never reach Kindred lands through the Glass Fields anyway. No, she tried to thwart us, and she failed." He fixed Cyril with a stern glare. "Be glad she was merely turned away, and not trapped within the Glass Fields forever. Shade is where she needs to be at last."

"Where is she?" Raiden asked, emerging from the grove. His voice was sharp.

Again, Korin's gaze turned west as if drawn by an invisible cord. His long, lean frame tensed. "She is on her way to the Nexus," he said. "She's going to raise her Veil."

"She can't do it," Raiden said softly, almost to himself, his face sallow. "She can't raise a Veil."

"What are you saying?" Dante demanded.

Raiden's dark eyes fixed on him, wide with horror. "If she raises the Veil, she'll bring destruction. By the gods of my father, I swear it!"

For a moment, only stunned silence answered him, but then Cyril exploded. "What lies did those priests put in your head, boy?"

"Is Cyril right?" Dante approached him menacingly. "Did the Brotherhood tell you this? You can't believe a word they say!"

Raiden started, and he glanced at Cyril, despair on his face. Despair, and utter certainty. His lips grew pinched as if he might be sick, and he looked away. Suddenly, his eyes locked on Korin. The old healer had turned to face them at Raiden's shocking words. Unlike the rest of them, there was no horror on his face, no doubt or anger. He stared at Raiden with a clear amber gaze, his back straight and his face stern.

"It's not a lie," Raiden said faintly, and he pointed at Dante's mentor and lifelong friend. "Ask Korin…"

"Korin?" Dante said faintly. A roaring started in his ears as he waited for Korin's outraged denial and none came. The look on his face told him everything he needed to know.

"What is he talking about, Korin?" Dante couldn't keep the anguish from his voice. It cracked on his next despairing plea. "Is he right?"

Korin's eyes shifted to him, but just as abruptly slipped aside. Dante's heart sank and he felt as ill as Raiden looked. Cyril watched Korin like he was an adder dropped in their midst, waiting for his answer, his hand on the hilt of his knife. With a deep sigh, Korin drew himself straight.

"It is the Coterie's belief," he began, no hint of shame or regret in his voice, "that when she raises her Veil at the Nexus, it will fail. That failure will tip the balance which has been so precariously maintained for centuries. The other Veils will fall, even the oldest and the strongest. The qaraz will be fully corrupted, and there will be nowhere left for any of us to hide." His hands bunched into fists and his voice rose, became strident. "This time, all of Malavita will be forced to rise up against our ancient enemy. Every wizard with a blade will be forced to fight our true enemy. Not the Capos and their Corsaro, not the Brotherhood, but the Unseen! At long last, we will have the chance to destroy them and finally cleanse Malavita of the blight!"

They stared at him in open-mouthed shock. A shiver rippled through Dante. "Faces turn from me," he said. "The Unseen are shadows, Korin, only their taint remains. Starting a war with phantoms won't rid our land of the blight. How many will die when the Veils fall? Without the protection of a Veil, the entire city of Sicaria could be wiped away by a single Blackstorm!"

"It is a small price to pay." Korin leaned closer to him, his nostrils flaring and his eyes wild. "The Unseen are not gone, only imprisoned, and that prison grows weaker by the day. Some have escaped, and they spread their evil across the land. The Guardians – those few Sicani left – they hide like frightened rabbits in their holes, allowing the creatures to infest Malavita, too afraid to hunt them down. Dropping the Veils is the only thing that will drive my people out to join our fight – the screams of thousands suffering and dying."

Dante jerked back. "Your people? What are you saying...?"

"Yes, my people. I am a Sicani, one of the few, true Sicani left, and I am ashamed at the cowardice of my kind. It has been my driving purpose to destroy the last of the Unseen and cleanse our land. Once the Veils fall, the prison which holds the Unseen will crack open like a rotten egg. My people will have to fight or be swept away by the demonic hordes. The Sicani will cleanse the land at long last. Don't you see, my son?"

Fury replaced his shock. "I am not your son!" he shouted. He stepped toward Korin, his hands knotting into fists. "How could you do this to me? All this time you've listened to me

talk of raising a Veil and said nothing! You knew it would lead
to disaster. You knew!"

"I tried to warn you," Korin shouted back, his face wrinkling
with anguish. "I tried to warn you away from *her*! I never
wanted to hurt you, Dante, but this is the only way."

Horrified, Dante could only stare at him. "You're mad."

"What of Shade?" Cyril said. "What will happen to her
when she raises the Veil?"

Korin's lips thinned. A mask seemed to drop over his face,
and he wouldn't look at Cyril. His heart pounding with sudden
fear, Dante grasped him by the collar, shaking hard. "Answer
him!"

Gripping his wrists, Korin stared down at him. "We lost
everything when we lost Mercedes' child. Elena was the
culmination of a century's planning – a weapon we created
to use against the Unseen. A power strong enough and pure
enough to heal the world. When the flames took her, we had
to find another way. The witch was always a poor replacement,
but she was the best we could hope for. She will serve a greater
purpose than you could ever understand." His words turned
bitter. "I warned you not to get close to her, and instead you
took her into your bed like a smitten fool."

Dante's lips drew back from his teeth and he gave Korin
another, harder shake. "Tell me what will happen to her, or I
swear I'll gut you like a pig right here and now."

"The moment she crafted her blades, we knew she would
serve us. This Veil will be her gift to the world. But when it
falls – and it *will* fall – she will fall with it."

A fierce cry burst from Cyril, an enraged denial. His knife
appeared in his hand as he lunged at Korin. He pressed the
sharp blade against the old man's neck, drawing blood. His
mustache quivered over his bared teeth. "Let me slit this dog's
throat," he rasped. "He deserves no better!"

"No," Dante said, knocking Cyril aside. "There's still time!
We can stop her. We can save her."

"You cannot!" Korin declared angrily, or tried to, but Dante's hands closed around his throat, cutting him off.

"Only your years of service to my family is keeping you alive right now, Korin. I owe you my life, I owe you my hands, old friend." His fingers squeezed tight and Korin's eyes bulged. "But I will gladly use them to choke the life from you if anything happens to Shade Nox."

CHAPTER TWENTY-FOUR

The journey through the qaraz was like being plunged into a raging river. The golden light was blinding and made her eyes ache even though she kept her lids squeezed shut. She tumbled helplessly and clung to Matteo as if he were a sturdy branch. How long would it take to reach the Nexus from the center of the Glass Fields? She couldn't take much more of this!

Then, suddenly, the world stabilized. There was ground beneath her feet, and the light faded to comforting darkness. Cold struck her and she shivered violently. In her arms, Matteo was sobbing. He clutched at her, his legs giving out. Shade made soothing noises, easing him to the ground, holding him close while he wept.

They were in the Wastes, she knew by the cold and the hard sand beneath her knees, but beyond that she knew nothing. It was hard to think, hard to do anything but feel. They had lost Angelo, she had lost Satine – again. She wasn't even sure where they were; she couldn't focus enough to get her bearings. By the light, she thought it might be dusk, and a vague alarm filled her. Night was coming. They had to draw circles of protection. Every moment they wasted their danger grew.

"Matteo," she said, taking his face in her hands. "Matteo, listen to me. We aren't safe."

"Why did he do it?" He grabbed her, his entire body shuddering. His wild, red-rimmed eyes fixed on her. "Why?"

She shook her head, her throat aching. "I... I think he had to," she said at last when she could speak. "He did it for us."

"He's gone." His face crumpled, his eyes squeezing shut. "He's gone forever."

"No. No. I refuse to believe that. Please, Matteo, please..."

She kissed him gently to calm him, to ground him. He started, his eyes flying open in shock. Holding his gaze, she stroked his cheeks. He took a deep, shuddering breath. His entire frame trembled, but he grew calm. Relieved, she kissed him again, intending a chaste, sisterly peck on his lips, but his arms went around her, pulling her hard against him. His lips devoured hers, and fire roared in her belly, rose up her chest and shivered through her limbs. His hands slid beneath her vest, hot against her bare back and she cleaved to him, seeking his heat in the frigid air.

Grief and fear and pain vanished in a whirlwind of desire and need. She pulled Matteo down to the hard sands, stroking his muscled flanks and broad chest, reveling in the feel of him – so solid and strong and real. His burning hands moved to cup her breasts, trapped beneath her vest. Moaning, she tugged at the ties of her vest, ripping it open for him. His mouth found her skin, teasing and warm. She arched her back, rising to meet him. The cold air struck her hot skin, making her shiver, and she clasped his warm body closer. Her hands moved to his armored kilt, pulling it up to get at the linen bindings wrapped around his loins while he worked to remove her skirt with deft, eager motions.

"Shade," he murmured, his lips roaming her body when they both lay naked together. He groaned as her hand grasped his ready member. Breathing heavily, he rose onto his hands, letting her guide him to her. Desire contorted his face, and his burning gaze met hers as they joined. Shade let loose a wild cry, heedless of attracting enemies.

With the cold blackness of the Wastes the only witness, they lost themselves, finding heat and joy and comfort. Grief hovered at the edges of their awareness, and neither wanted to face it. They chose to drown in each other instead. They rose together to the peak, moving as one in an urgent rhythm, then fell together afterwards into sweet oblivion.

Later, stars bright above them, limbs entwined in a tangled heap, panting, satiated, Shade held Matteo close and ran her fingers through his dark, silky hair. His chest rose and fell in untroubled sleep. No circles had been set, but she felt no concern. If there were beasts close enough to threaten them, they would have come by now. Even the blight seemed distant. Satine had not sent them out to die. The earth beneath them radiated warmth and peace, something she hadn't noticed in the throes of passion. They lay upon a qaraz – no, several qaraz, and it formed a node of clean power, stronger protection than any circle she could have drawn.

They were at the Nexus.

The warmth of the sun pulled Shade up from the depths of exhaustion. The ground was hard beneath her, small rocks jabbed her back and buttocks, and a warm body lay close, a heavy arm and a muscular leg thrown across her. It was late, she could tell by the heat in the air, but she was sore and tired and chilled after a freezing night spent without shelter – the Nexus had kept the beasts away, but not the cold – and her heart ached with loss. She had promised to keep her companions safe, vowed to take them through the Glass Fields unscathed, and she had lost Angelo. It was cold comfort to know he had stayed behind willingly.

When Matteo woke, would he hate her? Gently, she stroked his arm, tracing his tattoos – disembodied claws and nightmarish faces growing from branches and vines. Strangely violent imagery for such a gentle man. Their night of passion replayed itself in her mind and she felt a warm ache pinch her belly. Before last night she hadn't considered Matteo as anything other than a friend, though he was strong and handsome, brave and funny. She couldn't bear the thought that he would blame her for Angelo.

She ran her fingers up his arm to his shoulder and down again, gently stroking his tattooed skin. Her sensitive fingertips felt the tracery of healed scars across his skin, the same faint scars she bore as well. One cost of their magic. Dante Safire had more scars on his skin, she recalled with a vague sense of guilt. It passed swiftly. Things between her and Dante would always be complicated. She and Matteo had turned to each other out of need, pure and simple. They had nothing to feel guilty about. She shifted closer to him, pressing her face into his chest, breathing in his scent.

Matteo stirred. He adjusted himself to take his weight off her and gathered her into his arms. She felt him kiss the top of her head and the heat in her belly flared. His reaction to her was immediately apparent since they lay skin to skin. Absently, she hoped they hadn't ruined any of their clothing in their eagerness to remove it. They weren't exactly well-equipped out here, even if this Nexus would keep them relatively safe.

Thoughts of survival and safety slipped to the back of her mind as her body's response to his caresses consumed her.

The sun's heat beat down on them when they finally collapsed together in a sweaty knot of limbs and tangled hair. Panting, Shade managed a soft laugh. "You certainly know how to wake a girl."

He rolled onto his elbow to look down at her. His cheeks were flushed and his brow creased. "Shade, I didn't... I mean, I'm sor–"

"Don't." She put her fingers over his lips. "Don't say you're sorry. I'm not. We needed comfort last night, and we found it." She smiled. "This... This was for us. I don't regret any of it."

His eyes were still troubled, appearing almost gray in the bright light. "I know you and Prince Safire…" His voice trailed off, and he looked away, loose strands of his dark hair falling over his brow. "I know I shouldn't have let this happen. I shouldn't have given in to…to my feelings. But I've wanted you for so long."

"Have you?" Surprised, she reached up to brush his hair back from his face. "You never acted like it."

He looked down at her with a crooked smile. "I thought it was obvious. Angelo was always warning me not to stare at you." A chuckle rumbled deep in his chest, then his expression darkened, and his eyes squeezed shut in sudden pain.

She caressed his face. "Matteo," she whispered.

His eyes opened, desire smoldered in their depths, and his hand tightened on her hip. "Keep saying my name like that, and I may be ready to 'comfort' you again."

Regretfully, Shade extricated herself from his arms. Her clothes were scattered nearby, thankfully intact. She got to her feet and dressed while Matteo did the same. The sun was brutal above them, they needed shade and water. She was buckling on her knife belt when Matteo called to her. He was kneeling beside two satchels resting on the red earth, rifling through their contents. Grim-faced, he looked at her. "I guess they didn't dump us out here to die, at least. We have rations, and a water skin apiece."

Well, that was one less thing to worry about. Hills surrounded them, some broken and jagged, others smooth-sloped and almost whole. The Razor Ridge mountains rose to the west, but the hills hid the land in all other directions. She faced the mountains and felt a moment of disorientation. This place was… familiar. A valley between two broken hills. A valley she recognized.

"This is the place," she whispered. She closed her eyes briefly and gripped her blades. "Thank you, Satine…"

"Do you know where we are?" Matteo asked, coming to

stand beside her. He stood close but didn't touch her as if suddenly shy even after all that had happened.

"The Nexus," she said. "This is where I was meant to come, not the lands of the Kindred. Here." She looked at him. His jaw was clenched as he stared at the hills. "You know what I have to do now, don't you?"

He tensed and his hands went to his blades reflexively. "I know, but... do you really have to? The magic," and he shivered in spite of the heat. "It's so dangerous. Are you sure you want to do this?"

"No," she admitted with a shaky laugh. The memory of that awful magic filled her with a bone-deep terror, and she began to shiver. By the Faces, what was wrong with her? Why was she being so weak?

"Shade..."

Matteo gathered her into his arms. He was tall – her head fit neatly beneath his chin. Her shivers turned to uncontrollable shaking as she fought the fear rising within her. She released her blades and clung to him, her arms wrapping around his waist.

"I don't want to do this," she said, and felt his arms squeeze tight.

"Then don't. I won't tell anyone."

Her laugh was half-sob, but, slowly, her trembling ceased, and she no longer felt overwhelming terror. She released a long, shuddering breath, relaxing against him. "I don't want to do this," she repeated, more firmly this time. She could feel the slow thump of his heart where her ear was pressed against his broad chest. It calmed her, steadied her. "But I will."

CHAPTER TWENTY-FIVE

When they left the shelter of the thorn trees, the sun sat low in the sky and their long shadows chased them. It was dangerous riding in the worst heat of the day, but even more dangerous to ride at night. Time was against them. They rode hard, racing against the dying day as they followed a faint qaraz through the rough terrain of broken hills and twisted scrub. The strange power which had alerted Korin to Shade's location in the first place had faded, but he knew where she was. He'd set them on this particular qaraz – however reluctantly – assuring them it would lead them to the Nexus by the quickest route. Dante had a hard time believing anything he said at this point, but he didn't know how else to reach Shade.

Korin rode with him. Dante had wanted to keep him close. He was a Sicani, who knew the depth of his power?

Sicani...

It explained so much. Korin's extraordinary ability to heal, his longevity, his knowledge of those ancient people – *his* people. No wonder he'd been able to sense Sicani blood in others. Blood called to blood. He'd said it to Dante his whole life. Still, it was one thing to be strong in Sicani blood, quite another to *be* a Sicani. A legend come to life. Which meant he was probably right about the Unseen. He would know his ancient enemy, wouldn't he?

The uneven stride of his struggling horse jarred Dante from his thoughts, and he focused on riding and keeping the beast to the proper path. It was a constant fight to keep the terrified animals from bolting. A constant cost of blood. Behind him, Korin gasped at a particularly hard jolt and clung to his belt. Dante grimaced. This was hard travel for a man his age, however old he was. He crushed every bit of sympathy he might have normally felt for his mentor. His actions had set them on this path – racing to save Shade, racing to save all of Malavita.

"Will you know if she begins the Veil magic?" he said gruffly. He didn't want to talk to Korin, but he needed some answers. He snarled, and added angrily, "Would you even tell us if you did?"

"You'll know if she works such magic," Korin replied grimly. "We all will. Any bloodwizard within miles will feel it."

"For your sake, you'd better hope she waits to raise her Veil."

"I have done what must be done; these are plans a century in the making. Malavita will be free of her blight at long last. I only wish you could understand the true threat we face. Sacrifices are necessary."

"I never took you for a fanatic, Korin. Of course, I never took you for such a talented liar, either." Bitterness laced his words; he'd pushed the pain of betrayal to the back of his mind, but it struck him at times like the thrust of a knife. Fear for Shade drove him to shove aside his personal agony, though. She was all that mattered.

"I never lied. Not to you. We didn't lie to Shade, either. She only heard what she wanted to hear. Her fate is her own."

Korin's grim words should have stoked the rage Dante already felt deep in his belly. But instead, a strange and sudden hope filled him, a soul-deep certainty. As sure as the sun rose, he knew Shade would find a way to change the fate others had planned for her.

"I guarantee all your plans will come to nothing," Dante said, confidence raising his spirits. His horse's stride smoothed beneath him as if the animal sensed his renewed faith. "You may think Shade is your tool, and your sacrifice, but she's bent the world around her to suit her goals more times than I can count. If anyone can upend a century's worth of planning, it is Shade Nox."

From their perch atop one of the high, broken hills looming over the valley, Shade and Matteo watched darkness creep over the land as they laid fuel for a fire. The sun had slipped behind the mountains, leaving them in shadow. Matteo had drawn the circles of protection, sparing Shade her strength, and they were ready to settle in for the night.

They had climbed to this place earlier in the day after exploring the valley first for a suitable location to lay the Quattro Canto. Because of the confluence of several qaraz, the Nexus managed to be shielded from the worst of the blight. The grass – not exactly green or healthy – was nonetheless more akin to normal grass than not, and the stunted scrub and twisted trees were merely unsightly rather than lethal. Upon further exploration of the valley, they had managed to find a small spring trickling from the base of a rocky cliff. Tasting the clean, clear water convinced Shade she had been led true by her visions. Not even the power of the qaraz reassured her as much.

"The Quattro Canto should be placed somewhere high," she had said as they'd refreshed themselves at the spring. Hot and sweaty from the day's exertions, Shade soaked a kerchief in the cold water and wiped her face clean while Matteo filled their water skins. "We have to be able to protect our position until the Veil is raised."

"A high place," he murmured, shading his eyes with his hand and peering up the cliff. It was steep, rocky and covered in brambles, but the top of it clearly rose above the valley. "Would that be high enough?" he asked, pointing straight up.

Shade followed his hand, squinting against the bright sun. It wouldn't be an easy climb, and her limbs shook at the thought, but she knew in her bones it was the right spot. Nexus or not, once she called her magic, the beasts would swarm like flies to blood. They needed a defensive position.

"We'll have to climb using our own good hands and sure feet," she said, wiping her neck with her damp kerchief. "We can't call any magic until we're ready, agreed?"

He nodded. "It's going to be tough," he said, and flashed her a smile. "I could carry you on my back if you want. You don't look too heavy."

"Maybe it'll be tough for you," Shade scoffed and poked him in the chest. "But I'm half mountain goat."

"Ow." Matteo rubbed his chest and squinted at her doubtfully. "I think I'd remember that."

Grinning, she ducked past him and leapt at the cliff, fingers and toes finding cracks and handholds effortlessly. "How about I race you to the top?" she said, throwing him a wink over her shoulder.

"You're on, lady witch!"

Despite her bravado, the climb up the cliff was a brutal test of endurance in the late afternoon heat. Breath searing in her lungs, Shade struggled to hoist herself to each new handhold, sweat stinging her eyes and her muscles quivering. Below her and to her left, Matteo kept pace but never managed to reach her, let alone surpass her. Not because he wasn't a good climber. Each time she faltered – her feet slipping once and leaving her dangling by her fingertips, and another when a shrub she grabbed loosened in her hand – he was there to catch her or lend a hand. More than once, his sure grip was all that had kept her from tumbling to the ground far below.

By the time she reached the top and hoisted him up beside her, she could do nothing but lie on the hard, red earth and heave for breath. The blistering sun finally drove her to her feet. They needed to find shelter. The top of the cliff was a wide plateau covered by twisted scrub and clumps of sharp grasses. The ground was blood-red sand; it crunched beneath their feet as Shade led them to a clump of trees offering some protection from the sun.

"This is the place," she said, turning in a slow circle. The rightness of her decision settled on her like a cloak. She smiled at Matteo and took his hand, squeezing. "You feel it, too, don't you?"

"Yes." He peered at the land below. "I can keep watch while you work your magic. I'll protect you as best I can."

"I know you will."

She had given his hand a final squeeze and let go.

And now, with the sun tucked behind the mountains and the sky turned to a dusky rose, Matteo prepared a meal for them over the low, hot fire they'd managed. He'd spread out their blankets for the night, positioning them as he had the whole journey until Shade raised an eyebrow at him. With a shy grin, he rearranged them together, making a cozy nest.

"I wasn't sure," he said, coming to sit beside her while she ate the thick porridge he'd made them. "And I didn't want to presume…"

"How gentlemanly of you," she murmured, nudging him with her elbow. "But I think I'd rather be warm tonight than well-rested."

He chuckled and gave her a look which made her belly tighten pleasantly. She held his gaze for a moment. How had she not noticed his eyes? They were blue with an inner ring of green, but more, they were kind and expressive.

Not a hard, intense cobalt full of shadows and mystery. And pain…

Shade looked away, her heart aching. She'd never noticed Matteo's eyes because of Dante Safire. She'd wanted him almost since the day she'd met him. His honor and integrity, his strength of will and determination had attracted her. He'd treated her with respect, never doubting her power, or her word. No man had ever intrigued her as much as he had. It didn't hurt that he was tall, well-built and darkly handsome. There had always been heat between them, a mutual attraction, but they could never be together, not openly. It would cause far too many problems. Dante was a city-prince, the last scion of a First Family. He couldn't be lovers with the Black Witch. And if she hid herself behind a dress, in some new aristocratic persona, how could she live with herself? Besides, she would be tied to her Veil soon, and he had to stay in Sicaria to conduct his business. Perhaps she'd turned to Matteo because she knew she and Dante were doomed?

She shifted on the hard earth, no longer interested in her dinner, and stared at the glowing coals. Beside her, Matteo grew still. "Are you not hungry?" he asked quietly.

"No, I'm–" She shook her head. How could she tell him what she was thinking? Shrugging off her sour thoughts, she gave him a smile and picked up her spoon. "I'm fine."

Silence settled between them and the day grew dark around them. The broad dome of sky turned from a dusky purple to a pure black spangled with stars. The glowing coals of their fire was small competition for the myriad stars spinning overhead. They seemed to spiral upwards into an endless nothingness. Despite the hot fire, Shade shivered, feeling tiny next to this infinity. She moved closer to Matteo, comforted by his warmth and solidness. He was real, at least, and here beside her.

And where is Dante? And Raiden? My friends? Why do I feel like I'm facing everything alone?

"When will you begin?"

Shade looked at Matteo. The fire burned hot but didn't produce much light. Strange shadows played across his face, outlining his sharp jawline and straight nose. His eyes looked dark as he regarded her.

"As soon as I can," she replied, feigning confidence. She sighed and leaned against him. She wasn't alone. "Maybe tomorrow, or maybe the day after that. I do need to rest. This journey has been difficult."

He shifted and put his arm around her, pulling her close. "Take a few days if you need to. We have enough supplies to last a week if we stretch things, and there's water close." He grew still. "What happens after the Veil is raised?"

"I will send for the clans and call them home." It would be a simple thing; she would send birds made of fire and air to any Golondrina clan within reach. They would bring their wagons, their supplies, and their herds of goats. Hopefully, the Veil would be big enough to shelter them all even in its nascent state. She supposed it would depend on her will and power.

"Lord Safire will come, as well, I should think," he said.

"If he's able, I have no doubt. His wealth will fund our efforts after all." Shade frowned. Where was Dante? Had he freed Raiden from the Brotherhood yet? Or were they all languishing in a polizia cell? She pushed the thought aside. It didn't matter. She couldn't help them until after her own work was finished. And she couldn't put off what had to be done, no matter how tempting it was. She knew she didn't have time to waste. Satine had made that much clear; if she was to make a difference, she had to make it sooner rather than later. The Wastes hung in a precarious balance. She had to set it right.

"I will take a little time to prepare," she said, molding herself to him. She was *not* alone. "Tomorrow, then one last night. On the second morning, I will raise my Veil."

He gave her a comforting squeeze. "As you say, my lady."

His touch stirred a response deep in her belly, and she turned to him, lifting her face to his. He kissed her, his lips soft, gentle. Gripped by sudden need, she reached up and buried her hand in his hair, pulling hard. She was not alone. He was here. And Dante was far away.

Matteo groaned and his kiss deepened, gentleness swept

away by her passionate response. They tumbled into their blankets, wrenching away clothes and seeking bare flesh. Shade reveled in the feel of him, hard muscles beneath surprisingly soft skin, and her hands and mouth played across his body until he was gasping in delight. He returned the favor with remarkable skill, leaving Shade to wonder if her cries might attract unwanted attention. In the moment, though, she could hardly bring herself to care.

An urgency gripped them as their bodies joined at last, a frantic need to feel and be felt. They made love as if tomorrow would never come. As if this night, this moment, might be their last.

CHAPTER TWENTY-SIX

It was full dark when they finally stopped to make camp. They found shelter in the lee of a cluster of hills, though the rocks might also shelter a myriad of Waste beasts. Dante didn't care. He trusted his blades and the strength of his companions to keep them all safe from whatever might come. Beast or man...

Korin's betrayal burned in his gut like a bad piece of pork, the pain of it second only to his worry for Shade. Any second, he expected to feel her magic on the wind. He knew it intimately. Even before they'd shared a bed, he would have known her magic across half the world. The intensity of his feelings toward her surprised him even after all that had happened between them. It was more than lust and desire for her, more than just wanting to be with her again. He needed her. He needed her *power.*

Dante's hands trembled as he walked the perimeter of their hasty camp, working with his blades to lay a circle of protection. The sapphire gleamed with his blood and pulsed slightly in reaction to his emotions. He stumbled to a halt, wondering at the feeling which gripped him. It wasn't lust, and it certainly wasn't love. He licked his lips as if he might be able to taste her still. It had been intoxicating – the taste of her power. The power in her blood. Like his, yes, but not. Was she... was she a Sicani? Or just strong in Sicani blood?

Korin had always said she wasn't strong in Sicani blood, but how could Dante believe anything he'd ever said? He shook his head and resumed his work. Whatever made Shade Nox special didn't much matter. Sicani or something else, her power would give him what he so desperately wanted – the Veil.

She'll find a way. Dante found himself back where he'd started, near where Raiden was tending to their exhausted horses. *Some way to raise the Veil without destroying everything, and I must be there when she does.*

"The circle is set," Dante announced, emerging from the shadows to join Raiden. Cyril and the boys already had a fire blazing nearby. "How are the horses?"

Giving the tall, red mare he'd been riding with Manoli a comforting pat, Raiden turned to him. Frown lines marred his forehead and his eyes were shadowed. "They are suffering, but they have more to give." He blew out a breath, adding grimly, "Not much, I'm afraid."

Dante grimaced. It was unfortunate, but unavoidable. He'd run a hundred horses into the ground to get to Shade, and he knew Raiden felt the same. But neither had to like doing it.

"How far away are we?" Raiden asked, stroking the mare.

"Korin thinks maybe a few days, depending on how hard we push the animals."

Raiden's hand paused a moment, then resumed stroking. "Will we be in time?"

"We have to be."

Raiden glanced over his shoulder toward the others. "Are you sure we shouldn't leave Korin behind?"

"Believe me, I've asked myself the same, but I can't abandon him to the Wastes. Though it is tempting." Dante followed Raiden's gaze, and ruthlessly suppressed a wave of pity to see his old mentor hunched in on himself in misery. He grinned humorlessly. "Besides, I want to see what Shade will do to him."

Raiden's gaze grew shadowed, turned inward. "I fear what Shade will do before we reach her. What if she raises the Veil? She'll bring doom to everyone, herself included."

"Don't be so certain. Where is your faith, captain? I thought you believed in her."

"There is too much at risk this time. We can't be blinded by our faith." He paused. "Or our love."

"*Our* love?" Dante echoed with a touch of anger. He fought to control a rising wave of feeling: jealousy, possessiveness, rage. Shade was his. She *belonged* to him–

The ferocity of his emotions hit him like a shock of cold water. Belonged? She *belonged* to him? He blinked, a chill replacing the heat of anger. How could he think such a thing? Shade would knife him in the belly if she ever heard him say it out loud.

"We all love Shade," Raiden was saying, but Dante barely heard him through the roaring in his ears. What was wrong with him? He hadn't been so obsessed with Shade before. He'd been attracted to her, certainly, and he cared about her deeply. Sleeping with her had been wonderful, but these feelings coursing through him bore no resemblance to love.

"I do love Shade," he said slowly, trying to work through a cascade of feelings.

"I know." There was a resignation in Raiden's voice that pulled Dante out of his circling thoughts. He shook his head, trying to clear it.

The taste of her on his lips, the taste of her power. The Wild Power, so dangerous yet so intoxicating...

A shudder rolled down him, and he had a moment of stark clarity. "I love Shade, how could I not? But she and I–" He shook his head again, in sorrow this time. "We can never be more than what we are. I need her power, her magic. She needs my wealth and my ties to the Empire. Together, we will build something grand, something new, but we have our places in this world. And those places exist far apart from one another."

A soft, bitter laugh broke from Raiden. "Not so long ago, I thought I knew my place in this world, my purpose. I was bound by duty and loyalty; my fealty was to my royal blood. Every day of my life was spent in service to it. Then I was cast out by my family. Sacrificed without a thought. I didn't expect to feel such resentment, such bitterness and hate. It consumed me. And I felt that way until a man I barely knew sacrificed himself to save me. Because he saw honor in me, worth." Raiden's hand lifted to stroke his mare again. "Sometimes, the best thing that can happen is finding a new place in this world. You might want to try it."

"It's not so simple," Dante said. "If we married, she'd have to give up her blades, become a proper lady. Can you see her doing that? I could never ask it of her."

"Is that the only way to be together? For her to fit into your world?"

It was Dante's turn to laugh bitterly. "I worked my whole life to regain my family's wealth and position in Malavita, do you think I would toss it away to go live among the Golondrina?"

"Wouldn't it be worth it? If that's what it took to be with her?"

"No," he admitted grudgingly. "Not to me." Dante sighed. It was a terrible thing to say, but it was the truth. He was glad the darkness hid the flush of shame on his cheeks. He'd been so afraid to let himself care about Shade, so afraid of getting hurt again. It hadn't occurred to him he might hurt her. By the Faces, had he taken advantage of her? Of her love for him?

"Then you shouldn't let her think you have a future together. If she's in love with you, it will only hurt more if you try to spare her the truth. Especially if you truly care about her."

"I do, I care about her a great deal. But you're right, I must tell her the truth. We can never be together."

It hurt to say it out loud, but not as much as he'd expected. Dante exhaled and looked at Raiden. A small smile played about his lips, and his gaze had turned inward.

"She never said she loved me," Dante said suddenly, watching him closely. The man blinked and looked down.

"Oh?" he said, a bit too casually. "Then maybe her heart is safe. That should be a relief to you."

"Yes," Dante murmured. His fear and worry roared back to the forefront. "If only a broken heart was the worst thing that could happen to her."

Raiden took third watch, relieving a yawning Petra.

"Any trouble?" he asked the russet haired Golondrina.

Petra shook his head and shot a glance toward Korin's blanket-shrouded figure. "The old man's been sleeping like a baby. I think I watched him more than the Wastes." He grinned, his face wan with exhaustion. "Mostly to make sure Cyril or Manoli didn't knife him in his sleep."

"Hmm." Raiden clapped him on the shoulder. "Go to sleep, my friend."

Yawning wide enough to crack his jaw, Petra nodded and dropped into his blankets. His soft snoring rose above the crackle of the fire a moment later. Smiling, Raiden stirred the fire, added a clump or two of dung – he had no idea from what animal – and took his place at the perimeter of camp. Just after dusk, they'd had two incursions of Waste beasts, but between Dante and the Golondrina, they had managed to drive them off. Even the horses weren't tempting enough with such strong wizards to hand, and Dante's circles were powerful. Standing watch at this point was more about human trespassers.

None of them believed they had escaped pursuit so easily. And all of them feared their pursuers were hanging back and waiting for them to reach Shade. But it couldn't be helped. They had to reach her. And soon.

Urgency gripped Raiden, a desire to be moving. Though exhausted himself, sleep had proven elusive. Standing watch at least gave him something to do. Raiden adjusted his sword and began a slow circuit of camp. He checked on the horses, his mare whickering to him softly in greeting. They were as anxious as he was, fearful and stressed. He spent a moment soothing the animals then moved closer to the steep slopes rising away from their camp.

The rocky hills held shadows and hidden crevasses perfect for concealment. Away from the fire, he let his eyes adjust to the darkness and watched for any movement. If someone intended to approach them unnoticed, they would come through the hills.

"Captain..."

The word was a breath of wind against his cheek. Startled, Raiden drew his sword. He held still, searching the darkness. Shrubs and twisted brush threw shadows across the rocks, shadows which moved in the dancing campfire. He watched for movement counter to the flames.

There. An outline of neither shrub, nor rock, nor skulking beast. A man... made entirely of darkness.

"Who's there?" he said, but pitched his voice low. He didn't want to rouse his friends for nothing.

But was it nothing? Or did he not want them to wake for another reason?

"Thank the Faces, I have found you, my son." The voice, not the wind, was close to a whisper. "The time draws near. Disaster is imminent."

He recognized the voice and blinked in surprise. Lowering his sword, he stepped closer to the man hidden in darkness. A face emerged atop a long, flowing cloak of black. Jacobis.

A sudden warmth sprang to life at his chest. It filled him to the ends of his toes. His limbs trembled with it as he sheathed his weapon. "Brother Jacobis," he whispered. Shock faded in the warmth. Of course, he was here. Why wouldn't he be?

"My dear captain, I fear you must come with me," the priest said, approaching slowly, one hand raised, fingers crooked. Like a reaching claw. A dark ruby glowed softly on his chest – twin to the one beneath Raiden's jacket. It pulsed, and he felt an answering throb against his heart.

"I have felt a bending, an ancient power which has no place in this land." Jacobis' eyes looked black. His gaze bored into Raiden. "The woman will work terrible magic soon, and it cannot be allowed."

Shade...

A vision surfaced in Raiden's mind: a woman with gleaming blond hair and a smattering of pale freckles across her cheeks, smiling at some secret only she knew. Emotion filled him, and he struggled against the warmth holding him. This wasn't right. Something was wrong about–

Heat beat against his breast. Jacobis' fingers tightened as if he held Raiden's heart in his hands and was squeezing. Shade's face faded. Jacobis' fingers clenched into a fist and a red haze dropped over Raiden's vision. For a moment, he gasped for breath, fighting even though he wasn't moving. He couldn't move. Sweat slipped down his face, dampened his uniform.

"She is going to raise her Veil. It will destroy us, my son. Protect us, protect everyone from her folly..."

The Veils will fall... thousands will die...

Shade would never do that; she would never harm an innocent. He'd watched her show mercy to her enemies...

And felt her call on power strong enough to shatter the world.

"The woman will break the world if she isn't stopped. Only you can stop her."

The words were thunder. A shudder racked him, and peace followed. He knew what he had to do.

"How soon?" he asked. The haze had lifted, and the world around him developed a sudden clarity. "Can I still stop her?"

"Yes." The word was a strange hiss, and Jacobis' face lit with triumph before dissolving into a mask of concern. "It's not too late. We have a little time. Perhaps until dawn."

"Dawn?" Raiden rubbed his chin. The night was sharp and clear around him, but his thoughts seemed slow. Thick. "But Korin thinks we are days away from her."

"You are. But there are ways to travel more quickly, ways only we know."

"The Brotherhood?" Raiden blinked at him. Jacobis had come rather close; he loomed over him almost menacingly. Nostrils flaring, the priest took him by the arm. "Not the Brotherhood," he said. His eyes slid sideways toward their camp, and he grimaced as if in distaste. "He may be able to follow us, but it can't be helped."

"Who can follow? Dante? I should let him know–"

"There is no time!"

With his free hand, Jacobis grasped Raiden's jacket. No – he grasped the amulet hidden underneath and wrenched him forward. Raiden stumbled a few steps, and darkness surrounded him. He felt as if he'd been dropped into a well of ink. Another step forward – he felt Jacobis dragging him but could see nothing. Then the world settled around them once more.

They were still in the Wastes, but not near the hills where he and his friends had camped. A grove of twisting, black trees surrounded them, casting strange shadows. From beneath the trees, glowing eyes appeared. The hair on Raiden's neck rose as low growls erupted from the darkness. Frowning, unconcerned, Jacobis stepped into the closest shadow, dragging Raiden with him. The world seemed to shift around them once again.

"Here. She's here…"

The words drifted to his ears as if from a great distance. "Jacobis!" Raiden gasped as he was suddenly released, his arms pinwheeling to keep his balance. The ground was hard and sandy beneath his boots, and the sky overhead was bright with stars. There were hills, but at a distance. The trees and the creatures lurking among them had vanished. He was somewhere else.

Here, Jacobis had said, where was here?

Slowly, Raiden turned. The priest was gone, and he was alone in the Wastes. His heart still pounding from the strange

experience – how far had they traveled in those few seconds? –
he focused on his surroundings. Jacobis had brought him here
for a reason. *She* would be nearby.

A light flickered atop a distant hill, one higher than the
others and broken along its face. It would be a difficult climb
up the rocky cliff, but not impossible. Much faster than trying
to navigate its bramble-clogged slopes. The amulet pulsed, and
Raiden pulled it from beneath his shirt. It would lead him to
her, he was sure of it. Clutching the stone until his fingers
ached, Raiden started toward the cliff.

The cold woke Shade from an unsettled sleep. Disjointed
dreams had chased her through a broken rest: her friends
running, fighting, dying, a vast, red globe of black-laced fire
growing ever-larger, ever-stronger, a priest with blood-colored
hair and a blood-covered face, grinning at her in triumph.
When the dream-skies began to rain blood, she'd felt the bone-
deep chill of the night and awakened shivering.

Beside her, mere inches away, Matteo slept with his broad
back to her. It felt like a chasm separated them. A chasm, and
a wall. She only needed to shift, ever-so-slightly, and she could
wrap her arms around him. Find warmth. Comfort. But she
didn't move. Couldn't move. Something more than cold had
awakened her.

The night lay heavy still, dawn was a few hours away. She
needed rest, more sleep. Her body ached, her muscles stiff
from the day's exertions. It would be so easy to nestle against
Matteo and fall back into oblivion, even if it meant a few bad
dreams.

But… had they been more than dreams?

Yes. The certainty sent a tremor through her. Not bad
dreams. A warning. Something dark had uncoiled in the
Wastes. Something ancient and evil. Something that wanted
her dead. No, not dead. *Obliterated.*

Shade sat up, her blanket falling from her. She was dressed but for her knife-belt which she'd been using as a pillow. Without disturbing Matteo, she rose and buckled it on. Immediately, she felt better. Not only did she have her blades, she had the stones her father had died for. She wouldn't let it be for nothing. They held pure magic, the elements encapsulated. She would use their power when she raised the Veil, releasing it as needed. It might make all the difference between success and failure.

Her breath frosted with every exhalation. The sand crunched beneath her sandals as she slipped away from her blankets. The vast sky above wheeled with stars. She craned her head back to stare at infinity. But for the sense of an evil presence nearby, she could have been the only person in the world. She took a deep breath, held it, then let it stream from her in a crystalline cloud.

Soft steps crunched behind her. She smiled. Matteo. Of course, he'd awakened, too. He'd vowed to protect her. He would give his life for her. She knew this, though she had no intention of letting him. But she did need his help for what came next.

"Shade?" he asked, his soft question like a thunderclap in the silence.

"I need you to draw more circles," she said, her eyes on the stars overhead. It was a shame a Veil dimmed their glory. A small price. "Circles upon circles. Strong enough to withstand a Blackstorm. I can't wait another day. It's time."

CHAPTER TWENTY-SEVEN

Seated at the center of the hilltop, Shade watched Matteo draw blood with his tourmaline blades. The stars had faded to pinpoints but dawn was still an hour or more away. His tattoos gleamed in the dimness, and the pale green stone of his knives pulsed like fireflies. She ached to add her blood to his. Tourmaline was strong, but it could only manipulate the Four Faces. Matteo was strong, but she was stronger. If she didn't add the Hidden Face to the circles, would they fail when she needed them most?

Shade kneaded the hilts of her blades, finding both comfort and trepidation in the feel of the well-worn bone. Since she'd crafted them in the shadow of Mount Sera, the very earth steaming and rumbling beneath her, she'd depended on her blades like her own limbs. They were the source of her power, and the source of her greatest fear: the Wild Power.

I can't lose control. I cannot.

She'd repeated it to herself ever since she'd decided to raise her Veil. It was starting to lose meaning. No longer words, but some nervous tick.

I can't lose control. Can't lose control. Don't lose control...

Every time she called her magic, she knew the danger, but she'd always accepted it. No, *relished* it. The fear of the Wild Power was almost as intoxicating as the power of the Four and the Hidden. But this, this was different. If she lost control of the Veil magic – if she summoned the Wild Power during it – she might unleash the lowest hells across all of Malavita.

You wanted me to raise my Veil to stabilize the Wastes, Satine. What if I destroy the world instead?

She released her blades and ran her sweaty palms against her thighs, over the twin, green-eyed dragons Satine had inked. Now was not the time for second-guessing. She understood the magic – Satine's vision had ingrained the ritual within her. But for the creation of the cornerstones, it wasn't far from what her father had taught her. She knew what she had to do, and she was ready to do it. And she wasn't alone; Matteo was here.

For a moment, she missed Angelo sharply. He'd been a solid, stable presence. His absence was palpable in every move Matteo made. Setting up camp or searching for fuel took twice as long for him alone. Some tasks were left undone, and Shade had tried her best to fill in for Angelo, but she knew it wasn't nearly the same. Angelo's absence hung like a shadow over them.

Satisfied with his work, Matteo gave a nod, sheathed his blades and returned to her. He handed her the water skin they'd filled from the spring. He didn't sit beside her, but stood over her, alert and watchful. Shade drank. She might not be able to drink again for some time. Once she started, she would not be able to stop until it was finished.

"Dawn's close," Matteo said. He looked down at her. "The circles will hold, Shade."

Shade lowered the water skin. Their eyes locked. "I know. I trust you."

He helped her to her feet. For a moment, they stood facing each other, only their hands touching. Shade could see the worry in his gaze, even in the darkness.

No, it was no longer dark. She could see his face, the lines and planes of it. He was pale in the gray light. His fingers tightened on hers. "I swear my life to you, lady witch." He spoke gravely, his eyes serious. "I will protect you until my last breath. If you fall, it is only because I have fallen."

"Don't fall then," she said, her throat suddenly thick.

A smile flashed on his face. Sun from behind a dark cloud. He stepped back, giving her hand a final squeeze before releasing it. "I don't plan on it."

"At least we're in agreement – no one falls today. Now." She took a deep breath and made sure she was in the center of the circles he'd drawn. Marking the cardinal points, she placed the cornerstones at their respective directions. When she needed to unleash their power, they had to be close. "Don't stop me once I've begun. No matter what happens, no matter how much I might scream. This will be ugly, bloody, frightening. Just… let me do what I have to do."

"I understand," Matteo said, though he didn't look happy about it. "No matter what happens, I won't interfere."

"Good." She took one last look at him and turned to the east. The sky was brightening rapidly.

The bone handles of her obsidian blades were cool in her grip, familiar and comforting. She drew both blades. They were extensions of her hands, her body, her soul. The sharp obsidian parted the skin on her forearm. Blood welled from the cut, black against the bright colors of her tattoos. A rush of ecstasy followed the sting of pain. She hissed a breath, and the air between her teeth tasted like the finest wine.

With the first drops of spilled blood she called to the Eastern Face – Air – and felt the wind rise around her. Shade caught it, spun it into a funnel, and wrapped it around her like a cloak. The sun broke the horizon, bathing her in light. A chime rang out. The raw, uncut diamond she'd placed at the eastern point rose, pulsing faintly.

Again, she touched obsidian to her flesh and drew a parallel line to the first. A deeper cut, more blood, more magic. She turned and called upon the Southern Face of God: Fire. The air grew hot around her, throbbing and pulsing against her skin. Sweat popped from every pore and she found it hard to breath. A ruby as deep red as pigeon's blood lifted from the earth and she turned to the west. Now, she drew blood from her abdomen, slipping her blade between her vest and her kilt to slice the hard muscles across her belly. Water. The Western Face. One of the most powerful of the elements in the dry land of Malavita. Pure and clean, life-giving.

Shade added water to her funnel of magic. The hot, dry air grew muggy. Heavy. Every movement was an effort. And a sapphire the color of the ocean on a clear day rose before her eyes.

Excitement shivered through her. The power of the Brotherhood stones was immense, and she would need every scrap of it to call the true stones.

The blood she'd called vanished in the weave of her tattoos. But there would be more blood to pay.

A final turn. The Northern Face. Earth. Solid and sure beneath her feet. Stability, security. A deep power, an enormous power.

Not her strongest element, by far, though her blades had been born from the earth's deepest fire. To call earth, she drew blood from her thigh. A thrum started beneath her feet, pounding up through her soles, her calves. Her knees ached with it. She felt it in her bones. Strength eternal. She was a pillar connected to the world, channeling its power.

Green as grass, the emerald floated up to join its counterparts, spinning and throbbing eye-level to Shade.

Only the last Face remained. The Hidden Face. Spirit. In Satine's vision, the Sicani had been the one to call it. Those fledgling bloodwizards had not mastered such complex magic yet. Even now, only the strongest of the strong called upon the Hidden.

I am the strongest of the strong. I am Obsidian.

Shade gripped her blades until her knuckles whitened. This power would come from her alone. Whenever she called great amounts of Spirit, it left her open to the Wild Power. She hesitated, her heart hammering. Briefly, she met Matteo's gaze through the maelstrom of her magic. He nodded once. Shade gritted her teeth and slashed at her flesh with both blades, drawing blood from her arms, her legs, her chest. Swift, shallow cuts.

She called the Hidden Face.

Dante snapped awake. The earth beneath him was trembling. He sat up, blinking in the pre-dawn grayness. What in the lowest hells?

Then he felt it... a wave of power on the wind, through the earth. Elements colliding, coalescing. The beginning of something extraordinary.

"Shade," he whispered. His hands tangled in his blanket and he clutched it to him like a shield. Fear fought with wonder. She was raising the Veil, and he was too far away to stop her. Too far away to help her...

"Safire!" cried Cyril. He rose from his bedroll on the other side of the fire, a hand to his head. Even in the darkness, the whites of his eyes shone clearly, his mouth slack with panic. "It's Shade – she has begun!"

Dante tossed aside his blanket and stood. Cyril's panic was contagious, but he fought to calm his wild pulse. "Yes, I felt it. We have to go to her – now!"

Manoli and Petra had risen, as well. Any bloodwizard within miles, no matter their strength, would feel such magic. Both men were as wide-eyed as Cyril. A shudder rolled through Petra and he put a hand to his mouth.

"She can't," Manoli said, shaking his head wildly.

"She is," Dante countered grimly. He strode to Korin's bedroll, and shook the old man awake. "Get up! How far away are we? Wake up, old man!"

Korin blinked at him, his amber eyes unfocused. He seemed

dazed. Was Shade's magic affecting him, too? Angrily, Dante shook him again.

Suddenly, Korin's gaze sharpened. He gripped Dante's wrist, his lips peeled back from his teeth. "Unseen!" he hissed. "I feel their darkness."

"What? What are you talking–"

"Where's Raiden?" asked Petra, his voice rising. "He took last watch. Where is he?"

"Faces!" Manoli dashed toward the horses. They snorted and whinnied at his sudden movements, shuffling in their hobbles. He ignored them, searching the perimeter of their camp. There was no sign of Raiden. Manoli clutched his knife hilt. "Could something have dragged him off in the night?"

"Impossible." Cyril shook his head. "Not him. No beast would have gotten the better of him."

"Not a beast," Korin said. Fear had entered his eyes.

"Do you know what happened to him?" Dante hauled Korin to his feet, preferring anger to the dread rising in his chest. "Tell us!"

"I–I can't be certain." He put a shaking hand to his head. He was pale, drawn. Every year he'd lived seemed to crash down on him at once. "There's an… echo. A dark power was worked very near here."

Korin pushed past Dante and stumbled toward the hills. Cyril gave a low growl and shadowed him, but Korin wasn't trying to escape. He stopped at the perimeter of the camp. Shadows clung to the rocks in dawn's pale light, draping them in inky darkness. His head down, he seemed to be searching the ground for something. Abruptly, he stopped. "Here," he said. He spun back toward them. His golden eyes gleamed like torches. "A demon passed through the shadows here. I fear it may have taken the Imperial with it."

"A demon? Are you mad?"

"No, he's not," Cyril said grimly. He dropped into a crouch and examined the earth near Korin's feet. "I see Raiden's tracks, and another's. Both vanish in the same spot. As if they took a step together and fell off the earth."

"The Unseen use the blight to travel the Wastes," Korin said. "To them, the shadows are doorways."

"Your demon has the body of a man, Sicani. Look here, boot tracks. And here, at the feathering around them. He was wearing robes."

Manoli cursed at Cyril's words. "A priest! Faces spit on me, of course they harbor demons among them."

"I know who it was," Petra exclaimed, his eyes wide. "That red-haired priest. Manoli, you remember him? He talked to Raiden the night we escaped, pulled him aside for some secret exchange."

"You're not saying Raiden went with him willingly?" cried Manoli. He grasped his cousin's arm. "He wouldn't betray us!"

"I… I don't know." Stricken, Petra ran a shaking hand through his tangled hair. "I don't want to believe it…"

"Raiden Mad would not betray us," Cyril said. Wiping dust from his hands, he stood and faced Korin. The old man met his gaze, and something passed between them. An understanding. "The Unseen are powerful. They can bend even the strongest man to their will."

Korin nodded, not questioning how Cyril would know such a thing. "They have power, but it is limited. They use others as their tools. I fear they have a use for the captain."

"They want to kill Shade," Dante growled. He could feel her power on the wind. It had grown stronger. He strode to the horses and began to release their hobbles. "Raiden has an innate resistance to our magic, and his sword is quick. We have to stop him. He can't be far ahead of us–"

"They rode the shadows," Korin cried. "They've crossed miles with a few steps. We'll never reach her in time. Not on horseback."

"We have to try!" Dante tightened his mount's saddle with sharp, angry motions. "We'll run the horses into the ground if we have to. I'm not going to abandon her." He spun on Korin. "It won't serve your purpose for her to die *before* she raises the Veil!"

He recoiled as if Dante had struck him. "I was wrong, my son," he said softly. His eyes grew distant and he turned toward the southwest. Toward Shade. "I wanted to bring about the final war, no matter the cost, to destroy the Unseen at last, and I didn't see Shade as anything but a means to that end. But I was wrong. I thought the Unseen would want her to raise a Veil if it meant unleashing ruin. They revel in chaos, in death. That they are so desperate to stop her – to reveal themselves like this. I was wrong. Shade is… She's–"

Tears welled in the old man's eyes, and his lips trembled as emotion overwhelmed him. Dante stared at him in shock. What had changed his mind? He shook his head. It didn't matter.

"She's dead if we don't get to her in time," he said harshly, moving to Raiden's chestnut mare. "We have to ride."

"We can reach her in time," Cyril said, and Dante stopped, his hands on the girth strap. He looked over his shoulder at the Golondrina elder, not daring to let himself feel hope. Cyril glanced at Manoli, then Petra. Both men wore matching expressions of grim determination. "The Golondrina can travel the qaraz faster than a horse can run. Much faster." His lips thinned briefly, and he grimaced. "But only Golondrina have the ability. Only the three of us can get to her in time."

"Just show me the magic. I carry sapphire. Surely I can master this ability?"

"It is our Golondrina blood which grants us the power, Prince Safire." Dante's heart sank at the kindness in his tone. The regret. "It has nothing to do with blades or the Four and the Hidden. We can no more show you how to do it than a bird can show you how to fly."

His fragile hope shattered with Cyril's words. The world spun around him. It wouldn't be enough, just the three of them. They wouldn't be able to stop Raiden Mad. If he was in a demon's sway, he would kill them all. Dante turned away from Cyril, and rested his forehead on the hard, leather saddle. He could taste Shade's power on the wind. She was everywhere, but completely out of reach.

"The Golondrina are correct. They cannot grant you this power."

Korin spoke into the agonized silence, his voice clear and strong. Teeth clenched, Dante turned on him, ready to unleash bitter words. But a flare of blue light blinded him, and he shielded his eyes with his arm. "What–?" he gasped.

The blue light faded. Dante blinked spots from his eyes and focused on his mentor. Strength had returned to Korin. He stood tall and straight, his face was still wan but no longer slack with grief. Blue flames danced on his palm.

"But *I* can."

Korin tossed the fire into the air above them, and it rivaled the new risen sun. "It was my ancestors who tasked the Golondrina with maintaining the qaraz," he said. "The Coterie is wrong to think them oath breakers. They may have forgotten why after all these centuries, but the Golondrina have been diligent in their duties. Riding the qaraz is their gift, and their responsibility."

Dante eyed the globe of blue flames spinning above them. "We can travel the qaraz?" he demanded. "All of us?"

Korin nodded. "The Unseen travel in darkness and shadows, but we will travel in light."

A glow appeared beneath his feet. It banished the shadows around him and unfurled along the ground, splitting their camp in half and aiming into the Wastes. A pathway. Dante looked closer. Not quite. Currents flowed in its depths, moving swiftly toward the southwest. Petra gasped, but Manoli stooped down and touched it. His hand slipped into it and a laugh burst from him. Tendrils of light clung to his fingers as he pulled his hand free. Grinning, he straightened. "I'm glad we didn't kill you, Illario!"

"I've never seen it so strong," Cyril said, his gruff voice soft with awe. He narrowed his eyes at Korin with a grudging respect. "I guess your pet Sicani has finally come in handy, Safire."

Dante stepped to the edge of the flowing path, leading the horses. He couldn't leave them behind – they would be easy pickings. He stared into the river of light and felt a sudden urge to leap into it. This magic was familiar, yet so very alien. "What do we do?" he asked. "How do we…?"

"Just take a step, my lord," Korin said. His golden eyes gleamed and he beckoned Dante onto the path. The Golondrina had already taken the first step. They stood together, waiting. The currents of the shining qaraz flowed around them. Dante stepped onto the path.

CHAPTER TWENTY-EIGHT

Shade floated above the ground, her body caught in a swirl of power. Waves of energy poured off her, expanding in ever-greater circles. They pushed Matteo backward, toward the edge of the plateau. Distantly, she heard him shout. Lazily, she gestured with a blade and parted the waves. It sent a thrill through her to see the power respond so readily.

Matteo slipped inside her burgeoning creation and approached her cautiously. His eyes shone as he stared at her. "You're glorious!" he cried.

She couldn't speak. Fire roared through her veins, not blood. Her body was air, her bones the branches of a tree. An ocean embraced her. It would be nothing to sacrifice herself to this magic, to be connected to it for eternity. This was her purpose.

Suddenly, Matteo looked beyond her, and his eyes narrowed. She felt a slight concern, but it was distant. Matteo drew his blades and threw her a look. "Don't stop," he said. "I'll keep them back."

Them? Shade turned on a pillar of energy. Dark shapes slunk at the edges of her fledgling Veil, snuffling about for openings. She spotted lupari – black-scaled wolf-like creatures with razor sharp claws and teeth – and other vile creatures. All out for blood. *Her* blood.

The beasts of the Wastes both feared and craved the bloodwizards of Malavita. She was alone and caught in the throes of magic. To the beasts, she must seem like easy pickings. Matteo's circles of protection were holding them back, for now. He launched attacks at them, his pale green blades flashing. It worked. The dark forms scattered.

But even as he drove away beasts, more appeared to replace them. Urgency beat at her breast, pulsing in time to the growing waves. She turned again to the east, lifted one obsidian blade, and drove it deep into her belly. The razor-sharp obsidian parted skin and muscle with ease. It felt like a punch, and the shock made her gasp. And then—

Agony. It burned through to her spine, sending weakness down her legs. If power hadn't been holding her, she would have collapsed. Her arms trembled, and her gasp turned into a sobbing scream. Blood poured from the wound, but she couldn't draw the blade free, not yet. Not until…

A shriek rattled from her. Her vision dimmed and she reached for more power. The diamond hovering at the east swelled with light then burst like an overripe melon. Pieces of it landed on her skin and she absorbed its released strength gratefully. Bending over, she dug deeper into her flesh, searching with the tip of her sharp blade, sweating and panting. And then she felt it. A hardness against the tip of the obsidian.

Fighting nausea and a darkness at the edge of her vision, she levered at the object, tipping it closer to the surface of her body. When she felt it was close enough, she withdrew her blade. Blood washed over her hip in warm cascades. She held her blade between her teeth and reached in with her fingers. They closed around a smooth, cool object and she pulled it free.

Immediately, her abused flesh began to close, her tattoos working desperately to seal the wound. The blood clotted, ceased to flow, and the pain eased. The borrowed power from the shattered diamond rolled through her veins. She could breathe again, though tears blinded her. She lifted her prize. A new diamond. More perfect than any she'd ever seen, already cut and polished. Letting the power guide her, she released it and it stayed aloft, pulsing in time to her heart.

One...

Raiden climbed the cliff with preternatural ease. It had taken him longer to reach it than he'd expected. Fear and desperation chased him, driving him unerringly upwards. He had to stop her before she finished. All was lost otherwise. All those Veils, all those helpless people.

The amulet Jacobis had given him hung around his neck, tucked inside his uniform. It pulsed against his skin, emitting heat. Part of him wanted to tear it away and drop it to the earth far below, but something stayed his hand. He might need it on the hilltop; Jacobis said it would protect him.

The sun had broken the horizon by the time he reached the top of the cliff. Red light bathed a large plateau dotted with twisted scrub and small trees. He emerged in a tangled copse of stunted witch hazel and slowed his frantic pace. Caution made him crouch among the vegetation. The amulet burned even hotter and he clutched at it, hissing quietly. What was wrong with it? He took it by the chain, yanking the stone out of his uniform jacket. It glowed like a red-hot coal. He let it fall against his jacket.

A small voice deep inside urged him to toss it aside, but it was easy to ignore it. Especially with what he was witnessing on this high plateau.

Creatures growled and barked all around the edges of a vast, scintillating dome of energy. It gleamed red in the morning light, but blues and greens and bright white light splashed across its surface. Waves cascaded down it and rippled out from its edges. He felt those waves pass over his skin, tingling not unpleasantly. The amulet emanated an angry light in reaction to the waves of power. Raiden felt a matching anger rise within him. This could not be; this thing could not exist! It would ruin everything!

Raiden spotted a man inside the large dome. He was slashing at himself with pale green blades edged in pink and directing attacks at the amassing creatures. The beasts seemed intent on breaking into the energy field, slavering and snarling in blood lust. Raiden knew him. Matteo, one of Dante's men. Where was Angelo? Quickly, he scanned the area, but saw only Matteo and–

Shade.

She was at the center of the dome of power. An agonized cry split the air, echoing across the hilltop. Raiden straightened. Had she been attacked? She screamed again, one hand twisting against her belly; she was nearly bent in two. Sudden fear broke through the anger building within him. It shocked him into stark clarity. He was here to save her, to protect her from herself. He raced forward, but the dome stopped him.

"Shade!" he cried, but the howls of the beasts drowned the word.

He spotted the hilt of a knife in her hand. Gods of his Fathers! Was she *stabbing* herself?

There was an explosion in the air before her, a burst of blue light and the next instant she pulled her knife away, took it in her teeth, and dug a gemstone from her belly with her own fingers. His mouth fell open and he staggered back a step. What was she doing? What horrible magic was this?

Wrong, terribly wrong! A thousand voices screamed in his mind. Raiden grabbed his head, feeling as if his skull would split. *It is an abomination. She must be stopped! Stop her! Do as we command!*

The shouts faded abruptly, but the urge to act pounded through his muscles. He drew his sword, his eyes pinned on Shade. A blue stone was floating to the ground at her feet, there to join a clear gem and a red one. They shone like miniature stars, and the sight of them filled him with terror. It wasn't his terror, though; he knew it somewhere deep inside.

The quiet voice which had urged him to rip off the amulet whispered against a maelstrom of dark energy and was lost within it.

Distantly, Raiden watched her turn without moving her feet – was she floating above the ground? – and face north. Her hair flowed loose around her, torn from its braid. Her tattoos gleamed with color and light. More light shot from her eyes and the top of her head. She was a goddess come to earth.

And he had to destroy her.

NO! By all the gods, I won't!

Desperately, Raiden fought the power controlling him, hoping against hope the dome of energy would be enough to stop him. He had no control. The amulet urged him to strike her down, and even as he hoped the dome would hold him back, he struck at it with his sword, drawing sparks from it. There had to be a way in, a weakening in the structure. Those beasts were working against it, as well; they would break into it soon enough, giving him a way inside.

If she called forth the last stone, she would only have to bind them with spirit and the Veil would be complete. He had to stop her before she reached that point. The perfect moment would be when her blade was deep in her gut, seeking the last stone.

No, no, I won't do it! I can't hurt her! Nothing in this world can make me!

We are not of this world, fool...

A wild howling to his left told him at least one of the beasts had found an opening. He raced toward the sound, a savage grin pulling at his lips. The beast turned on him before he could slip into the dome, growling. Raiden ran it through without pausing and leaped over its corpse.

It was quieter inside the dome, despite the power flowing from Shade in unceasing waves. The howls of the beasts grew dim. She was there at the center, floating like an angel above the earth, surrounded by light and energy. Her arms were outspread as she faced the north, faced him, and then, suddenly, she plunged a blade into her midsection. Her screams cut through him, and he sprinted toward her. To save her… to kill her…

The last stone. The power of earth encapsulated in an emerald. Her blade cut into her flesh yet again, drawing a hoarse scream from her raw throat. It didn't get any easier, each time she brought forth a gem. Even knowing this was the last time didn't ease her pain. The agony was endless, but she worked through it, seeking as she'd sought each stone, limbs shaking, vision dimming, nausea threatening to overwhelm her.

The last physical stone exploded as she called its power to her. A swirl of gemstone fragments whipped around her, the remnants of the stones her father had given her, though he had never known. Despite the complexity of her feelings toward Bishop Raphael, she sent him a prayer of thanks. Without him, she never would have made it out of those Brotherhood mines.

There. Now she recognized the feel of the stone immediately. She withdrew her blade, dropping it from numb fingers this time, one would be enough for the next step, and plunged her hand into her flesh. The stone was slippery, elusive. She looked up, seeking strength from the swirling energy of the broken cornerstones while her fingers sought the prize.

A lean shadow raced toward her across the plateau, a long, thin streak of silver in its hands. She froze, the sight so unexpected it distracted her from her pain and her task.

Raiden…?

A red-black stone lay against his chest, stealing all light. Terror rose in her, a primal fear which made the hairs on her neck stand on end.

And suddenly, she knew: death was coming for her.

Frantically, she dug out the last stone. She barely had time to register its perfection before she released it. She had no time. Only an instant before Raiden's sword found her neck and took her head from her body.

He was close enough now she could see his dark eyes. They held agony, fear, and despair. He raised his sword in a graceful arc. *Fight it*, she willed him, never taking her eyes from his.

Her eyes were locked with Raiden's, so she never saw Matteo leap between them and lunge at the Imperial. Not until Raiden's sword cleaved into his shoulder, through his chest, and buried itself in his heart.

Eyes wide with shock, Raiden staggered backward, and yanked his sword from Matteo's limp body. The younger man hung a moment as if suspended by strings. Then the strings snapped, and he fell, blood spraying, to land on his face on the hard, red earth.

Finally, Shade found words. One word.

"NOOOO!"

It tore from her throat, shredding her.

The power surrounding her trembled, pulsed wildly, and failed for an instant before she regained control.

Grief as terrible as any Blackstorm roared up from her soul, bursting out of her in another wave of energy. Energy which strengthened the dome of power surrounding them. Pure Spirit, the Hidden Face, the fifth and final power needed to complete the Veil.

The Veil stabilized above her, a shimmering dome of power strong enough to repel the Unseen's blight and anything born of it. Free of the calling, Shade dropped to the earth, the light fading from around her, leaving her bereft and shaking. Her heart thundered in her ears and she could barely see for the tears blinding her. She could feel the Veil. It pulsed rhythmically, filling a part of her soul she hadn't known was empty. For a breath, she felt joy.

In the next–

Rage and grief gripped her. Teeth clenched and tears streaking her face, she lunged at Raiden, her blade slicing toward his neck. White-faced, stricken, he didn't move, merely lifted his chin to make her strike easier. Her blade flashed near the vein pulsing beneath his fragile skin but did not hit flesh. Instead she sliced through the golden chain encircling his neck. The chain slithered free and the amulet fell to the ground between them. Shrieking, Shade stomped it into the earth. It shattered beneath her heel.

Raiden staggered as if she'd struck him. She grabbed his jacket, shaking him hard. Tears nearly blinded her, but she saw the confusion then the growing horror in his eyes. His face crumpled and his legs collapsed beneath him. "Faces turn from you, you bastard!" Shade cried, dragging at his jacket. "You have to fight! You have to help me!"

In that moment of stunned anguish when Raiden struck down Matteo, she had let the Veil waver. Only a moment, a flash of weakness, but it had been enough. All the beasts desperate for her blood had swarmed inside it.

She got him to his feet just in time. Slavering creatures bounded on them, eager for blood. Shade spun, and stood over Matteo's body, a single blade left to her. Driven by despair, she drew blood from her chest and side and upper thigh, calling magic indiscriminately. All she could do was lash out and kill. Kill until there was nothing left to kill. She struck down creature after creature, dimly aware of Raiden fighting beside her, at her back, reminding her painfully of her companions doing the same not so long ago.

Angelo...

Matteo...

A scream ripped from her, full of more pain and wretchedness than any she'd uttered earlier. The pain she'd suffered all day to create her Veil was nothing compared to what she felt now. The Unseen had managed to hurt her even as she'd struck a blow against them. Now she knew her enemy, by the Faces, she knew them all too well.

The sun was high above them when the last of the creatures fell to her magic and Raiden's sword. It was Raiden who fell to his knees first, weeping inconsolably over Matteo's cooling body. He flung himself face first on the hard earth. "Forgive me!" he cried. "I couldn't stop myself. I had no control–"

"Get up." Her grief-ravaged voice stopped his weeping. He grew still, and then slowly climbed to his feet, leaving his sword on the ground beside Matteo. Swaying slightly, he kept his eyes down, unable to look at her. Awaiting her judgement. She wanted to hate him, to blame him, but she could do neither. It wasn't his fault Matteo was dead. The fault was hers. She'd left Raiden to the Brotherhood.

"It's not your fault," she said hoarsely. "It's not–"

Her throat closed on further speech. Exhaustion made her list like a holed ship. Raiden grabbed her before she could fall, and pulled her against him, holding her tight. She didn't fight his embrace; instead, she leaned into him and let her tears fall silently on his shoulder.

"How did this happen? How, by all the Faces, did you fail me, my son?"

Raiden stiffened, and before Shade could even register what was happening, he'd shoved her behind him. "You," he growled, shielding her from the newcomer as if she were a helpless maiden. "You lying bastard!"

A priest with flaming red hair stood not far from them. Frowning, he glanced at what she had wrought, looking displeased. Shade recognized him – the priest who'd chased them from Dante's villa. A ruby hung on his chest. A twin to the one Raiden had worn. Even from a distance, she could feel its dark energy. The energy of the Unseen, the same as she'd felt in the Bastion. Eyes narrowed, she stayed behind Raiden, her hand tightening on the hilt of her lone blade.

"You've ruined everything, you fool," the priest said, his eyes on Raiden alone. "You let the witch succeed in her folly, and now all of Malavita will suffer."

"You're wrong!" Raiden slashed the air with his hand. "I don't believe your lies any longer, Jacobis. Look around you! Shade's Veil is strong, stronger and brighter than anything I've seen in this shattered land."

The brother turned a disdainful gaze on Shade, though it felt as if he looked right through her. "She's blinded you with her charms and dragged you into sin." His nostrils flared and his lip curled. "I can smell the stink of lust on you. I should never have entrusted my amulet to such a weak-souled messenger. Now, I have no choice but to destroy you both, and declare this Veil an abomination. The Brotherhood will deal with it in time. Dismantling a Veil is far easier than raising one."

"If you could destroy me, brother," Shade said, "you would have by now."

Brother Jacobis smiled and shook his head. "Silly woman, I have never tried to destroy you. My brethren might have, but not I. Your obsidian blades do not frighten me; you play with forces you barely understand. In spite of all this." And he waved a dismissive hand to encompass her fledgling Veil. "You are weak, damaged. A mistake I will correct for the good of my land."

A mistake? Shade's breath grew hoarse in her lungs. She tried to stoke rage at his words, but her limbs trembled. She had no strength. Grief had wrung her dry, and she was empty of magic. And the Veil. She had raised it, yes, but it hadn't kept the beasts away. She had wavered at the peak of her calling. The connection she'd felt to it suddenly became a dissonance. Even with the Veil a reality around them, nevertheless, she asked herself: had she failed?

As if clouds had blotted out the sun, darkness settled over them. Shadows. The sun shone above the Veil, but the Veil itself swirled with a strange blackness. Shade felt a stab of pain in her belly and groaned. She recognized this power; her Veil was blighted. Was he right? Was her Veil an abomination? She had sacrificed Angelo for this, and Matteo had given his life to protect her when she should have been strong enough to protect them both.

"Stop, don't give into it." Raiden shook her, dragging her back from the brink of despair. He stared into her eyes. "It's his amulet," he whispered. "Can't you see how it pulses? He's trying to trick you. Don't let him. We can fight him. Together."

"No, we can't fight him." The tears slid down her cheeks, and she felt her spirit slipping toward despair once more. She was too weak to fight and it had all been for nothing. She had failed. The priest would kill her, kill Raiden. Matteo would have died in vain. Angelo's sacrifice would come to naught. The Bastion would fall. The Unseen would break free from their prison, but by then the Veils would be corrupted, twisted beasts would hold dominion over men. All would be lost. Forever…

"We can't fight them!" Shade cried, the vision of the future crystallizing into unavoidable certainty. Desperate sobs wrung from her. "I can't fight them!"

"You don't have to."

A river of light split the earth in front of them. It drove back the shadows. Brother Jacobis cursed and fell back, shielding his face from the brilliance. Through her tears, Shade watched men emerge from the effulgence. They faced the priest and stood like a shield before her. She knew them. Knew them all. Her friends…

"Dante," she whispered, shocked. Was she dreaming this?

He turned toward her, his eyes gleaming in the strange light he seemed to have brought with him. Cyril and the boys stood alongside him, and Korin Illario of all people. Now she knew it wasn't a dream. If she was going to dream a miracle, he wouldn't be part of it.

Dante drew his sapphire blades. "We can fight for you."

Manoli and Petra flashed her matching grins, and Cyril gave her a two-fingered salute. "Stay behind the Imperial, little swallow. We'll deal with this scum."

"Cyril," she said numbly. How were they here?

"You caught Shade in a moment of vulnerability, priest," Dante said. "But you forgot she has powerful friends. Leave now and return to your master. Tell Arturious he failed to stop the inevitable. We have raised our Veil, and the Brotherhood can't do a thing about it."

Dante's words rang across the plateau, but Jacobis merely sneered, entirely unimpressed.

"Do you think that pompous clown is my master?" He drew his long, ruby blade, unconcerned at being surrounded and outnumbered. "I serve a higher power. The Four Faces and the Hidden guide me in all I do."

"No." Shade pulled away from Raiden. Strength had returned to her limbs with her friends' arrival. Her despair lifted, even when her eyes fell on Matteo's still form. Rage filled her, growing from her gut like a thorn bush. The red priest had killed him, not Raiden Mad. "You serve evil," she spat. "Your masters are the Unseen. You are a pawn, nothing more."

Rage distorted Jacobis' face. He lifted his blade, his robes billowing. The fabric was slashed for easy access to his skin below, but he made no move to draw blood. Instead, the amulet on his chest began to gleam. Shade stiffened. Jacobis' magic was not born of his blood.

"I serve all the Faces of God!" he screamed at her. The amulet began to pulse with a black light. She couldn't take her eyes off it. "You are an abomination, a whore, and a blight upon the land!"

The dark power grew, the shadows strengthened.

"Strike him down!" cried Korin. "Don't let his power build!"

Dante stepped in front of Shade and unleashed his magic against the mad priest. Cyril and the cousins added their power, striking him simultaneously. Fire and earth, wind and water ripped at him, but Jacobis stood in the maelstrom, unaffected. Laughter rumbled from him. He seemed to grow under the attacks, absorbing the power as it struck him. The amulet created a dark aura around him, and it drew energy from Dante and the others. Manoli cried out a second before Petra screamed. They both dropped to the ground as if felled by unseen weapons.

Struck down, as Matteo had been struck down...

The thorny rage tangled around her heart, piercing deep. Shade grasped the bone handle of her obsidian blade and watched Cyril fall, as well. Dante went to his knees, leaving only Korin still standing. The river of light had faded beneath them, and the old man looked frail. Yet he raised his hands anyway. Blue fire sprang from him, streaking toward the priest.

Shade gasped. Sicani magic!

Hope rose in her. Would it be enough?

The priest's laughter turned wild. Korin's attack struck the aura around him and dissipated like fog before sunlight. Korin swayed, his eyes wide in disbelief. Jacobis raised his hand disdainfully and gestured as if flicking a fly away. Korin was lifted and tossed aside.

A shout tore from Dante and he called more magic. His attack sent Jacobis back a few steps, but it wasn't enough to stop him. Face ecstatic, Jacobis strode toward them, hands raised.

Beside her, Raiden moved. He stooped to grab his sword and leaped across the ground toward the priest. Shade knew it would be useless; she'd already seen that priest best Raiden in a fight. And now he was filled with dark power. She stumbled to where the Quattro Canto lay contentedly in its setting of light, and retrieved the blade she'd dropped. There was only one power which might stop him now.

It was already rising within her, the Wild Power. Emotion drove it, rage and despair. And now desperation. She remembered this power, the danger of it and its vast potential. The obsidian, born from the deepest fires of the earth itself, held within it a dangerous flaw. A wildness that could change the world or destroy it. An elemental power stronger than any other. Beyond earth, fire, wind, water, and spirit. A Sixth Face.

As Raiden fought fruitlessly to strike down Jacobis, Shade called upon the Wild Power, letting it fill her until she thought she might burst. The world trembled beneath her. She felt a thousand possibilities stretch in all directions. She had only to choose the one she wanted, and the world would realign itself to suit her.

The ruby priest laughed contemptuously, his arms spread wide, dark energy bursting from the amulet he wore. Raiden was on the ground, struggling to rise. Shade felt the Unseen's blighted power descend upon her, unafraid. She knew the path she desired. She would set things right. Or the world would die with her...

The world trembled, shifted. Shade unleashed the Wild Power. Time flowed backward, turned sideways...

...she was floating on a pillar of energy, her feet no longer touching the ground. Raiden was rushing toward her, a dark amulet hanging around his neck. He was Death. His sword flashed in a wide, silver arc. Unstoppable.

Shade watched as Matteo stepped in front of her, shielding her, aware of every moment, every movement. Raiden's sword streaked toward him–

Set it right...

And it was not Matteo before her with his dark hair and gleaming tattoos, but a man in black robes. A man with red hair smoothed against his scalp in a severe braid.

Jacobis. The Unseen's avatar.

Raiden's sword cleaved into him, through him. Through the amulet. Blackness exploded from it, and the amulet Raiden wore shattered. His eyes grew wide, met hers – and the world vanished into black silence.

Shade felt herself falling, the Wild Power gone. Falling, falling. Terror pounded through her veins. She would shatter against the earth–

Someone caught her. A smile gleamed in the darkness. Sunlight through the clouds. Her heart lurched as green eyes ringed with blue met hers, and light flooded the world.

"Shade," Matteo whispered. "I have you."

CHAPTER TWENTY-NINE

The world shifted around him, and suddenly Dante Safire found himself plunged into the light of the qaraz again.

No, not again. *Before...*

The light surrounded him, and he felt the current propelling him forward. Each step he took covered miles. Somewhere near him, Cyril and the others rode the qaraz and a gentle power embraced them all. It was his old friend Korin who'd made this possible. His friend, a true Sicani from out of legend. Dante would forgive Korin everything if they reached Shade in time to save her.

But... they had reached her. They'd fought a red-headed priest swollen with the dark power of the Unseen. And they had been struck down one by one. Even Korin. Only Raiden had remained to protect Shade. No, the Imperial swordsman had been felled, too. None of them had been able to withstand that alien power.

So. Why were they in the qaraz? If they had all been struck down, why were they as before? He was remembering things which hadn't happened yet!

One of those memories surfaced unexpectedly. A memory of Shade, black blades gripped in her hands as she drew blood recklessly, calling a forbidden power. Her green eyes had gleamed with it, along with a fury he shuddered to recall. And then, the world had *shifted.*

Dante rose from the light of the qaraz. The earth became solid beneath his boots and he reached for his blades, expecting battle. But no enemies waited for them on the empty plateau, only sand, scrub and a few groves of stunted trees. The sun shone down from a cloudless, afternoon sky – warm, hot even, but not forge-like. His heart pounding in anticipation of a fight, Dante fought to make sense of it. Flanking him were Cyril and the cousins, all of them tense and ready for a fight. Only their harsh breathing disrupted the quiet.

Frowning, Cyril took a step forward, staring at the empty plateau before them as if he expected something quite different to be there. He tilted his head, squinting up at the sun. Dante followed his gaze. Something was strange about the sky. It was… hazy.

"We were…" Manoli began then shook his head. He put a hand over his heart, his brow furrowing. "I was hurt. A man, no, a priest. He attacked us."

Wide-eyed, Petra placed a hand on his cousin's shoulder. "We couldn't stop him. Even Korin."

Korin? Where was Korin? Dante turned slowly, feeling unsettled. Out-of-place. Korin was nowhere to be seen. Or…

"Shade," he whispered, both wonder and fear edging the word. "She did this. We were losing the battle. She called the Wild Power."

"Where is she?" Cyril said, the words grating from him. The elder Golondrina spun on his heel, searching anxiously.

Yes, she'd been behind them. *Before*. With Raiden Mad. And a dead man, Dante remembered abruptly. They had risen from the qaraz to fight for her against the Brotherhood priest, and in the chaos he had barely registered the man lying lifeless on the ground. A man he knew, unfortunately. A loyal soldier, and a good man. Matteo Ignaza.

But it wasn't Matteo lying there when he turned around. It was a man in black robes split open from shoulder to hip. Already flies buzzed and swarmed over the sticky blood.

Sightless eyes stared at nothing from a narrow face. Dante recognized him. Brother Jacobis, a Blademaster and Ruby Pontifex. Dead.

But… what had happened to Matteo?

The world had *shifted.* "Now" had become "before". Somehow, Shade had changed things.

A flash of red caught his attention. Another man lay beyond the dead priest. His crimson uniform jacket was scorched and torn, and blood streaked his face, but as Dante stumbled toward him, Raiden sat up, groaning. Alive. He was alive, thank the Faces.

Cyril had spotted the dazed Imperial, as well. But his reaction wasn't joyful, or relieved. He strode to him in quick, stiff strides, took handfuls of Raiden's jacket and hauled him to his feet. "What did you do?" he demanded. "Where's Shade?"

Blinking, Raiden opened his mouth and struggled to speak. He lifted a hand to his head, sagging in Cyril's grip. "I–I… don't know. I was coming to stop her, to save her."

Cyril shook him, his lips drawing back from his teeth. "He sent you here to destroy her, you weak-minded fool! Did you do it? Did you kill her?"

"Wait, Cyril, he didn't do anything to Shade." Dante reached them and grabbed Cyril's arm. The elder Golondrina turned his rage-filled eyes on Dante. There was a wildness in their depths that made his mouth go dry, but Dante didn't back down. It was grief and fear driving Cyril's anger. "She's not dead," he said quickly, daring to believe it even though she'd vanished. "And he didn't do this. Shade did! She used the Wild Power. Even now I can feel its echo. Can't you?"

His brow clouded and his teeth bared, Cyril nevertheless loosened his hold on Raiden's jacket and took some deep breaths. After a moment, his eyes widened and snapped up, meeting Dante's gaze. "I feel it," he said, his usually gruff voice dropping to an awed whisper. He shook his head, his eyes closing briefly. "I remember seeing that priest. I remember fighting him. But I thought it was a strange dream. Sometimes in the qaraz there are…visions."

"She called the Wild Power," Dante repeated, squeezing Cyril's arm. "And we're all still alive."

Anguish crumpled his face. "But is she?"

"I saw her…"

Raiden's soft words drew their attention. Although Cyril's grip tightened, Dante didn't think he wanted to kill the Imperial anymore. Whatever power had controlled Raiden was gone. His eyes were distant, and full of wonder, but they were his.

"What did you see?" Cyril growled.

Blinking, Raiden focused on Cyril. "She fell into the light," he said, sounding confused. "I–I don't know what happened exactly. But the last I saw of her, she was falling into a pool of light."

"The qaraz." Cyril released a long, relieved breath and set Raiden on his feet, dusting the handprints from his jacket. A grin split his face, and his long mustaches quivered. "She's in the qaraz."

"But… how?" Dante said, searching the ground at their feet as if he'd be able to see the shining path of light again. Instead of the qaraz, though, he found a set of four gemstones embedded in a square of light. He inhaled sharply. As a boy he'd had the chance to see a Quattro Canto. He'd wanted to play with his friends and had been bored and restless, but the minute he'd laid eyes on the glittering gemstones, he'd forgotten everything else in the world. It was the holiest of objects, and the most powerful magic in the land. And here one lay at his feet. At last he understood why the air felt different, why the sky looked soft and the sun wasn't boiling them. He looked up. That was a shield above them, softening the harsh glare of the sun. A Veil.

It was nascent, covering not much more than the plateau upon which they stood. But with time and blood and magic, it would expand. The land beneath it, sheltered from the blight, would be reclaimed, made fertile. As small as it was now, he could already feel the great strength of it. Not like the newer Veils in the interior, those thin, frail things, but like the Veil above Sicaria. In his wizard's blood, he felt the potential in this new Veil.

"She did it." He lowered himself to his knees beside the Quattro Canto. He wanted to reach out and touch it but didn't dare. "She did it."

"As if we ever had any doubt," Cyril scoffed, slapping him on the shoulder. "You should have had more faith in our witch, Safire."

"She was never my witch," he whispered absently, staring at the miracle. The gems pulsed and glittered even in the bright afternoon sun. Beautiful. But what had it cost? Shade was in the qaraz. Somehow. Had she sacrificed herself to save them from the Unseen?

"Korin has her," Cyril said suddenly. Dante lifted his eyes to find him standing on the other side of the Quattro Canto. Manoli and Petra flanked him, their eyes unfocused and their hands hovering near their waists as if they were feeling the air itself. All three men seemed in a strange communion with something only they could see and sense. Dante held his breath, afraid to interrupt whatever they were doing. If anyone could find her in the qaraz, it would be one of them.

"I came here in shadows," Raiden said. A haunted look darkened his face and horror had entered his black eyes. "He sent me here to kill her. I nearly struck her down, but a man stepped in front of me. A man...I knew him." He squeezed his eyes shut, gripped by a shudder. "But it wasn't him, it wasn't Matteo! It was Jacobis I killed, thank all the gods of my Fathers!"

Dante stared at him, watching as he struggled to come to grips with all that had happened. It was hard for him to understand, he had to admit, but at least he could feel the residue of the powerful magic Shade had called. The Wild Power was rightfully feared, rightfully shunned, but he couldn't help but feel awe at what Shade had wrought with it. Already, the events leading to this moment were growing fuzzy in his mind. Time had been set on a new path. His memories were adjusting to fit. And before they could fade entirely, he wanted Raiden to know what Shade had done for him.

"You did kill him," he said ruthlessly. "I saw Matteo dead on the ground. Shade bent the world to–" Dante stopped, a realization making his throat tighten suddenly. She'd bent the world for him. "To bring him back," he finished, the words rough. "That is the debt you owe her."

The color drained from Raiden's face, his eyes wide with shock. He swayed briefly and put a hand over his eyes. Tears streaked the dust on his cheeks when he pulled his hand away. "If he's alive, then where is he?" he demanded hoarsely. He swallowed, and his face grew haggard. "Is he with Shade?"

"I don't know." Dante forced himself to rise. The priest might be dead, but he knew the danger hadn't passed. What had been wrought here today would have been sensed for miles. Perhaps all of Malavita had felt the raising of a new Veil. His own feelings didn't matter. "All I know is what Cyril said: Korin has her. Maybe Matteo is with them. Just be glad he isn't lying dead at your feet."

He knew his words sounded harsh, but he didn't care. The ache in his chest was unexpected and unwelcome. It made no sense, feeling this way, but he couldn't control it. He'd already decided he and Shade had no future together. He'd come to accept it. Hadn't he? It didn't make any sense, but he couldn't help his feelings. He felt... betrayed.

She'd bent the world to bring *him* back...

"There are men approaching."

Manoli's sudden announcement jolted Dante from his bitter ruminations. A shiver rolled through him and his heart raced. He turned, his hands going to his blades, and found Manoli standing alert beside his cousin and Cyril. The other two Golondrina were still focused on the hidden qaraz, but Manoli's head was lifted and his body tense as he stared toward a line of trees at the eastern end of the hilltop. Dante moved to his side.

"That side's an easier climb than the cliffs, but it would have taken time to go all the way around this hill."

Dante started at the voice so near his ear, then ground his teeth. Raiden could move silently when he wished. "I don't see anyone," he muttered.

"Trust me, they are there," Manoli said, and before the last word passed his lips a man appeared from among the trees. Then another. And another. They moved slowly, hesitantly, emerging from the shadows into the sunlight. Tattooed men in the distinctive garb of Corsaro soldiers. And among them, flowing with serpentine grace, were men in black, hooded robes.

Two, no three Ruby Pontifex. Dante ground his teeth and he drew his blades. Three Ruby Pontifex and a dozen Corsaro. Faces. How had they followed so quickly?

Each Pontifex would bear ruby blades – no priest achieved the status with anything less. The Corsaro soldiers were strong, also, none lower than amethyst. And there was a sapphire wizard among them, too.

"Valentine," he growled, catching sight of the Capomajus among his soldiers. The older man seemed just as disoriented as his men, but once he spotted Dante and the Golondrina alone on the plateau a satisfied smile split his face.

"What now?" Manoli asked, eager even after all they'd been through. He had his blade drawn and ready. "We can't leave until we know what's happened to the boss. I say we fight."

Dante scowled. "We can't fight them. We'd lose. We must stall them until we know what's happened to Shade. With her, we might have a chance."

"So that priest didn't lead us astray," Valentine said once they had come closer. His men fanned out around him. The three Ruby Pontifex stood directly behind the Capo, their faces hidden in the shadows of their hoods. "He said we could travel swiftly using some 'secret' Brotherhood magic, but I had my doubts." A shadow passed over his face, and for a moment he looked disturbed. "It wasn't like any magic I've ever used."

"It wasn't Brotherhood magic," Raiden said. At some point, the Imperial had retrieved his sword and he held it loosely at his side as if it were of no account at all. "Brother Jacobis brought you here through the shadows and he used demonic power to do it. I know, because he brought me the same way."

Mutters erupted among the Corsaro, and a few exchanged pensive glances and disbelieving scowls. Valentine frowned, but the troubled look on his face only deepened. His hands went to his knife hilts, though not in any aggressive move. Dante would have bet half his lands that the battle-hardened bloodwizard was seeking comfort.

"Why should I believe anything you say, Imperial?" he demanded. He loosened one hand from the death-grip on his blades and waved it dramatically. "You said a new Veil was impossible, so what is this?"

"I said the Brotherhood couldn't give you a Veil," Raiden countered. "The Brotherhood didn't raise this one."

Valentine grunted and glanced to one of the priests beside him. "Is that true?" he snapped.

The Pontifex was silent, but then he gave a stiff nod. "It is an abomination," he said, his voice grating and angry. "We will deal with it in time."

"Deal with it?" Anger distorted his features and Valentine looked all around him, taking in the state of the Veil and the land beneath it. Already the grass had started to green, and even the trees looked healthier. "It seems to me this is a genuine Veil, and a strong one to boot. I'll 'deal' with it, priest! I'll pay your bishop what he demands, but this Veil will be mine and mine alone!"

"It is not theirs to give or yours to take!" Dante stepped forward, fury rising in his voice. "No one has a claim on this Veil but the wizard who raised it!"

"Who? You?" Valentine scoffed, and his men muttered derisive laughs right on cue. "You don't have the power to raise a Veil. I don't know how you managed, and I don't care. This Veil will belong to whoever is strong enough to claim it like every Veil in Malavita. And I am far stronger than you, Safire!"

"Older maybe, but I doubt you're stronger."

Valentine guffawed. "You always were an arrogant bastard. Even outnumbered and outmatched, you still think you're better than us."

"I don't think it." Dante smirked even as his heart threatened to pound out of his chest. "I know it." He kneaded his knife hilts and narrowed his eyes at the older man. "Care to let me prove it?"

It was a long shot, goading Valentine into a one-on-one match, but Dante was desperate. Unfortunately, the Capo was too canny to fall for it. "Why would I fight you when I have them?" He jerked his head toward the Ruby Pontifex, matching Dante's smirk. And he had a right to his smugness. There were few bloodwizards who could stand against one of them. He'd run from the last assassin he'd faced. "The bishop sent them along to make sure you were dealt with, Safire." He flicked his eyes toward Raiden briefly, contemptuously. "You and the nuisance. Maybe he didn't think there'd be a Veil waiting for us, but his wishes were clear. The Veil is just a bonus for a loyal servant."

A crackling of power rippled around the three assassin-priests even though they had made no move Dante could see. He felt sweat pop out on his upper lip. One Ruby Pontifex was bad enough, but three were impossible. Arturious wanted them all dead. He swallowed, his thoughts spinning rapidly for a way out of this. The priest to the right of Valentine moved forward, drawing his blade as he came.

Cursing, Dante fell back, drawing his own blades. It was futile to fight, but he had to do something. If he died here, at least he might give Shade a chance–

Even as he fell back, he felt the breeze of Raiden's lunge. Sword raised, the slender man leaped to meet the ruby-bladed assassin, moving with blinding speed. Incredulous, Dante could only stare, unable to fathom what was happening. Raiden's sword moved like lightning, flashing too fast to follow. The first priest toppled, his head following his black-robed body a moment later. Blood splattered across Valentine's face, and he gaped.

Ignoring him, Raiden streaked toward the second priest who had already drawn and called his magic. Maybe Raiden had caught the first assassin by surprise, but once they unleashed power, the highly trained killers were impossible–

Fire and wind swept around Raiden, but he passed through the attack like sunlight through fog. An upward strike of his deadly sword opened the stunned man from crotch to neck, but Raiden didn't stop there. A second stroke took the priest's head.

The ground opened beneath his feet, but Raiden leaped like an acrobat across the sudden chasm and landed atop the third Pontifex, taking the man down even as he desperately tried to call more magic. Raiden didn't even use his sword this time – his hand flew like a striking snake and rose with the man's beating heart grasped within it. The grumble of earth magic settled into sudden silence with the death of the last assassin. Raiden rose slowly, blood dripping from his hand and his sword. He faced a stunned Valentine – who gripped his blades uselessly, his mouth open and his eyes wide. The seasoned Capomajus was crouching like a boy afraid of a deserved punishment, and a whimper slipped from him when Raiden took a step closer.

"This is not your Veil," Raiden said, speaking in a low, calm voice which was far more terrifying than if he'd shouted and raved. "Shade Nox has raised this Veil for the Empire. It is ours by right and by law. Dante Safire will control this venture. Not the Brotherhood, and not you."

Valentine's jaw worked. His men watched him, wavering.

Dante couldn't believe he would back down with so many men around him, but Raiden was close enough to kill him with a flick of his wrist. Valentine was a thug, a murderer and a criminal, but he was not a coward. Slowly, he took his hands from his blades and straightened. He squared his shoulders and drew on all the bravado he could muster. "You can't kill all of us, Imperial. I don't care how fast you move. You'll be struck down, as will all your friends. And then who will be left to protect your witch?" He glanced around, sneering. "Wherever she's hiding…"

"You're wrong." Raiden stepped forward again and it was as if he was gliding over the ground. The look on his face made Dante's stomach lurch. Beside him Manoli was grinning with savage glee. He wondered briefly if Cyril and Petra were any closer to retrieving Shade – if it were even possible – but he couldn't take his eyes off the scene unfolding before him.

"I can kill you all," Raiden said to Valentine in that same, soft voice. "This entire nation couldn't hold all the men I've killed." He stood nearly toe-to-toe with the Capomajus. A smile curved his lips, and Dante shuddered. A smiling corpse would have been less disturbing. "I've held myself back all this time, you see. I won't hold back now."

The color slid from Valentine's face and his features slackened. Not one of his men made a move to draw; they stood uneasily, glancing among themselves, seeking some sort of guidance. Clearing his throat, Valentine made one last bid to save face. "It doesn't matter what you can do – I won't fight you." His throat bobbed with a hard swallow. "You're the son of the Emperor." He nodded as if he'd convinced himself of something. "I'd be a fool to harm you. The Emperor wouldn't tolerate such an insult. And not even the Brotherhood can stand against the entire might of the Bhaskar Empire!"

Raiden cocked his head. "You are a wise man, Capomajus Valentine. My father will be pleased you've shown such restraint."

"Yes, well, I'm no priest." He moved back a few steps, putting a measure of sunlight between him and Raiden. "I know how to be reasonable." He took another step backward, and nearly fell over a black-robed corpse. If possible, his face grew whiter. "How do I explain so many dead priests to Arturious?" he muttered. He lifted his hands in placation when Raiden frowned. "I don't want any trouble, mind you. Not with you, but not with the Brotherhood, either."

"Tell him his men used forbidden powers to get you here," Dante suggested, finding his voice even though his mouth was as dry as sand. "They were under the control of the Unseen; they had to die. I'll vouch for you if I must. In Sicaria, before the First Families."

Valentine glared at him, his nostrils flaring, but after a moment his expression grew thoughtful and he nodded slowly. "Demon-possessed. Yes." He allowed himself a tentative smile. "The bishop would never want a scandal like that to get out."

"No, I don't believe he would."

Dante held his gaze and understanding passed between them. Whatever grievance the Bishop Arturious had with Dante, Valentine seemed likely to keep himself out of it. Wise, indeed.

"You and your men will leave this Veil, Capomajus," Raiden spoke up. His voice sounded closer to normal, and every man in the vicinity let loose a breath. "Spread the word: a new Veil has risen, a Veil free of your corruption and the Brotherhood's control."

Never taking his attention from Raiden, Valentine retreated. Finally, when he was surrounded by his men, he stopped and spoke. "Our business is done here!" His voice carried across the plateau. No one argued with him. His men looked shocked, and their superior numbers suddenly seemed meaningless after Raiden's display. Battle was not the Corsaro way after all; a knife in the dark was far more effective. "Is there peace between us, Safire?" he demanded.

"Until you decide to break it, Valentine," Dante said. And he had no doubt from the look in his eye before Valentine nodded and turned to leave, that he planned to break it as soon as he could.

They watched the Corsaro soldiers file after their Capo and disappear back among the trees, and only when the last man was gone did Dante breathe a sigh of relief. His legs trembled slightly in the aftermath. He'd thought they were all dead. "Could you really have killed them all?" he asked Raiden.

Raiden shrugged, and flashed his teeth in chagrin. He ran a hand through his short hair, pulling the tangled mop back from his forehead. Like a boy guilty of some mischief. But the disarming gesture didn't fool Dante. Mostly because it left a smear of blood on his skin. "Luckily we didn't have to find out," he said.

Dante didn't press him. Bluff or not, it had worked. And there were three fewer Ruby Pontifex in the world, thank all the Four and the Hidden. His eyes lingered on one black-robed corpse and he suppressed a shudder before turning away. Surprisingly, Cyril and Petra stood as they had before. Had they even noticed all that had happened? He looked at Manoli.

"They are trying to find Shade," he said, lifting his chin as if Dante might be criticizing his kin. "We can search the qaraz without entering them, but it takes concentration. Not even a Blackstorm could have broken their focus with her life at stake."

"Her life?" Dante said. With clenched fists, he took a step toward Cyril. "Cyril never said her life was at stake. He said Korin had her!"

"He does," Manoli said swiftly. He frowned. "He did, anyway. I wasn't as deep in the magic, so I'm not sure what they found. I felt those soldiers coming and I had to warn you." He looked stricken suddenly. "I didn't abandon her. She would have wanted me to warn you!"

"Of course, Manoli, no one thinks that." Raiden laid a blood-stained hand on his friend's arm.

"I just… I don't want the boss to think I didn't try to help her."

"How do we help her?" Dante asked. "We have to do something!"

"Calm yourself, Prince." Cyril's rough voice cut him off abruptly. The elder Golondrina lifted his head. "We have her…"

CHAPTER THIRTY

Golden light surrounded her, embraced her. She floated in a pool with no water, held aloft by the gentle radiance. Her chest ached and she knew something was broken inside, but she felt only peace. The light was keeping the worst of her pain away, though tears leaked down her cheeks.

"Shade..."

She lifted a head as heavy as a stone and blinked to clear the moisture from her eyes. Why were her eyes watering so badly? Was it the light? Slowly, she wiped the tears away and lowered a hand covered in blood. Not tears, then. It should have shocked her, but it didn't. There was always a price to pay for bending the world to suit you.

"You're terribly hurt."

She recognized the voice speaking from the radiance. At last she felt something – rage.

"Korin... Illario..."

She said his name slowly, the rage building. It jolted through her like a knife hitting bone. Pain rose with the anger, and her awareness expanded. Yes, she was floating in a pool of brilliance – the qaraz – but she wasn't alone. Nearby, Matteo floated beside her, his eyes closed and his face peaceful. Her heart lurched. No, not the peace of death. His eyelids fluttered open as she watched. His brow wrinkled in concern when he spotted her. Her pain and rage retreated momentarily as he reached out and took her hand, their eyes meeting. "You're hurt!" he cried. "What's happened?"

"Ask him," she said, her voice rough. She lifted her chin toward the other man floating with them, unable to make a more aggressive motion. Faces, she *was* hurt.

"I took you both into the qaraz," Korin said. He stood facing them. Not floating but standing. He had control here, she realized. Of course, he was a Sicani, and she was a broken wreck. She wasn't even sure if her blades were at her waist – it seemed too great an effort to check. All she had was Matteo's hand in hers. She squeezed slightly, hoping he would take it as a warning and not some loving gesture.

"Why?"

Korin's gaze – as golden as the light around them – met hers. "Because you would have died in moments if I hadn't. Here, with all the pure magic left in this land to hold you, there is time to heal you. And the magic *is* pure again. You cleansed the qaraz, my child. Now, it is your turn to be saved." He stepped closer, his hands raised.

Shade jerked and cried out as pain burst through her. "Don't touch me!"

"Shade, stop, don't move," Matteo said, moving closer to her and trying to hold her in place. "You're bleeding. You're in pain. Let him help!"

"No! Don't trust him. He wanted me to die." Her breath wheezed in and out of clenched teeth, her words harsh grunts. It was taking everything she had left to keep away from him. She leaned into Matteo, her strength draining from her. "He sent me here to die."

"He wouldn't do that, he's Lord Safire's most trusted friend. Let him heal you!"

"It is alright, Matteo," Korin said. He hadn't come any closer, but he hadn't lowered his hands either. "She speaks the truth. As she knows it, anyway."

"I know the truth," Shade said hoarsely. "I know you and the Coterie wanted me to destroy everything, including myself." She panted heavily once she'd gotten the words out. She'd never felt so weak…

"We were wrong," he said simply. "I was wrong. All this time, I thought there was only one way to fight the Unseen. I wanted to force my people from hiding, make them finish the war those demons started. You were a useful tool. Or so I believed."

She couldn't do anything but grunt in disgust. Matteo's arms tightened around her, but her body had gone numb.

Korin's face looked suddenly haggard in the soft light. He tapped a finger against his chest. "I was wrong," he repeated, and tears silvered his eyes. "You are not a tool to be used, you are something I never thought to see again. The power in you, the light. It's this!" He waved at the radiance. "Already I can feel your power streaking through the qaraz – it has reached every Veil in the land and strengthened them. Don't you understand what that means? What we thought lost, or at the very least, corrupted beyond saving, still exists. In you! Somehow…"

"I don't… I don't know what in the hells you're talking about…"

He was trying to confuse her. Faces, she felt so cold. A shiver racked her, but it didn't bring the pain she expected. She felt nothing… not even Matteo's arms around her. And she was tired. Terribly tired. Her eyes closed and she hadn't the strength to open them.

"Shade! Shade!"

She wanted to tell Matteo to be quiet, but his shouting started to fade, and she felt a heaviness grip her. It would be so easy to sink into it…

"Korin! She's fading – she's dying!"

Poor Matteo. He sounded so desperate, so sad.

"Please, help her!"

It didn't matter. She was beyond help, and she didn't even

care. No wonder Raiden always faced death so calmly. It wasn't so bad…

"You are the most stubborn girl I have ever met. You'd rather die than listen to a word I say." There was no terror or desperation in Korin's voice, only annoyance. Shade wanted to smirk, but she couldn't feel her lips. Why would it bother him if she died? It's what he'd wanted.

"I already admitted I was wrong, my child. Now, this will hurt…"

Suddenly, she could feel her lips again. She could feel everything. A scream ripped from her throat as her entire body was dropped into molten fire. Her back arched and her limbs stiffened. The violence of her reaction knocked Matteo aside, but someone still held her. Someone cruel and vindictive. Wherever his hands touched, agony followed. She could do nothing but scream. Scream until her throat burned as badly as the rest of her.

And then there was solid earth beneath her. It embraced her as the light had moments before. The pain vanished, leaving her gasping. She stared at a hazy sky – not colorless with heat, but a soft magenta. A Veil sky. Her Veil. No longer racked with pain, she could think. It was her Veil; she felt it in her soul. Joy welled up in her chest – a chest free of aches in a body whole and strong.

Faces blocked the marvelous view and she frowned in disappointment until she realized she knew them. Her friends. Yes, they were all here. They had come to fight for her… before she had bent the world with the Wild Power.

"Cyril?" she said, and her voice was no longer ragged and hoarse. "Are you crying, old man?"

"Yes, little swallow." Cyril knelt at her head, leaning over her. His roughened hand stroked her hair back from her face, and he was grinning even as tears leaked into his grizzled mustache. "What of it?"

She stared up at her friend in consternation. Had she ever

seen him cry before? By the Faces, they were all crying. Even Manoli, though he was laughing at the same time and pounding his cousin on the back who wept unabashedly at her side. Ever the healer, though, Petra was feeling her limbs and probing at her midsection.

"I'm fine," she insisted, but he held her wrist, his fingers against her pulse point. She doubted he heard her, though, he was crying so hard.

"We thought we'd lost you."

Shade turned her head and found Dante Safire. Tears streaked the dust on his cheeks, but his eyes were clear as he looked at her.

"You shaved," she said.

He rubbed his stubbly chin, flashing a smile. "It'll grow back."

Her belly did a strange flip. She remembered him standing in front of her like a living shield and felt her heart swell with gratitude. "I like it," she said. "You look like a scoundrel."

"Can you stand up?" he asked, and she nodded. Suddenly, several pairs of hands were helping her rise.

When she reached her feet, the first thing she saw was Matteo standing over Raiden Mad. Raiden was on his knees, his head bent, but he was lifting his sword toward a confused Matteo. Offering it to him with both hands.

"What is this?" Shade demanded. She took a step and nearly fell. Hells, her knees were weak. But Cyril and Dante were there to aid her, and her next step was stronger, surer. "What in the hells are you doing, Raiden?"

He wrenched his head toward her. His eyes were red-rimmed and wild. "I owe him a blood debt. My life is his to take if he wants it."

"You don't owe me anything!" Matteo blurted, waving his hands in refusal. "I'm not going to lop your head off, captain!"

Shade wanted to scoff at Raiden's offer, she wanted to kick that sword out of his hands and shake some sense into him.

But she did none of those things. Instead, she went to him and laid a hand on his bent head. At her touch, he began to sob. She took his sword and handed it to Matteo, giving him a look. He didn't need any other explanation from her. He nodded and stepped away, holding the sword like it was a sleeping snake.

"Raiden," she said, and she went to one knee beside him. Her hand tightened in his hair and she forced him to look at her. "It was not your fault. Do you hear me? And I fixed it. Matteo is alive. I'm alive. So, you can keep your head, understand?"

He began to tremble, his face crumbling. Beneath her hand, he nodded, and she let go of him. "Shade," he said, and his voice trembled as badly as the rest of him. She gathered him to her, holding his shaking body tightly.

For a long time, his wretched sobs were the only sounds beneath the newly raised Veil.

By the next morning, a collection of colorfully painted carts had gathered at the base of the broken hill where Shade had placed her Quattro Canto. The newly raised Veil had grown in the night, expanding over the land like a rain cloud and the carts resided within its shelter. Golondrina moved among them, laughing and calling and singing to one another as they set up their low-slung tents. The multi-colored felt and canvas structures looked like a scattering of blossoms across the greening grass. With the rising sun, more carts snaked into what had once been the Nexus, each Golondrina band following one of the several qaraz crisscrossing this powerful place.

Made more powerful by the Veil above it.

My Veil...

Shade stood watch from the top of the cliff she and Matteo had climbed just a few short centuries ago, observing the arrival of her clan and others, Jolynn's among them. She'd have to greet the matriarch at some point, but not now. There would be pleasantries and discussions, celebrating and planning, greetings… and farewells. Right now, she didn't want to deal with any of that. She wanted a moment to savor her triumph.

The awareness of her Veil rested at the back of her mind, curled there like a sleeping cat. A sleeping, purring cat. It was strange. Even after interacting with that harmless creature at Satine's cottage, she still hated and feared the beasts. But it was exactly what her Veil felt like – a cat. She touched her bare midriff, feeling a faint tracery of scars across her tattoos. Even sleeping cats had claws.

Even stranger was the fact she was still standing. Standing strong. And whole. She'd paid the price for her Veil, nearly the ultimate price, but she'd been given a reprieve. All the Faces and the Hidden had spared her.

No, the Faces of God didn't save me. Korin did…

In the aftermath of her return from the qaraz, once Raiden had pulled himself together, they'd started to relate their adventures to one another when Dante had realized one of them was still missing. In their joy and excitement at reuniting, none of them had noticed Korin Illario had not returned from the qaraz. Immediately, Cyril had fallen into a trance to try to locate him while the rest of them waited pensively.

"He healed me," Shade had said, taking Dante by the hand. "Maybe he just needs a moment more in the qaraz to recover."

White-faced, Dante shook his head, his hand squeezing hers. Tears silvered his lower lids. "There is only so much strength in him, even if he is Sicani. We had days of hard travel, and it cost him. He made it possible for me to travel the qaraz, too. I fear–"

His words ended sharply, and she released his hand to slip her arm around his waist. A tremor shook him as he leaned against her. "He is a Sicani," she whispered. "None of us can possibly understand his power. He'll be alright."

Shade looked up, feeling eyes upon her. Standing with Manoli and Petra, Matteo was watching her and Dante. His gaze was shadowed, but he flashed his usual smile when he caught her look.

"Did you see what happened?" Shade asked him, feeling an unexpected distance open between them. They had been through so much together, but everything seemed different.

His brow furrowed and his eyes grew dark. "I saw him lay his hands on you, then you screamed." He shuddered, blinking at the memory. "There was so much light. It was too bright to see anything. Like… like being dropped into the sun. Korin… I couldn't see anything but you, Shade."

Their eyes met again, and this time Shade held his gaze until he gave her a crooked smile. She smiled back and felt the camaraderie they'd shared return. No matter what happened between them from this point forward, Matteo would always be her friend and protector. He'd sworn his life to her. And paid it… once. She vowed he would never pay such a price again.

Finally, after an hour had passed, Cyril emerged from his trance. He turned stricken eyes to Dante and said what they'd all dreaded, "I cannot find him. Korin Illario is gone…"

Dante's agonized shout had rung across the plateau, and once again Shade found herself embracing a weeping man. The others had stood watching helplessly, until Cyril ordered them to set up a campsite as evening fell.

With the Veil above them, they hadn't needed to draw circles against the coming night, but no one had slept easily after darkness fell. The following morning, Shade hadn't been the only one to watch the sun lift above the horizon.

With the sun, the Golondrina began to arrive, drawn by the surging in the qaraz. Tied to those magical pathways, they'd been called to her Veil. Manoli and Petra had gone down the cliff to greet them, eager to see their people again. When Shade told Cyril he could go, too, if he wanted to, he'd gruffly told her to kiss her own behind if she didn't stop pestering him, and he set about making breakfast. He and Matteo had fallen into an easy rhythm preparing the camp for the day, and Shade was reminded of how Matteo had worked so effortlessly with his brother. It had been good to see, but it made her wonder if he would leave with Dante or stay with her. And how would Dante react if Matteo asked to stay?

"Shade."

Shade stepped back from the cliff's edge and turned to face Dante Safire, her heart racing. Unexpectedly. Would he always make her heart pound? But so much had happened since she'd seen him last. So much had changed. While she wasn't *in* love with Matteo, their relationship was becoming something else. Something beyond lovers. Dante, on the other hand...

"Dante," she said, feeling suddenly awkward. Which wasn't entirely new around him. "How are you?"

He grimaced and rubbed his chin. His beard was still mostly stubble. She wanted to run her hand over it and see how it felt. But she kept her hands at her sides.

"I have received what I wanted after all this time," he said. "You delivered the impossible, and though I never doubted you, it's still a shock. It's also only the beginning. There's so much work to be done here, but..."

Now it was his turn to look awkward. And somewhat ashamed. Shade knew what he was going to say, so she said it for him. "But you need to return to Sicaria."

"I'm afraid so. Bishop Arturious is trying to start a war. I must gather the allies I have left, those on the city council, and put a stop to it before the whole city is awash in blood. With Raiden's help, we can convince everyone there is no Veil to fight over. And once word of your Veil spreads, we can build a coalition to break the Brotherhood's hold on our land, to end the Capo's corruption, to–"

"Our Veil," Shade interrupted him. "It's our Veil, Dante. Well, technically, I believe it's yours. You hold the charter."

A rueful smile crossed his lips. "We both know the charter is merely a legal document granting me rights to the land." He lifted a hand, gesturing. "This Veil belongs to you, to you and your people."

She lifted a brow. "But you'll happily collect the tax revenue from it, and any gems we might mine, won't you, my prince?"

Her tone was light, and he chuckled, giving her a small shrug. "I have to make a living. And since you won't be paying tithes to the Brotherhood, or tribute to the Capos, you'll be making quite a decent living yourself."

Shade kicked at the sandy ground beneath her feet, seeing in her mind her true goal: bloodwizards, *Golondrina* bloodwizards, bearing the blades she would create for them. "Eventually," she said, keeping her thoughts to herself. "In the meantime, we'll need your help."

"And you'll have it."

"All the way from Sicaria?"

Dante sighed, and he looked out over the cliff. The breeze ruffled his dark hair. He'd grown rather scruffy since the last time she'd seen him. Life on the run didn't suit him. "Do you really think your people would welcome a Malavitan Prince among them? Would I rule them, or would we rule them together?" He faced her again, his blue eyes piercing deep. There was regret in his gaze, and something like... hope. Did he want her to say they could rule together? Shade held her breath, wondering at such a possibility. Briefly. She shook herself from the fantasy.

"No one rules the Golondrina," she said at last. "Certainly not me, and definitely not you. They live in the Wastes to be free, to be a community not a kingdom. I might have raised this Veil, but it belongs to them." She smiled at him, and felt tears prick her eyes. "If you stayed, would you have to be a prince?"

His expression softened. He lifted a hand to touch her cheek and she stepped into his embrace. They held each other, and Shade felt an overwhelming sadness. They could have been good together, she knew it in her soul. But their worlds would always be separate. Dante's reply confirmed it. "If you returned to Sicaria with me, would you have to be a bloodwizard?"

Her eyes squeezed shut and she buried her face against his chest. "Dante," she whispered. "I–"

"I know."

For a long moment they stood together, the sun warm on their heads. Until finally, Shade released him and stepped back. She didn't bother to wipe the tears from her cheeks as she stared up at him. "When will you leave?" she asked, glad she could keep her voice steady.

"As soon as my men arrive. I sent a message early this morning, and it will take a few days for them to reach us. Once they've gathered, I'll return to Sicaria."

Her eyes went to Matteo again. He and Cyril were sitting together beside the fire, Raiden near them seemingly lost in his own misery until Matteo handed him a tin cup of steaming tea. Surprise crossed Raiden's features, shifting quickly to gratitude. He accepted the tea and Matteo clapped him on the shoulder, flashing a smile Raiden tentatively returned.

Dante had followed her gaze, and sudden understanding relaxed his expression. "I have to take Raiden with me, for now," he said. "I'll need him as my liaison with the Empire, but I think he'll be our liaison, as well. I know he wouldn't be happy if I kept him in Sicaria all the time. And we both know he can take care of himself. He can address any issues you might have and let me know how you're managing." His eyes flicked toward her. "I think it might be a good idea for Matteo to stay here, though. It would be good for me to have a man I trust so near you. To keep you out of trouble."

His last words drew a laugh from her. "You think one man will be enough to keep me out of trouble?"

He grinned. "No, but it's worth a try."

"Are you so sure he'll want to stay?" she asked, feeling her throat tighten unexpectedly. The sadness returned, along with a chasm of loss opening in her belly.

Dante fixed his blue eyes on her. "I would stay if I were him. I would stay forever. If I were him..."

He reached for her and pulled her into his arms once again. This time, he kissed her. Hard enough to make her toes curl and her stomach burn, but there was a rock in her throat. This wasn't love, or passion, this was goodbye.

Raiden watched Dante and Shade over the brim of his cup, and nearly choked when they embraced for a passionate kiss. The kiss was brief, but they stood clinging to one another after it ended, and he wondered what had been decided. Dante hadn't said much since rising that morning, his face haggard with grief over Korin. The Prince had sent a bird made of air and fire to his men waiting in Enrice before he'd sought out Shade. Raiden had assumed to say farewell, but now he wasn't so sure.

"Parting is painful," Cyril said gruffly, tossing the last of his tea into the fire.

"That doesn't look like a parting," Matteo said. He stirred the fire with a crooked stick, dropping his gaze from the scene. Was he bothered by seeing Shade in another man's arms? Raiden eyed him, unsure what had gone on between the two of them. Only... she'd risked the whole world to bring him back to life. He had to be important to her. Just... how important?

His attention returned to the couple on the cliff's edge. They had parted, but still stood close together, their hands joined and their eyes locked. A dull ache rested in Raiden's chest, but he ignored it. Shade would never be his, and he had to accept it. And he had to be glad she didn't hate him after all he'd done. He glanced at Matteo. The man's focus was intent on the fire. A little too intent. He felt a sudden camaraderie with the man he'd killed.

"It is a parting," Raiden said as much to convince himself as to convince Matteo. "Dante has to return to Sicaria. We all do. The bishop might have started a war with that damnable false charter, and we must put a stop to it. We have to make it clear the Empire stands with Dante Safire. He'll need good men at his side."

Matteo shifted, looking suddenly uncomfortable. "I'm not going," he said. "I... My place is here." He looked up at Raiden, his features crumpled. "I pledged my life to her. I'm her man, now, not Dante's. I will guard her to my last breath."

You already did, Raiden wanted to say, but shame held his tongue. The young man's earnest gaze was too much, and he looked away. "I understand," he said softly, his eyes falling on Shade. Light bathed her; she seemed to glow from head to toe and it reminded him of the first time he'd laid eyes on her. He'd thought she was an angel come to earth. Silently, he made the same vow as Matteo: his life was hers. To the last breath.

"Korin said she was made of light, of magic," Matteo said in a low, wondering tone. "I don't know what he meant, but I believe it."

"Korin said what exactly?" Cyril asked sharply.

"He said Shade was something he'd thought lost. Some ancient magic even older than him, than the Sicani, I guess. Neither one of us understood what he was saying." Matteo shook his head, stabbing at the fire with his stick. "It had to do with the qaraz."

Cyril grunted and rubbed his hands on his knees, watching Shade with Dante. "The qaraz are ancient," he muttered. "As old as the land itself. Sometimes my people will catch glimpses of... things when we travel the qaraz. Shapes made of light, human but not human. Visions of something lost." He shook himself. "Korin was dying," he said in his rough voice. "Perhaps he was seeing things."

"Perhaps," Raiden said. "But I think Matteo may be right. If there is light left in this world, it's in her."

The three of them fell silent as Dante and Shade crossed the plateau to the campsite. Their hands were clasped, but as they neared they broke apart. When they reached the fire, there was a distance between them. A strange relief filled Raiden. It *had* been a parting. But even as relief filled him, anxiety followed. As an Imperial envoy, his place was with Dante Safire. If Dante was leaving, he would have to go, too.

"We should go down and greet the clans," Shade said to Cyril, smiling. "You up for the climb, old man, or do you want me to toss you off the cliff?"

"Only if you jump first." Cyril rose, stroking his long mustaches, but he was grinning. "And it's about time you decided to go down there. Jolynn will be hopping mad if you put her off any longer."

She frowned. "I hope Jolynn understands this Veil isn't going to work like a caravan."

"And how is it going to work, little swallow?"

Uncertainty clouded her features briefly but vanished in a sudden grin. "I haven't figured it out yet, but I do know one thing – our days as Waste-walkers are ending."

Cyril shook his head, still smiling. "I wouldn't count on that."

"I never count on anything but my blades and my magic," she said, but then she gave each of them a look, adding softly, "And my friends."

Beside her, Dante cleared his throat. "You can always count on us, my lady. Even when we aren't with you."

She lowered her head to him, as close to a bow as he'd ever get. "I know, my prince." Her attention shifted to Raiden. "You're going to be our liaison, Captain Mad, are you up for the task? It will mean a lot of traveling back and forth between my Veil and Sicaria, but I think you'll prove to be a capable Waste-walker. Your immunity to our magic will be a definite boon."

"I... Yes, of course," Raiden said, a stunned pride filling him. He rose and bowed to her deeply, his hand on his sword hilt. "I offer my services, my lady. Proudly."

Beside him, Matteo jumped to his feet. "Prince Safire! My lord. I… I have to tell you–"

"Ah, Matteo," Dante interrupted him as if the younger man hadn't said anything at all. "I'm afraid you won't be returning to Sicaria with us. I believe you would serve me best by remaining with Shade and the Golondrina. I need a good man in our new Veil, a loyal man. Shade's already agreed to let you stay."

Agape, Matteo blinked rapidly, looking from his prince to Shade. A slow smile crossed his lips and he ducked his head, tugging his broad-brimmed hat low over his eyes. "Of course, my prince. I'm honored to serve the Lady Witch. For you, my lord," he added hastily.

"We are all honored to serve the Lady Witch," Dante said, his gaze returning to Shade. He bowed to her as deeply as Raiden had without a hint of mockery. When he straightened, his eyes gleamed. "To the last breath."

"To the last breath," Raiden echoed, at almost the same instance Matteo spoke the words.

Shade looked shocked, and Cyril chuckled. "Close your mouth before you swallow a bug," he said, and she snapped her lips closed, giving him a glare. Still chuckling, he held out a hand for her. "Let's welcome our people home."

ACKNOWLEDGMENTS

Though writing is a solitary pursuit, publishing requires a team effort.

I want to thank the team at Angry Robot Books. First, for opening the pod bay doors and allowing my submission to sneak in without an agent. And second, for telling me you loved my book – what every writer hopes to hear someday about their life's work.

I especially want to thank Gemma for always being responsive and understanding; your help has been invaluable. And Eleanor, who walked this newbie through her contract with utmost patience and professionalism.

To Simon, my editor, thank you for digging out the deeper parts of this story and making it a better book. Your questions and comments took me in directions I hadn't planned and for that I am grateful. And thanks to Andrew who handled the copyedits and found mistakes I never would have. Thank you, Mark Ecob for the fabulous cover which inspired me more than you know. Thanks to Caroline, Angry Robot publicist extraordinaire, and to the Robot Army for promoting everyone's work so diligently.

I need to thank my husband, Bob Daley, for reading a version of this book many years ago, for always encouraging my writing pursuits and for reading this current version during a pandemic. You told me I needed to put my work out into the world, and you were right. Just this one time, though. Don't get cocky.

Thanks to everyone who kept asking me if I was still writing, to those who said they believed in me, and thanks to Andrea, my first (non-relative) reader. Also, thanks to all my friends who responded to the news about my debut novel with unabashed support and genuine happiness for me.

And a special thank you to my fellow writers in the #TranspatialTavern. You welcomed in this orphan writer no questions asked, and for that I am heartily appreciative. I never expected to find such a fantastic group of friends from all over the world united by a common goal, a common joy, a common love. What an incredible pool of talent; I'm honored to be included.

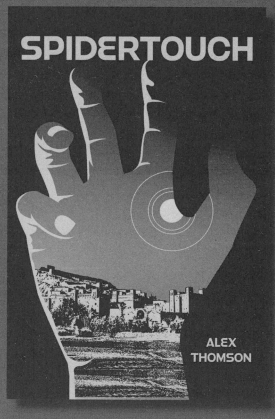

1.

The touch for /*Donkey*/ is infuriatingly close to the touch for /*Mother*/ in fingerspeak.

For /*Donkey*/, the forefinger and thumb squeeze the middle band, and then the little finger taps the lower band twice, whereas /*Mother*/ uses the middle finger.

This is just a small example of why whoever came up with this bastard language should be thrown from Traitors' Rock into the Southern Sea.

Unlike the handful of other known languages, fingerspeak also has no permanence. You can repeat a foreign word in your head, and then mull it over until you can winkle out its meaning, but you can't repeat someone's touch to yourself, or replicate a sensation. If you had to dream up the most inconvenient language for us to learn, you would be hard pressed to improve on fingerspeak.

Which is bugger all use complaining about in my current position. I say 'current' as though it's a choice, like I'm weighing up a range of exciting career opportunities. The truth is that the elders will never let me leave; there's too few of us who can interpret fingerspeak. That fact used to make me think I was a cut above the other kids from the quarter – you could see their limited lives mapped out for them in the wrinkles of their fathers' leathery skin – but who turned out to be the fool in the end?

I stand in the High Chamber and wait my turn, watching the councillors in conversation. They all wear hooded cowls and their crimson robes denote the highest rank of the Keda. They are in pairs, each with their right hand on the other's bare left arm, fingers dancing between the three silver bands worn there.

There is one advantage of fingerspeak: it's virtually impossible for anyone to eavesdrop on your conversation. Even now, ten paces away – I'm not stupid or vulgar enough to stare at the Keda – I can see Double's fingers moving, but I don't have a clue what xe might be saying.

For over a century the Keda have ruled Val Kedić, and yet there's still so much we don't know about them. The language barrier keeps us apart, with us translating to maintain a purely functional relationship. The majority of Keda, in their blue robes, have next to no contact with citizens; it's only the councillors and Justices who matter. And the less we know of them, the greater power they have over us. Gender, for example, is a closed book. Someone introduced the pronoun "xe" to describe them a century ago, and there's been no advance ever since. Their mouths are another example: hidden by their cowls, but thanks to servants' gossip, we know they do have them – twisted and grotesque, but mouths for eating, all the same. Just not speaking.

There's only a handful of the Council I know by name – Double, because xe's the main contact for my quarter. Xe is the one who summons me to pass on instructions and information. Xer name is, by its nature, untranslatable to our tongue – being a mixture of taps and squeezes and no spoken words – but I know xer as Double because it's a repeated sequence of taps.

Then there's Giant, who I've never fingerspoken with, but xe is unusually tall for the Keda. Xe is the same height as me so xe always stands out.

The most senior member of the Council, though – they have no leader, but it is clear that xe is the top dog among them – is known to us as Eleven, because of the complicated series of eleven taps that make up xer name. At a rough guess, it means something like "xe-who-lives-by-the-eastern-something-something-tranquil-grove". But who knows. The taps all blur into one.

Then there's Chicken. Now xe, I can't stand. I mean, obviously, I hate all the Keda – they stole my son, they squeeze us dry, they've sucked the life out of our city. They are our captors. But Chicken? Xe is a real pain in the arse.

It pleases us to call xer Chicken because xer given name is not far away from the touch for /Chicken/. It also reduces xer somehow, takes away some of xer power over us. But no matter what we call xer, I can't forget the way xe looks at me.

You don't see much of a Keda beyond the bare left arm – their cowls cover most of their heads, so you can only see their flat noses and threatening eyes in the gloom of the hood. But I'll never forget that one time when we were fingerspeaking, I had to ask xer about the quotas due from our quarter. I essayed a phrase, something like:

(Question) / Number / Barrel /.

It was a simple squeeze and trill of the fingers. But the look of disgust xe gave at my clumsy accent took my breath away. The contempt blazing from xer flared nostrils and eyes felt like hard chips of marble cutting my skin. I wanted to scream at xer, "Don't blame me for not being touch-perfect in your stupid language!"

Needless to say, I sucked it up, received xer answer, and bowed before withdrawing.

Anyway. What I'm trying to say is, there are Keda and there are *Keda*. Most are anonymous; you see their robes, their piggy little eyes, you hear the occasional snuffly exhalations they make to express shock, pleasure or humour. While they're all scum, the ones I can't stand are those like Chicken, who treat us with open contempt.

I catch Ira's eye. She's standing by a column twenty paces away, waiting, as I am, for the Keda to summon her services. I raise my eyebrows a fraction, trying to convey "how boring is this?" But she studiously ignores me.

I used to do that with Borzu all the time, trying to read each other's minds and having a whole conversation with eyebrow twitches, side-eyes and grimaces. Afterwards, we'd compare notes, see how much of each other's part of the conversation we had understood. Very little, was the usual answer. But Borzu... well, it doesn't do to dwell too much on what happened to him. He is a salutary lesson as to why the best thing to do is keep your head down among the Keda and be as dull and obedient as possible, as Ira has clearly set out to be.

Astonishingly, some people act like it's a cushy number being an interpreter for the Keda. Some resent the occasional perks given to us: our interpreter's residence, and the fact that we skipped our seven-year service in Riona. It was only so that we could learn fingerspeak. But people ignore those years of study and the fact we're now on the front line, dealing with the Keda and their banal whims every day. Trained monkeys that appear at the snap of a finger. Our lives are not our own, not in the way most citizens can say, and I sometimes wonder why anyone would choose this path on purpose.

As if on cue, Double inclines xer head towards me and beckons with xer forefinger. Xe stands a foot shorter than me, but xe stands imperiously as if towering above me. I approach, bow, and xe places xer long, cadaverous fingers on my left arm. Like all the Keda, xer right-hand nails curve round like vicious scimitars, the better for fingerspeaking. Although I've been doing this a while, I can't help but swallow a grimace when I feel the nails' prickly caress on my skin.

In preparation, the rest of my body zones out and my whole attention focuses on the three bands that enclose my arm. Murky bronze, of course, unlike the delicately engraved silver ones that the Keda earn the right to wear on their thirteenth birthdays. It pays to keep ours unpolished – these small status signifiers mean a lot to the Keda, especially anything to do with fingerspeak.

I close my eyes and shut out the distant whisper of the sea, and the buzz of Val Kedić outside. I switch off everything that I don't need right now, and I feel.

Visitor / (Future) / Day /, Double says without preamble, *From / (Unclear) /*.

It's some distant land; I don't know the touch and don't need to know.

Pulse / Fish / Vegetable / Nut / Date / – xe breaks off to make a gesture with xer left hand, like "etcetera, you get the idea".

(Positive) /, I say. *Prepare / Many / Good / Food / Council /*.

Double does not react. There is no word for "thankyou" in their language. Or perhaps there is, and we've just never heard it. Then xe frowns, and grasps my upper band: *(Past) / Fish / Small / (Disgust) / Many / Bone / (Question) / Reason /*.

I ache to make a sarcastic retort, to say, "A million apologies, Excellency, our lazy fishermen must have guzzled all the plump mackerel themselves, I'll have them whipped." But I stifle my irritation and take xer bare arm to respond. It tenses, like it always does.

(Regret) / Councillor /, I say, *(Negative) / Many / Fish / Now / (Question) / More / Vegetable /*.

Double listens to me, then replies with a curt series of touches.

More / Fish /. Then, as an afterthought, xe spreads xer fingers and taps, *Girl / Send / Many / Girl /*.

It was my old teacher I have to blame. Myriam, I think her name was. I adored her, and her classroom. It was down by the beach, next to the wharf where most of us lived, where our fathers fished. The rest of Val Kedić called our quarter The Stain – a fetid blot that festered outside the city walls – but we didn't care. The shacks sprouted from each other like a fungal growth, staggering off in all directions, creating twisted alleys, and eaves that jabbed into other buildings. A reek of fish clung to the walls and our clothes. It was a dirty slum, but it was *our* dirty slum, and most of us stayed happy there, insulated from the rest of the world.

We knew little of what was going on in the city proper, still less of the Keda who rarely troubled to come out to such a distant fringe of Val Kedić. Occasionally, you might see a green-robed Justice striding down the alleys, but we were warned to keep clear of them, and they were the bogeymen in our bedtime stories.

By the time I was seven, I was helping my father unload his fish in the market each morning, and in the afternoon I would go down to the school by the beach. There we learned our numbers and letters, and, if the heat was tolerable, Myriam would take us outside to the famous black sands, and we would practise counting with shells and pebbles.

I found it all easy – couldn't understand the trouble numbers and letters caused the others – and I soon found Myriam was taking a special interest in me. At first, I noticed the lessons were increasingly directed towards me as the sole audience, while the others were allowed to play and bicker. Then, around the time of my eighth birthday, I took the first steps towards becoming an interpreter.

Myriam had sent the other children home, and sat down by me, unrolling a piece of parchment. She spread it across the table, displaying two lists of words in scratchy calligraphy.

"What's this?" I asked her.

"This is a different language," she said. "It might look funny, but just think of it as a secret code."

"Like the one they use in the market?" I said, thinking of the argot they all used to describe fish and customers – gillies for sunfish, stump for the massive lobsters that were considered a Val Kedić delicacy, dryden for outsiders who were ripe to be exploited, and so on.

"Exactly," she said. "I want you to take a look at the code, and see if you can learn it."

So I sat there, greedily drinking it up. I started to understand that I was good at this, and that not everyone could do it. Sometimes I asked her about a word from the list, checking how it sounded, but mostly I absorbed it alone. Years later, I realised she'd given me a glossary of Gerami, a creole from Mura – our nearest neighbours over the Southern Sea and a major trading partner. At the time, all I saw was the magic of language, and the realisation that the concept of bread was no longer just "bread" but had doubled in size to both "bread" and "deenah".

I learned it as best I could, allotting two names to every one of the concepts. Then she quizzed me: "*Three lemons?*" she would say in Gerami, and I, with the parchment in front of me, would have a go at understanding the message, and coming up with a suitable response. I loved it. It was a game, a good one, and my brain started creaking into life after years of fiddling around with numbers and letters.

We did that for a while, gradually getting harder, Myriam taking away the parchment, and giving me more complex constructions to decipher. I found it a challenge, and struggled to remember everything, but she didn't seem to mind.

Then, one afternoon, she took me to the beach, and told me to sit on a boulder. "There's someone who wants to meet you," she said. "He'd like to have a chat with you about what you've learned. Could you do that for me, Razvan?"

I nodded, a wary eye on the man who had emerged from behind the limestone steps that led up to the wharf. He was small, Mecunio, clean-shaven back then, a young man but already wearing the black sash of the city elders. He approached me with a bland smile on his lips, and Myriam turned away, leaving us to go back to her classroom.

"Your teacher's told me all about you, Razvan," he said in a deep, raspy voice that didn't sound right for such a small man. "She says you're a bright boy. That right?"

I didn't know what to say, so stayed silent.

"Show me," he said. "Show me what you can do." Then, in rough Gerami, "*Where do you live?*"

I recognised the words, and pointed towards the slum beyond the wharf. "The Stain," I said.

"Describe it for me. In the words you learned."

"*Small house*," I said in Gerami, "*near... fish shop.*"

It was a long way from perfect, but he seemed impressed. We did a few more exercises like that, with him probing to see the extent of my knowledge, trying to trick me with some words that could easily be confused. Then he took out a baat pipe, tapped the stem, and lit it. It was an odd habit for someone his age, but I was to learn he had always been a septuagenarian, trapped in a younger man's body.

"Have you ever thought, Razvan," he said, "that languages don't just have to use sound?"

I didn't answer, so he went on. "What's that smell?" he asked, sniffing.

"The sea."

"The sea. Right. But go a hundred paces to the east, and you'll receive a different message to your nose – the stink of The Stain. The fish market."

"I suppose."

"Same with taste. I could blindfold you, give you a variety of foods, and each one would be sending you a different message. You'd be able to work out what food I was giving you, even though you couldn't see it. And touch is no different. Close your eyes."

I shut them, and he grabbed my hand and shook it twice. "What message is that?"

"What?"

"What am I saying to you with this touch, this movement? Translate it for me, just like you did with the words."

"Pleased to meet you?"

"Good. What about this?" He delivered a stinging slap to the back of my head, and I opened my eyes, and glared at him.

"Ow!"

"Translate." He raised his hand, palm open.

"I'm cross with you?"

"Right. But what if we could make it more complex than that, base the whole language on touch alone…?"

And that was how it began. Mecunio came to my father's stall with me that afternoon, and I sat by the fountain while the two of them had a long conversation in the shade of the tattered awning. At one point, my father turned to look at me, as if seeing me for the first time. Finally, they shook hands and Mecunio walked out of The Stain without another glance at me. When it was time to pack away, the two of us worked side by side, lifting the wicker baskets and putting the leftover stock in crushed ice.

"So," he said, "the man says you're clever. Says you could learn another language."

"The touch language?"

"That's it. Spidertouch, they call it. The one the Crawlers use." Nobody would risk calling the Keda "Crawlers" in public, but the market was nearly deserted, and we knew everyone who was in hearing distance.

We'd never talked about the Keda – I'd never heard of fingerspeak before Mecunio mentioned it – but I was beginning to realise my father knew more than he let on.

"Not sure I like the idea of you mixing with Crawlers," he said. "But it's a way out of your service in the mines. A way out of The Stain. What do you think?"

I had the arrogance of youth, the belief that I was destined for better things. "I like it," I said. "I could do it."

"You're sure you want to do this?"

I nodded. I wish now I could remember his face, but all I can see are his clothes, frayed at the edges and covered in oily streaks.

I didn't see Mecunio again for a few years. But a fingerspeak interpreter came to see me once a week, an old woman with knotted grey hair and a white armband on her right arm, and she began my training. Most families had to pay for private lessons like this, but I later learned that Mecunio had arranged it all – he took an interest in finding new interpreters.

The woman gave me three copper bands and we started by learning the different positions and signals – the taps, the squeezes, the finger trills. She didn't say a lot – she wasn't the mothering type, and we didn't have much else to talk about – but she was a good teacher. We would sit on the rocks, facing each other, holding each other's left arm. She loved the sun, and when we took breaks she would unravel her shawl and munch on dates, while I retreated to the shade. Once I had learned the positions and signals, she began teaching me the touches, and it started to get difficult. When I disappointed her or was too slow, she would show her displeasure with a tsk or a rap with a birch cane that she carried.

When I turned eleven, I left the black sands and The Stain for good. They moved me to a compound in the centre of Val Kedić to become an apprentice in the guild of interpreters. There were nearly thirty of us there, ages ranging from eleven to eighteen, and they expected more than half of us to fail.

On my first day, I realised how massive the city was. I saw Keda strolling up the broad avenues, and the alchemical plumes of silver smoke that hung high in the air. I met Borzu and all the other savvy apprentices, and for the first time I was ashamed of The Stain. I can draw a clear line between my life before that day and my life after.

My father left the city a year later. The Stain never really forgave him, I think, for keeping his son from the mines, for avoiding what they had all endured. The guilt became too much, and they say he sailed across the Southern Sea. I never saw him again.

I walk back from the High Chamber with Ira, along Victory Avenue, lined with palm trees. Until we reach the Bridge of Peace, we are on proper Keda territory – Val Firuz is an island-citadel at the heart of Val Kedić, and the only place in the city where they outnumber us. Some elders and high-ranking citizens are permitted to live here, but I'm not sure why you would want to. Ordinary, blue-robed Keda are all around us, though it's noticeable that they veer away from us as we cross paths, as though a bubble surrounds us.

"They seemed jumpy today," says Ira in a low voice.

"Who?"

"Council, of course. These visitors that are coming. They're nervous."

"How could you tell? Double was just ordering food for a feast. Yours?"

"Same, but xe was quite stressed by it. Got me to repeat back to xer what xe had said. And they were going in and out all morning, all these hurried conversations – Crawlers everywhere."

I glance at her in surprise. Most elders, interpreters and influential citizens don't use that word, not if they want to get ahead. But she's young, no children – she doesn't have the fear yet.

"Well," I say, "if it makes them jumpy, can't be a bad thing."

"Perhaps. It depends. An unhappy Crawler can be a dangerous one."

We pass the statue of Kedira, an enormous stone monstrosity that celebrates the victories of their ancestors. Keda are milling around in groups here, and we walk in silence. Nearby is the alchemical institute, and we both keep our eyes on the silver smoke billowing into the sky. Round the corner, and we come to the Bridge of Peace. A pair of iron gates frame either end of the bridge, with a Justice barring entry. Even if some foolhardy citizens managed to rush the first gates, the second pair would be long closed and bolted by the time they had crossed the bridge. Underneath, you can see the Little Firu, a horseshoe-shaped moat that winds its way around the island of Val Firuz, until either end meets the Firu River. This bisects the city in the east and rushes down to the Southern Sea. Between them, they lock the Keda in. Or us, out.

We approach the gates and come to a halt in front of the green-robed Keda. If the councillors are the Keda's brains, the Justices are the fists. Their job is to enforce discipline, exact punishments, and generally inspire fear in the populace. Like the councillors, I can't distinguish many Justices by sight – they all look the same to me. I know Scorpion, of course. Xe is one of the Justices who manage my quarter. Supposedly, xer name comes from how xe administers punishment – whipping with a studded belt, leaving the victim covered in xer "stings". But honestly, I wonder if they come up with these names themselves, and make sure they spread to build up their reputation. Any of the Keda who are particularly brutish or sadistic get put in line to be a Justice, that's for sure. The exemplar of this is Beast, a legendary Justice, known throughout Val Kedić for xer viciousness and rhino-like build.

The one here, however, looks like a run-of-the-mill Justice – xe takes xer time, checking our pass, despite the fact xe must remember us from earlier in the day when we entered Val Firuz. Eventually, xe lowers xer poleaxe, and allows us to pass through to the bridge.

The Little Firu is twenty paces wide here. We stop and watch the surface of the water, looking for the eels that swim there. I exhale noisily, and Ira smiles.

"How long you been doing this?" she says.

"Twenty-two years now."

"It get any easier?"

"Nope," I reply. A pause. I look at her curiously. "They say you quit, after you finished your apprenticeship. And travelled, before you came back here."

"They're right. I thought there had to be a better world than this out there. I went out to find it."

"And?"

"Turned out I was wrong."

I snort. "Didn't have you down as a cynic."

"Ah, I'm no cynic. Just a good old-fashioned disillusioned optimist."

"Right. What's the difference?"

"Don't know. Put it into fingerspeak, that'll get rid of the nuance for you."

"Was that a… *joke* about fingerspeak?"

"Don't sound so disgusted." She smiles. "I remember you, you know. When I was fifteen, you gave us classes for a year. We had you every few days."

"Really? I haven't had to teach for a while now. How was I? Was I terrible?"

"Not bad. Better than some, who were deathly boring. Mind you, you never looked like you enjoyed it much."

"No, I don't think I did. Imagine what it's like telling a group of hormonal teenagers how to touch and squeeze each other in the right way, *and* keep them all focussed."

She laughs, and we fall silent for a moment. I feel a wave of relief that working with Ira is going to be all right. She may play it prim and proper with the Council, but outside, she's a real human being.

I could stand here watching the Little Firu until dusk – the thought of having to see the elders bores me beyond words. But Ira jabs me in the ribs, nods at the Justice on the other gate, who is glaring at us for daring to dilly-dally on xer bridge.

"Come on," Ira says. "We'd better go before xe comes over for a frank exchange of views. Even your fingerspeaking skills won't get us out of that one."

ANGRY ROBOT

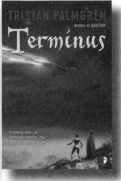

We are Angry Robot

angryrobotbooks.com